EVERYMAN'S LIBRARY
EDITED BY ERNEST RHYS

FICTION

LETTERS FROM THE UNDERWORLD
BY FEDOR DOSTOIEFFSKY. TRANS-
LATED BY C. J. HOGARTH

THE PUBLISHERS OF *EVERYMAN'S LIBRARY* WILL BE PLEASED TO SEND FREELY TO ALL APPLICANTS A LIST OF THE PUBLISHED AND PROJECTED VOLUMES TO BE COMPRISED UNDER THE FOLLOWING THIRTEEN HEADINGS:

TRAVEL ❧ SCIENCE ❧ FICTION
THEOLOGY & PHILOSOPHY
HISTORY ❧ CLASSICAL
FOR YOUNG PEOPLE
ESSAYS ❧ ORATORY
POETRY & DRAMA
BIOGRAPHY
REFERENCE
ROMANCE

IN FOUR STYLES OF BINDING: CLOTH, FLAT BACK, COLOURED TOP; LEATHER, ROUND CORNERS, GILT TOP; LIBRARY BINDING IN CLOTH, & QUARTER PIGSKIN

London: J. M. DENT & SONS, Ltd.
New York: E. P. DUTTON & CO.

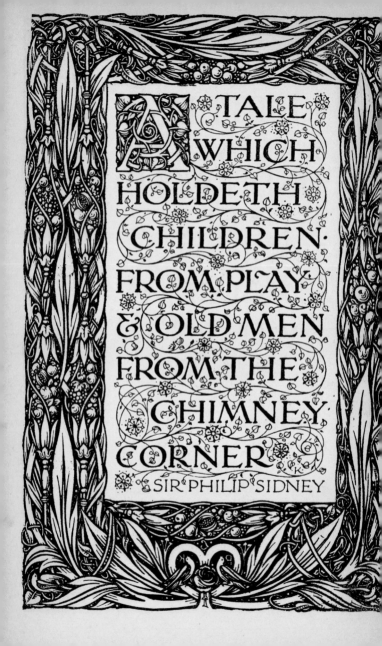

A TALE WHICH HOLDETH CHILDREN FROM PLAY & OLD MEN FROM THE CHIMNEY CORNER

SIR PHILIP SIDNEY

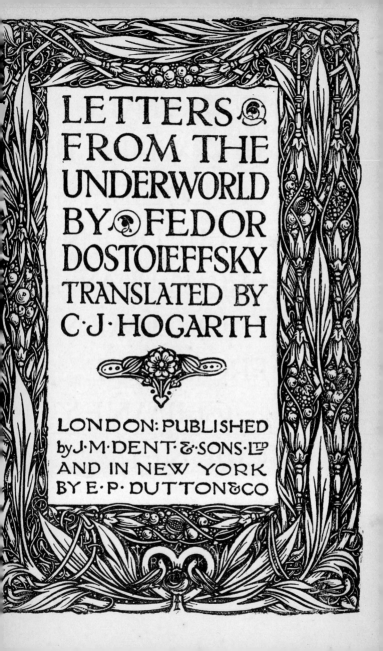

LETTERS FROM THE UNDERWORLD

BY FEDOR DOSTOIEFFSKY

TRANSLATED BY C. J. HOGARTH

LONDON: PUBLISHED
by J. M. DENT & SONS LTD
AND IN NEW YORK
BY E. P. DUTTON & CO

INTRODUCTION

A GRATIFYING sign of the times is the fact that the merits of Theodor Dostoievsky, the greatest of Russian realistic writers, are becoming increasingly realised by the reading public of this country, who no longer look upon the works of Tolstoi, Turgeniev and Tchekhov as the be-all and end-all of Russian fiction. Dostoievsky may be said to constitute particularly healthy reading for the "comfortable" section of society, for he lays bare some of the worst of our social sores, and invites all men and women to contemplate the putrescent foulness which civilisation permits to exist, even if it has not brought into existence. That it is Russia of which the author speaks does not make the picture any the less applicable to other modern communities, our own included, since moral plagues and plague-spots of the kind which he describes exist everywhere, and seem to form a necessary concomitant of the system upon which modern society is based.

Unlike what so many realistic writers portray, his descriptions of the terrible things of this world are descriptions written at first hand, for he himself had descended into, had dwelt in, the Inferno; not merely as a spectator, but as a captive in, an inmate of, Hell— an outcast who had been forced to rub shoulders with the lost souls who herd there, and to endure their bodily pains and mental sufferings. Drawing us pictures of what he has seen and heard in those murky depths, he, by implication, asks of the comfortable section of society what it thinks of it all. Yet he does not seek to extenuate, any more than he seeks to condemn, the vices and foulnesses, moral and physical, of the underworld. He does not lay the blame for what he has witnessed at the door of any particular social system, any particular social class. He merely invites the reader to look, and

then to go away and think over what he has beheld.
Dostoievsky is no preacher like Tolstoi; he does not even
indulge in gentle satire, after the manner of Tchekhov;
yet also he is no pessimist.   Even in the blackest of
surroundings, even in the most degraded of human
beings, he can discern, if not a ray of light, at all events
the possibility of a ray eventually penetrating the darkness, and coming to redeem and make glorious the
whole.   Sonia and Marmedalov in *Crime and Punishment*, Lisa in *Letters from the Underworld*, and many
another one—in all such Dostoievsky can discern the
potentially godlike, the inextinguishably spiritual.   But
how, he asks, is their redemption to be brought about?
By love in the higher sense of the term.   Yes, love, love,
and again love, is Dostoievsky's one remedy for the ills
of life, his one medicine for the sicknesses of humanity.
Yet he never actually *puffs* his panacea.   He only shows
us what it can do, and then leaves the reader to draw
his own inference from the demonstration.   Tolstoi,
taking from the easel the picture which he has painted,
raises it on high, and, with pointer in hand, proceeds
to particularise the moral lessons which he intends to be
drawn from the details on the canvas.   Dostoievsky, or
the other hand, paints his picture, leaves it where ·
stands on the easel, and quietly withdraws from the
room.   You can go and look at the picture if you like,
and you can think of it what you like; but it needs no
pointer, no insistence upon the manner in which its
details are meant to be understood.   If there is any
humanity within you, the humanity of the picture will
speak to yours; and if within you there is no such spirit
of understanding—well, it does not greatly matter.   At
least the artist does not intend to *preach* to you, for he
too has been a sinner with the sinners whom he portrays.

Thus in this volume we see the author representing
love, in the higher sense, as able to redeem the most
ignoble of natures.   In all its phases, says Dostoievsky,
love of the higher and purer sort is competent to save
and to purify.   "If, when I was a child, I had been
blessed with parents I should never have become what I

am to-day"; "The father himself wears but a threadbare
coat; yet for her (his daughter) no gift is too costly. . . .
He will spend his last coin for her . . . if, in return, he
shall receive but a smile"; "Where there is no love there
is no wisdom"; "It is sufficient to love steadfastly, and
work will become a pleasure"; "Think" (a cynical
debauchee is speaking to an outcast of society) "if you
had but a little child to dangle at your breast! . . .
Is it not perfect happiness when all three are united in
one—husband, wife and child?"; "Love is the whole
world, love is the most precious of jewels. . . . Love is
what men will give their very souls, their very lives,
for." Many another such passage might be quoted which
Dostoievsky has put into the mouths of drunkards,
epileptics, misers and prostitutes. In one of the stories
in this volume we have the remorseful ravings of a man
who, though intrinsically mean of soul, has loved greatly
and with his whole heart. Under the influence of this
true and sterling passion he, a sordid moneylender, has
learnt to be at once generous and a hero, despite the
fact that with his opinionated severity he has broken his
wife's heart, and driven her to suicide. In another of
these stories we read of the ruin of an unbalanced nature
which passes, through the throes of a purely amorous
affection, to its undoing. Lastly we read how a poor
outcast upon whom a half-crazed, embittered cynic has
planned to vent his wrath and disappointment with
the world catches eagerly at what she believes to be the
true and generous love which he is offering her, and, in
doing so, reveals, as in a flash, all the higher, better
and purer nature which still lurks within her woman's
soul. That tender soul, yearning for what fate has
denied it, offers the man its all; and he—he turns upon
and rends her, though, in the act, he rends also himself.
It is a terrible picture—perhaps some might say too
terrible. To such persons one might almost imagine the
author retorting: "Do not look at it, then. Continue,
good people, to be—comfortable."

C. J. HOGARTH.

BIBLIOGRAPHY

Translations of Dostoïeffsky's novels have appeared as follows: Buried Alive; or, Ten Years of Penal Servitude in Siberia, translated by Marie v. Thilo, 1881. In Vizetelly's One Volume Novels: Crime and Punishment, vol. 13; Injury and Insult, translated by F. Whishaw, vol. 17; The Friend of the Family and the Gambler, etc., vol. 22. In Vizetelly's Russian Novels: The Idiot, by F. Whishaw, 1887; Uncle's Dream; and, The Permanent Husband, etc., 1888. Prison Life in Siberia, translated by H. S. Edwards, 1888; Poor Folk, translated by L. Milman, 1894.

See D. S. Merezhkovsky, Tolstoi as Man and Artist, with Essay on Dostoïeffsky, translated from the Russian, 1902; M. Baring, Landmarks in Russian Literature (chapter on Dostoïeffsky), 1910.

CONTENTS

LETTERS FROM THE UNDERWORLD

B

PREFACE BY THE AUTHOR

IT need hardly be said that both the writer of these
"Letters" and the "Letters" themselves are
creatures of the imagination. Nevertheless, in
view of the circumstances under which, in general,
our community has become formed, such men as
the writer in question not only may, but are bound
to, exist. I have tried, therefore, to set before the
public, in more striking guise than usual, a character
which is peculiar to the present age—a representa-
tive type of the generation which has not yet passed
away. In the "Letter" headed "The Underworld"
this individual presents himself and his views of life,
and purports to explain the causes which have
created his personality—a personality due to the
milieu which all of us share in Russia; while in the
second of the two "Letters" he describes certain
incidents which are supposed actually to have
occurred during his life.

THEODOR DOSTOIEVSKY.

1846.

PART I

THE UNDERWORLD

I

I AM ill; I am full of spleen and repellent. I conceive there to be something wrong with my liver, for I cannot even think for the aching of my head. Yet what my complaint is I do not know. Medicine I cannot, I never could, take, although for medicine and doctors I have much reverence. Also, I am extremely superstitious : which, it may be, is why I cherish such a respect for the medical profession. I am well-educated, and therefore might have risen superior to such fancies, yet of them I am full to the core.

Also, I have no real desire to be cured of my ill-humour. I suppose you cannot understand this? No, I thought not; but *I* can understand it, although it would puzzle me to tell you exactly whom I am vexed with. I only know that I do not choose to offend the doctors by telling them that I am unable to accept their treatment. Also, I know—better than any one else can do—that I alone am my worst enemy, and that I am my own worst enemy far more than I am any one else's. However, if I am not to be cured, so much the worse for me and my evil passions. If my liver is out of order, so much the worse for my liver.

I have been living like this for a long while now —for fully twenty years. I am forty years old, and, in my day, have been a civil servant. But I am a civil servant no longer. Moreover, I was a

5

bad civil servant at that. I used to offend every one, and to take pleasure in doing so. Yet never once did I accept a bribe, though it would have been easy enough for me to have feathered my nest in that way. This may seem to you a poor sort of a witticism, yet I will not erase it. I had written it down in the belief that it would wear rather a clever air when indited, yet I will not—no, not even now, when I see that I was but playing the buffoon— alter the *mot* by a single iota.

Whenever people approached my office table to ask for information, or what not, I used to grind my teeth at them, and invariably to feel pleased when I had offended their dignity. I seldom failed in my aim. Men, for the most part, are timid creatures—and we all of us know the sort of men favour-seekers are. Of such dolts there was one in particular—an officer—whom I could not bear, for he refused to defer to me at all, and always kicked up a most disgusting clatter with his sword. For a year and a half we joined battle over that sword; but it was I who won the victory, I who caused him to cease clattering his precious weapon. All this happened during my early manhood.

Do you wish to know wherein the sting of my evil temper has always lain? It has always lain (and therein also has always lain its peculiar offensiveness) in the fact that, even at moments of my bitterest spleen, I have been forced to acknowledge with shame that not only am I not at all bad-tempered, but also I have never received any real cause of offence—that I have been but roaring to frighten away sparrows, and amusing myself with doing so. Foam though I might at the mouth, I needed but to be given a doll to play with, or a cup of sweet tea to drink, and at once I sank to quiescence. Yes, I have always grown calm for the moment—even though, later, I have gnashed my teeth at myself, and suffered from months of insomnia. Such has invariably been my way.

For a long time past I have been belying my own personality by calling myself an irascible fellow. It has been pure rancour that has made me tell that lie against myself. As a matter of fact, I only played, so to speak, with my office callers, and with that officer, while all the while it was impossible for me to lose my temper. Every day I keep discovering in myself elements of the most opposite order conceivable, and can feel them swarming within me, and am aware that, to the very end of my life, they will continue so to swarm. Yet, often as they have striven to manifest themselves outwardly, I have never allowed them to do so. Of set purpose I always prevent that from happening, even though they torture me shamefully with their presence, and sometimes throw me into convulsions of *ennui*—ah, of how much *ennui* indeed ! . . . Would not all this lead you, gentlemen, to suppose that I am expressing a sort of regret—that I am asking, as it were, your pardon? I am sure that you think so? Well, I can only say that I do not care a rap for your opinion.

No, I am not really bad-tempered. Rather, the fact is that I have never succeeded in being anything at all—whether kind-hearted or cruel, a villain or a saint, a hero or an insect. I just crouch here in this den of mine, and worry myself with the irritating, the useless, reflection that, after all, a man of parts cannot become anything; for only a fool does that. Yes (I say to myself), a man of the nineteenth century is morally bound, above all things, to be a colourless being, since a man of character, a man of action, is a being who is essentially limited. Such is the conviction which forty years have forced upon me. Forty years have been the span of my life, and forty years are a lifetime—they are the most extreme limit of old age. To live longer than that seems indecent, base, immoral. Who would want to live longer than that? Answer me—sincerely, and from your heart. Well,

I will tell you who want to live longer. Only fools
and rogues. This I say to all old men in the world
—to respected old men, to silver-haired old men, to
old men of repute. Yes, I say it to the whole
universe. And I have the right to say it, for I
myself am going to live to be sixty, or seventy, or
even eighty ! . . . Wait a minute. Give me a
moment to recover my breath. . . .

Probably you think that I am trying to make fun
of you? If so, you are wrong. I am not such a
merry fellow as you suppose, or as you *may* suppose. At the same time, if, in irritation at my fool-
ing (and I suspect that you *are* so irritated), you
were to ask me exactly what sort of a man I am,
I should reply that I am a college graduate who,
for my living (and for that purpose alone), served
the State for a season, but who last year, on the
death of a distant relative who left me six thousand
roubles, retired from the service, and settled down
in this den which you see. I used to live in it
before, but since then I have taken up my abode in
it for good. It is a mean, shabby room on the
outskirts of the city, while for servant I have an old
country-woman whose deafness makes her crusty,
and whose person smells to heaven. They tell me
that the climate of St. Petersburg is doing me harm,
and that, in view of my insignificant means, it is
sheer extravagance for me to go on living in the
capital. Well, I know all that. Yes, I know it
better than all the wisest and most experienced
counsellors and tossers of heads in the world could
possibly do. Yet I remain in St. Petersburg, nor
do I intend to leave it. No, I intend to remain
where I am . . . Ah ! As though it matters one
way or the other whether I stay here or take my
departure !

By the way, what is it that all respectable men
talk about most readily? Answer—about themselves. So I too will talk about myself.

II

I WISH to tell you, gentlemen (no matter whether you care to hear it or not), why I have never even been able to become an insect. I solemnly declare to you that I have often *wished* to become an insect, but could never attain my desire. I swear to you, gentlemen, that to be overcharged with sensibility is an actual malady—a real, a grievous malady. For humanity's daily needs mere ordinary human sensibility ought to suffice, or about one-half or one-quarter of the sensibility which falls to the lot of the average educated man of our miserable nineteenth century, if he has the additional misfortune to reside in St. Petersburg (the most abstract, the most deviously-minded, city on this terrestrial sphere of ours, where towns, in their psychology, may be complex or non-complex). At all events such sensibility as falls to the lot of (for instance) the generality of so-called independent persons and men of action ought to suffice. I dare wager, now, that you think that I am writing this with my tongue in my cheek, and solely to make fun of men of action; that you think that it is sheer bad taste that is making me rattle my sword in the way that that officer used to do? Yet, to tell the truth, gentlemen, who would be vain of one's weaknesses while at the same time one is using them as a means for poking fun at others?

Yet why should I *not* do this? All men do it. All men are proud of their weaknesses, and I, perhaps, more so than my fellows. Let us not quarrel about it. It may be that I have used an awkward expression. Yet I am persuaded that not only is excess of sensibility, but also sensibility of any kind whatsoever, a malady. Of that I have not the smallest doubt in the world. For the moment, however, let us drop the point. Tell me this: how is it that always, and of set purpose, as it were, and at the very moment—yes, at the very moment—

when I have appeared to be most in a position to appreciate the finer shades of "the great and the beautiful" (to use the term once current amongst us), I have not only invariably failed to recognise as unseemly, but also have never failed to commit, actions which—well, in a word, actions which all men commit, but which I have always perpetrated just when I was most acutely sensible that I ought not to do them? The more I have recognised what is good and what constitutes "the great and the beautiful," the deeper I have plunged into the mire, and the more I have been ready to smear myself over with the sticky stuff. But the most curious point of all is this—that the mood which I have described never seemed to be a mere fortuitous happening with me, but my permanent, my normal, condition, and therefore neither a weakness nor a vice. Consequently I have gradually come to lose all desire to combat this failing of mine. Indeed, things have reached the point that I almost believe (I might almost say, I *wholly* believe) that it is my normal condition. At first, however—*i. e.* at the actual beginning of things—I suffered terrible pangs in the struggle against my weakness, for I never could bring myself to believe that other men were not in the same position as I. Yet I kept the fact a secret close-locked in my breast, for I was ashamed of it then, and am ashamed of it now —yes, ashamed of the fact that I used to experience a sort of mysterious, abnormal, base gratification in recalling to my memory (say) some filthy nocturnal revel in St. Petersburg, and in recognising that once again I had acted foully, but that what had been done could never be undone. Inwardly and secretly I often licked my lips at the thought of these revels, and chewed the cud of my recollections until their bitterness turned to a sort of base, accursed sweetness, and then to an actual, an assured, sensation of delight. Yes, I say of delight, of delight. I insist upon that. I often told myself

that I would greatly like to know whether the
same delight fell to the lot of other men. First of
all, however, let me explain to you wherein that
delight lay. It lay in a clear consciousness of my
degradation—in a feeling that I had reached the
last wall, and that the whole thing was base, and
could never be otherwise, and that no escape therefrom was to be looked for, and that it was not
possible for me to become a different man, and
that, even if I still retained sufficient faith and
energy to become a different man, I should not wish
to become so, but that I would rather do nothing at
all in the matter, since to undergo such a change
might not be worth my while. And the chief thing
about it was that one felt that the process was
ruled by the normal, the fundamental, laws of acute
sensibility, added to the inertia which arises from
the working of those laws; wherefore one was never
likely to alter, nor yet to lift a finger to effect an
alteration. Hence may be deduced the fact that
over-sensibility causes a villain to hug his villainy
to himself if he really *perceives* that he is a villain.
. . . However, enough of this. Have you understood all that I have said? Can you explain to me
what that delight of mine consisted of? No; so I
will explain it myself. I will pursue the matter to
the end, seeing that I have taken up my pen to
write.

I am extremely self-conscious. Also, no hunchback, no dwarf, could be more prone to resentment and to offence than I. I have been through
moments when, had I happened to receive a blow
in the face, I should have been glad ! Yes, I say
it in all seriousness, that I should have derived the
greatest possible gratification from a blow—the
gratification of being able to feel desperate (since
it is in desperation that one finds one's most glorious
moments, especially when one has recognised that
one cannot possibly draw back from the position
taken up). Yes, a blow, and nothing but a blow,

can wholly erase the consciousness of the grease in which one has been rubbed. Yet, averse though I am to scenes, it has always befallen me that *I* have been the offending party; as well as that (a still more shameful thing) I have been at fault without actually having transgressed—I have been, as it were, guilty through the mere working of the laws of nature. In the first place, I have often been at fault in that I have thought myself cleverer than any one else with whom I have come in contact. Such has always been my way. Sometimes, though —would you believe it?—I have felt sorry for this. At all events I know that, all my life long, I have preferred to look people under the eyes rather than in them. And in the second place, I have often been at fault in that, if there lies within me any nobility of soul, such ability has never been able to do anything for me beyond torment me with a consciousness of the utter uselessness of possessing it. I have never been able to *do* anything with that nobility, for the reason that, however much an offender might strike me in obedience to the laws of nature, it is not feasible to forgive laws of nature, nor yet to overlook them, while, despite the existence of those laws, an insult still remains an insult. Hence, were I able to divest myself of all magnanimity, and to take revenge upon each and every person who offended me, I should never really be able to revenge myself upon such persons, for the reason that, in all probability, I should never be able finally to make up my mind to any given course of action, even if I had the power to carry it out. Why should I be so unable to make up my mind? On that subject I have a word or two to say.

III

PEOPLE who are able to wreak vengeance upon an assailant, and, in general, to stand up for them-

selves—how do they do it? It can only be supposed
that, momentarily, their whole being is possessed
by a desire for revenge, and that no other element
is, for the time being, within them. A man of that
sort goes as straight to his goal as a mad bull
charges with lowered crest; and nothing but a stone
wall will stop him. (*Apropos,* such persons—that is
to say, independent persons and men of action—
make no bones about *yielding* to the wall. For them
a wall is not an excuse for turning aside [as it is
for us, the men of thought, and therefore the men
who do nothing]; it is not a pretext for swerving
from the path [a pretext in which, as a rule, no one—
not even oneself—believes, but for which one is
nevertheless thankful]. No, they just come to a
halt before it. For them a wall connotes something
calming, something morally decisive, final, and
even mystical. . . . But about the wall later.) I do
not consider an independent man of that type to be
the real, the normal, man as his fond mother,
Nature, who has borne him upon earth, would have
him be. Yet I envy such a man with all the power
of my spleen. True, he is gross—but then the
normal man may *have* to be gross. How, indeed,
do you know that his grossness is not one of his
very best points? Anyway I daily grow more and
more confirmed in my suspicion that if he were to
take the antithesis of the normal man—that is to
say, the man of acute sensibility, the man who
hails, not from Nature's womb, but from a chemical
retort (this approaches a little nearly to mysticism
—a thing which I also suspect)—the man born of
the retort would sometimes feel so conscious that
he was outclassed by his antithesis, the man of
action, that he would come to look upon himself,
despite his acute sensibility, as a mouse rather than
as a human being. A very sensitive mouse, it is
true (he would say to himself), yet none the less a
mouse; whereas the other is a man, and therefore,
etcetera, etcetera. Above all things, it would be

he—he, the man of sensibility—who, of his own volition, would dub himself a mouse. He would ask no
one else's opinion on the matter. This is an important
point. Next let us observe the mouse in action.
Suppose, for example, that it receives an insult (and
it nearly always *is* so receiving an insult), and that
it wishes to revenge itself. Perhaps it will be
capable of harbouring malice in its breast to an
even greater extent than *l'homme de la nature et
de la vérité*. Yes, a mean, debased little yearning
to repay the offender in his own coin might wax in
that mouse's bosom in an even meaner way than
it would do in that of *l'homme de la nature et de la
vérité,* since the innate grossness of the latter would
cause him to look upon revenge as bare justice,
whereas the mouse, with its hypersensibility, might
very possibly deny the existence of such justice.
Lastly we come to the act itself—to the actual deed
of revenge. By this time the unfortunate mouse
will have augmented the original insult by sur-
rounding itself, through doubts and questionings,
with such a number of other insults—it will have
added to the main question such a string of questions which are still undecided—that involuntarily it
will have collected about itself a fatal quagmire, a
stinking morass, of misunderstandings, emotions,
and, lastly, spittle discharged at it by the independent persons, judges, and dictators who are
solemnly standing around it in a ring, and salut-
ing the little animal with full-throated laughter.
Naturally nothing will be left for the mouse to
do but to make a disdainful gesture with its little
paw, indulge in a smile of deprecatory contempt
wherein even the smiler itself will have no belief,
and retire shamefacedly into its hole. There, in
its dirty, stinking underworld, our poor insulted,
brow-beaten mouse will soon have immersed itself
in a state of cold, malignant, perpetual rancour.
For forty long years (so it may very well be) it will
continue to recall to its mind the most minute, the

most shameful, details of the insult which it has sustained, and to add to them, as it does so, other details more shameful still, and to taunt and worry itself with its own fancies. Of those fancies it will be ashamed, yet it will nevertheless remember them all, exaggerate them all, and even imagine to itself things which have never happened, on the mere pretext that one day it may obtain its revenge, and that therefore it must, in the meanwhile, forget nothing. Or perhaps it *will* actually embark upon a scheme of revenge; but if it does so the thing will be done only by fits and starts, and from behind a stone, and incognito, and in a manner which makes it clear that the mouse distrusts alike its right to wreak vengeance and the ultimate success of its scheme, since it knows in advance that its poor attempts at retribution will bring upon its own head a hundred times more suffering than will fall to the lot of the person against whom the vengeance is aimed, but upon whom not so much as a scratch will be inflicted. Yes, upon its very deathbed the mouse will again recall the whole story, with compound interest added.

Now, it is just in this same cold, loathsome semi-mania, this same half-belief in oneself, this same conscious burying of oneself in the underworld for forty years, this same voluntarily imagined, yet privately distrusted, powerlessness to escape from one's position, this same poison of unsatisfied wishes that for ever penetrates inwards, this same fever of vacillation, of resolutions adopted for all eternity, and of regrets that come upon one in a moment, that there lies the essence of the strange delight of which I have spoken. So subtle is this delight, so elusive to the senses, that merely limited persons, or persons who merely possess a strong nervous system, cannot grasp a single one of its features. "Perhaps, too," you may add with a simper, "persons who have never received a blow in the face cannot understand it?"—thereby implying that,

at some date or another during my life, I have
received such a blow, and therefore am speaking as
an expert. Yes, I dare wager that that is what
you are thinking. Do not disturb yourselves,
gentlemen. Never once have I received a blow in
the face—though I do not care a pin what *your*
imaginings on the subject may be. My only regret
is that I have dealt so few blows in my life. . . .
But enough of this. Suppose we say no more concerning this theme which you seem to find so extraordinarily interesting? Let me quietly continue
what I was saying about strong-nerved individuals
who do not understand the higher refinements of
the pleasure which I have described.

Good people who, under other circumstances,
bellow as loudly as bulls (of course, we must suppose
that the performance does them infinite credit) at
once become mute in the face of the Impossible. By
the Impossible I mean the stone wall of which I have
spoken. What stone wall, do you say? Why, the
stone wall constituted of the laws of nature, of the
deductions of learning, and of the science of
mathematics. When, for instance, people of this
kind seek to prove to you that you are descended
from an ape, it is of no use for you to frown; you
must just accept what they say. When, again, they
seek to prove to you that a single drop of your fat
is of more essential value to you than the bodies of
a hundred thousand men who resemble yourself,
and that by this deduction there become finally
resolved the so-called virtues and duties and other
inventions of unreason and prejudice, you must just
accept what they tell you, and make up your mind
to do nothing at all, since the formula that twice
two make four is mathematics. To that find an
objection if you can !

"Pardon us," so these people bawl, "but you
simply *cannot* refute what we tell you. Twice two
make four; Nature does not ask *your* leave for
that; she has nothing to do with *your* wishes on

the subject, no matter whether you approve of her
laws or not. You must just take her as she is, and,
with her, her results. A wall still remains a wall,"
—and so forth, and so forth. . . . Good Lord!
What have *I* to do with the laws of Nature, or with
arithmetic, when all the time those laws and the
formula that twice two make four do not meet with
my acceptance? Of course, I am not going to beat
my head against a wall if I have not the requisite
strength to do so; yet I am not going to *accept*
that wall merely because I have run up against it,
and have no means to knock it down.

Does a wall, forsooth, constitute a full-stop, a
signal for a cessation of the struggle, for the mere
reason that it and the formula that twice two make
four are one? Oh, blindness of blindnesses! What,
rather, we should all do is to comprehend everything, to envisage everything—to comprehend and
to envisage every impossibility and every stone wall;
to accept no single impossibility, no single stone
wall, if we do not feel inclined to accept it; to attain
(in spite of the most inevitable combinations and the
most refutative conclusions of logic) to the eternal
truth that one may be at fault even in regard to
a stone wall, no matter how much one may *seem*
not to be at fault; lastly, on recognising that fact,
to subside silently, and with lips compressed to
resignation, and with a bitter-sweet feeling in one's
heart, into a state of inertia, there to dream that
one need not *really* be angry with any one, since
one's reasons for being so never existed, and never
will exist, and have become changed, and shuffled,
and substituted for one another, and half obliterated
(though how, or by whom, one cannot think, except
that those unknown factors and changes cause one's
head to ache more and more as the mysteries in the
the question remain unsolved).

C

IV

"Ha, ha, ha! Then we presume that you would find pleasure even in toothache?" you say to me with a grin?

"Well, why not?" answer I. "Even toothache may afford one gratification. I myself have had it for a month, so I know what it means. When one has toothache one does not, of course, sit glowering in silence; one groans aloud. But those groans are not candid ones—they are uttered with suppressed venom; and in such a venomous state as that anything may turn to a jest. In reality those groans express the sufferer's *delight*. If he found no pleasure in them, he would not groan."

Yes, you have suggested an excellent theme to me, gentlemen, and I will hasten to exploit it. Those groans express, firstly, the degrading futility of one's complaint, a legalised tyranny of nature which one despises, but from which one, unlike nature, is bound to suffer. They also express a sense of the fact that at the moment one has no other foe than the pain; a sense of the fact that one is utterly at the mercy of one's teeth; a sense of the fact that Providence is in a position either to will that your teeth shall cease on the instant to ache or to will that they shall go on aching another three months; and, lastly, a sense of the fact that if you do not agree with, but, on the contrary, protest against, the situation, your only resource, your only comfort, will be either to cut your throat or to go on beating the walls of your room ever harder and harder with your fists, since there is nothing else for you to do. Now, all these dire self-insultings, self-mockings, at length lead to a pleasure which often attains to supreme heights of voluptuousness. Let me beg of you, gentlemen, to seize the first opportunity of listening to the groans of a cultured man of the nineteenth century who is suffering from toothache. But this you should do

only on the second or the third day of his malady,
when he is beginning to groan in an altogether
different manner from what he has done on the
first day (when he will groan simply from the pain);
when he is beginning to groan, not as a rude
peasant, but as a man who has felt the touch of
European progress and civilisation; when he is
beginning to groan as a man who has "divorced
himself from the soil and from vulgar principles"
(to use the phrase now current). Well, by that time
his groans will have become malicious and meanly
irascible; and though he may continue them whole
nights and days at a stretch, he will be aware all
the time that he is doing himself no good by his
utterances, but merely uselessly angering and annoying himself and others. Better than any one else
will he be aware that his family, as also the public
before whom he is cutting such a figure, have for
a long while been listening to him with disgust;
that they think him an utter rascal, and have it in
mind that he might just as well have groaned in
a simpler manner (that is to say, without any turns
or roulades), since his present style of groaning
is due simply to temper, and is leading him to
play the fool out of sheer viciousness. Now, all
this self-expression, all these insults to others, con-
note a certain voluptuous delight. "I am disturbing you," you can say to your friends, "and driving
you to distraction, and preventing every one in the
house from sleeping. Very well. Pray do not
sleep, but join me in my constant recognition of
the fact that I have got the toothache. I am no
longer the hero whom I have hitherto seemed, but
only a public nuisance. Very well; be it so. I am
very glad that you have found me out. Do you
dislike having to listen to my villainous groans?
Then go on disliking it, and I will execute a few
more of these infernal roulades." Do you understand it *now*, gentlemen? No, I wager that you
do not. It is clear that I must develop and expound

my theme much further if you are ever to comprehend all the ins and outs of the pleasure which I
mean. You laugh, do you? Then I am delighted.
If my jests are in bad taste, and rude, and obscure,
and halting, that arises from the fact that I have
no self-respect. Indeed, what man of sensibility
could possess self-respect?

V

How could any man respect himself who wilfully
takes pleasure in a consciousness of his self-abase-
ment? I do not say this out of any feeling of puling
regret, for never at any time have I found it possible
to say, "Father, forgive me, and I will sin no
more." This is not so much because I have actually
felt myself *incapable* of uttering the words as
because they have always come too easily to my
lips. And whenever I have said them, what has
happened next? Why, that, as though bound to
fall, I have plunged straight into sin, when all the
time I have been innocent both in thought and intent.
A worse thing could not be. Next I have felt
softened in heart, and shed tears, and reproved
myself, and seen things as they were, and felt
unclean of soul. Yet for this I cannot very well
blame the laws of Nature, since to offend against
them has been the chief, the constant, occupation of
my life. It is a degrading fact to have to recall,
but the fact remains. Then, a moment or two
later, I have always angrily reminded myself that
my whole conduct has been false — horribly,
gratuitously false (by "it," of course, I mean all
my regrets, my softenings of heart, my vows of
regeneration). So I would ask you, gentlemen—
what caused me to rack and torture myself in
this way? Well, the answer is that I always
found it irksome merely to sit with folded hands.
That is why I have given myself up to so much

wrongdoing. Mark what I say, gentlemen, for what I say is true, and will give you the key to the whole business. Of set purpose I used to devise opportunities for ordering my existence in such a way as to—well, as at least to see a certain amount of life. For instance, I have often been *careful* to take offence at something—not for any good reason, but merely because I wanted to. Gentlemen, you yourselves know that if one takes causeless offence—the sort of offence which one brings upon oneself—one ends by being really, and in very truth, offended. I have been at pains, all my life, to play tricks of this sort; with the result that I have come to be destitute of any sort of selfcontrol. Also, I have twice tried to fall in love; but I can assure you, gentlemen, that I suffered greatly in the doing so! One's heart may not *seem* to be suffering as the smiles pass over one's face, yet one *is* in pain all the while, and that in a very real, a very demonstrable, fashion, since at such times one is jealous, and above oneself. The sole cause of it all, gentlemen, is *ennui;* yes, the sole cause of it all is *ennui.* The fact is that one comes to feel crushed with the tedium, the conscious folding of the hands in contemplation, which is the direct, the inevitable, the automatic outcome of sensibility. Of this I have spoken above. . . . I repeat, therefore, I earnestly repeat, that all men of independence and action—men who are men of action because they are *prone* to action—are both gross and limited in their purview. How is this to be explained? Thus. Such men are led by their limitations to mistake approximate and secondary causes for primary, and so to persuade themselves, more easily and more readily than other men do, that they have an assured basis for their action, and therefore may cease to trouble themselves further. That is the truth, and the whole truth, of the matter. To embark upon action one must first of all feel perfectly sure of oneself, so that no doubts

as to the wisdom of that action may remain. But
how does a man like myself bring himself to the
requisite state of assurance? Whence do I derive
my primary causes? Whence my bases? Well,
first of all I begin thinking things over; which has
the effect of leading each original cause thought of
to attract to itself some cause a good deal more
primary, more original, still. And it is in this that
there lies the essence of self-realisation and thought
(though perhaps it is also the law of Nature).
What is the result? Always one and the same
thing. You will remember that, just now, I spoke
of revenge (though perhaps you did not altogether
follow me?). I said that a man may wreak
vengeance because he believes it to be justice;
wherefore he has found his original cause for action
in justice, and may feel sure of himself, and proceed to wreak his vengeance quietly, and with
success, since he is persuaded that what he is doing
is altogether right and honourable. But, for my
part, I never can perceive either justice or virtue in
such a course : wherefore, if I embark upon a scheme
of revenge, I do so, rather, out of malice. Of
course, malice *may* succeed in overcoming one's
doubts—it *may* serve (and with perfect success, too)
as a first cause for action (though it is nothing of
the sort); but what am I to do if even malice be
wanting in me (which is the point whence I
originally started)? Under the accursed laws of
sensibility, malice becomes subject to a process of
chemical disintegration, since it always happens
that if a given object of action be volatile, the
reasons for such action easily turn to gas, and
responsibility disappears, and the offence ceases to
have been an offence at all—it becomes merely a
delusion wherein (as in toothache) no one is guilty,
and wherefrom there is no other way of escape than
from toothache—namely, by beating one's head
against the wall. Perhaps, in despair of finding a
first cause for action, one shrugs one's shoulders?

Well, my advice is blindly and unthinkingly to leave first causes alone, and to give oneself up to one's impulses, and, for once in a while, to let volition lie altogether in abeyance. That is to say, either hate or love, but in any case do anything rather than sit with folded hands. If you do this I wager that by the day after to-morrow (at the very latest) you will have come to despise yourself for having ever got into a fluster at all; with the result that once again you will relapse calmly into inertia and the blowing of soap-bubbles. Ah, gentlemen, at least I can look upon myself as a wise man in that I have never succeeded in beginning or ending *anything*. Grant that I am a foolish, useless, troublesome chatterer, as we all are—yes, grant that: yet may not the one true function of every man of sensibility be to act as a chatterer—to act, that is to say, as a dissipator of airy trifles into space?

VI

If only I had never done anything but out of sheer laziness! How I should have respected myself! Yes, I should have respected myself for the reason that I *was* capable of being lazy—that in me there *was* at least one positive quality of which I could rest assured. If you were to ask me, "Who are you?" I should be thankful to be able to say, "A lazy man." Yes, I place it beyond doubt that I should like it to be said of myself that I am a sluggard. "A lazy man"—in that there is connoted a whole calling, a whole destiny, a whole career! Do not laugh at me. What I say is true. Once upon a time I used to belong to a leading club, and to cultivate the art of self-respect; and among my club acquaintances there was a man whose lifelong boast it was that he was an infallible judge of "Chateau Lafitte." Upon this accomplish-

ment he looked as a positive merit, and was never
in doubt about it; with the result that he died, if
not with a quiet conscience, at all events respect-
ably. And he was right in his way of life. I, too,
used to wish to have a similar career. I, too, longed
to become a sluggard and a glutton—though not
merely a sluggard and a glutton, but a sluggard
and a glutton who could sympathise with "the great
and the beautiful." Does that meet with your
approval? It is a long time now since I had such
fancies; yet all through my forty years of subterranean
life that craze for "the great and the beautiful" has
remained as an obsession. Once upon a time things
were different. Once upon a time I longed for a
congenial sphere of activity in which I should be
able ceaselessly to drink to the health of "the great
and the beautiful." Yes, I used to seek every
possible opportunity of dropping a tear into my cup
before emptying a bumper to the health of "the
great and the beautiful." I used to refer everything
in the world to that standard, and, even in regard
to the most damnable and indisputable rubbish,
would first of all consult "the great and the beautiful," and be as ready with my tears as a wet sponge.
For instance, an artist would paint some picture
or another, and I would hasten to drink to the health
of the artist who had painted that picture, since I
loved only "the great and the beautiful." Or an
author would write some book or another, and
again I would hasten to drink to the health of the
author who had written that book, since I loved
only "the great and the beautiful."

Also, I was firmly persuaded that I ought to be
looked up to for this; so that at any time I was
ready to put a man through his paces who refused
to show me that respect. To live in peace, and to
die with *éclat*—yes, that constituted my whole aim
and object in life. I even dreamed of growing a fat
stomach, developing a triple chin, and fashioning
for myself a purple nose, in the hope that every one

who met me would exclaim as he gazed upon my
figure, "See, there goes something *substantial*,
something *positive!*" Well, they might have said
that as much as they liked; for, in this negative
age, gentlemen, it is always pleasant to hear of
anything positive.

VII

BUT these are mere golden dreams. Who was it
first said, first propounded the theory, that man
does evil only because he is blind to his own interests, but that if he were enlightened, if his eyes were
opened to his real, his normal interests, he would
at once cease to do evil, and become virtuous and
noble for the reason that, being now enlightened
and brought to understand what is best for him,
he would discern his true advantage only in what is
good (since it is a known thing that no man of set
purpose acts against his own interests), and therefore would of necessity also *do* what is good? Oh,
the simplicity of the youth who said this! Oh,
the utter artlessness of the prattler! To begin
with, since when, during these thousands of years,
has man ever acted solely in accordance with his
own interests? What about the millions of facts
which go to show that only too often man knowingly (that is to say, with a full comprehension of
what is his true advantage) puts that advantage
aside in favour of some other plan, and betakes
himself to a road, to risks, to the unknown, to which
no agent nor agency has compelled him, as though,
unwilling to follow the appointed path, he preferred
to essay a difficult and awkward road along which
he must feel his way in darkness? Would it not
almost seem as though the directness, the voluntari-
ness, of such a course had for him a greater attraction than any advantage? Advantage, indeed?
What, after all, *is* advantage? Would *you,* gentle-

men, undertake exactly to define wherein human advantage consists? What if human advantage not only *may,* but *does,* consist of the fact that, on certain occasions, man may desire, not what is good for him, but what is bad? And if this be so, if this really be so, the rule falls to the ground at once. What is your opinion about it? Can it be so? I see you smiling. Well, smile away, gentlemen, but also answer me this : Can human interests *ever* be properly reckoned up? May there not always remain interests which never have been, never can be, included in any classification? You, gentlemen, take your lists of human interests from averages furnished by statistics and economic formulæ. Your lists of interests include only prosperity, riches, freedom, tranquillity, and so forth, and any one who openly and knowingly disagreed with those lists would, in your opinion (as in mine also, for that matter), be either an obscurantist or a madman. Would he not? But the most surprising point is this—that statists, savants, and lovers of the human race never fail, in their summing up of human interests, to overlook *one interest in particular.* This interest is never taken into account in the shape in which it ought to be taken ; and this fact vitiates all their calculations. Yet, were they to add this interest to their summaries, no great harm would be done. The mischief lies in the fact that this particular interest declines to fall under any particular heading, or to enter into any particular schedule. For instance, I might have a friend—as also might you yourselves, gentlemen (for who has not?)—who, when about to embark upon a given piece of work, might tell one, clearly and grandiloquently, that he intends to proceed strictly on lines of truth and reason. He might even go so far as to speak with emotion and enthusiasm of the nature of true, normal human interests, and with a smile to inveigh against shortsighted dolts who do not understand either their own interests or the proper meaning of virtue. Yet within only a quarter of an hour, and without any sudden, unforeseen event having arisen—merely in accordance with something which is stronger than all his other interests put together—this same man may cut straight across what he himself has said—that is to say, cut straight across both the dictates of reason and his own true interests and everything else! Yet this friend of mine is but one of a type; wherefore the fault cannot be laid at his door alone. May there not, therefore, exist something which to most men is even dearer than their true interests? Or, not to infringe the logical sequence, may there not exist some supreme interest of interests (the additional interest of which I am speaking) which is greater and more absorbing than any other interest, and for which man, if the need should arise, is ready to contravene every law, and to lose sight alike of common sense, honour, prosperity, and ease—in a word, of all the things which are fair and expedient—if haply he can gain for himself that primal, that supreme, advantage which he conceives to be the dearest thing on earth?

"Ah well, there are interests and interests," you might interrupt me at this point. Pardon me, gentlemen, but I ought to make it clear that, not to juggle with words, this interest of which I am speaking is a notable one, and escapes all classification, and shatters every system which has ever been established by lovers of the human race for that race's improvement. In short, let it be understood that it is an interest which introduces general confusion into everything. Before naming to you that interest I should like to damn myself for ever in your eyes by telling you bluntly that all those fine systems of, and schemes for, demonstrating to mankind its true, its normal, interests, and for explaining to it that, so long as it strives to attain its true interests, it will ever grow better and more noble, are so much dialectic. Yes, I say so much dialectic.

To maintain theories of renovating the human race through systems of classification of true interests is, in my opinion, about the same thing as—well, about the same thing as to maintain that man grows milder with civilisation, and, consequently, less bloodthirsty, less addicted to fighting. Logically, perhaps, that *does* happen; yet he is so prone to systems and to abstract deductions that he is for ever ready to mutilate the truth, to be blind to what he sees, and deaf to what he hears, so long only as he can succeed in vindicating his logic. Of this let me give an example which will be clear to all. Look around you at the world. Everywhere you will see blood flowing in streams, and as merrily as champagne. Look at our nineteenth century; look at Napoleon—the great Napoleon and the modern one; look at North America, with its everlasting "Union"; look at the present caricature of Schleswig-Holstein. What has civilisation done to instil greater mildness into our bosoms? Civilisation develops in man nothing but an added capacity for receiving impressions. That is all. And the growth of that capacity further augments man's tendency to seek pleasure in blood-letting. Nothing else has civilisation conferred upon him. You may have noticed that the most enthusiastic blood-letters have almost invariably been the most civilised of men— men whose shoes even Attila [1] and Stenka Razin [2] would have been unworthy to unloose; and if such men as the former have not bulked in the public eye quite so largely as have Attila and Stenka Razin, it is only because the former have been too numerous, too transitory. At all events civilisation has rendered man, if not more bloodthirsty, at least a worse (in the sense of a meaner) thirster after blood than before. Once upon a time he considered blood-letting to be just retribution, and could therefore,

[1] Chieftain of the Huns who conquered Rome.
[2] Leader of a Cossack rebellion during the reign of Catherine the Great.

with a quiet conscience, exterminate any one whom
he wanted to; but now we account blood-letting a
crime—and indulge in that crime even more than in
former days.   Which, then, is the worst of the two?
Well, judge for yourselves.   It is said that Cleopatra
(if I may take an instance from Roman history)
loved to thrust golden pins into the breasts of her
slaves, and took pleasure in the cries and contor-
tions of her victims.   Possibly you may say that all
this happened in a comparatively barbarous age—
that even at the present day the times are barbarous
—that golden pins are still being thrust into
people's breasts—that though man, in many things,
has learnt to see clearer now than he used to do
in *more* barbarous ages, he has not yet learnt to
act wholly as reason and science would have him
do.   Yet all the while, I know, you are persuaded
in your own minds that man is bound to improve
as soon as ever he has dropped some old, bad
customs of his, and allowed science and healthy
thought alone to nourish, to act as the normal
directors of, human nature.   Yes, I know that you
are persuaded that eventually man will cease to err
of set purpose, or to let his will clash with his normal
interests.   On the contrary (say you), science will
in time show man (though, in our opinion, it is
superfluous to do so) that he does not possess *any*
will or initiative of his own, and never has done,
but that he is as the keyboard of a piano, or as the
handle of a hurdy-gurdy.   Above all, science will
show him that in the world there exist certain laws
of nature which cause everything to be done, not of
man's volition, but of nature's, and in accordance
with her laws.   Consequently, say you, those laws
will only need to be *explained* to man, and at once
he will become divested of all responsibility, and
find life a much easier thing to deal with.   All
human acts will then be mathematically computed
according to nature's laws, and entered in tables
of logarithms which extend to about the 108,000th

degree, and can be combined into a calendar. Better still, there will be published certain carefully revised editions of this calendar (after the manner of modern encyclopædias) in which everything will be enumerated and set down so exactly that henceforth the world will cease to know wrong-doing, or any occasion for the same.

Then (I am supposing *you* still to be speaking) there will arise new economic relations—relations all ready for use, and calculated with mathematical precision, so that in a flash all possible questions will come to an end, for the reason that to all possible questions there will have been compiled a store of all possible answers. Then there will arise the Golden Palace of the legends. Then—well, *then*, in a word, there will dawn the millennium ! . . . Of course, though (it is *I* who am now speaking), you cannot very well guarantee that things will not have come to be excessively dull, seeing that there will be nothing left for us to do when everything has been computed beforehand and tabulated. By this I do not mean to say that things will not also be excessively *regular*. I only mean to say, is there anything which dullness will not lead men to devise? For instance, out of sheer *ennui*, golden pins may again be inserted into victims' breasts. That is all. It is shameful to have to think that into everything which is goodly man loves to thrust golden pins ! Yes, he is a gross animal, phenomenally gross. Rather, he is not so much gross as ungrateful to a degree which nothing else in the world can equal. For instance, I should not be surprised if, amid all this order and regularity of the future, there should suddenly arise, from some quarter or another, some gentleman of lowborn— or, rather, of retrograde and cynical—demeanour who, setting his arms akimbo, should say to you all : "How now, gentlemen? Would it not be a good thing if, with one consent, we were to kick all this solemn wisdom to the winds, and to send

those logarithms to the devil, and to begin to live
our lives again according to our own stupid
whims?" Yet this would be as nothing; the really
shameful part of the business would be that this
gentleman would find a goodly number of adherents.
Such is always man's way. And he might act thus
for the shallowest of reasons; for a reason which
is not worth mentioning; for the reason that, always,
and everywhere, and no matter what his station,
man loves to act as he *likes,* and not necessarily as
reason and self-interest would have him do. Yes,
he will even act straight against his own interests.
Indeed, he is sometimes *bound* to do so. Such, at
least, is my notion of the matter. His own will,
free and unfettered; his own untutored whims; his
own fancies, sometimes amounting almost to a madness—here we have that superadded interest of
interests which enters into no classification, which
for ever consigns systems and theories to the devil.
Whence do savants have it that man needs a
normal, a virtuous, will? What, in particular, has
made these pundits imagine that what man most
needs is a will which is acutely alive to man's interests? Why, what man most needs is an *independent*
will—no matter what the cost of such independence
of volition, nor what it may lead to. Yet the devil
only knows what man's will——

VIII

"Ha, ha, ha!" I can imagine you interrupting
me with a chuckle. "Whether you choose to think
so or not, there is no such thing in the world as
human will. Science has so far dissected man as
to make it absolutely clear that his volition and
so-called freewill are but——"

Wait a moment, gentlemen. I was just going
to say the same thing myself, though I confess that
I was feeling a little nervous about it. I was just

going to observe that the devil only knows what
man's will depends upon, when suddenly (the Lord
be thanked!) I recalled that precious science of
yours, and broke off short. However, you have
now said it for me. As a matter of fact, if ever
there shall be discovered a formula which shall
exactly express our wills and whims; if ever there
shall be discovered a formula which shall make it
absolutely clear what those wills depend upon, and
what laws they are governed by, and what means
of diffusion they possess, and what tendencies they
follow under given circumstances; if ever there shall
be discovered a formula which shall be mathematical
in its precision, well, gentlemen, whenever such a
formula shall be found, man will have ceased to
have a will of his own—he will have ceased even
to exist. Who would care to exercise his will-
power according to a table of logarithms? In such
a case man would become, not a human being at all,
but an organ-handle, or something of the kind.
What but the handle of a hurdy-gurdy *could* a
human being represent who was devoid either of
desires or volition? Is it not so? Reckoning all
the possibilities, could things ever come to be thus?

"Hm," you might conceivably reply, "our wills
mostly err through adopting false views of our interests. Sometimes we will what is sheer rubbish,
for the reason that in such rubbish we foolish fellows
perceive the easiest way to the attainment of some
presupposed advantage. But if all were to be
tabulated and set forth on paper (which it would be
quite an easy thing to do, seeing that to assume
that man is incapable of learning a few laws of
nature is senseless and absurd), there would, of
course, be an end to our so-called power of volition.
If, on the other hand, our volition were always to
march with our reason, we should invariably exercise
that reason in preference to our freewill, since such
exercise of one's reasoning powers would prevent
us from ever again desiderating foolish things, or

wilfully cutting across our own judgment by desiderating for ourselves what would be harmful." Well,
if all desires and resolutions (of course, it is *I* who
am now supposed to be speaking) can be exactly
computed, for the reason that they are revealed to
us beforehand by the laws of our so-called freewill,
I do not really see that I am jesting when I say that
something after the manner of tables *might* be compiled, and that we should be forced to exercise our
volition only according to what might be found in
them. Yet were those tables to tell me, to reckon
for me, that, should I (say) point with my finger
to an object, I should be doing so simply because it
would have been impossible for me to do otherwise,
or even to point to the object in question with any
other finger than the one I used—well, in that
case what element of freedom would remain to me,
even though I were an educated man, and had gone
through a course of science? In short, if things
were so arranged, I might be able to forecast my
life for (say) the next thirty years, and there would
be nothing left for me to do, and I should not so
much as require an intelligence. All that I should
need to do would be to keep on reminding myself
that never, and under no circumstances, will nature
ask me what I *desire* to do, but must be taken just
as she is rather than as what we would have liked
her to be. Therefore, if our tendency is towards
tablets and calendars—yes, or even towards retorts
—we shall just have to accept them. Nature is
always herself, and therefore requires her retorts
to be taken with her.

For me, however, all such matters are bagatelles.
Pardon my philosophising like this, gentlemen, but
it is the fruit of forty years in the underworld, and
you must not mind my building castles in the air.
See here : reason is an excellent thing—I do not
deny that for a moment; but reason is reason, and
no more, and satisfies only the reasoning faculty in
man, whereas volition is a manifestation of all life

D

(that is to say, of human life as a whole, with reason and every other sort of appendage included). It is true that, in this particular manifestation of it, human life is all too frequently a sorry failure; yet it nevertheless *is* life, and not the mere working out of a square root. For my own part, I naturally wish to satisfy *all* my faculties, and not my reasoning faculty alone (that is to say, a mere twentieth portion of my capacity for living). For what does reason know ? Reason only knows that man possesses a certain capability of apprehension. Anything else, believe me, it does *not* know. This may be poor comfort, yet why should it not be said? On the other hand, human nature acts as a whole, and with all that is contained in it; so that, whether conscious or unconscious, sane or mad, it is always human nature. Now, I suspect, gentlemen, that you regard me with pity, for you keep telling me that man can never be really enlightened or developed—he can never be what the *future* human being will be—through the fact that he knowingly desiderates for himself what is harmful to his best interests. This is mathematical deduction, you say. I do not dispute it. It *is* mathematical deduction. Yet *I* tell *you* (and for about the hundredth time) that there is one occasion, and one occasion only, when man can wilfully, consciously desiderate for himself what is foolish and harmful. This is the occasion when he yearns *to have the right* to desiderate for himself what is foolish and harmful, and to be bound by no obligation whatsoever to desiderate anything that is sensible. It is his crowning folly; it is wherein we see his ineradicable waywardness. Yet such folly may also be the best thing in the world for him, even though it work him harm, and contradict our soundest conclusions on the subject of interests. This is because it is possible for his folly to preserve to him, under all circumstances, the chief, the most valuable, of all his possessions— namely, his personality, his individuality. Yes, it is not I alone who maintain that this is the most priceless asset whereof man can boast. Of course, he *may* make his volition march with his reason, and the more so if the former does not abuse the latter, but uses it with moderation. Such a proceeding is expedient, and may, at times, even be praiseworthy; but only too often do we see volition clashing with reason, and—and—— Yet, do you know, gentlemen, *this too*, at times, may be both expedient and praiseworthy. For suppose man *not* to be innately foolish (in reality this could never be said of him, except in so far as that it might be urged that, if he be foolish, who in the world is wise?); yet, though he may not be foolish, he is at least monstrously ungrateful, phenomenally ungrateful. In fact, I believe that the best possible definition of man would be "A creature which walks on two legs and is devoid of gratitude." And this is not all—this is not his principal failing. No; his greatest failing is his constant immorality, which began with the Flood, and has lasted up to the present Schleswig-Holstein period of human history. Consequently, immorality being his leading weakness, so also is unreason, for it is an axiom that unreason arises from immorality. Try if it does not. Glance at the history of mankind, and tell me what you see there. Immensity? Well, what availed even the Colossus of Rhodes? Not for nothing did some people maintain that it was the work of human hands, while others asserted that it had been fashioned by nature herself. Variety? Well, in all ages and in all nations, what has been the use of discriminating between certain uniforms worn by military men and civilians, so long as there were no non-uniformed people, nor yet any men of learning? Uniformity? Well, in history men fight and fight, and are fighting now, and have always fought, and fought again. I should imagine that *here* you see an *excess* of uniformity! Everything, therefore, which could possibly enter into the most disordered

of imaginations might well be said of the history of
the world. Yet there is one thing which could *not*
be said of it—and that is, that it affords much of a
spectacle of reason. If one were to state the contrary one would choke at the very first word. In
particular, we are continually confronted, in history,
with the diverting circumstance that there continually
figure in its pages large numbers of moral, sensible
men and scholars and lovers of the human race who
make it their prime object in life to behave as morally
and as sensibly as possible—to, as it were, enlighten
their neighbours by proving to them the possibility
of leading, in this world, both a moral and a sensible
existence. Yet what is the good of all this? We
know that, sooner or later, many of these philan-
thropists undergo a change, and display phases of
a most unseemly order. Consequently, I would ask
you—what are we to expect from man, seeing that
he is a creature endowed with such strange qualities?
You may heap upon him every earthly blessing, you
may submerge him in well-being until the bubbles
shoot to the surface of his prosperity as though it
were a pond, you may give him such economic
success that nothing will be left for him to do but
to sleep and to eat dainties and to prate about the
continuity of the world's history; yes, you may do
all this, but none the less, out of sheer ingratitude,
sheer devilment, he will end by playing you some
dirty trick. He will imperil his comfort, and purposely desiderate for himself deleterious rubbish,
some improvident trash, for the sole purpose that
he may alloy all the solemn good sense which has
been lavished upon him with a portion of the futile,
fantastical element which forms part of his very
composition. Yes, it is these same fantastical
dreams, this same debased stupidity, that he most
wishes to retain in order to feel assured of the one
thing with which he cannot dispense—namely, of
the knowledge that men are still men, and not key-
boards of pianos over which the hands of Nature

may play at their own sweet will, and continue so
to play until they threaten to deprive him of all
volition, save by rote and according to calendars.
Moreover, even if man *were* the keyboard of a piano,
and could be convinced that the laws of nature and
of mathematics had made him so, he would still
decline to change. On the contrary, he would once
more, out of sheer ingratitude, attempt the perpe-
tration of something which would enable him to
insist upon himself; and if he could not effect this,
he would then proceed to introduce chaos and disruption into everything, and to devise enormities of
all kinds, for the sole purpose, as before, of asserting his personality. He would need but to launch a
single curse upon the world, and the mere fact that
man alone is able to utter curses (the one privilege
by which he is differentiated from the other animals)
would, through the very act of commination, effect
his purpose for him—namely, the purpose of con-
vincing himself that he really *is* a man, and not the
keyboard of a piano. But if you were to tell me that
all this could be set down in tables—I mean the
chaos, and the confusion, and the curses, and all
the rest of it—so that the possibility of computing
everything might remain, and reason continue to
rule the roost—well, in that case, I believe, man
would *purposely* become a lunatic, in order to become
devoid of reason, and therefore able to insist upon
himself. I believe this, and I am ready to vouch
for this, simply for the reason that every human
act arises out of the circumstance that man is for
ever striving to prove to his own satisfaction that
he is a man and not an organ-handle. And, however
devious his methods, he *has* succeeded in proving
it; however troglodyte-like his mode of working may
have been, he *has* succeeded in proving it. So in
future, perhaps, you will refrain from asserting that
this particular interest of his is nugatory, or that
his volition depends upon anything at all?

Also, you often tell me (or, rather, you tell me

whenever you deign to favour me with a single word) that no one can deprive me of my freewill, and that I ought so to arrange matters that my freewill shall, of its own volition, coincide with my normal interest, and with the laws of nature, and with arithmetic.

Ah, gentlemen! How much freewill should I have left to me when we had come to tables and arithmetic—when only the rule that twice two make four had come to hold the board? However much twice two might make four, my will would, to the end, remain my will.

IX

GENTLEMEN, I need hardly say that, so far, I have been jesting. Yet, poor as my jests may have been, not everything which I have said has been uttered in mockery : for some of my jests have been spoken through clenched teeth. Certain questions are disturbing my soul, and I beg of you to solve them. For instance, you say that you desire man to unlearn certain of his old customs, and to regulate his will according to the dictates of science and of sane thought. But how know you that man not only *can,* but *must,* change? What leads you to suppose that the human will stands in need of being regulated? In short, how come you to feel certain that such regulation of man's will would bring him any advantage, or that if he refrained from flying in the face of his real, his normal interests (as guaranteed by the deductions of reason and of arithmetic) such a course would *really* be good for him, or require to be made the law for all humanity? So far all this is only a proposition put forward by yourselves—a mere law (we must suppose) that has been made by logicians rather than by humanity as a whole. Perhaps you think me mad, gentlemen? Well, if so, I plead guilty; I quite agree with you. Man is essentially a constructive animal—an animal for ever destined to strive towards a goal, and to apply himself to the pursuit of engineering, in the shape of ceaseless attempts to build a road which shall lead him to an unknown destination. But that is just why man so often *turns aside* from the road. He turns aside for the reason that he is *constrained* to attempt the journey; he turns aside because, being at once foolish and an independent agent, he sometimes takes it into his head that, though the road in question may eventually bring him to a destination of some sort, that destination always lies ahead of him. Consequently, as an irresponsible child, he is led at times to disregard his trade as an engineer, and to give himself up to that fatal indolence which, as we know, is the mother of all vices. Man loves to construct and to lay out roads—of that there can be no question; but why does he also love so passionately to bring about general ruin and chaos? Answer me that. First of all, however, I myself have a word or two to say about it. May not his passion for bringing about general disorder (a passion which, we must admit, allows of no dispute) arise from the fact that he has an instinctive dread of *completely* attaining his end, and so of finishing his building operations? May it not be the truth that only from a distance, and not from close at hand, does he love the edifice which he is erecting? That is to say, may it not be that he loves to create it, but not to *live* in it—only to hand it over, when completed, to *les animaux domestiques*, in the shape of ants, sheep, and so forth?

Ants are creatures of quite a different taste. They are constantly constructing marvellous edifices, but ones that shall be for ever indestructible. From the antheap all respectable ants take their origin, and in it (probably) they meet their end. This does credit alike to their continuity and to their perseverance. On the other hand, man is a frivolous, a specious creature, and, like a chess-player, cares more for the process of attaining his goal than for the goal itself. Besides, who knows (for it never does to be too sure) that the aim which man strives for upon earth may not be contained in this ceaseless continuation of the process of attainment (that is to say, in the process which is comprised in the living of life) rather than in the aim itself, which, of course, is contained in the formula that twice two make four? Yet, gentlemen, this formula is not life at all; it is only the beginning of death! At all events men have always been afraid to think that twice two make four, and I am afraid of it too. Can it be, therefore, that, though man is for ever working to attain this formula, and though, in his search for it, he sails all the seas and sacrifices his whole life to the acquisition of his end, he fears *really* to succeed in the quest, for the reason that, if he were suddenly to come upon the formula, he would feel that he had nothing left to look for? Workmen, on completing their weekly tasks, receive their wages, and betake themselves to the tavern to make merry. Such is their weekly diversion. But whither can man in the mass betake himself? It is plain that he feels ill at ease when the end of his labour has really been reached. That is to say, he loves to attain, but not *completely* to attain; which, of course, is an exceedingly ridiculous *trait* in his character, and would appear to contain a paradox. In any case the formula that twice two make four is the factor which, of all others, he cannot stomach; nor do *I* look upon it in any other light than as an abomination, since it is a formula which wears an impertinent air as, meeting you on the road, it sets its arms akimbo, and spits straight in your face. True, I agree that, in its way, it is well enough; yet I also beg leave to say (if I must apportion praise all round) that the formula "Twice two make five" is not without its attractions.

Why, then, are you so absolutely, so portentously, certain that one thing, and one thing only, is normal and positive—in a word, good—for mankind? Does reason never err in estimating what is advantageous? May it not be that man occasionally loves something besides prosperity? May it not be that he also loves *adversity?* And may not adversity be as good for him as is happiness? Certainly there are times when man *does* love adversity, and love it passionately; so do not resort to history for your justification, but, rather, put the question to *yourselves*, if you are men, and have had any experience of life. For my part, I look upon undivided love of prosperity as something almost indecent; for to cause an occasional catastrophe, come weal come woe, seems to me a very pleasant thing to do. Yet I am not altogether for adversity, any more than I am altogether for prosperity; what I most stand for is my personal freewill, and for what it can do for me when I feel in the right mood to use it. I know that adversity is not thought acceptable in vaudeville plays, and that in the Palace of Crystal [1] it would be a thing quite unthinkable, for the reason that, since adversity connotes a denial and a doubt, no edifice of the kind could exist wherein a doubt was harboured. Nevertheless, I feel certain that man never wholly rejects adversity (in the sense of chaos and disruption of his schemes); for adversity is the mainspring of self-realisation. When beginning these letters I said that, in my opinion, self-realisation is, for man, a supreme misfortune; yet I am sure that he loves it dearly, and that he would not exchange it for any other sort of delight. For example, adversity is immeasurably superior to the formula that twice two make four; for if the latter were ever to be found, what would there remain for us to do or to realise? All that there would remain for us to do would be to muzzle our five senses, and to relapse into a state of perpetual contemplation. The same result (namely, that there might remain nothing for us to do) might arise from self-realisa-

---

[1] A Russian expression for the millennium.

tion; yet in that case one could at least give oneself
an occasional castigation, and revivify oneself. This
might be a retrograde course to take, yet at least it
would be better than nothing.

X

You believe, do you not, in a palace of crystal
which shall be for ever unbreakable—in an edifice,
that is to say, at which no one shall be able to put
out his tongue, or in any other way to mock? Now,
for the very reason that it must be made of crystal,
and for ever unbreakable, and one whereat no one
shall put out his tongue, I should fight shy of such
a building. For do you not see that if the edifice
were not a palace, but a hencoop, and rain were to
begin falling, I might take refuge in that hencoop,
yet should hardly be likely, out of mere gratitude
for its shelter, to mistake it for the residence of a
king? At this you may laugh, or you may even go
so far as to say that, in such a matter, a hencoop
would do as well as the most stately fane. If so, I
should retort, "Yes—provided that one's sole object
in life is to avoid getting wet."

But how if I were to take it into my head that
one need not live for that purpose alone, and that if
one *must* live, it were best done in a palace? I am
supposing such to be my will, my desire. In that
case you could not rid me of my desire by any method
save that of abrogating my will-power. And even
supposing such abrogation to be possible for you to
accomplish, and that you had some counter attraction
to offer me, and that you could provide me with a
new ideal, I might *still* decline to mistake a hencoop
for a palace. And even if a palace of crystal were
only a thing of dreams and, by the laws of nature,
a sheer impossibility, and even if only my individual
folly, added to certain old-established, irrational customs of my generation, had made me imagine it,

what, even then, should I care if it *were* an impossibility? Would it not be all one to me whether it
existed or not—or, rather, whether it existed or not
so long as my desire for its existence ceased? . . .
Again I see you smiling. Well, smile away. I take
your smiles for what they are worth, for at least I am
not in the habit of saying that I am surfeited when
I am hungry, or that I do not know that my hopes
are based upon something better than a mere com-
promise, an ever-recurring nought, which the laws
of nature may (and, indeed, *do*) allow to exist. The
crown of my desires is not a block of flats, with its
tenements let as offices to dentists, or as homes to
poor lodgers on thousand-year leases; but if you
were to annul my volition, to erase my ideals, and
to show me something *better,* I might then come
to fall in with your views. To this you might reply
that to convince me would not be worth your while;
whereupon I might make a similar retort: after
which we might solemnly discuss the matter a little
further, until finally you decided that I was not
deserving of your attention. I should not greatly
care. For me there will always remain the underworld.

Meanwhile, I go on living, and exercising my
volition : and may my hand wither ere ever I use it
to add so much as a brick to any block of tenements !
Never mind that only a short while ago I rejected
the idea of a crystal edifice, for the sole reason that
I should not be able to put out my tongue at it.
What I then said I did not say because I am fond
of putting out my tongue at things, but because, of
all buildings, an edifice whereat no one can mock
is the only one that has not yet come into existence.
On the contrary, of sheer gratitude I would cut out
my tongue if matters could be so arranged that I
should never at any time feel a desire to protrude
that member. What care I that an edifice of such
a kind is impossible, and that I must rest content
with my present lodgings? Why should such desires

occur to me at all? Merely in order that, eventually,
I may come to the conclusion that my whole organ-
isation is a fraud? Is that the object of it all? I
do not believe it.

Yet of one thing I am certain—namely, that a
denizen of the underworld ought always to ride himself upon the bit; for although for forty years he
may sit silently in his den, let him once issue into
the light of day, and straightway he will take the
bit in his teeth, and continue talking, and talking,
and talking. . . .

XI

So at length, gentlemen, we have reached the
conclusion that the best thing for us to do is to do
nothing at all, but to sink into a state of contempla-
tive inertia. For that purpose all hail the underworld! True, I said above that I profoundly envy
the normal man; yet, under the conditions in which
I see him placed, I have no wish to be he. That is
to say, though I envy him, I find the underworld
better, since at least one can—— Yet I am lying.
I am lying because, even as I know that two and
two make four, so do I know that it is not the
underworld which is so much better, but something
else, something else—something for which I am
hungry, but which I shall never find. Ah no! To
the devil with the underworld!

At least, though, I should find things better if I
could bring myself to believe a single word of all
that I have written. I swear to you, gentlemen,
that not a single syllable of what I have been jot-
ting down enjoys my confidence. That is to say, I
believe it all, but at the same time I suspect—somehow I feel—that, throughout, I have been lying like
a bootmaker.

"Why, then, have you written it?" you might
ask me; to which I should reply—

The Underworld

"Supposing I were to submerge *you* somewhere
for forty years, and that you had no occupation to
beguile the time, and that, during the whole of
those forty years, you were forced to keep peering
out of the underworld, what would become of *you*
under such circumstances? Can a man spend forty
years alone, yet do nothing at all?"

"But it is no shame, no degradation, to you,"
you might retort, with a toss of the head. "It is
only natural for you to hunger for life, but the
mischief is that you seek to decide the *questions* of
life by a mass of logical tangles. How daring, how
insolent, are your sallies, though all the while you
are shaking with fear! You talk arrant nonsense,
yet you are delighted with it. You give vent to
impertinences, yet you are afraid of them, and hasten
to beg our pardon. You assure us that you care
for nothing, yet in the same breath you come cring-
ing to us for our opinion. You declare that you
speak through clenched teeth, yet the next moment
you attempt witticisms in order to make us laugh.
In short, though well aware that your witticisms are
not witty, you appear to rest perfectly satisfied with
them, so long only as they are orthographically correct. Possibly, in your time, you have had to suffer,
but at least you do not show any respect for your
suffering. A grain or two of truth may lie in you,
yet not an atom of reticence, since your petty vanity
leads you to make a show of everything—to befoul
it, and to air it in the market-place. You try to
speak concisely, yet your nervousness leads you to
spin a perfect web of words, for the reason that you
have not a particle of self-confidence, but only a sort
of pusillanimous knavery. You keep praising self-
knowledge, yet at the same time you continue to
vacillate, for the reason that, though your mind
be working, your heart is befogged with corruption.
Without a pure heart there can be no full, no true,
realisation of self. And what an impudent way you
have with it all! What strings of questions you

ask, and what fearful grimaces you make! Yet all of what you say is lies, lies from beginning to end."

This speech I have, of course, invented for you out of my own head—another trick which the underworld has taught me. You must remember that for forty years I, in my cranny here, have been listening to the kind of stuff which you usually utter. Yes, I have been listening to it, and thinking it over, until it is no great marvel that I have learnt it all by heart, and can set it down in more or less literary form.

But are you actually so credulous as to suppose that I intend to have it all printed, and to give it to you to read? True, I myself am rather puzzled to know why I keep on calling you "gentlemen," and addressing you as though you were destined to be my readers. Confessions such as mine should never be printed, nor handed to others for perusal. At all events *I* have not sufficient self-confidence for that course, nor do I think it necessary. My reason for writing must be that the idea of it has entered my head and stuck there. That is how it must be.

Every man's reminiscences include things which he reveals, not to all men and sundry, but to his friends alone. Again, every man's reminiscences include things which he does not reveal even to his friends, but to himself alone, and then only under a close seal of secrecy. Lastly, every man's reminiscences include things which he hesitates to reveal even to himself. Of this latter category there soon becomes accumulated in the mind of every decent man a large store. The more decent he be, the larger will his store of such recollections become. Recently I decided to recall to my memory certain of my old experiences, but until now have always deferred doing so, through a feeling of uneasiness even at the idea. Now, however, that I am minded, not only to recall things, but to write them down, I wish, in particular, to try whether one can *ever*

be really open with oneself—*ever* be really fearless
of any item of truth. *En passant*, Heine has said
that a true autobiography is practically impossible,
since every man lies to himself. In his (Heine's)
opinion, even Rousseau, in his *Confessions,* lied—
partly out of set purpose, and partly out of vanity.
And I believe that Heine is right. I myself know
how vanity may lead a man to impute whole crimes
to himself; of the working of such vanity I have a
good idea. But Heine was speaking of men who
write their confessions *for the public eye,* whereas
I wish to write but for myself alone. Let me therefore state, once and for all, that, though I may seem
to be writing for the eye of a reader, I do so out of
mere show, and for the reason that I find that that
kind of writing comes easier. It is all mere form
—all a mere empty form, for I shall never have a
reader. This I have explained before.

Moreover, I do not wish to be restricted in the
scope of my writing. Consequently I intend to
observe therein no order or system. What I
remember, that I shall write down.

Upon this you might catch me up, and say: "If
you do not count upon being read, why is it that
you make these compacts with yourself, and set
them down on paper?—the compacts, we mean, that
you will observe no order or system in your writing,
and that you will write down just what you remember, and so forth? To whom are you speaking? In
whose eyes are you seeking to excuse yourself?"

I should merely reply: "Wait and see."

For it may be that there is a whole psychology
of reasons for what I do. Possibly I am simply a
coward. Or possibly it is that I have purposely
imagined to myself a public in order to cut the
better figure when I *really* come to write for the
public. In short, there may exist a thousand reasons
for my action.

Again, for precisely what reason, for precisely
what purpose, do I desire to write? If not for the

benefit of the public, why cannot I remember things without committing them to paper?

Certainly I *could* adopt that course; but on paper my reminiscences are more likely to come out regularly and in order. Besides, in doing so there will be something inspiring, and I shall be able to keep a better rein over myself, and to add a word or two here and there. Again, it is possible that I shall gain from the mere labour of writing a certain *relief*, for one oppressive reminiscence in particular is weighing heavily upon my mind—a reminiscence which recently came back to me, and remains in my thoughts like a musical *motif* which refuses to be banished. I must banish it somehow! A hundred others like it there are, yet at times this one in particular persists in standing out from the rest, and troubling me. Somehow I feel confident that, once it were written down, it would vanish for ever. Why should I not try the experiment?

Lastly, I wish to write because I am *ennuyé*, and have nothing in the world to do; whereas writing is at least work of a kind. They say that labour renders man good-hearted and honourable; wherefore I wish to avail myself even of *that* chance.

To-day half-melted, yellow, dirty snow is falling. It was falling yesterday, and it does so nearly every day. I believe that it is that same half-melted snow which has once more recalled to me the episode of which I cannot rid my thoughts; so here goes for my confession *ápropos* of the fall of sleet.

PART II

APROPOS OF THE FALLING SLEET

When from th' abyss, the darkness,
  A word of earnest prayer
Plucked your soul for an instant—
  For an instant dulled its care;
Wringing your hands, black curses
  You heaped upon your sin
As memory, that dread rider,
  Spurred with the rowels in.
Then did you, weeping, tell me
  The secrets of the past,
Till, torn, at bay, shame-stricken,
  Your soul stood bare at last.

From a poem by NEKRASSOV.

I

I WAS then thirty years old, and, so far, had lived a dull, ill-regulated existence that was wellnigh as solitary as that of a savage. I had no friends or intimates, and was gradually coming to confine myself more and more to my lodgings. In the same way, when working in my office, I never even looked at those around me, for I knew that my colleagues not only regarded me as an eccentric, but also felt for me a distinct distaste. Often I would ask myself why *I*, of all men, should excite such aversion. For instance, one of my comrades had a repellent, pox-riddled face that was almost ruffianly in its expression; it was a face of the kind (so it always seemed to me) with which no man would care to face the world; while another of my office-associates was so dirty in his person that he smelt aloud. Yet neither of these two gentlemen seemed in the least put about by this. They seemed to care not a pin

about their faces, their clothes, or anything else.
Neither the one nor the other of them seemed to
think that he was detested; or, if he thought so, at
least he did not care, so long as his superiors
approved of his work. On the other hand, *I* was
led by my boundless vanity and pretentiousness to
look upon myself with a dissatisfaction that, at times,
amounted almost to loathing. Consequently I attributed to every one the view of my personality which
I myself took. For instance, I detested my face
because I thought it had a knavish expression. I
even suspected it of looking a little vicious. The
result was that, while working in our office, I used
to make constant and desperate attempts to look
as "pure" as possible, in order to escape any imputation of viciousness, while I would also endeavour to make my face express the utmost possible
refinement. "Even if I *have* an ugly face," I used
to say, "at least I will force it to look distinguished,
speaking, and, above all things, clever." Yet I
knew, I knew only too painfully well, that my face
would never come to express any one of those things.
Worse still, I would take it into my head that my
countenance looked positively stupid, and feel over-
whelmed with despair. Indeed, I would not have
minded its vicious expression if only I could have
ensured its also being thought extremely clever.

Of course I hated and despised my colleagues.
Yet somehow, also, I was afraid of them, and at
times felt them to be my superiors. Yes, though I
despised them, there were times when I rated them
above myself. In fact, a man of the nineteenth
century who is at all educated and refined cannot
be vain without alternating between boundless self-
assertion and envious self-depreciation. Contemptuous or respectful, I lowered my eyes before persons
with whom I was brought in contact; and though
sometimes I would try to outstare them, I always
proved the first to avert my gaze. Also, I was
desperately afraid of appearing ridiculous, and paid

slavish heed to routine, and to everything that partook of an external nature. Yes, I took great care to walk always in the general rut, and dreaded lest I should discover in myself anything that savoured of eccentricity. But how was I to keep this up? I was a man of advanced tendencies, as befits a gentleman of the nineteenth century, whereas my comrades were men of dull habit, and as like one another as a flock of sheep. Probably I was the only man in our office who thought himself a poltroon and a slave because he was also a gentleman. Moreover, not only did I *think* myself a poltroon and a slave, but I was so in very truth. I say this without the least tinge of shame. Every educated man of the nineteenth century is, and must always be, a poltroon and a slave; it is his normal condition. Of that I, in those days, felt perfectly certain. Modern man is fashioned and constructed to that end and no other. Nor is it *now* only, and owing to fortuitous circumstances, that an educated man is bound to be both a coward and a bondsman; but for all time, and generally. Such is the law of nature for every educated man on this earth. If there should be anything upon which a man of refinement has cause to congratulate himself, he will derive no comfort or solace therefrom, since in all other matters he will still have to truckle to his neighbours. It is the inevitable, the eternal, result of his being what he is. Only the asinine family and its derivatives practise self-congratulation; and that only to a limited extent. But *them* we need not heed, since they signify precisely nothing.

One circumstance in particular used to torment me—namely, the circumstance that no one else was like me, and that I was like no one else. "I am a person to myself, whereas they are *everybody*," was my usual thought whenever I engaged in meditations on the subject. From this you will see that I was also extremely young.

In some ways, too, I was inconsistent, for

though at times I would find my office work perfectly
abhorrent—so much so that I often returned home
from it ill—at other times I would fall into an unexpected vein of scepticism and indifference (this often
occurred), and laugh at my own impatience and
distaste, and blame myself for what I called my
"romanticism." At such times I would talk with
any one, and not only argue with him, but also
consort with him on terms of friendship. Yes, my
dislike of my fellow men sometimes disappeared
entirely. Possibly I never really possessed that dislike, but derived it from books. Even to this day I
cannot quite decide the point. However, no sooner
had I broken the ice then I used to visit these friends
of mine, to play cards with them, to drink vodka,
and to talk "shop." . . . Here let me make a
slight digression.

Generally speaking, we Russians have never gone
in for that stupid transcendental romanticising of
German and, still more, French origin in which
nothing is ever done by anybody, though the ground
be shaking beneath one's feet and all France be
going to pieces at the barricades, so long only as
decorum forbids one to change, and one can go on
singing transcendental songs in what I might call
the grave of one's existence, for the reason that one
is a fool. In the Russian land there *are* no fools.
That is a fact, and one that distinguishes us from
all the other Germanic countries. Consequently,
Russia contains no transcendental natures in the
pure meaning of the term. Yet many of our public-
ists and critics have been in the habit of imagining
that our romanticists are similar to those of France
and Germany! On the contrary, the qualities of
our romanticists are directly opposed to the trans-
cendental-European standard, and not a single stanza
in the European style finds acceptance here. (You
must not mind my using the term "romanticism."
I do so only because it is an old and a respected one,
and has seen much service, and is familiar to every-

body.) The nature of *our* romanticists is to comprehend everything, to see everything, and frequently to see everything incomparably more clearly than do more practical intellects; not to accord offhand acceptance to anyone or anything, but nevertheless to be squeamish of nothing; to skate around everything, to yield politic way in everything; never to lose sight of the useful and the practical (as represented by such things as lodgings at the State's expense, pensions, and medals); to keep that end in view through all the enthusiasms and depressions of lyrical poetry; to cherish always within themselves "the great and the beautiful"; and to devote their own personalities, like so many precious jewels, to the furtherance—no matter in what trifles—of "the great and the beautiful." Yes, our romanticist is a man of wide sympathies, and the chief rogue whom we possess—that I can assure you from personal experience. Or at all events he is so if he is a wise man. But what am I saying? The romanticist is *in any case* a wise man. Rather, I mean that, though we used to have some mad romanticists among us, we need not take *them* into account, since, when just in the flower of their vigour, they became converted into Germans, and, the better to safeguard their treasures, went and settled in Weimar or Schwartzwald or some other German town. For my part, I used to have a sincere contempt for my official work, over and above the necessity which compelled me to sit on a stool and receive money for that work—an obligation, mark you, which I did *not* so greatly regret. On the other hand, if the ordinary foreign romantic were to lose his senses (though this does not very often happen) he would not feel in the least distressed at the prospect of having to be taken to the madhouse as "the King of Spain" or some such personage (that is to say, if he had gone *sufficiently* out of his mind); whereas with us only frail and aged romantics lose their reason. Moreover, the number of romantic

writers could never be computed; which fact has led
to their being divided into hosts and hosts of grades.
Also, their many-sidedness is astonishing. For instance, what a faculty they possess for combining
within themselves the most opposite of qualities! I
used to derive great amusement from the fact—from
the fact, that is to say, that among us there are
numbers of "broad-minded" writers who never lose
their ideals, and who, though unwilling to stir a
finger on behalf of those ideals, or to cease to be
anything but declared robbers and brigands, continue, to the point of weeping, to cherish their
original aspirations, while at the same time showing extraordinary singleness of heart. Yes, it is
only in Russia that the most abandoned of rascals
can be wholly, even splendidly, honourable men,
while also continuing to be rascals. Therefore I
repeat that the ranks of our romantics have given
rise to bands of such absolute scoundrels (I use the
term "scoundrels" with particular pleasure)—to
bands of men who display such a sense of the
realities, such a knowledge of the practical—that a
bewildered Government and public can but stand
and gape at them!

Yes, their many-sidedness is astonishing, and
God only knows whither at the present day it is
being bent and developed, or what it promises for
the future. Yet, after all, it does not make bad
material. I do not say this out of patriotism, nor in
a sour or sneering way, though I have an idea that
once more you will believe me to be poking fun at
you. Well, I greatly value and appreciate your
opinion, and would ask you to pardon me if I have
offended.

With my comrades I, of course, maintained no
intimacy, and soon grew tired of them. Indeed,
my then youthful inexperience led me not to curse
them, but simply to drop them. At home I read
a great deal, in a vain endeavour to drown in a flood
of external impressions what was seething within me.

The way to attain this lay, so far as I could see, only in reading. Books helped me, for by turns they soothed, stimulated, and pained my intellect. Yet at times I grew terribly weary of it all, and felt that, come what might, I must embark upon some kind of activity. Hence I would suddenly plunge into the lowest depths of foul, dark—well, not so much debauchery, as lewdness, for at that time my passions were keen, and derived all the greater heat from the aching, perpetual discontent with the world of which I was full : and to these bouts there would succeed intervals of hysteria which threw me into convulsions of weeping. I had no resource beyond reading. That is to say, there was nothing in my daily life which attracted me, or which I could respect. Above all things, constant depression seethed within me—a depression which, causing me to thirst for something different, for some sharp contrast, plunged me into vice. This I am not saying merely out of self-justification—— But again I have lied. I *am* saying it merely in order to justify myself. I make this confession for my own eyes alone, since I do not wish *you,* gentlemen, to think me a liar.

Stealthily, and by night, I used to indulge in solitary rounds of dissipation, but always with a timid, blackguardly, shamefaced sort of feeling which never deserted me even in my moments of greatest abasement (though at such times, true, it caused me to curse myself). It was the fruit of my long carrying of the underworld within me. Always, too, I had a great dread of being seen, or met, or recognised by any one; wherefore I would frequently change the venue of my dark proceedings.

One night, when passing a tavern, I saw, through some lighted panes, a party of gentlemen playing at billiards. Presently they fell to fighting one another with their cues, and one of their number was thrown out of the window by his companions. At any other time I should have felt only disgusted

at this, but on the present occasion I conceived a
sort of envy of the expelled individual—so great an
envy that I entered the tavern, and approached the
billiard-room. "Come," I thought to myself, "let
me but pick a quarrel, and they will expel me too."
I was not drunk; I was merely ready for anything
—to such a pitch can hysteria and depression eat
into a man's soul. Yet nothing happened. Seeing
that I could not, if necessary, spring from the
window, I was on the point of departing without
joining in the brawl when I was brought up short
by an officer. At the moment, all unwittingly, I was
blocking the door of the room, and he was trying to
pass out of it. Taking me by the shoulder, and saying not a word of warning or explanation, he pushed
me aside, and pursued his way as though he had not
noticed me. Under ordinary circumstances I should
have apologised to him, but, as it was, I felt that
I could not do so, seeing that he had not only thrust
me out of his path, but also departed without
deigning me a single glance.

The devil only knows what, at that moment, I
would have given to pick a real, a regular, a more
decent, a more (if I might use the term) literary,
quarrel! I had been treated like a fly! Whereas
the officer had been a man of six feet, I was only a
thin, mean little fellow; yet the quarrel had lain
entirely in my hands, and, had I protested, I too
could have been thrown out of the window. But I
had wasted time in a mass of thinking and propos-
ing, and so had incurred the shame of seeing myself
snubbed!

So angry and disturbed was I that when I left
the tavern I went straight home, and next day continued my course of dissipation—but in an even more
timid, cowed, and lugubrious manner than usual.
Indeed, I did so with, as it were, tears in my eyes.
Yet I *did* continue it. Do not think that I was *afraid*
of that officer. I have never yet been a coward at
heart, however much I have been so in action. No,

you need not smile; I have an explanation for this, even as I have, you may rest assured, an explanation for everything else.

Oh, if that officer could have been one of those who will fight duels! But no, he was essentially one of those gentlemen (now, alas! a vanished race) who prefer to take action with billiard cues, or, like Gogol's Colonel Pirogov, in obedience only to orders. Such men do *not* fight duels; a duel even with a fellow fire-eater they consider inexpedient, since they look upon the duel as a senseless, free-thinking institution which savours of Frenchism. Consequently they remain ever ready to insult others—especially if they (the aggressors) can boast of six feet of stature!

No, it was not out of cowardice that I held my hand, but through boundless vanity. I feared neither six feet of stature nor the fact that I might be beaten and thrown out of the window. *Physical* courage has never been wanting in me: what I then lacked was *moral* courage. I was afraid lest every one present, from the head marker to the lowest official, with his blotched and pimpled face and greasy collar, would fail to understand me, and laugh when I protested and addressed them in really literary language. For of the point of honour—not of honour pure and simple, mind you, but of the *point* of honour—it has never been the custom to speak in any but the most refined and literary diction. No ordinary words have I ever heard spoken concerning that same point of honour. Therefore I felt certain (it was due to the practical sense in me, as distinguished from the romantic) that every one present would burst their sides with laughter, while the officer would not merely—that is to say, inoffensively—thrash me, but also trip me in the back with his knee, lead me a dance around the billiard-table, and, finally, have sufficient pity upon me to expel me through the window. But of course I could not let this wretched episode end where it

was. Frequently in after days I met the officer in
the street, and took the most careful note of him.
I do not know whether he recognised *me*, but I think
that he did not. None the less I always regarded
him with hatred and envy. Thus things continued
for several years, my grudge against him growing
ever deeper and stronger as the years passed on.

Early in the proceedings I tried to make some
cautious inquiries about the man, but found the
task very difficult, for the reason that I knew no
one. At last one day some one spoke to him in the
street (I was then following him as closely as though
I were tied to his person), and I learnt his name.
Another time I followed him home to his flat, and
for the sum of one *grivennik* [1] ascertained from the
porter what number the officer lived at, on which
floor, and whether alone or with some one else—in
short, all that *could* be ascertained from a porter.
Another morning, though it was my first essay in
literature, I took it into my head to indite this officer
a letter, in the form of a caricature embodying a
story. With great zest I wrote it, and, making it
fairly scurrilous, at first appended to my enemy a
name which he was bound to recognise at first sight;
but later I decided to change it for another one, and
then sent the whole to *Tales of the Fatherland*.
But, to my grief, it never got into print. Sometimes my wrath almost stifled me; so much so that
at length I decided to challenge the foe to a duel.
To this end I composed a beautiful, a most attractive
letter, wherein I adjured him to expiate his fault,
and hinted that, in case of refusal, I should call him
out to fight me. Yet the missive was couched in
such terms as would lead the officer, if he were at all
capable of comprehending "the great and the beautiful," to at once seek me out, fall upon my neck, and
proffer me his friendship. "And how splendid that
would be!" I said to myself. "We will have such

---

[1] Ten kopecks, or 2½*d*.

a time of it together—yes, such a time of it! He
shall hold over me the ægis of his professional position, and I shall give him the benefit of my refinement—er—and—and of my ideas. Much, much will
come of it!" You must remember that it was now
two years since he had offered me the insult, and
my challenge was simply a gross anachronism, without mentioning the added *gaucherie* of my letter,
which at once disclosed and concealed that anachronism. However, thank God! (even to this day I can
never bless the Almighty without tears), I failed
to send the letter. Indeed, whenever I think what
might have happened, had I sent it, I turn cold.
In the end it befell that I wreaked vengeance in the
most simple, the most genial, of fashions, for a
brilliant idea suddenly occurred to me. You must
know that, at four o'clock on the afternoon of festival
days, I would go for a walk along the sunny side
of the Nevski Prospect; or, rather, I would not so
much go for a walk as go to indulge in a series of
annoyances, humiliations, and outpourings of spleen
—things which seemed to me an absolute necessity.
Like a lamprey, I would, in uncouth fashion, go
wriggling my way through the throng, and give
room, now to a general, now to an officer of the
Horse or of the Foot Guards, now to a civilian, and
so on. Yet all the while there would be spasms of
pain at my heart, and shivers running down my
back, at the mere thought of the wretched appearance that my costume and figure must be presenting.
To me it was sheer misery and degradation—sheer,
ceaseless, unbearable misery and degradation—to
have to think, always and *apropos* of everything,
that, in the eyes of this shining world, I was no
more than an unclean and useless fly. True, the fly
was one that was much cleverer, better educated,
and better born than those who were jostling him,
yet none the less it was a fly that had to give way
to every one, to be looked down upon by every one,
to be scorned by every one. *Why* I should volun-

tarily have incurred the misery which I used to suffer
on the Nevski Prospect I do not know.   I only know
that I found myself drawn thither on every possible
occasion.

It was at that period that I began to experience
the species of delight to which I have referred in
Part I; and after the incident with the officer I began
more than ever to be attracted to the Nevski Prospect, for it was there that I most often encountered
and found myself obsessed by him.   He, like myself,
walked there mostly on festival days; he, too,
stepped aside to make room for generals and big-
wigs; he, too, wormed his way along like a lamprey,
while common folk like myself he merely jostled, or
else walked straight into, as though the space in
front of him were perfectly clear.   Never did I see
him make way for such people, and as I gazed at
him I used to feel perfectly drunk with rancour—
though I gave him room with the rest whenever I
met him.   How it hurt me to think that even in the
streets I was powerless to get on even terms with
him.   "Why the devil *do* you step aside?" I would
ask myself in a sort of idiotic, hysterical way when
I awoke, say, at three in the morning.   "Why is it
always *you*, not *he*?   Is there no law for such a
man—no precept?   Supposing that we were to meet
on equal terms, in the usual way that gentlemen meet
one another, what would happen?   Well, he would
yield me half the path, and I the same to him, and
we should pass one another with mutual respect."
Yet never did this befall.   Always I turned aside for
him, whereas *he*—he never even seemed to notice
that I had done so.   It was then that there first
occurred to me the brilliant idea of which I have
spoken.   "What," was my thought, "if I were to
meet him and *not* leave the path—to *purposely* not
leave it, even though my not doing so should entail
a collision?"   This daring notion gradually obsessed
me until I could not rest.   Ceaselessly, deeply I
pondered over it, while of set intent I patrolled the

Prospect more frequently than ever, so as to realise the more clearly what I ought to do when actually I *did* come to make the attempt. All the while I was in transports, for more and more it was dawning upon me that my scheme was not only feasible, but a very good one. "Of course, I shall not actually *push* him," I would add to myself, anticipatorily considerate in my joy, "I will simply omit to turn aside, so that without coming into violent contact with him, I may rub shoulders with him so far as the conventions ordain. Exactly as he jostles *me* so will I jostle *him*." At length my mind was made up, though the preparatory process had taken a long time. In the first place, I felt that at the moment of execution I should need to be looking my best, and therefore must take some thought for my raiment, seeing that, if a public scene should ensue (the public itself, of course, did not matter, but promenading there would also be the Countess A. and the Prince B. and the whole of the literary world), I should require to be at least *decently* dressed. To be so would inspire respect, and at once place myself and my antagonist on an equal footing in the eyes of society. Accordingly I drew some salary in advance, and bought, at Tchurkin's, a pair of black gloves and a smart hat. Somehow black gloves seemed to look more respectable, more *bon ton,* than the yellow ones which I first tried on. "Coloured gloves are too loud, and make a man look too conspicuous," said I to myself as I rejected the yellow articles referred to. As for a shirt, I had long had one ready—one that was not only in pretty good repair, but also was fitted with white bone studs. The only thing that gave me pause was my overcoat. In itself it was not a bad one, for it was at least warm; but it had a wadded lining and a raccoon collar, and both of those things were the height of flunkeyism. Consequently it would be necessary to change the collar for a beaver one, such as all the officers wore. For this purpose

I made the round of the shops, and at length lit
upon a piece of beaver of cheap German extraction.
Though German beaver soon comes to wear shabby
and present a miserable appearance, it easily passes
muster at first, if properly furbished up. Consequently a piece of it would do well enough for this
occasion only. On asking the price, however, I
found that it was too dear; so, after further grave
consideration, I decided to sell my raccoon collar,
and to borrow the deficit from the head of my
department, Anton Antonitch Sietochkin. The
latter, though an easy-going man, was of serious
and opinionated bent, and anything but a moneylender; wherefore, despite the fact that on my entry
to the service I had been highly recommended to
his favour by the gentleman who had procured me
my nomination, I dreaded the prospect of begging
a loan of him. Somehow it seemed such a monstrous, such a shameful, thing to do that for three
whole nights I never slept, little though my fevered
condition had for some while past inclined me to
slumber. By turns my heart would sink to nothing
and turn to throbbing and throbbing and throbbing.
At the first blush Anton Antonitch seemed surprised
at my request; then he frowned, considered the
matter again, and, finally, handed me the cash in
exchange for a note of hand which empowered him
to recoup himself, in two weeks' time, out of my
salary. Thus I had everything prepared. The
beautiful beaver had now dethroned the miserable
raccoon, and I could set myself to the work in hand.
No rash decision must be come to, I felt; the affair
was one which called for gradual and guarded
management. Yet it must be confessed that, though
I made many attempts to carry out my enterprise,
I soon found myself beginning to despair of ever
coming into actual contact with the enemy.

For instance, on one occasion I was not ready;
on a second occasion I had not properly thought the
matter out. More than once the officer and myself

were on the point of colliding when—again I stepped aside, and he passed me by without looking at me. Sometimes I even went so far as to mutter fervent prayers as I approached him—prayers that God might steel me to the effort. At length I had really made up my mind to jostle him when, at the very last moment, when only a couple of paces from him, my breath failed, and I tripped and fell under his feet. Nonchalantly he stepped over me, and I rolled away out of the throng like a ball. That night fever again seized me, and I became delirious. However, the affair ended in the best way possible, for it struck me, the next afternoon, that I might as well desist from my abortive enterprise, and accordingly I made my way to the Nevski Prospect for the last time, to see whether I really could effect my purpose. Suddenly, when my foe was within three paces of me, I came to a sudden decision, put on a ferocious scowl, and—and came into violent collision with his shoulder! Not an inch did I budge, but continued my way with unshaken stride. Again he did not look at me, again he did not appear even to have noticed me; yet I felt certain that he was shamming. Yes, to this day I am sure of it. In any case it was I who had gained the most from the encounter. Though he might remain the stronger of the two, that did not matter. What really mattered was that I had attained my end, I had upheld my dignity, I had not yielded to him an inch, and I had publicly placed myself on an equality with him in the eyes of society. I returned home revenged, revenged! I felt transported with delight, and trolled an Italian aria as I proceeded. I need not tell you how I spent the next three days. Those of you who have read my *Underworld* will be able to guess it for themselves. Later, the officer was transferred to another station, and it is fourteen years since I last saw him. What has become of my idol? Whom is he now bullying?

II

AFTER this my phase of dissipation came to an end, and I found the time hang heavy on my hands. Occasionally repentance would seize me, but I always drove it forth again, for I was too weary to do aught but fall in with—rather, put up with— whatsoever chanced to happen. Yet all the while there was a way of escape which reconciled me to everything—namely, the way of escape contained in my visionary cult of "the great and the beautiful." I did nothing but dream and dream of it; for three whole months on end I, crouching in my den, did nothing else. You may be sure that at this period there was nothing in common between myself and the individual who, in chickenish perturbation of heart, had sewed a piece of German beaver on to the collar of his overcoat. No; of a sudden I had become a hero. Even my six-foot colonel I would not have deigned to admit to my rooms. As a matter of fact, I had forgotten all about him. What my dreams were, and how I was able to rest satisfied with them, it is difficult, at this distance of time, to conjecture, but at all events they *did* give me plea- sure. Moreover, they always came to me with greater strength and sweetness after a bout of dis- sipation; they came in company with tears and regrets, transports and curses. Indeed, such moments of rapture, of happiness, had I that, thank God, it never entered into my head to deride them. Ah, how full they were of faith and hope and love for my fellowmen ! That is to say, I had a sort of blind belief that one day some miracle, some external circumstance, would suddenly cause the present to break and become widened, and that suddenly there would dawn before me a horizon of congenial, pro- ductive, fair, and, above all things, *instant* activity (though in what manner *instant* I did not know), and that at last I should issue into God's world,

mounted on a white horse, and crowned with laurels.
Any secondary rôle I found myself unable to
envisage, and that is why I thought so much about
the subject. Whether a hero, or whether a groveller
in dung, for me there could be no medium. Hence
my undoing; since, when grovelling in dung, I
always comforted myself with the reflection that at
other times I was a hero, and that the hero over-
laid the dung-groveller; for, thought I, though a
man is usually ashamed when he bathes in mire, a
hero stands on too lofty a plane ever to be wholly
immersed in the stuff; wherefore he may grovel as
he pleases. It is curious that my aspirations towards "the great and the beautiful" should always
have come to me precisely in moments of dissipation
—on the very day that a bout of debauchery had
occurred. Yes, they always came to me in isolated
bursts, as though to remind me of their existence,
but without repairing the dissipation by this manifestation of themselves. On the contrary, they
seemed, through the mere force of contrast, to
revivify my debauched instincts—to arrive, as it
were, in time to make a sauce for those instincts.
Of that sauce the ingredients were remorse and a
sense of contradiction, added to torturing self-
analysis; all of which pains and torments communicated to my degradation a sort of piquancy, and even
a meaning. In short, my aspirations towards "the
great and the beautiful" fulfilled all the functions of
a relish. Yet behind this there was something else;
for how, otherwise, could I have reconciled myself
to debauchery that was worthy only of an under-
clerk, or have covered myself to such an extent with
mire? What was there in it all to attract me, or
to lead me to cheat the night in brothels? Ah, I
had a good excuse for everything. . . .

How much love—my God! how much love—I
used to expend in those dreams, in those yearnings
for "the great and the beautiful"!—yes, even
though my affection was of a fantastical order which

F

could not possibly have been applied to a human
being, but the abundance of which was such that I
never felt any need so to apply it, seeing that,
throughout, it was love of a superfluous, luxurious
kind. Fortunately, it usually ended by turning to an
indolent, sensuous cult of art, in the shape of beautiful forms of life which I borrowed readymade from
poets and romanticists, and then adapted to every
possible use and requirement of my own. In those
visions I would rise superior to all mankind; all
men were in the dust before me, and forced to
recognise my perfection as I extended to them my
pardon. Rapturously I would imagine myself to be
a famous poet or courtier, or the fortunate possessor
of untold millions which I was devoting to the benefit
of the human race, while confessing to the latter my
sins—though not sins in the actual sense of the
word, but, rather, acts which partook of "the great
and the beautiful" (something after the Manfredian
style). Yes, I would picture the whole world weeping and embracing me (it was bound to do so if it
were not wholly gross), and myself walking abroad,
barefooted and hungry, to preach my new ideas, and
to deal out to reaction its Austerlitz. Then a grand
march would sound, and a general amnesty would
be issued; after which the Pope would consent to
leave Rome for Brazil, and a ball to which all Italy
would be invited would be held at the Villa Borghese
(the said Villa Borghese being situated, for that
occasion only, on Lake Como, which, also for that
occasion only, would have been transferred to the
neighbourhood of Rome). Then, again, the scene
would become shadowy—— But does not every one
know the kind of thing? Not long ago you said that
it is wrong for a man to expose his all in the market-
place—to expose such tears and raptures as those
to which I have confessed. But why? Do you
really think that I am ashamed of them, or that
any of them were a whit worse than is anything in
your own lives? Moreover, not *all* my ideas were

badly conceived; not *all* of them centred around Lake Como. However, you may be right; they *may* have been low and degraded. The lowest thing of all is that I should have sought to justify my conduct in your eyes. A lower thing still is the fact that I have said so. . . . However, enough of this, or I shall never have finished with it. Always one thing lower than the last will keep occurring to me.

Yet I had not spent more than three months upon these ecstasies of mine when I began to feel a renewed inclination for intercourse with my fellow-men, although, for me, the social round meant only an occasional visit to the house of my official superior, Anton Antonitch Sietochkin. Indeed, he was the one friend whom ever I have permanently retained; and to this day I marvel at the circumstance. Even him, however, I never visited except when one of my curious moods had come over me, and my dreams had reached a pitch of delight which impelled me forthwith to embrace humanity at large (which I could not well do without having at hand at least one concrete, one existing, human being). Also, since my calls upon Anton Antonitch had always to be paid on a Tuesday (such being his reception day), I had to make my yearnings towards humanity also fall upon the second day in the week. His abode consisted of four rooms on the fourth floor of a block in Five Corners Street—rooms poorly furnished, and charged with the most penurious, the most jaundiced, air conceivable. With him lived two daughters and an aunt; the last-named of whom always poured out tea. At that time the daughters were thirteen and fourteen respectively, and had flaxen hair; while their habit of whispering and giggling together used greatly to embarrass me. As for the master of the house himself, he usually passed the time on a horsehair sofa near his study table, while beside him would sit a grey-haired guest who was one of the officials of our (or, possibly, some other?) office. In all, I never encountered more than two or three guests at these gatherings, and their conversation invariably turned upon the Stock Exchange, the last debate in the Senate, salaries, routine business, the Minister of our Department, and the best means of winning that Minister's favour. For some four hours or so I would sit stupidly beside these people, and listen to them without either a smile or a chance of joining in the conversation. Very dull I found it; but since, at times, I became so stricken with shyness that I would actually break out into a sweat, the whole thing did me good, since on the way home I would find no difficulty whatever in temporarily ridding myself of any desire to fall upon the neck of humanity.

Also, I had an acquaintance named Simonov, an old schoolfellow of mine. At that time many of my old schoolfellows were residing in St. Petersburg, but in most cases I had dropped them, and ceased even to salute them in the street. Moreover, I had gone so far as to procure my transfer to another department, for the sole purpose of severing all ties with my hateful boyhood. Yes, a curse upon the school at which I studied, and upon its horrible years of servitude! In short, from the moment when I regained my liberty I broke with the majority of my old comrades, save two or three. Of these, Simonov was one, since his retiringness and docility had saved us from any serious difference at school, and I could discern in him a certain amount of independence and uprightness of character. Nor did I look upon him as wholly a limited man; wherefore I spent many a friendly hour with him, and it was only comparatively recently that these reunions had ceased to be, and a mist had descended over their brightness. The truth was that suddenly he seemed to have grown weary of exchanging confidences, and to have taken fright lest we should again slip into the old footing. Yet, despite the fact that I gathered that I was no longer a *persona grata* with him, I still continued to pay him occasional visits.

So, one Thursday evening, when I felt unable any longer to bear my loneliness, and knew that on Thursdays Anton Antonitch's door would be closed to me, I bethought me of Simonov. As I mounted the stairs to the fourth floor where he lived I remember I felt more than ever assured that he had grown tired of me, and that I had come in vain; but considerations of this sort invariably ended by drawing me on the more to fill ambiguous positions, and I therefore entered his apartments. It was now almost a year since I had last seen him.

III

With him I found two other old schoolfellows of mine who were discussing what appeared to be a very important subject. On my entry neither of them paid me the least attention: which seemed to me an odd thing, seeing that I had not seen either of them for the space of a year. Evidently they looked upon me as some kind of ordinary fly. Even at school, much as, in those days, they had disliked me, they had not treated me so. I, for my part, felt sure that their contempt was due to my unsuccessful career in the service, my social descent, my shabby clothes, and such other things as, in their eyes, would constitute signs of my incompetence and low standing. Yet I had not expected quite such a lack of ceremony as this. For his part, Simonov seemed surprised to see me enter—though it had always been his way to appear so (a circumstance which had never failed to annoy me). Consequently I seated myself in rather a dejected mood, and set myself to listen to the conversation.

A grave, and even heated, discussion was in progress concerning a farewell dinner which these three gentlemen wished to offer, the next evening, to a friend of theirs named Zvierkov, an officer in the army, who was about to leave for a distant post.

He too had been a companion of mine at school,
but during our latter days he had led me to conceive
an intense dislike for him.   Even when we were
juniors I had envied him because he was a gay, good-
looking young fellow whom every one liked. Yet he
had never done his lessons aught but badly, and
the more so as time went on.   Indeed, that he passed
his examinations at all was due to the fact that he
had some influence behind him, for during his last
year at school he had inherited a legacy of two
hundred souls; [1] and since nearly all of us, his
schoolfellows, were poor, he had taken to assuming
rather grand airs over us.   Yet, though in the highest
degree vicious, he was also good-natured, even when
swaggering his worst; with the result that, despite
our purely external, fantastic, stilted forms of honour
and *esprit de corps,* we all of us, except a few,
grovelled before him, and the more so in proportion
as he played the lord.   Nor was it altogether out of
self-interest that he was fawned upon; it was equally
because he was so favoured of nature.   Moreover, it
was, with us, an accepted axiom that he was a
specialist in good manners and deportment.   But
the latter assumption simply maddened me.   I could
not bear either the grating, boastful intonation of
his voice, or his admiration of his own stupid witticisms, or the sight of his vapid, handsome face
(gladly though I would have given in exchange my
own supposedly "clever" one), or his free and easy
assumption of the manners of an officer of forty
years' standing, or his talk about his intended con-
quest of the fair sex (which, since he had decided
to leave it unentered upon until he had assumed an
officer's epaulets, he was the more eager to initiate),
or his everlasting prattle about his future prowess in
duels.   Once, when, during a play hour, he was
holding forth to his comrades about the property
which was one day to be his, and sporting at the

[1] That is to say, land sufficient to employ two hundred serfs.

prospect of it like a young puppy in the sun, and stating that he meant to take stock of every serf girl on the estate (he asserted that this would be no more than his *droit de seigneur*), and that if the peasants dared to utter a protest he would flog them all, greybeards included, and impose double tithes upon their holdings; when, as I say, he was declaiming all this, I suddenly dropped my customary rôle of silent auditor, and joined issue with him. Some of our fellows clapped their hands at this; which made me fasten upon my antagonist the more, since my prime motive was not so much pity for the serf girls and their fathers as rage at the thought that such a louse of a fellow should ever have his utterances applauded. True, on this occasion I won the day, but Zvierkov, though foolish, was also proud and good-tempered, and contrived to laugh off the affair in such a manner that I was partly cheated of the fruits of victory, and forced to see the laugh remain on the other side. Several times afterwards he managed to turn the tables upon me in the same way, but this he did without malice, and merely in jest, or in passing, or with a smile, though I felt too angry and contemptuous to respond. Nay, when our school days were over, he even made overtures of friendship which I did not altogether resist, since they rather attracted me; but soon we drifted apart again. Next, I heard of some doings of his in barracks, and of the dissipated life that he was leading there; subsequently of the fact that he was getting on in the service. Yet whenever he passed me in the street he used to give me the cut direct; wherefore I suspected that he was afraid of compromising himself by being seen in converse with such an insignificant individual as myself. Also, on one occasion I saw him in a third-tier box at the theatre—already adorned with shoulder-knots, and engaged in bowing and scraping to the daughters of an old general. During the last three years, however, he had become much thinner in the face, though

he was still handsome and engaging; his body had
grown bloated, and it was clear that by the time he
had reached the age of thirty he would have come
to be a mass of wrinkles.   Such was the Zvierkov
to whom the farewell dinner was to be given by my
fellow guests at Simonov's.   For the last three years
these gentlemen had been his constant companions;
although, as I could easily discern, they in no way
considered themselves his equals.

Of Simonov's two guests one was Ferfitchkin—a
Russo-German of dwarfish stature and ape-like face,
who, in his stupidity, laughed at everybody, and had,
from our earliest school days, been my bitterest foe.
Yet, though a vicious, conceited *farceur*, he aspired
to the nicest sense of honour—he a man who, all the
while, was essentially a coward !   Lastly, he was
one of those panderers of Zvierkov's who openly
flattered him, and secretly borrowed of him money.
The other of the two guests was a military nonentity
named Trudoliubov—a man of tall stature and frigid
mien, but possessed of a certain notion of honour,
even though he worshipped success in every form,
and could talk only "shop."   In addition, he could
trace a certain relationship to Zvierkov; which
fact, I am ashamed to state, conferred upon him
a certain standing in our circle.   Me, however, he
seemed to rate very low, for he treated me, if not
with actual rudeness, at all events with the barest
toleration.

"Seven roubles apiece," said Trudoliubov.   "In
all, that will make twenty-one roubles, and provide
us with a very good dinner indeed.   Of course
Zvierkov need not pay his share."

"Of course not, seeing that he is the guest,"
agreed Simonov.

"But do you suppose," put in Ferfitchkin, with all
the insolence of a valet who is flaunting his master's,
the general's, medals, "do you suppose that he will
permit us to pay his share?   In all probability he
will accept the invitation rather than hurt our feel-

ings; yet he will be sure also to contribute at least half-a-dozen of champagne."

"Then how are we to apportion the other half-dozen among ourselves?" asked Trudoliubov—his attention now riveted upon the wine question.

"I propose that the three of us (each of us contributing seven roubles) meet Zvierkov at the Hôtel de Paris at five o'clock to-morrow evening," said Simonov, who appeared to be the prime organiser of the feast.

"What? Only twenty-one roubles?" I put in, in as excited a tone as though I were offended. "Then accept me also as a guest, and we shall raise the total to twenty-eight roubles."

The truth was that there had suddenly come to me an idea that to cut in unexpectedly in this fashion was a clever thing to do, and would be sure to win the respect of all present.

"So *you* wish to take part in it?" exclaimed Simonov, though without looking at me. He always avoided my gaze, because he knew me by heart, and I felt furious that he should do so.

"Why not?" I spluttered. "I also am a comrade of Zvierkov's, and might well have taken offence at being passed over like this."

"We did not know where to find you," said Ferfitchkin brusquely.

"Besides, Zvierkov and yourself are not exactly *friends*," added Trudoliubov, with a frown.

Nevertheless, I stuck to my idea, and retorted with a stutter—

"I—I do not consider that any one has the right to judge between Zvierkov and myself. It is precisely because we *have* been on bad terms that I now wish to meet him again."

"Oh, who could understand *your* fine ideas?" said Trudoliubov, with a sneer.

"Well, well," decided Simonov, "you *shall* form one of the party. To-morrow, then, if you please, at the Hôtel de Paris, at five. And mind you come."

"And mind you bring the money, too," added Ferfitchkin gruffly, with a wink at Simonov. Further than this he did not venture, for even Simonov looked confused at what he (Ferfitchkin) had just said.

"All right," said Trudoliubov, rising. "If he wants to come, *let* him come."

"But the affair is a private party, not an official reception," persisted Ferfitchkin as he too rose and reached for his hat. In leaving the room he omitted to accord me any salute whatever, and Trudoliubov gave me only a very faint one as he averted his eyes. Simonov, too, seemed annoyed when he found himself left *tête-à-tête* with me, and kept throwing stealthy glances in my direction.

"Hm! Yes, to-morrow," he stammered. "Er— by the way, would you mind handing me your contribution *now*, so as to make quite sure of it?"

For the moment I felt beside myself with rage; but the next minute I remembered that for a long while past I had been owing him fifteen roubles, which, though never paid, I had not wholly forgotten.

"Surely," I replied, "you yourself see that I could not be expected to know what was in the wind when I came? Of course I regret my negligence."

"Very well, very well. You can pay me to-morrow, after dinner. I merely wanted to know; that is all. Pray do not——"

Without finishing his sentence he began to pace the room with an air of ever-growing annoyance, and a constant clicking of his heels.

"No," he went on. "That is to say, yes. . . . However, I must be off now. I am not going far." This last he said almost apologetically.

"Why did you not tell me before?" I cried, as I seized my hat.

"Oh, it is not very far—merely a couple of steps," he repeated, as he escorted me to the door with a preoccupied air which did not sit well upon him.

"To-morrow, at five," he cried for the last time, as I was descending the staircase—doubtless signifying that he was only too glad to see me go. I felt furious.

"May the devil take the lot of them!" I thought, as I wended my way home. "Why on earth have I gone and mixed myself up in the affair? Why, indeed? And to entertain an idiotic pig like Zvierkov, too! Good Lord! Of course, I *need* not go. But how am I to get out of the engagement? To-morrow I shall send Simonov word that——"

What really maddened me was the knowledge that I *should* go to the dinner. The more tactless, the more out of place it seemed to me to go, the more was I bent upon going. Yet one difficulty confronted me: I had no money. True, I had nine roubles in my possession, but, to-morrow, seven of these would need to be paid over to my servant, Apollon, who received from me, as wages, board and lodging and the monthly sum specified. Not to pay his wages punctually was, for me, a thing impossible, owing to his character. But of this brute, of this plague of my life, more anon.

All the time I knew that I should *not* pay those wages, but, on the contrary, go to the dinner.

I had terrible dreams that night—a not very remarkable thing, seeing that I had spent the evening in company with memories of my servitude at school—memories which I could not banish. To that school I had been sent by some distant relatives in whose care I had been, and of whom I had long since lost sight. They had sent me to that school an orphan whom they had cowed with scoldings until I had become a prematurely silent, introspective, curiously observant boy; and there I had been saluted by my comrades with nothing but cruel, pitiless jeers, owing to the fact that I was not like any of them. Those jeers I could not stand; I could not get on good terms with my companions in the easy way which *they* could with one another, but conceived an

instant grudge against them, and shut myself up in
a world of nervous, sensitive, boundless pride. My
comrades' roughness was a sheer torture to me, for
they never grew tired of making cynical jests on the
subject of my face and ungainly figure. Yet how
stupid their own faces were! Indeed, our school
fostered a sort of facial expression that was unique
for its innate, ever-growing dulness. However
good-looking a boy might be when he first came to
us, a few years would succeed in making him look
simply repulsive. Even at sixteen I found myself
astonished at the pettiness of my companions'
thought, and at the inanity of their pursuits, games,
and subjects of conversation. They did not understand even the most ordinary things of life, while
things that were at all striking or inspiring aroused
in them no interest whatever. Consequently I had
no choice but to regard my fellow students with
disdain. Yet it was not mere wounded vanity that
impelled me to do so, so for the love of God do not
pounce upon me with the sickeningly hackneyed
phrase that "you were then only a boy of dreams,
whereas *they* knew what life meant." I tell you
that these boys knew simply *nothing,* whether of
life or of anything else : and this incensed me all the
more against them. On the other hand, the plainest,
the most evident, actuality was viewed by them in
fantastically stupid fashion, for they were already
accustomed to worship only success. Everything
which, though of good report, was also lowly and
unassuming they flouted with insults and cruelty.
Rank they mistook for brains, and even at the age
of sixteen they could speak familiarly of places of bad
resort. Of course, much of this *may* have arisen
from the crass, debased conditions which surrounded
their early boyhood and adolescence; yet, even so,
it must be said that, taken as a whole, they were
almost monstrously vicious. True, that viciousness
may, in its turn, have been largely cynical and external, for at times a certain youthful freshness glim-

mered amid the vice; yet even that freshness was devoid of all attractiveness, and showed itself mostly in a sort of premature pruriency. In short, I had the greatest horror of them all, even though I myself may have been the worst of the lot; and this detestation they repaid—and very openly, too—in kind. However, I did not want their liking. On the contrary, my one desire was to see them humbled to the dust. As a means of escaping their ridicule I set myself earnestly to pursue my studies, and soon had risen almost to the top of the school. This *did* make a certain impression upon them, for it gradually dawned upon them that I could read books which they could not even decipher, and that I understood things (beyond the school curriculum) which they had never so much as heard of. Of this they took their usual derisive, barbaric view, but, morally, it gave me the whip hand over them—and the more so since the circumstance led the tutors themselves to pay me some respect. Thus the sneers died away, but there still remained a feeling of hostility which caused cold, constrained relations to subsist between my schoolfellows and myself. Indeed, the situation was too irksome to be borne, and as the years passed on I developed a yearning for *real* comrades, *real* friends. But, try though I might to form some extraneous intimacies, the latter always seemed unnatural, and soon came to an end of their own volition. True, I had *one* school friend for a while, but at heart I was tyrant enough to try to exercise an excessive sway over him as, in an endeavour to inspire him with dislike for our environment, I demanded of him a final, an unconditional divorcement from everything. The result was that I only frightened him with my passionate friendship, and reduced him to tears and sullenness. By nature he was unspoilt and of a yielding disposition; yet no sooner had he surrendered to me his all than I disliked him as much as I did his companions, and drove him from me as though he had been congenial

to me only so long as I could hector him and keep
him in subjection. Yet it was not *all* my companions
that I could bully in this way, for my friend was
unlike the rest of the gang, and constituted a bright
exception.   On leaving school, my first act was to
refuse the post to which I had been nominated; my
object being to sever all ties with the past, and to
bury it wholly in the dust. . . . And God only knows
what, later, drew me towards the man Simonov of
whom I have just spoken !

Early next morning I sprang out of bed in as
agitated a state as though something important were
soon about to happen. Somehow I had an idea that
some radical change in my life was approaching,
inevitably approaching.   All my life it has been my
way, on the least external occurrence, to feel that
some fundamental break in my existence is at hand.
However, I went to my office as usual, and slipped
away home again two hours before the usual time,
to prepare myself for the dinner.   "Above all
things," I thought to myself, "I must not be the
first arrival, or I shall be thought over-eager about
the thing."   Important points like this seemed to
multiply by thousands, and worried me until I
almost fainted. Next with my own hands I cleaned
my shoes, for Apollon would never have done them
twice in the same day; he would have thought such
a proceeding quite irregular. That done, I swept the
hall clear of the litter which I had made, in order
that he should not afterwards see the remains and
despise me for what I had done.   Then I looked
through my wardrobe in detail, and found that it
was old and worn and creased. Yes, I had grown
very slovenly in my dress. True, my uniform [1]
looked decent, but one cannot very well go out to
dinner in a uniform. Worst of all, my trousers had
a large yellow stain on one of their knees, and I
felt that that stain alone would deprive me of nine-

---

[1] In Russia even officials of the civil service wear uniform.

tenths of my dignity, well though I knew it was beneath me to feel like that. "Come, come," I thought to myself with a sinking of the spirits, "enough of what I may or may not think. I have now to deal with *reality*." Yet, though well aware that I was exaggerating everything to a perfectly monstrous degree, the thought of what lay before me shook my soul as with ague. Distractedly I pictured to myself the cold, superior manner in which "that rascal" Zvierkov would greet me; the dull, invincible contempt with which "that blockhead" Trudoliubov would eye me; the rude, insulting giggles which "that skunkish" Ferfitchkin would vent at my expense (if by so doing he could curry favour with Zvierkov); the manner in which Simonov would size me up, and despise me for my wretched vanity and want of spirit; and, lastly, the degree to which the affair, from start to finish, would be sordid and shameful rather than "refined." Of course, it would be best for me not to go, but this was impossible, since no sooner do I take a thing into my head than it drags my head along with it. That is to say, it is always *after* the event that I reproach myself. "But why," was my reflection, "should I be afraid of, play the coward before, reality?" Yet, passionately desirous though I was of showing all this riff-raff that I was not the coward whom I imagined myself to be, it was in a perfect storm of pusillanimous agitation that I fancied myself getting the better of the company—first snubbing them, then attracting them, then forcing them to like me for "the elevation of my thoughts and my undoubted wit." Zvierkov I should first of all displace from his perch, and then force to sit in shame and silence while I simply *crushed* him. Lastly, if you please, I should have pity upon him, and drink his health, and address him in the second person singular.[1]

---

[1] In Russia, as in France, the second person singular denotes familiarity, intimacy, or condescension.

None the less, the cruellest and most shameful thought of all was the knowledge—yes, the certain knowledge—that none of these things would *really* happen; that, as a matter of fact, I had no desire to crush, or to get the better of, or to attract my fellow guests, and that for such a result (were it even attainable) I should be the last man in the world to care. Oh, how I prayed God that the evening might pass as quickly as possible! Finally it was in inexpressible anguish that I went to the window, opened the sliding pane, and looked out into the dim swirl of wet, falling snow. . . .

At length my shabby wall clock whirred, and struck the hour of five. Instantly I seized my hat, and, trying not to catch Apollon's eye (ever since the morning he had been awaiting receipt of his wages, yet had been fool enough never to speak of them), I darted past him through the door, and, in a cab which I had ordered beforehand, drove in state (and in return for my last half-rouble) to the Hôtel de Paris.

IV

As long ago as the previous night I had known that I *should* be the first to arrive. Yet that did not greatly matter. What really mattered was that I had great difficulty in finding our room. Nor, as yet, was the table even laid! What could this mean? After many inquiries of the servants, I learnt that dinner had been ordered for six o'clock, not for five; and this the attendants in the buffet confirmed. It was bad enough even to have to ask them! As yet the clock showed twenty-five minutes to six. If the change of hour was in any way due to my fellow guests they ought to have let me know by post rather than have lowered me in my own eyes and in those of the servants. However, I sat down, and a waiter began to lay the table—greatly embarrassing

me by his presence as he did so. Towards six
o'clock candles were brought in, to aid the lamps,
though the waiter evidently had not thought it worth
while to bring them in when I first arrived. In a
neighbouring room there were dining two sombre-
looking customers who appeared, from their mien,
to be out of temper and disinclined to talk; while
in a room further on a considerable noise, and even
some shouting, was in progress—the chattering of a
whole party of people being audible, with stray little
exclamations in French. Evidently the company
included ladies. In short, I found the time of waiting excessively tedious—so much so that when
(exactly at six o'clock) my fellow guests arrived *en
masse,* I felt momentarily so delighted (as if they
were my deliverers) that I almost forgot my rôle of
an offended personage.

Zvierkov entered at the head of the band, as their
manifest leader. At the moment he and his companions were laughing loudly, but when he became
aware of my presence he straightened his face, came
forward slowly, and with a sort of coquettish
wriggling of the waist, gave me his hand with a
faintly benevolent, yet faintly reserved, air in his
manner, as though, even in the act, he desired to
guard himself against something. On the other
hand, I had expected him to break into his old
thin, high-pitched laughter, and, at the first word,
to lapse into his old way of cracking sorry jests
and witticisms. Indeed, ever since the previous
evening, I had been looking for this to happen.
Consequently I was the more dumfounded by his
condescending and superior *bonhomie.* Could it be
that he conceived himself immeasurably above my
level in all the relations of life? If so, and if his
design was only to insult me by his patronage, it did
not greatly matter, since I could get even with him
somehow; but what if, without actually intending
to offend, he really cherished in his sheep's brain the
idea that he was the better man of the two, and

G

therefore in a position to treat me with condescension? The very supposition made me gasp!

"I have learnt with pleasure of your wish to join us," he began, with a drawl and a lisp and an even greater mouthing of his words than in the old days. "Somehow we never seem to meet one another now, for you keep so much to yourself. Yet you need not do so, for we are not nearly such queer creatures as you think. At all events I am very glad to renew your acquaintance now," and he turned away with a slighting air to lay his hat upon the window-sill.

"Have you been waiting long?" Trudoliubov asked me.

"Yes," I replied in a voice which presaged a coming explosion. "I arrived exactly at five o'clock, as warned to do yesterday."

"Then did no one let him know that the hour had been changed?" cried Trudoliubov, turning to Simonov.

"No; I forgot to do so," answered the latter in an unrepentant tone, as, without a word of apology to myself, he departed to order dinner to be brought in.

"So you have been here an hour, my poor fellow!" cried Zvierkov with a laugh (naturally it would seem to him a laughing matter). In imitation of his patron, Ferfitchkin also burst into a shrill, mean chuckle like the barking of a small dog, for he too evidently thought my position an extremely ridiculous and absurd one.

"There is nothing to laugh at," I exclaimed to Ferfitchkin, growing more and more exasperated. "It was somebody else's fault, not mine. No one ever warned me. It was, it was—well, it was simply rude."

"Not only rude, but something else," remarked Trudoliubov, naïvely taking my part. "You put things too mildly. It was simply an insult—though, of course, not an intentional one. How Simonov could have done it I—— Ahem!"

"If *I* had been played such a trick," said Ferfitch-kin, "I should have——"

"Yes, you would have ordered up something to go on with, or simply have told them to lay dinner," concluded Zvierkov for him.

"Certainly I *could* have so acted without any one's permission," I rapped out. "If I waited, it was only because——"

"Well, well; let us take our seats, gentlemen," said Simonov, at that moment re-entering. "Everything is ready, and I will answer for it that the champagne is well iced. You see," he added to myself, "I did not know your address, nor where to find you." Again he avoided my eye, for he evidently bore me a grudge of some sort. After my experiences of last night I was determined to find out what it was.

Every one—myself included—seated himself at the table, which was a circular one. On my left I had Trudoliubov, and, on my right, Simonov; while Zvierkov confronted me, with, between him and Trudoliubov, Ferfitchkin.

"Tell me, are you in a government department?" Zvierkov said to me. Clearly, seeing that I was ill at ease, he had decided to interest himself in my affairs, and really thought that he ought to be kind to me—to, in a way, "hearten" me.

"Does he want me to throw a bottle at his head?" thought I to myself. Somehow, the strangeness of the situation had made me unnaturally prone to take offence. But aloud I said drily, with my eyes on my plate—

"I am in the Ministry of ——."

"And do you like it? Also, tell me—what led you to resign your former post?"

"What led me to resign my former post?" I re-echoed, involuntarily assuming a drawl thrice as pronounced as Zvierkov's own. "I resigned it simply because I wanted to."

Ferfitchkin giggled, and Simonov looked at me

with an ironical air.   As for Trudoliubov, his fork remained poised in the air, so petrified was he with astonishment.

Zvierkov winced, yet he did not mean to show it.

"And what is your present income?" he continued.

"My present income?"

"Well, your *salary*?"

"Am I, then, to be put through a regular examination?" I retorted.   However, I told him the amount of my salary, and grew very red in the face while doing so.

"Not much indeed!" he observed pompously.

"No, one couldn't afford good restaurants every night on *that*," added Ferfitchkin mischievously.

"In my opinion it is sheer poverty," was Trudoliubov's comment.

"And how thin you have grown!   You have changed a good deal since I last saw you," continued Zvierkov, with a glance of impertinent commiseration at my person and clothes.

"Come," said Ferfitchkin, with a snigger, "we have put our good friend sufficiently out of countenance."

"Sir," I retorted, "it is not in your power to put me out of countenance.   Do you hear?   I am dining in this restaurant at my own expense, at my own expense, and not at that of some one else, Monsieur Ferfitchkin."

"What?" cried Ferfitchkin, turning as red as a boiled lobster, and looking at me with fury.   "*Which* of us is dining at the expense of some one else?"

"Never mind," I replied, feeling that I was in for it.   "We should do well to talk on some more intellectual topic."

"Yes; to give you an opportunity of airing your wonderful gifts, eh?"

"No, not at all.   That would be out of place here."

"More so than in your *leper*-tment?" [1]

---

[1] A play upon the Russian word *departament*.

"Enough, gentlemen, enough!" cried Zvierkov imperiously.

"What folly this is!" murmured Simonov.

"Yes—and utter stupidity!" assented Trudoliubov. "We have met here to spend a few friendly hours together, and to wish our friend *bon voyage;* yet *you*"—this was addressed to me exclusively—"must start quarrelling! Since you invited yourself to the dinner, pray do not disturb the general harmony at it."

"That will do, that will do," said Zvierkov again. "Let us drop the subject, gentlemen. Allow me to tell you how, three days ago, I came very near to getting married." And he embarked upon a story which bore no relation at all to marriage, but only to the amorous exploits of some old generals, colonels, and court chamberlains, with the narrator himself as the leading spirit. A general chorus of laughter followed, and Ferfitchkin fairly shrieked. No one noticed me any longer, and I sat crushed and humiliated.

"My God! Look at the company that I am keeping!" thought I to myself. "Yet what a fool I must look to them all! And I used to forgive Ferfitchkin so many things! Do these blockheads really imagine that they are doing me an honour by giving me a place at their table? Cannot they understand that it is *I* who am doing *them* an honour? I have grown thin, have I? I wear shabby clothes? Oh, the cursed clowns! Long ago Zvierkov must have noticed the yellow stain on my knee. What then? I have a great mind to rise—yes, this very minute —from the table, and to take my hat, and simply go without another word. Yes, go out of sheer contempt. To-morrow, perhaps, there will be a duel? Oh, the blackguards! But I do not think that they would miss my seven roubles very much. Perhaps they intend to—— Oh, the devil take them all! I don't care a hang for the seven roubles. I'll go this very instant."

However, I stayed, and kept drinking glass after glass, both of claret and sherry. Lack of usedness to wine soon began to turn my head, and my anger increased with my fuddlement. Suddenly I felt as though I should like to insult every one in the rudest possible fashion, and then go. I had an idea that I should like to seize a favourable moment to show myself in my true colours. "Let them say what they like!" I thought to myself. "Even if I *am* ridiculous, I have some brains in my head, and—and—in short, they can go to the devil!"

From time to time I glared at the company, but every one seemed to have forgotten my existence, and to be merged in a din of shouting and merriment. Zvierkov was holding forth, and I set myself to listen. His story related to a fine lady whom he had induced to confess to a passion for himself (of course the fellow was lying throughout), as well as to an intimate friend of his—a certain Prince Kolia, of the Hussars, the alleged owner of three thousand souls [1]—who had rendered him valuable assistance in the affair.

I broke into the conversation. "This Prince Kolia," I said, "this owner of three thousand souls, how comes it about that *he* is not here to entertain you to-night?"

For a moment or two no one spoke; but presently Trudoliubov threw a contemptuous nod in my direction, and even went so far as to remark that for some time past I had been drunk. Zvierkov, for his part, sat gazing at me like a cow, until I was forced to lower my eyes, while Simonov seized the opportunity to pour out fresh bumpers of champagne. As soon as he had done so, Trudoliubov raised his glass, and every one except myself did the same.

"Your very good health, and a pleasant journey to you!" he cried to Zvierkov. "Let us drink to the

---

[1] *i. e.* three thousand serfs.

years which are gone, and to the years which are coming! Hurrah!"

The whole company honoured the toast, and then rushed to embrace Zvierkov. I alone did not stir, and my glass remained untouched upon the table before me.

"And are not *you* going to drink it? " rapped out Trudoliubov impatiently, as he turned to me with a threatening air.

"Yes; but first of all I wish to make a speech of my own, Monsieur Trudoliubov. When I have done *that* I will drink the toast."

"Oh, the abominable cad! " muttered Simonov.

I straightened myself with the aid of the table, and feverishly clutched at my glass. I felt as though I were preparing to say something very important, yet had not a notion what it was going to be.

"Silence! " cried Ferfitchkin. "We are about to hear something worth hearing! "

Zvierkov sat waiting gravely. He had an inkling of what was coming.

"Monsieur le Lieutenant Zvierkov," I began, "please to know that I detest phrases, phrasers, and fools with waists. That is my first point. Follows my second."

There was a general stir of astonishment.

"My second point is that I detest blackguards and blackguardism, but more especially the former. My third point is that I love truth and frankness and honesty." I was speaking almost mechanically, and beginning to shiver with apprehension at my own words. "Yes, and I love high thinking, Monsieur Zvierkov, and I love genuine good-fellowship and equality and—— No. Ahem!—I love—I love—— However, Monsieur Zvierkov, I drink to your good health. May you conquer the whole Caucasus, and slay your country's enemies, and—and—here is your very good health, Monsieur Zvierkov."

He rose, bowed, and said, "Thank you." Plainly

he was very much put about, for he had turned quite pale.

"The devil take it!" exclaimed Trudoliubov, striking his fist upon the table.

"That sort of thing ought to have been answered with a blow on the mouth," squeaked Ferfitchkin.

"Let us throw him out," muttered Simonov.

"Not a word, gentlemen! Do not lose your tempers!" cried Zvierkov, endeavouring to appease the general indignation. "I thank you, but *I* shall know what value to set upon his words."

"Monsieur Ferfitchkin," I shouted at the top of my voice, "to-morrow you shall make good to me what you have just said."

"A duel?" he replied. "Then I accept." Yet so absurd did I look as I challenged him, and so ill did it consort with my figure, that every one—Ferfitchkin included—burst out laughing.

"Oh, leave him alone," said Trudoliubov disgustedly. "He is drunk."

"I shall never forgive myself for having included him in the party," added Simonov.

"Now is the time for me to throw bottles at them," thought I to myself. I seized up one, and—calmly poured myself out another glassful.

"I had better stay on to the end," I reflected. "I dare say you fellows would be thankful to see me go, but I don't intend to do so. I intend, rather, to sit on here and drink, as a sign that I think you of no importance whatever. I intend to sit on here and drink because the place is a tavern, and I have duly paid my entrance money. I intend to sit on here and drink because I look upon you all as so many unsubstantial dummies. I intend to sit on here and drink because—yes, and to sing too if I want to, and because I have the right to sing, and because—ahem!"

As a matter of fact, I did *not* sing that night, but exerted all my faculties to avoid meeting my companions' eyes, the while I struck attitudes expressive

of independence, and impatiently waited for some
one to be the first to address me. But, alas! no
one was so. How I wished, how I wished that
at that moment I could have made my peace with
my companions! The clock struck eight, and then
nine. Presently the revellers moved from the table
to a divan, where Zvierkov stretched his full length,
and rested one foot upon a what-not. Also, more
wine was handed round—he producing three bottles
of his own, but omitting to include me in the invitation. Round him sat his admirers, who seemed to
listen to him with such absolute veneration that it
was clear they really liked him. "But why, but
why?" thought I to myself. From time to time,
in their drunken rapture, they actually embraced him
as they talked of the Caucasus, of the nature of true
passion, of lucrative service posts, of the astounding
income of the hussar officer Podcharzhevski (whom
none of them personally knew), of the marvellous
beauty and grace of the Princess D—— (whom
none of them had even seen), and of the immortality
of Shakespeare.

I smiled contemptuously, and, placing myself in
front of the divan, started to pace the length of the
room—from the table to the stove, and back again.
My one desire was to show my companions that I
could get on without them; wherefore I purposely
clicked my heels together, and stamped a good deal
with my soles. Yet it was all to no purpose, for the
party paid me no attention whatever. Thus, from
eight o'clock to eleven, I tramped to and fro before
the company, always keeping to the same beat
(namely, from the table to the stove, and back again).
"Here I walk," was what my attitude expressed,
"and no one can prevent me from doing so."
Several times, when he entered the room, the waiter
stopped to stare at me, while the frequent turning
and turning made me giddy, and every moment I
thought that I should have a fit, seeing that three
times, during those three hours, I burst into a sweat,

and then grew dry again. Also, every now and then there pierced my heart, with deep and venomous pain, the thought that ten, twelve, or, maybe, forty, years might pass, yet I should still remember, with horror and humiliation, the most ridiculous, the most degraded, the most disgusting evening of my life. More unconscionable, more gratuitous, my degradation could not have been, and I fully understood that as I paced up and down between the table and the stove. "Oh, if you only knew what thoughts and feelings I am capable of, and what a man of refinement you have in me!" was my incessant reflection as I purposely turned towards the divan where my enemies were seated. But my enemies comported themselves as though I were not so much as present. Once, and only once, did they pay me the slightest attention—namely, when Zvierkov was speaking of Shakespeare, and I gave a contemptuous laugh. So scurrilous, so mean was my snigger that, as with one consent, they stopped speaking, and for two or three minutes gazed at me gravely and in silence, the while I continued pacing the room, and making as though I had not noticed them. Yet nothing came of it. None of them spoke, and the next moment I was again forgotten. At length eleven o'clock struck.

"Gentlemen," cried Zvierkov as he rose from the divan, "let us now go to the place of which you know."

"Of course, of course!" came the general exclamation.

Upon this I moved sharply towards Zvierkov. I felt so tortured and shattered in mind that I could almost have cut my throat, and put an end to things then and there. A sort of fever had got hold of me, and my sweat-soaked hair was clinging to my forehead and temples.

"Zvierkov," I said harshly, but firmly, "I beg your pardon. Ferfitchkin, I beg yours also, as I do that of every one present; for I have done a wrong to each one of you."

"Aha! So a duel is not in your line, after all?" hissed Ferfitchkin venomously.

This cut me to the heart.

"Do not think that I fear a duel, Ferfitchkin," I retorted. "I shall be ready to fight you to-morrow, but only after a reconciliation. Upon the latter I insist, and it is not for you to refuse it me. Yet, to show that there is no duel of which I am afraid, I propose that you shall fire first, and that I shall fire in the air."

"He is only playing the fool," remarked Simonov.

"Or clean gone out of his mind," added Trudoliubov.

"Please let me pass," said Zvierkov contemptuously. "Why do you block my way like this? What is it you want?"

Every one was red in the face, with glittering eyes, for much wine had been drunk.

"I only seek your friendship, Zvierkov," I replied. "I have offended you, but——"

"Offended *me*? *You* offended *me*? Please to understand, my good sir, that never, and under no circumstances whatsoever, could you offend *me*."

"Besides, we have had enough of you," growled Trudoliubov. "Come on, you fellows. Let us be off."

"Olympia for me, gentlemen!" cried Zvierkov. "That was a bargain."

"Yes; we don't dispute it," came the laughing response.

I remained alone in my shame as the party left the room. Trudoliubov drawled out some idiotic song or another as they went. Only Simonov lingered a moment to tip the waiters. Suddenly I approached him.

"Simonov," I said in a tone of absolute despair, "please to lend me six roubles."

Extreme astonishment dawned in his stupid eyes (for he too was drunk).

"Do you also wish to go *there* with us?" he inquired.

"Yes."

"Then I have no money to lend you," he retorted with a contemptuous smile as he moved towards the door.

I seized him by the greatcoat, for a sort of nightmare was upon me.

"Simonov," I remonstrated, "I have just seen that you *have* some money. Why do you refuse me? Am I such a rascal? Besides, mind how you refuse me, for you cannot know the real reason why I make the request. Everything depends upon this —my future, my plans, my——"

Taking some money from his pocket, he almost threw it at me.

"Here you are, then!" he said in a hard voice, "if you care to be such a cur." Then he left the room at a run, to rejoin his companions.

For a moment or two I remained where I was— alone with the litter, the leavings, the dregs of liqueur, the spilt wine, the odds and ends of cigarettes; alone with the fumes and the fever in my head, and the aching depression in my heart; alone with the waiter, who, having seen and heard all, was now staring at me with intense curiosity.

"Yes; *I* will go there too!" I cried. "Either they shall kneel to me, and clasp me by the feet, and beseech my friendship, or—or I will hit Zvierkov full in the face!"

V

"So, at length, *this* is contact with reality!" I muttered as I tore down the staircase. "Surely to learn *this* it was not necessary that the Pope should leave Rome and go to Brazil, or that a ball should be given on Lake Como?"

"You cur!" I went on, in objurgation of Zvierkov. "What if you should get the laugh of me even now?"

"No matter if he does," I cried the next moment, in answer to myself. "By now you have lost everything."

The scent of my quarry had now had time to grow cool, yet I knew where to find the man for whom I was seeking.

At the door of the hotel there was lounging a solitary night cabman, with his greatcoat dusted over with the moist—almost warm—snow which was still falling and making everything look dim and oppressive; while his shaggy little piebald pony also had a powdering of snow upon its back, and from time to time, I remember, kept coughing. Leaping into the rough bark sledge, I was in the act of bending my legs to sit down when the recollection of Simonov's recent loan of six roubles threw me into such a state of mind that I rolled backwards on to the seat like a sack.

"Yes, it will take a great deal to set all this right," I exclaimed as I did so. "Yet I *will* set things right, or perish in the attempt. Forward!"

Off we started—I with a veritable whirlwind circling in my brain.

"Yet it is unlikely that they will go upon their knees to win *my* friendship," I reflected. "It is all a mirage—a horrible, disgusting, romantic, fantastic mirage, like the ball on Lake Como. Consequently I shall have no choice but to strike Zvierkov in the face. I shall simply *have* to. *That* at least is decided upon. Get on with you, cabman!"

The cabman gave his reins a jerk.

"I shall deal Zvierkov the blow as soon as ever I enter the room. But ought I first of all to say a few words, by way of preface? No, I shall just enter and hit him. They will all be in the salon together, with Zvierkov seated by Olympia's side, on the divan. That cursed Olympia! Once she refused me, and laughed in my face. I will pull out her hair by the roots, and Zvierkov's ears as well! Or, rather, I will take him by one of those ears, and drag him

about the room! Perhaps his companions will hurl
themselves upon me, and beat me. At the very least
they will throw me out of doors. What then? At
all events I shall have dealt him the blow; I shall
have taken the initiative, and branded him, and
placed it beyond his power to efface my blow with
one of his own—only with a duel. Yes, he will
simply *have* to fight me. But suppose they should
beat me first? Well, let them, the brutes! Trudoliubov would do the most in that way, for he is
very strong, whereas Ferfitchkin would probably
steal up from behind, and hang on to my hair.
However, be it so, be it so! I am going there for
that very purpose. Yes, at last their sheep's brains
shall be forced to taste the tragic note in this. And
when they are dragging me to the door I shall cry
to them that the whole gang is not worth my little
finger. . . . Drive on, drive on!" I shouted to the
cabman, who started, and then flourished his whip,
for my shout had been a wild one.

"Yes, at dawn we shall fight," I went on. "That
is decided. Likewise, my work in the office is ended.
I remember Ferfitchkin making a joke about a
department and a *leper*-tment. . . . But where am
I to get pistols? Pshaw! I shall draw an advance
of salary and purchase some. And powder and ball?
Oh, *they* are the business of the seconds. But how
is everything to be arranged by dawn to-morrow?
And where am I to get seconds? I have not so
much as a friend in the world. Pshaw! Why, the
first person whom I meet in the street will be glad
to act as my second, just as he would do if he were
asked to come and save a drowning man. Extraordinary circumstances must be specially allowed
for. Even if I were to ask the head of my department to second me to-morrow, he would consent out
of very chivalry, and keep my secret as well. Anton
Antonitch is——"

At that moment I suddenly realised, with absolute
and increasing clearness, the idiotic folly of my

plans. Yes, I saw the reverse side of the medal. But——!

"Drive on, cabman! Drive on, you brute! Drive on, I tell you!"

"Aye, aye, sir!" responded that son of the soil.

Next, a cold fit seized me.

"Would it not be better," I thought, "would it not be better if I were to go straight home now? Oh, my God! Why on earth did I ever invite myself to that dinner? It is impossible for me to go home after that three hours' walk between the table and the stove. They—yes, they and no one else— must reckon with me for that walk. They alone can purge me of my dishonour. Drive on, cabman!

"But what if they should give me into custody? No, they would never dare to do such a thing, for they would be afraid of the scandal. Again, what if Zvierkov should contemptuously refuse to fight a duel? It is quite probable that he would do so. Well, in that case I should show him that—— But no; I should wait for him at his door to-morrow, and, just when he was coming out, and about to get into the cab, I should seize him, and tear the great-coat off his back, and fasten my teeth into his hand, and bite him. 'See, every one!' I should cry. 'See to what lengths a desperate man may be driven!' Yes, even though he were striking me over the head, and the rest of the gang were clinging to me from behind, I should still continue to cry to the public: 'Look! Here is a young man going out to conquer the Caucasus! Look at the mark of my spittle on his face!'"

After this (so it seemed to me) all would be over, and my Department would, as it were, disappear from the face of the earth. I should be arrested, tried, dismissed the service, thrown into gaol, and, finally, sent to a penal settlement in Siberia. No matter! Five years later, when released from prison, I should set out—poor, and clad only in a shirt—to look for Zvierkov. Probably I should find him in some provincial capital—a married man, happy, and with a young daughter just beginning to grow up; and I should say to him: "Look, villain, upon my hollow cheeks and ragged clothes! Everything have I now lost—my career, my happiness, my art, my learning, the woman whom I love, and all because of you! Here are pistols. I had come hither to fight a duel with you, but—but now I pardon you." Then I should fire in the air, and be seen and heard of no more.

I could almost have wept at the pathos of my own imaginings. Yet all the while I knew that every one of them came out of *Sylvia*, or Lermontov's *Masquerade,* or some such piece. Suddenly I began to feel ashamed of myself—so ashamed that I stopped the cab, got out of it, and stood in the snow, in the middle of the street, with the driver looking on in open-mouthed amazement.

"What am I to do?" was my reflection. "It is clear that to go on is folly, while to stop at the present stage is impossible, now that I have got so far. Good Lord! I only wish that I could put an end to the matter! Yet how am I to do that after all the insults I have received?"

"No!" finally I shouted, as I sprang into the cab again. "It is foreordained! It is fate! Drive on, cabman!"—and, beside myself, I struck him a blow on the back of his neck.

"What are you hitting *me* for?" cried the little peasant; but nevertheless the blow had the effect of causing him to whip his steed until it began to kick. Wet snow was still falling in large flakes, but I took no heed of the elements as I sat there with my coat unbuttoned. Everything was now forgotten save that I had finally decided upon dealing the blow. With horror, too, I realised that, come what might, the blow must be dealt, and that no power on earth could save me. In the streets the solitary lamps glimmered dimly through the mist, like torches at a funeral, while snow was drifting under my greatcoat, jacket, and scarf, and melting there. Yet I scorned to wrap myself up, for I felt that all was lost.

At length we arrived at our destination. Leaping from the cab, I ascended the steps at a single stride, and banged with feet and fists upon the door. It opened as quickly as though I had been expected. As a matter of fact, Simonov had warned the people of the house that another member of the party might soon be following, and in houses of that kind it is best always to give warnings, and to take precautions. The house was one of those *magasins de modes* which used to be so numerous, but have now been closed by the police. During the daytime it was a dressmaker's establishment, but at night only those who had the *entrée* could resort thither for entertainment.

Passing rapidly through the show-room (which was unlighted), I reached a *salon* to which I was not altogether a stranger, and where a solitary wax candle was burning.

"Where are they?" I found myself asking of some one; but it turned out that they had that moment departed.

Presently I perceived that the proprietress herself —a woman with a foolish, smiling face, whom I knew a little—was standing before me. Then a door opened, and another person entered. Without paying any attention to either of them, I started pacing the room, and muttering to myself as I did so. I felt as though I had been saved from death. Certainly and beyond all doubt I should have dealt the intended blow, but my antagonist, by leaving the place, had altered the whole situation. I kept throwing vague glances around the room, for I could not properly rally my thoughts. Then, in mechanical sort of fashion, I looked at the woman who had just entered, and saw before me a pale, fresh young face which, though a trifle sallow, had straight black eyebrows and a serious, an astonished

H

sort of an expression. It was a face which pleased
me at once, for I should have detested it if it had
been a smiling one. As I looked at her with increased attention I could discern in that serious
countenance—a countenance that was grave almost
to the point of singularity—a species of good-
humoured *naïveté*. Assuredly she was not the sort
of woman to attract those sots, and probably had
passed unnoticed by them. True, she could not be
called exactly pretty, but her figure was tall, strong,
and well-made, and she was dressed in quite simple
fashion.

Then an evil impulse stirred within me, and I
approached her. At that moment I caught sight
of myself in a mirror, and could see that my face
was pale and agitated, my expression sullen, repellent, and vicious, and my hair dishevelled.

"So much the better!" I thought. "I would
rather seem to her disgusting than attractive. It is
just what I want."

VI

SOMEWHERE behind the partition-wall, and with
a strangled sound as though it were being violently
squeezed, a clock emitted a prolonged whirring.
Then, after continuing to do so for an almost unnaturally long time, it gave forth a thin, a mean,
and, as it were, an unexpected stroke with its gong,
as though some one had suddenly sprung at and hit
it. The gong struck twice. Hitherto I had been
dozing rather than sleeping—lying in a sort of half-
comatose condition.

The room—a low, narrow, confined apartment in
which there was a huge wardrobe, and which was
littered over with cards, rags, and every sort of odds
and ends of clothing—was almost dark, since a
candle which had been burning on a table at the
further end of the apartment had gone out, save

for an occasional flicker. In a few moments the darkness would be complete.

Soon I recovered my faculties. At once, without the least effort, everything came back to my memory, as though it had been watching its opportunity to revive. Yet all through my slumber I had seemed to be conscious of some point which had never quite sunk into oblivion, and around which all the fantasies of my sleep had laboured in anguish. Another curious circumstance was that all the events of the previous day now seemed, at the moment of my awaking, to have happened a long while ago, and as though I had lived through them at some far distant period.

My head was filled with fumes, for something seemed to have come over me—to be catching at, exciting, disturbing me, until my old bilious depression began again to seethe within my breast and to search vainly for an outlet. Suddenly, by my side, I perceived a pair of widely-opened eyes regarding me with intent curiosity. Their gaze was so cold, so detached, so sullen, that they seemed hardly to belong to a human being. Indeed, I found their inspection irksome to bear.

But presently a morose idea sprang to birth in my brain, and diffused itself over my body with a sort of unclean sensation which resembled what one experiences when for the first time one penetrates to the musty, fusty underworld. Somehow, too, I thought it unnatural that those eyes should have chosen such a moment to scrutinise me. Also, I remembered that never once throughout the two hours since I had entered the room had I spoken to this creature beside me so much as a word. I had not thought it necessary to do so. Indeed, it had been a sort of pleasure to me to preserve the silence unbroken. Now, however, there suddenly rose to my mind an image as uncouth and repellent as a spider—an image of the debased passion which, destitute of love, begins, grossly and shamelessly, where true love ought to receive its final crown. For a long time we lay thus—looking intently at one another. Yet at last, since she neither lowered her eyes nor once changed her expression, I could stand it no longer.

"What is your name?" I asked brusquely, and the sooner to put an end to the situation.

"Lisa," she replied in a half-whisper, and with a sort of reluctance. Then she turned her eyes away.

I remained silent for a moment.

"It is bad weather—snowy and horrible," I went on, though more to myself than to her, as I clasped my hands indolently behind my head, and lay staring up at the ceiling.

She said nothing. The whole thing was becoming unpleasant.

"Do you belong to St. Petersburg?" I continued, almost angrily, with a slight turn of my head in her direction.

"No."

"To where, then?"

"To Riga," she replied, with a very bad grace.

"You are a German, then?"

"No; a Russian."

"And have you been here long?"

"Where?"

"In this house?"

"Two weeks."

Her replies grew shorter and shorter. Soon the candle finally expired, and I could no longer see her face.

"Have you a father and a mother?"

"Yes—no—yes."

"Where are they?"

"There—in Riga."

"*Who* are they?"

"Somebody."

"How 'somebody'? What sort of people are they? What is their profession?

"They are *miestchané*." [1]

"And have you always lived with them?"

"Yes."

"How old are you?"

"Twenty."

"Why did you leave your parents?"

"Because——" Her "because" evidently signified: "Leave me alone, for I am tired." A silence
ensued.

God knows why I did not seize the opportunity to
get up and go, for I was growing more and more
disgusted and depressed. In spite of my efforts to
banish them, pictures of the happenings of the previous day would keep wandering through my brain.
Suddenly I recalled an incident which I had witnessed in the street when leaving the office early in
the afternoon.

"Yesterday," I said loudly, and as though I had
not wished to begin the conversation again, "I saw
some men carrying a coffin. They very nearly let it
fall."

"A coffin?"

"Yes; in Sennaia Street. It had just been brought
out of a cellar."

"Out of a cellar?"

"Well, out of a basement—you know the sort of
place—the basement of a brothel. There was mud
everywhere and filth. The place simply stank. It
was horrible."

Another pause ensued.

"Bad weather for a funeral," I went on, in order
at any cost to break the silence.

"That would make no difference," she remarked
after a further pause.

"Oh, but it would," I replied, with a yawn.

"How so?" she inquired—again after a pause.

"Because it *would*. In the first place, it would
wet the gravediggers' jackets and make them swear,

---

[1] Persons of the commercial class.

and, in the second place, it would fill the grave with water."

"Why with water?" she asked, with a touch of curiosity, and in a sharper, rougher tone than she had hitherto employed.   For some reason or another this irritated me.

"Because at any depth below six *vershoks* there is *always* water.   In Volkhovo cemetery it is impossible to dig a grave dry."

"Why so?"

"Why so?   Because it is a damp spot—marshy all over.   They just tip the dead into the water. I have seen it done myself—yes, several times."

(As a matter of fact, I had never once seen it done, for I had never been in Volkhovo at all—I was relying upon mere hearsay.)

"Does not that make you afraid to die?" I went on.

"Why should I be going to die?" she exclaimed, as though defending herself against some imputation.

"Well, you will have to die *some* day, and precisely as that woman of Sennaia Street died.   She, like yourself, was a young girl once, but now she lies dead of consumption."

"A woman should go and die in a hospital."

("Evidently she knows all about it," I thought to myself; "for she said, ' a woman,' not ' a young girl.' ")

"When that woman died she was deeply in debt to her mistress," [1] I resumed aloud (for I was growing more and more cantankerous).   "Yet up to the very end she was forced to serve her old woman, despite the consumption.   I heard some cabmen—probably they were old friends of hers—telling some soldiers about it.   Lord, how they laughed!   They were just about to repair to a neighbouring tavern to celebrate the funeral."   By this time I was inventing right and left.

[1] The proprietress of the brothel of which the woman was an inmate.

There fell a silence—a profound silence. Not a sound came from the woman.

"Then it is better to go and die in a hospital?" at length I asked.

"It is much the same thing, is it not?" she asked irritably. Then she added: "But *why* should I be going to die?"

"Not now; but, later on, will you not have to?"

"Perhaps—later on."

"But look here. As yet you are young and fresh and comely; consequently you can still name your price; but remember that after another year of this life your good looks will have faded."

"After *one* year only?"

"Well, after a year your value will at least have lessened." Somehow I felt inclined to be captious. "When that has come about you will be forced to leave this house, and to enter an inferior one, and then a third, and then a fourth, and so on, always descending lower and lower and lower, until, after some seven years of it, you will find yourself landed in a Sennaia Street cellar. That will be glorious, will it not? On the other hand, it is probable that some day you will catch a disease—pneumonia, or a chill, or something of the sort; and the kind of life that you are leading makes such an illness progress very rapidly. It will cling fast to you, and refuse to be shaken off until you die."

"Ah, well—then I must die, that is all." She spoke as though she were exasperated, and at the same time made a quick movement of impatience.

"But do you not at all regret it?"

"Regret what?"

"Your life?"

There came no answer.

"Have you ever had a sweetheart?" I resumed.

"What is that to you?"

"Oh, I do not wish to press you. Quite so; what is it to me? But why should you be so angry about it? However, probably you have your troubles like every one else, and they are no business of mine. Only, I am sorry for——"

"Sorry for what?"

"For you."

"You need not be," was her almost inaudible rejoinder, as again she made a movement of impatience.

This angered me the more. What? I had spoken to her kindly, and she——!

"Do you ever think?" I persisted. "Do you suppose, for instance, that you are treading the right road?"

"No, I *never* think."

"Ah, well, that is just where the evil lies. Open your eyes while there is yet time. There *is* yet time. As yet you are young and good-looking, and might fall in love, and marry, and——"

"But not all married people are happy, are they?" she interrupted in her old rough, rapid way.

"No, not all; but at least their life is better than yours. Indeed, in comparison with your life there could not be a better one. And if one loves, one can live even without happiness; and should sorrow come, such life is still good—it is still good to be alive and to live. But *here,* what is there but foulness? Pah!"

I turned away in disgust, for I could not reason with her coldly. Besides, I was beginning to feel the force of what I was saying, and to grow warm over it. Also, I was thirsting to expound certain ideas which I had long ago conceived in my solitary den. Something in me had suddenly caught fire; there had suddenly dawned before my vision a definite aim.

"Never mind the fact that I too am here," I said, "for I cannot be taken as an example, even though I may be worse than you. As a matter of fact, when I came to this house to-night I was drunk" (it will be seen that I was in a very great hurry to justify myself), "and in that respect a man is no example for a woman. You and I are different persons, for, however much I may bedaub and befoul myself, I am no slave. I come, I go, and it is as though I had not come. I can shake it off, and become, as it were, a new man. But you—you have been a slave from the beginning. Yes, a slave. For have you not surrendered your all, and even your freewill? Consequently, later on, when you may wish to break your chain, you will never be able to do so. It will fasten itself closer and closer upon you. And a right cursed chain it is, too! I know its nature only too well. But since, I suppose, you will not be able to understand me if I put it in any other way, I will ask you—Are you not in debt to your landlady? Ah! *Now* you see how it is; *now* you see your chain. Nor will you ever escape from it, for that is how it is done. The fact that your soul must go to the devil matters nothing to your employer. I, on the other hand, am an unfortunate who plunge into the mire simply out of despondency. Some men drink out of despondency, but I—well, I come *here*. Yet what good does it do? Here have we been lying together without a single friendly word to say to one another all the time. You have merely looked at me like a wild beast, and I at you. Is it *thus* that one should love? Is it *thus* that a man should mate with a woman? No, it is foulness, foulness, from start to finish."

"*Yes!*" came a hasty confirmation of all that I had said. Indeed, I was astounded at the precipitancy with which she accorded her assent. Surely it meant that similar ideas had been wandering in *her* brain also while she had been looking at me? Surely, then, she was capable at least of *some* thought?

"Devil take it all, but this is curious, for it comes so pat," I thought to myself, as I almost rubbed my hands with joy. "Why should I not probe a little further into this youthful soul?" By this time I was getting more and more excited with the game.

She turned towards me, and (so far as I could

judge in the darkness) raised herself upon her elbow. How I regretted that at that moment I could not watch her eyes! Yet I could hear her deep breathing.

"Why did you ever come to this house?" I resumed, with something of an authoritative air.

"For a certain reason."

"Would it not have been much better for you to have gone on living with your father? There you would have been at least safe and well. There you would have been, as it were, in the nest."

"But what if things were *worse* there than here?"

"It still remains for me to find the right note," thought I in passing; "for evidently she does not appreciate sentimentality."

Yet this was only a momentary thought. I swear that she really interested me. Also, I was feeling weak and unstrung, and knavery goes all too easily with such a mood.

"Who can say?" I hastened to answer aloud. "Such things often happen. Indeed, I feel sure that some one has ill-treated you, and that you have been sinned against rather than sinning. Of your history I know nothing, yet I *do* know that a girl of your type does not lightly enter a place like this."

"What sort of a girl am I, then?" she whispered almost inaudibly: yet I heard it.

"The devil take it all!" I reflected. "Here have I been actually flattering her! This is horrible. Yet it is possible that good may come of it.

"Look here, Lisa," I went on; "let me speak of myself a little. Had I, since childhood, had parents to live with, I should never have become what I am to-day. This often occurs to my mind, for, however miserable life at home may be, there has at least one's father and mother, not enemies or strangers. Yes, and even though those parents show one love but once a year, still one knows that one is at home. On the other hand, I had to grow up an orphan:

whence it has come about that I am what you see me now—a man of no feeling."

Again I stopped and waited. "Perhaps she does not understand me!" I thought. "Perhaps all this moralising seems to her ridiculous!"

"If I were a father," I continued, "and had a daughter, I should love her even more than I did my sons." I confess to blushing as I said this.

"And why?" she inquired (she *had* heard, after all!).

"Because—well, I hardly know, Lisa. I know a father—a stern, grave man—who adores his daughter, and often kisses her hands and feet, and never grows tired of looking at her. For a whole evening he will sit and follow her with his eyes as she dances. In short, he is absolutely mad about her, and I can understand his being so. When night time comes she may be weary, and goes to rest. Then the father arises, and folds her in his arms as she lies asleep, and makes the sign of the cross over her. He wears but a threadbare coat, for he is a miser; yet for her no gift is too costly—for her he will spend his last coin, and feel happy if, in return for the gift, he receive but a smile. A father is always fonder of a daughter than a mother is. Yes, young girls are indeed fortunate to be living at home with their parents. For myself, I think that I should never have allowed any daughter of mine to marry."

"Why not?" she asked, with a faint laugh.

"Because, by heavens, I should have been jealous. What? She to kiss another man—to love a stranger more than she did her own father? It hurts me even to think of it! Certainly, many follies are committed, and all men come to their senses at last; but I believe that to the very day of my death I should have hated giving my daughter away. On the other hand, I would have put every suitor in the world through his paces to ensure that she should fall to the man she loved. Unfortunately, the man whom the daughter loves is generally the man who cuts the worst figure in the father's eyes. 'Tis always so, and causes much trouble in families."

"Some parents prefer to *sell* their daughters rather than give them honestly away," she broke in quickly.

"Ah, ha!" I thought. "So *this* is how the wind lies!" Aloud I said, with some heat: "Lisa, that happens only in families which are unfortunate enough to be destitute either of love or of God. Where there is no love there can be no wisdom. True, I know that such families exist, but it was not of them that I was speaking. To judge by your words, I think that you yourself cannot come of a very loving family—that you have been made to suffer. On the other hand, conduct of that kind sometimes arises from poverty."

"Are things any better in gentle families? There are plenty of poor people who live honourably."

"Yes—perhaps. But, Lisa, man loves to count his misfortunes, and to forget his blessings. If he were a little juster he would admit that every one has an equal share of both—that, so long as all goes well in a family, God distributes His benefits to each member alike. The father will be jovial, affectionate, and faithful—a man who makes every one around him happy. Even in times of trouble everything, through him, will come to seem cheerful. For where, in marriage, does one not find trouble? If ever you should marry, you too will know trouble. But how happy is the honeymoon of a girl who has wedded the man she loves! Everywhere and always she will be happy. Even the most trivial disputes will be hushed during those few blessed weeks. At the same time, there are women who, the more they love, the more they desire to quarrel. I assure you that it is so. Once I knew a woman of that type. 'I love you,' they say, 'and it is *because* I love you that I wish to torment you. Do you not see how it is?' I wonder if you know what torture a man may be put to on this plea? Yes, there *are* such women. They think to themselves: 'How I mean to love him afterwards! I will caress him for ever if only I may tease him a little now.' Yet even *they* tend to happiness in the home—to the making of everything cheerful and comfortable and peaceable and in order. Then other women there are who are jealous. I myself used to know such a one. If her husband went out she could never rest quietly at home, but must go out (even in the middle of the night!) to see if he were not '*there*'—that is to say, in a certain house, or with a certain woman. Yet she knew better than any one else that it was all a mistake on her part. Yes, she suffered from it more than any one else could do. And that was her punishment. Yet such women love, and are all for love. How pleasant, too, are reconciliations after a quarrel! The wife of her own accord acknowledges her fault to her husband, and he and she pardon one another with equal delight. Both are so happy! 'Tis like a reproduction of their first meeting, a second nuptial, a rebirth of love. Nor has any one in the world a right to know what passes between husband and wife if they really love one another. However much they may quarrel, the wife's mother should never be called in to act as arbitrator. That she should so much as suspect the *existence* of a quarrel is wrong, for husband and wife are their own best judges. Love is a secret of two, and should live hidden from all eyes, whosoever they be. It is better so, it is more religious, and it tends to develop self-respect. Now, from self-respect there spring many things, and if love has come at the right time—if it is for love that a man and a woman have married each other—why should that love ever pass? Cannot it be fostered? If so, why not? Very seldom is such a thing impossible. Why should love ever pass if the husband be kind and honourable? Of course, the fervid passion of the first few weeks cannot last eternally; but to that love there sometimes succeeds another and a better love. When that has come about, husband and wife are twin souls who have everything in common. Not a secret is there between them, and if children should result of the union, even the most difficult moments in life will have a sweetness of their own. It is sufficient to love steadfastly, and work becomes a pleasure. A married couple will then be happy indeed, and tell themselves that one day their children will repay them with love for all the present pain, and that therefore it is for themselves that they (the parents) are working. In time, too, the children will begin to grow up, and you will feel that you must set them an example, and be their support, and that when you are dead they will, for all their lives, preserve in their hearts your precepts and your thoughts as they have received them from you. In short, you will feel that your children will ever cleave faithfully to your remembrance. But what an onerous duty does that impose upon you! Therefore, for the better ordering of your conduct, is it not better to be united in as close a bond as possible? It is said that child-bearing is a painful thing. Who said that? On the contrary, it is the happiness of heaven. Do you love little children, Lisa? For myself, I adore them. Think if you had a little child to dangle at your breast! What husband would harbour even a single bitter thought against his wife if he could watch her nursing her firstborn—a little, rosy, chubby thing that stretches itself, and rubs itself, with its tiny feet and hands all swelling with milk, and its nails clean and so small, so small, that it is laughable to see them, and its little eyes so full of intelligence that one could not say *what* they do not see? Yes, look at a baby sucking—how he shakes and plays with the breast! Presently the father draws near, and at once the baby drops the teat, and turns over upon his back, and, gazing at his parent, falls to laughing as

though he would never stop. Then he takes up the
teat again, and sometimes falls to biting it if he has
got sufficient teeth to do so, while at the same time
he looks at his mother, as much as to say, ' See how
I have sucked my fill of you.' Yes; is it not perfect
happiness when all three are united in one—husband,
wife and child? What would one not give to attain
such moments as they enjoy? No, Lisa; first one
must learn the lesson of life before proceeding to lay
the blame upon fate."

("By such pictures as these I shall certainly catch
you," was my secret thought the while. Yet what
I had said I had spoken in all sincerity.)

Suddenly I turned very red in the face, for it had
suddenly occurred to me, "What if I were to find
that all this time she has been bursting with laughter
at me?" The idea simply enraged me. Towards
the end of my speech I had grown really heated;
and to find that my conceit was in danger of being
wounded! The silence continued until I had a great
mind to nudge her with my elbow.

"What made you say it all?" she began, and
then stopped.

Even that was sufficient for me. In a flash I
understood the situation, for quite a new note could
be heard quavering in her voice. No longer was
there in it the old rude, brutal, obstinate intonation,
but, rather, an intonation eloquent of gentleness and
timidity—a timidity so great that even I felt touched,
as well as (it must be confessed) a little guilty
towards her.

"What do you mean?" I asked with intense
curiosity.

"Well, you——"

"I what?"

"Well, one would almost think that you were
speaking from a book," she said. In her tone I
could detect the mocking note.

The speech irritated me—it irritated me greatly.
Nor could I understand what point lay in that

mockery, seeing that such an artifice is usually the last defence of a heart which is not only diffident of itself, but, as yet, free from vice; of a heart which is holding out to the last against rudely insistent efforts to penetrate its recesses; of a heart which is seeking to conceal its true feelings. As a matter of fact, it was from those stray silences, during the period when she was making feeble attempts to rail and failing to accomplish it, that I ought to have derived enlightenment; but *that* I was not clever enough to see; and, moreover, I was blinded by my ill-humour.

"Wait a little," I thought to myself.

VII

"Really, Lisa," I said aloud, "had vice been foreign to me, I *might* have been speaking like a book; but, you see, it is *not* foreign to me. Consequently everything that I have said to you has come from my heart. Is it, then, possible that you are not conscious of the vileness of your present life? Truly, if you are not, then great must be the force of habit, and the devil only knows whither it can lead a human being! Do you in all seriousness think that you will never grow old—that you will always be comely, and allowed to stay here? I am not speaking of your infamy in general, but of the following consideration. As yet you are young and attractive and pretty, as well as not altogether devoid of feeling. Are you, then, aware that, no sooner had I recovered my senses to-night, than I felt disgusted at finding myself here by your side? To have the hardihood to enter such a den as this one needs to be drunk. But if you had been of a different kind, if you had been leading an honest life, I might have courted and fallen in love with you. Then your every look, your every word, would have been delightful to me. I should have

watched at your door, and knelt to you when you
came out, and it would have been my highest boast
to proclaim that I regarded you as my sweetheart.
Never should I have harboured—never *could* I have
harboured—a single impure thought concerning you.
But *here* I know that I have but to whistle for you,
and that you will come, since I need not consult
your pleasure, but, rather, *you* must consult *mine*.
The lowest peasant who sells his labour is none the
less not a slave, for the reason that he knows that
one day his labour will have an end.   But when, for
you, will that end come?   Think, then : what it is
that you have surrendered?   What is it that you have
delivered over into bondage?   Why, your very soul
—the soul of which you had no right to dispose, but
which you have none the less enslaved to your body !
You suffer your love to be profaned by drunkards
when all the while love is the whole world, love is
the most precious of jewels, love is the cherished
treasure of virgins, love is what men will give their
souls, their very lives, for !   But what is *your* love
worth?   You have sold it beyond redemption, for
who would seek to attain love where everything
may be attained without love's presence at all?
What worse offence could a woman commit?   Do
you understand me?   True, I have heard that you
wretched women are given a certain amount of
amusement, and, at times, are allowed to have particular lovers of your own.   Yet that is a mockery,
a mere make-believe.   You take what is given you,
and get laughed at for your pains.   For what sort
of a man would such a lover make?   Would he be
even capable of love?   Never !   How could a man
love you when all the while he knows that at any
moment you may be summoned to attend someone
else?   No, the whole thing, for him, would be a
piece of indecency, and no more.   And could such a
man have any respect for you?   Could there be anything in common between you and him?   No, he
would only laugh at you and plunder you.   Such

I

would be *his* way of loving.   You might consider yourself fortunate if some day he did not kill you. Could you ever be sure that he would not do so? Why, at the merest hint that he should marry you he would laugh in your face, even if he did not also spit in it, and then put you to death.   And all the while, save that you had grown used to him, you might not care for him the amount of a couple of cracked kopecks!   To think of it!   Then why have you buried your life here?   Is it because **you** are given coffee and fed well?   But for what purpose are you fed?   Food of that kind would choke any honest woman, since beneath such generosity she would always discern the hidden motive.   Besides, you are in debt to your landlady, and will always be so—to the very end, to the very moment when your customers have ceased to care about you. And that moment will soon come!   Do not trust too much to your youth, since in this place one year counts as three, and you will soon find yourself out-side, though not before there have been many intrigues against you, and disputes and revilings, even as though you had not already handed over your health and youth to your landlady, even as though you had not already lost your soul for nothing, even as though your taskmistress had not already despoiled and beggared you and stolen your goods!   No, do not trust to her always to keep you.   And, to please her, your companions will never be backward in attacking you, for they are slaves like yourself, and have long since lost sight of conscience and pity.   In your life the prize goes to her who is the most unclean, the most vile, the most abominable.   In your life, too, they know how to inflict such injuries as are undreamt of else-where.   All that you possess, all that you hold most dear—your health, your looks, your youth, your last remaining shred of hope—will soon be lost.   At twenty-two you will be aged thirty-five; and if by that time you have not also become diseased you may think yourself lucky, and render thanks to God. Perhaps you suppose that at least you do not *work* here, that you are always 'making holiday'? Wretched woman! I tell you that in all the world there is no more horrible trade than yours—in all the world there exists no form of forced labour which is even *comparable* to your existence. Ought not that one thought—let alone any others—to make your heart weep? And when you come to be turned out of this house not a word, not a syllable, will there be that you can say for yourself. For ever you will have to go your way an outcast. Yes, you will have to enter another brothel, and then a third one, and others, until at last you find yourself landed in Sennaia Street. There you will often be beaten, for the place has its own endearments, and its *habitués* are apt to confound caresses with blows. Its horrors pass belief! Pay but a single visit there, and when you have seen it for yourself you will believe the evidence of your eyes. One New Year's Eve, when I was walking through that quarter, I saw a woman outside a door. Her companions had turned her out of the house because they could not bear to hear her weeping. Despite the fearful cold, they had closed the door upon her! There she sat at nine o'clock at night—drunken, dishevelled, half-naked, and almost dead with the beating which she had received. Terrible was the contrast between her painted cheeks and blackened eyes; her nose and gums were running with blood from a blow which had been given her by a cabman. In her hands she was holding a piece of salt fish, and as she sat there on the pavement, and wept bitter tears of pain, and lamented her lot, she kept striking this piece of fish against the doorsteps of the house, while a group of cabmen and soldiers on the kerb were engaged in egging her on. Surely *you* do not wish to become like that? Personally I do not think that you ever will; but how can any of us tell? Perhaps, some eight or ten years ago, even that woman with the fish came to this house as fresh as a cherub, and innocent, and pure, and ignorant of evil, and ready to blush at the least word. Perhaps she too was once proud, like yourself, and sensitive, like yourself, and different to all her companions, and full of the idea that nothing but happiness awaited her and the man who said he loved her, and whom she loved. Yet see the end to which she has now come! Ah, can it be that, when, drunken and dishevelled, she was striking that fish against the dirty doorsteps, she was recalling to her memory her unsullied past, and her father's house, and her school days, and the road where the young man used to wait for her to swear that he would love her always and devote his whole future to her, and the moment when they decided that their affection would be eternal, and that they must marry as soon as ever they came of age? Lisa, it would be a sheer blessing for you if you were to die to-morrow, in some cellar, some hidden corner, like the consumptive woman who died the other day in Sennaia Street. You say you will go to the hospital, do you? But they would not receive you there, because of your debt to your landlady. Consumption is not a rapid sickness, like a fever, which to the last moment leaves the patient some hope of recovery. No, a consumptive woman goes on deceiving herself, and believing herself still strong and well, while all the time she is playing into her landlady's hands. Slowly and surely you will be dying, and seeing yourself dying, and gradually being cast aside; until, at last, what will there be left for you to say? True, you will have sold your soul; but you will still be owing your landlady money. Consequently you will be left alone, utterly alone, for what else could they do with you? Perhaps they will reproach you for not earning your keep, as well as for being so long a-dying! And should you be thirsty, they will give you water, and, with it, insults, and the words : ' When are you going to get out of this, you slut? You keep us

awake at night with your groans, and the customers
do not like it.' I myself have heard things like that
said to a woman. And at length, when death has
nearly come to you, you will be thrown into a corner
of some stinking cellar, to lie helpless in the darkness and the wet. What will you have to think of
during the long, long, endless nights? . . . And
when death has come, some strange, some grudging
hand will shroud you; and around your corpse there
will be heard, not prayers, but vile oaths. No one
will be there to bless you, no one to bewail you.
You will be placed upon a bier similar to that which
they allotted to the consumptive woman of Sennaia
Street, and when that has been done the bearers
will repair to a tavern and talk of you, while your
body will be left to lie in the mud and the filth and
the half-melted snow. And what of your funeral
rites? 'Lower away at that end, Vaniukha.[1] Even
here she keeps up her heels in the air, just as she
used to do when she was plying her trade. Yes,
that is the sort she was.' 'Don't bear too heavily
upon that rope there. Let it down a bit. Yes,
that's the way.' 'No, no; you will upset her if
you do that. After all, she was a human being
like ourselves.' 'Well, so much the worse for her!
On we go.' Nor will they quarrel long over you.
As quickly as it can be done they will throw over
you a few shovelfuls of wet blue clay, and then
betake themselves once more to the tavern. Such
is the future before you. Other women are accompanied to the graveyard by children, fathers, or
husbands; but for *you* not a tear will be shed, not a
sigh will be heaved, not a regret will be uttered.
Nor will any one come to pray over your grave, but
your name will vanish as utterly as though you had
never existed, as though you had never been born.
'Dust to dust!' And at night, when the dead raise
the lids of their coffins, you will cry aloud: 'Suffer

---

[1] A diminutive of Ivan.

me to go and live a little longer in the world, good people. I lived, but I never knew life, for my life served but as a cloth for others to wipe their lust upon. All my existence was drunken away in the mire of Sennaia Street. Suffer me to go and live a little longer in the world, good people.' "

Here my own pathos began to get the better of me, and I felt such a choking sensation in the throat that I was forced to stop. Presently a nervous feeling also came upon me, and with beating heart I raised myself to listen. I had good reason to do so.

For a long while past I had been suspecting that my words would probably end by overwhelming Lisa's soul, and breaking her heart; and the more assured that that would be so I had become, the more I desired to attain my end as quickly and as thoroughly as possible. It was a game which greatly attracted me. Yet it was not *all* a game.

Though I knew that, throughout, I had spoken in a sentientious, stilted, bookish manner, and could not have spoken otherwise, the fact in no way disturbed me, since I was well aware, and had a sure presentiment, that she would end by understanding me, as well as that my very bookishness would help me to further my plans. Yet even in the moment of success I recoiled and stood aghast at what I had done! For never, never in my life have I witnessed such despair as now came upon her! She lay there with her head buried in the pillow, her face pressed into its folds, and her frame shaken from head to foot with convulsive tremors. And just at the moment when her sobs seemed to be passing altogether beyond control, she broke forth into shrill cries and moans as she glued herself still closer to the pillow, in the hope that she might prevent any other inmate of the house—indeed, any living soul in the world—from hearing her agony. Tearing the sheet with her teeth, she bit her hands until (as I afterwards saw for myself) the blood came, while she twined her hands convulsively through her dis-

ordered hair. Lastly she lay motionless, almost
without breathing, and with her teeth tightly
clenched together. At first I tried to speak to her,
to calm her agitation, but I had not the requisite
courage. Shaking from head to foot, I groped my
way from the bed, with the intention of dressing
myself and departing; but the room was so dark
that, despite my efforts, my movements were greatly
retarded. At length I found a box of matches and
a new and unburnt candle. As soon as the flame
had lit up the room Lisa raised her form with a
sharp contortion, seated herself—a sorry figure—
upon the edge of the bed, and looked at me with a
gaze which had in it almost the smile of a mad
woman. Seating myself by her side, I took her
hand. Instantly she appeared to recall all that had
passed during the preceding hour, and, leaning in
my direction, as though to embrace me, seemed
suddenly to change her mind, and ended by gently
kissing my head.

"Lisa, my dear one," I began, "I did not mean it.
Pray pardon me."

Upon that she clasped my hands with such force
that in an instant I understood that I had said the
wrong thing. So for a moment I held my tongue.
Then I went on—

"Here is my address, Lisa. Come and see me."

"Yes, I will come," she murmured, though a
little irresolutely, and with her head drooping.

"Now I must go. Good-bye until we meet
again."

I rose, and she did the same. Suddenly I saw
her start and blush. Then she seized a shawl which
was lying on a chair, threw it over her shoulders,
and muffled herself up to the chin. After that she
threw me a half-whimsical glance—a sort of sickly
smile. It hurt me so much that I made all the more
haste to depart. I had a longing to be gone.

"Wait a moment," came her unexpected request
when we had reached the entrance-hall, and were

standing by the door while I put on my overcoat. Setting down the candle, she ran back into the house.

"She must have remembered something which she had wished to show me," thought I. "When she left me her face was red, her eyes were shining, and her smile had quite a different air to what it had before. What can it all mean?" I waited. Presently she returned with a sort of petitioning or deprecatory look in her face. Nor was it the same face as a few hours ago, for it no longer had in it the mournful, suspicious, obstinate eyes which I had seen before. On the contrary, those eyes were now gentle, beseeching, full of confidence and tenderness, yet timid. It was the face of a child who is gazing at some one whom it loves, and from whom it is hoping to receive a gift. They were clear and grey; they were beautiful, animated eyes which could with equal intensity express either love or hate.

Without any explanation, but as though I had been some sort of a superior being who could divine everything, she tendered me a paper. As she did so her face looked brilliantly radiant—naïvely, almost childishly, triumphant. I unfolded the paper. It was a letter from a medical student (or something of the kind) which, though florid in tone and highly coloured, expressed in an entirely respectful manner a declaration of love. I have forgotten its exact terms, but can remember that, despite its flowery diction, it contained between its lines a certain amount of genuine feeling of the sort which cannot be feigned. When I had finished reading it I chanced to encounter Lisa's gaze. It was eager, full of curiosity, and as impatient as that of a child. Next, since I was slow to make a remark of any kind, she told me rapidly, and in a few words (as well as with a kind of joyous pride), that, some few days ago, she had been to a ball at "a good house" where there lived people "who knew nothing of what I am now—no, nothing at all," since she was then

quite new to the brothel, and had once, only once,
etcetera, etcetera, and had now no intention of
remaining there, but was resolved to leave as soon
as ever she could get clear of the place.   Well, at
this ball she had met the medical student, and they
had danced and talked together the whole evening,
and the student had known and played with her as
a little girl at Riga, and had also known her parents.
Of *this,* however, he had known nothing, nothing
whatever—he had never even suspected it.   And,
the day after the ball (that is to say, three days ago),
he had sent her this letter by the hand of a friend
who had gone with her to the dance ; and—and—
well, that was all.   She lowered her eyes in
confusion.

Poor girl !   So she had been keeping this letter
as a precious thing, and had yearned to show me
her poor little treasure because she would not have
me depart without knowing that even *she* could win
honest, sincere affection, and be addressed with
respect.   Doubtless the letter was destined to lead
to no result, but only to grow old and faded in a
casket ; yet sure am I that she would have treasured
it to the end, as at once her visible trophy and her
visible excuse.   And now, in this moment of pride
and desire for extenuation, she had thought of bringing me this poor little missive, that she might naïvely
parade her triumph before me, and rehabilitate herself in my eyes, and (perhaps) even earn my con-
gratulations ! . . .   However, I said nothing ; I only
pressed her hand and departed.   Somehow I was in
a great hurry to depart.

Large flakes of snow were falling, but I walked
the whole way home.   Tired, overdone, astonished
though I was, there was yet dawning in me a
consciousness of the truth.   And a sorry truth it
was !

VIII

AT first I could not bring myself to accept that truth; but, next morning, on awaking from a heavy sleep of several hours, I at once recalled all the events of the night, and felt astounded at the sentimentality which I had displayed towards Lisa. "What was the use of that horror and that pity?" I said to myself. "Am I getting as nerve-diseased as an old woman? Pah! And why did I give her my address? What if she should avail herself of it? Well, *let* her come. It will not matter." Evidently the point—the chief, the most important point of all—was to hasten to retrieve my reputation in the eyes of Zvierkov and Simonov. Consequently for that morning, at all events, Lisa escaped my anxious mind altogether.

First of all it behoved me to repay Simonov my debt of last night; and to effect this I decided upon desperate means—namely, to borrow fifteen roubles from Anton Antonitch. As it befell, the latter was in an exceedingly good temper that morning, and acceded to my request at the first asking. This so delighted me that, in signing the promissory note, I told him negligently, but with some archness of bearing, that, the previous evening, I had "dined with friends at the Hotel de Paris." "The occasion," I went on, "was a farewell dinner to a comrade—I might even say, to a friend of my boyhood—who had gone the pace right royally. Of good family and unexceptionable standing, he has also had a distinguished career, is clever and good-natured, and can boast of very great success among the fair sex. We drank champagne by the dozen," —and so on, and so on. Rubbish though it all was, it nevertheless came quite easily, disconnectedly, and unbidden to my lips.

On reaching home I at once wrote to Simonov; and to this day I am lost in admiration when I recall the truly gentlemanly, the perfectly frank and good-humoured, tone of my letter. Easily and with grace —above all things, with no superfluous expenditure of words—I begged pardon for all that had happened, and justified myself—"if I may be permitted to do so"—by the fact that, from the moment when, between five and six o'clock (that is to say, previous to my companions' arrival), I had imbibed a first liqueur at the Hotel de Paris, sheer unusedness to wine had turned my head. Of Simonov I begged pardon by name, and then asked him to make my excuses to the rest of my fellow diners, but more especially to Zvierkov, whom I declared that I "remembered only as in a dream," but whom I must undoubtedly have offended. To this I added that assuredly I would have called upon each of my fellow diners in turn had not my head—still more, my conscience—been too sore to permit of my doing so. Upon this facile, this, as it were, careless (yet entirely becoming), touch which had suddenly manifested itself in my pen I particularly plumed myself, since, better than anything else, it would give my friends to understand that I took an absolutely independent view of "my unseemly behaviour of last night," and that I did not look upon myself as the crushed individual whom "you, my good sirs, may suppose me to be," but as a gentleman who knows how to respect himself. "Let me not be blamed for my youthful indiscretions," I wrote in conclusion.

"What marquis-like playfulness!" I commented admiringly, as I read the document through. "What a refined, what a well-mannered person it makes me appear to be! Others, in my place, would have been at a loss to extricate themselves from the difficulty, whereas I have wormed my way out, and can go to dinner again, simply through the fact that I am a refined, educated man of the nineteenth century. To think that all this should have arisen out of last night's wine! Hm! But no; it was not due to the wine, for, as a matter of fact, between five and six o'clock I never touched a single drop of vodka, and have therefore told Simonov a lie. Yes, I have lied to him most unconscionably; and to do so was wrong. No matter; the main thing is that I *have* got out of it safely.

With this letter I enclosed six roubles, and, having sealed the lot, requested Apollon to take it to Simonov's; whereupon, Apollon having learnt that the package contained some money, the rascal became more respectful, and consented to perform the errand. Towards evening I went for a walk, for the previous night's festivities had left me very bilious, and my head was swimming badly. The further the evening advanced, and the darker the shadows grew, the more did my reflections become varied and involved. In the recesses of my heart and conscience there seemed to be lurking something which would not die—a sort of mysterious feeling which hurt me even as a burn might have done. Generally, on such occasions, I directed my steps towards the most crowded spots and most populous thoroughfares—especially at dusk, at the hour when the throng of hurrying workmen and artisans (their faces worn almost to brutality) becomes denser, and the daily toil has reached an end. It was precisely the humble pursuits of these humble breadwinners—the blatant prose of life—that interested me most. Yet, that evening, the jostling of the pavements only served to exasperate me, and to prevent me from properly connecting my thoughts. Within me there was arising a carking uneasiness which would not be quieted. At length so unstrung was I that I betook myself homewards. Something like a crime seemed to be weighing upon my conscience.

Also, the thought that one day Lisa might call upon me kept torturing my soul. It was strange that, of all my recollections of the previous night, the memory of her should disturb me with a kind of a special, separate force. Everything else had by this time escaped my mind, since everything else had been put right by my letter to Simonov. Only as regards the point of which I have spoken did I still remain uneasy. It was as though only Lisa had the power to make me suffer. "What if she *should* come?" was my constant thought. "Well, it will not greatly matter. *Let* her come. Hm! Yet I cannot bear to think that she should see the way in which I live. Last night I must have seemed to her a perfect hero; whereas now——! Also, I cannot bear to think that I am so out-at-elbows. My rooms speak of nothing but poverty. Look at the suit in which I had to go out to dinner last night! Look at that deal sofa shedding its straw, and at the dressing-gown which barely covers me! What a set of rags! And to think that she should see all this, and see Apollon too! And the brute will be sure to insult her, and to pick a quarrel with her, if only he can do me a rudeness. And I, as usual, shall play the cad, and fall to prancing before her, and wrapping myself in the folds of my dressing-gown, and grinning, and telling endless lies. Oh, the foulness of it all! Yet even that would not be the worst thing that I should do, for in me there is something fouler, baser, more serious yet. Yes, in me there is something baser—something which will once more make me don the mask of falsehood and dishonour."

The thought of this fired my anger the more. "But why dishonour?" I cried. "What is there so dishonourable in it? What I said last night I really meant, for I genuinely felt it. What I did was to try and arouse her to better instincts. The fact that she wept was all to the good, and may prove the saving of her."

Yet somehow I could not reassure myself. Continually during that evening—even after nine o'clock, when (so my calculations told me) there was no chance of her coming that night—I could see her present before me, and always in the same attitude.   For, of all the incidents of the previous night, one in particular was for ever graven on my memory. It was the moment when the light of the match had revealed to me her pale, wrung face and martyred expression.   What a strangely pitiful, futile smile there had been playing on her lips !   Nor did I know that, even so long as fifteen years after the event, she would still be present to my mental eye, with that strangely pitiful, futile smile of hers.

But next morning I felt disposed to look upon the whole affair as nonsense and a mere lapse of the nervous system—above all, as an "exaggeration."   Of this latter weakness in me I had always recognised the existence, and was afraid of its effects.   "I invariably magnify things; wherefore I invariably come to grief," was what I kept saying from hour to hour.

At length I summed up my reflections in the thought that possibly she *might* come.   Yet still the uncertainty annoyed me.

"Yes, she *will* come," I burst out as I paced the room.   "If not to-day, at all events to-morrow. Oh, the cursed romanticism of these ' pure hearts ' ! Oh, the damnableness, the folly, the obtuseness, of pruriently sentimental souls like hers !   Yet how is it that I do not understand her ?   How is it, indeed ? "

I stopped in strange perplexity.

"To think," I resumed, "that a few words, a mere fragment of an idyll (and a bookish, artificial, invented idyll at that) should bring about such a revolution in the life of a human being !   It only shows of what a virgin, an untouched soil, is capable."

At times I even thought of going to see *her,* and telling her all, and asking her not to come; but at these times such wrath again seized upon me that I verily believe that, had she at that moment been within my reach, I should have fallen tooth and nail upon her.   Yes, I should have insulted her, spat

upon her, chased her out of the house, and beaten
her black and blue !

However, another day passed, and then another
one, and then a third; yet no Lisa came, and I began
to feel a little easier. Especially after nine o'clock
did I feel cheerful as I went out for my walk. In
fact, I came to take a brighter view of things
altogether, and would say to myself : " I will save
Lisa by having her to visit me, and talking to her.
Yes, I will develop and shape her mind. I know that
she loves me, and loves me passionately, yet I mean
to pretend that I am unaware of it (though *why*
I should so pretend I do not know, unless it be
because she is comely). Then one day, with an
air at once confused and beautiful, she will throw
herself into my arms, in a transport of tears and
tremors, and tell me that I have been her deliverer,
and that she loves me more than all the world
beside. Then I shall feign surprise, and say : ' Lisa,
is it possible that you suppose that I have never
divined your love? Why, I saw it, and understood
it, long ago, but dared not, of my own initiative,
lay siege to your heart, since I had an influence over
you, and feared lest, should you ever become aware
of it, you would think it incumbent upon you to
respond to my passion, and to force a similar passion
in yourself; which would never have been in accordance with my wish, since such a course would have
been sheer despotism and indelicacy on my part.'
At this point I shall plunge into a sea of Western-
European, George-Sandian subtleties, and then continue : ' But now you are *mine,* Lisa. Now you are
my own creation, a thing pure and beautiful, and my
fairest of wives. So—

> " ' Into my house, with daring step and free,
> Enter thou and reign.' [1]

"From that point onwards we shall tread the road

---

[1] From a poem by Nekrassov.

of life together, and travel abroad," etcetera, etcetera, etcetera.

But in the end I used to feel ashamed of myself, and to put out my tongue at my own folly.

"Perhaps," also I thought at times, "they will not let this tiresome woman leave the house. I believe such women are *not* allowed to go out very much—least of all in the evenings " (for some reason I always thought that she would come at night, and precisely at seven o'clock). "But," I suddenly remembered, "she told me that, as yet, she was not completely a slave—that she still stood upon a special footing. That means—hm! well, what the devil *does* it mean? Nevertheless, she will come some day; infallibly she will come."

Really I must think myself fortunate in that, throughout that time, Apollon's rudeness did much to distract me. He simply exhausted my patience. He was my prime cross, my constant plague, in life. For years we had been wrangling with one another, night and morning, until I had come positively to hate him. My God, how I hated him! Never before nor since have I so hated a human being! An elderly man of imposing aspect, he not only acted as my servant, but also did a little tailoring in his spare moments. Why he had such a contempt for me I do not know. For he *did* despise me, and that to an unreasonable extent. Yet, though he looked down upon me from heights of unspeakable superiority, he treated every one in the same way. Merely to see his tow-coloured head, his excessively sleek hair, the tuft which he grew on the top of his forehead (and which he periodically greased with olive oil), his huge mouth, and his V-shaped lips, made one feel that one was in the presence of a being who was supremely sure of himself. Besides, he was an intolerable precisian—the most precise person on earth, and could boast of a conceit which would have presumed to patronise Alexander of Macedon himself. Also, for every button on his

coat, and for every nail on his fingers, he cherished
an affection which positively amounted to adora-
tion.   Myself, however, he treated with a high
hand.   He always spoke to me very shortly, and,
when looking at me, did so with invincible self-
sufficiency, supreme hauteur, and a sort of rallying
mockery which drove me nearly to distraction.   Yet,
though he made such a favour of his services, those
services amounted to very little, for he appeared to
think himself under no particular obligation to work.
In short, there can be no doubt that he thought me
an absolute idiot; and if for a single moment he
endured my presence, it was only because he took
pleasure in drawing, at my hands, the seven roubles
per month which I awarded him for his idling.
Much, much may be forgiven me on his account.
Sometimes, owing to our mutual enmity, the very
sound of his footsteps would make me feel as though
an attack of nerves were imminent.   But the feature
in him which disgusted me most of all was a sort
of whistling noise which he always made when
speaking.   Surely he must have had a tongue too
long for his mouth (or some such deformity) to make
him suck his lips and whistle as he spoke?   Yet of
this circumstance he actually seemed proud—probably because he believed that it gave him a distinguished air !   Usually he spoke low, and very slowly,
with one hand clasped behind his back, and his eyes
cast down.   Above all things he infuriated me when
he was reading his nightly Psalms (between my
room and his there was only a thin partition-wall),
and we had many a battle over those devotions.   Yet
with him they were a sheer passion.   Every day he
would fall to conning them over in a voice that was
as level and devoid of intonation as the voice of a
man keeping vigil over a corpse.   Curiously enough,
the last-mentioned pursuit is the very trade that he
has now come to, for at the present time he is a
professional reciter of Psalms over the dead, while
the rest of his time he divides between the profes-

K

sions of rat-catcher and bottle-washer. However, I was powerless to dismiss him; he was, as it were, chemically soldered to my existence. Besides, nothing in the world would ever have induced him to give me notice; while, for my part, I could not have endured life in a furnished tenement. My present tenement was an isolated one, and therefore my sheath, my box into which I could withdraw from all humanity; and for some infernal reason or another Apollon always seemed to form part of it. Consequently for seven whole years I found myself unable to make up my mind to dismiss him.

As for my retaining his wages for a day or two, I had always found the scheme impossible, for the reason that whenever I had attempted to do so he had told me tales which had made me wonder where best I could flee to hide my head. On the present occasion, however, I was so exasperated with the world that I resolved (never mind why) to punish Apollon by making him wait as much as a fortnight for his emoluments. For the last two years I had been vowing to do this thing, even if it were only to show him that he could not take a high hand with me, and that I was his master; but on the present occasion I decided to say nothing to him about it, and so force him to take the initiative in referring to his wages. As soon as he should do so (I decided) I would go to my cash-box, show him the seven roubles in order to let him see for himself that they had duly been set apart for him, and say that I did not choose, *I did not choose,* to hand them to him now. Yes, I would say quite simply that *I did not choose* to do so, since I had a mind to be master, although for a long time past he had been rude and overbearing in his manner. On the other hand, if he chose to come and ask me for them respectfully, I would (perhaps) pardon him: otherwise he would have to wait fifteen days longer, or perhaps three weeks, or, possibly, a whole month.

Yet, for all my resolution, he proved the victor, for I failed to maintain the struggle longer than four days. He began in the manner which he always adopted on such occasions, and, since I had been making the same sort of attempt for three years, I knew exactly what to expect. Yes, I knew all his villainous tactics by heart. He would begin by staring me in the face with long-drawn-out severity; more especially if he met me in the street, or if he were leaving the flat at the same moment as myself. If I bore the ordeal well, or if I seemed to be paying him no attention, he would embark upon other, though always silent, persecutions. Unsummoned, he would suddenly enter the room on noiseless tiptoe, at a moment when I was either reading or quietly walking up and down. Halting on the threshold, he would then lay one hand behind his back, advance one foot a step, and train upon me a look less of severity than of absolute, whole-souled contempt. If I asked him sharply what he wanted he would return me no answer, but continue to stare me in the eyes. Lastly, with a very special, a very meaning sucking of the lips, he would turn on his heel, and slowly—very slowly—retire to his den. Two hours later he would return. This time, unable any longer to contain myself, I would not ask him what he wanted, but raise my head with a sharp, imperious movement, and fix him with my gaze. In this manner we would remain staring at one another for two or three minutes; after which, with great dignity, he would once more turn on his heel (even as he had done the first time), and take his departure for another couple of hours.

In case even *that* did not suffice to bring me to terms, and I still had the hardihood to continue rebellious, he would begin sighing as he looked at me—sighing long and deeply, as though by his sighs he wished to make clear to me the measure of my moral abasement. It need hardly be said that this last stratagem had always worsted me. I might

be beside myself, I might even foam at the mouth
with rage, but in the end I had always had to take
the road which he desired me to take.

On the present occasion, however, he had no
sooner reached the stage of "stern looks" than I
issued from my fastness and attacked him (I was
sufficiently irritated, you may be sure, for the deed).

"Stop!" I cried.   "Remain where you are!"

With slow, silent and dignified bearing he continued to leave the room, with his hand still clasped
behind his back.

"Return!" I cried after him.   "Return at once!"

My voice must have reached an almost super-
natural intensity, for he *did* return, and stood gazing
at me in some astonishment.   Not a word did he
speak, however, and that angered me the more.

"How dare you enter my room without being sent
for?" I shouted.   "And how *dare* you look at me
like that?   Answer!"

For fully half a minute he continued calmly to
look at me.   Then again he turned to depart.

"Stop!" I yelled as I made for him at a run.
"Do not move an inch!   Stop where you are, and
answer my questions!   For what did you come
here?"

"To see if you had any orders for me," he replied
with gentle deliberation after a moment's silence;
the interval having been employed in sucking his lips
and poising his head, first upon one shoulder, and
then upon the other.   His voice, his attitude, his
whole self exuded a lethargy which drove me to
distraction.

"It is *not* so, you ruffian!" I cried in a voice
which trembled with rage.   "I never sent for you
at all.   *I* can tell you why you have come here.
You have seen that I have not paid you your wages;
yet your vanity will not allow you actually to ask
for them.   *That* is what you have come here for,
with those damned looks of yours.   Yes, you have
come here just to punish and to torture me, without

having the sense, you brute, to understand what a damnable, damnable, damnable thing you are doing!"

Again he was on the point of turning on his heel when I caught him by the arm.

"Listen!" I cried. "Here is your money. Do you see it? It is *there!*" (I drew the sum from a drawer). "Yes, the seven roubles are *there!* But you are not going to have them until you choose, humbly and respectfully, to beg my pardon."

"That is impossible," he replied, with almost a superhuman amount of assurance.

"Very well!" I shouted. "Then I swear to you that you shall *never* have your wages at all!"

"There is nothing that I need beg your pardon for," he went on, as though he had not heard me. "On the other hand, you have called me a rascal, and I intend to go and see the superintendent about it."

"Go, then!" I yelled. "Go at once! Yes, this very minute, this very second! Go, you rascal, you rascal, you rascal!"

Scarcely looking at me, he moved towards the door; whence, paying me no further attention, nor once glancing in my direction, he re-entered his own room.

"But for Lisa, all this would never have happened," I reflected. I felt so agitated that my heart had well-nigh stopped beating as for a moment or two I preserved my solemn, dignified attitude. Then I pursued Apollon to his room.

"Apollon," I said in a voice the low, restrained tone of which was really due to the fact that I was half-stifled with rage, "go at once for the superintendent of the buildings."

Apollon had just seated himself at his table, after donning his spectacles, and begun to sew; but, on hearing my command, he burst into a loud snigger.

"Yes, go this instant!" I repeated. "Go this

instant, I tell you ! If you do not go, more will happen than you have bargained for."

"You yourself are not feeling very comfortable about it, I think," he observed. As he spoke he did not even raise his head, but sucked his lips in, and slowly threaded his needle. "Is it usual for a man to go for a policeman to effect his own arrest? And as for frightening me, you might as well save yourself the trouble, for you will never succeed in doing *that*."

"Nevertheless, I tell you to go !" Barking out the words like a dog, I had just seized Apollon by the collar when—the door opened, and slowly and softly a figure appeared, came towards us, and stood gazing in astonishment at the spectacle. I felt so overcome with shame that, diving hastily into my room, I seized hold of my hair with both hands, staggered back against the wall, and remained crouching there.

A couple of minutes later I heard Apollon's slow footsteps approaching.

"Some one to see you," he said, with a look of amazing severity. Then he stood aside for Lisa to pass. When she had done so, he made no attempt to depart, but stood there with his mocking smile.

"Go, go !" was my frantic command.

At that moment the clock, emitting a laboured whirring and creaking, struck seven.

IX

"Into my house, with daring step and free,
    Enter thou and reign."

I FOUND myself standing thunderstruck—standing shamed to the core. Yet I have an idea that I smiled, and tried to dispose my dilapidated dressing-gown to the best advantage—even as, in previous moments of doubting, I had imagined that I *should* do. She too seemed greatly confused—a thing for which I had been in no way prepared; yet it was my embarrassment which eventually rose superior to the occasion.

"Pray sit down," I said in mechanical fashion as, placing a chair for her near the table, I withdrew to the sofa. She seated herself obediently, and gazed at me in evident expectation that I should continue. I strove to keep myself in hand, but must confess that this artless attention on her part nearly drove me mad, for I conceived that she must be merely *pretending* to have noticed nothing, merely *pretending* to be looking upon everything as the normal state of things; whereas all the time she——! Inwardly I swore that I would make her pay for this.

"You have surprised me under odd circumstances, Lisa," I began, though somehow conscious that that was just what I ought *not* to have said. "No, no," I went on (for I saw her face suddenly colour), "I am not speaking of my *furniture*. I am not in the least ashamed of my poverty, but, on the contrary, am proud of it. I may be poor, but at least I am honourable. One *may* be poor and honourable, you know" (here I stammered a little). "By the way, will you have some tea?"

"No, thank you," she began, "but——"

"Wait a moment," I interrupted. Rising swiftly, I ran to Apollon's room, where, in default of any other resort, I was only too thankful to take refuge.

"Apollon," I stuttered, with feverish eagerness, as I threw him the seven roubles which I had been holding in my hand the while, "here are your wages—do you see? Yes, I will give them you *now*, but, in return, I beg of you to run to a shop, and get me some tea and a dozen lumps of sugar. If you refuse to do this, you will render me a dishonoured man, for you do not know who this lady is. Yes, that will be all. Er—perhaps you are thinking things about her? That is only because you do not know who she is."

Apollon, who had now resumed his work and

spectacles, squinted at the money without even laying aside his needle. Then, according me neither word nor glance, he continued to wrestle with his thread, which somehow seemed to be finding it difficult to pass through the eye of the needle. For fully three minutes, with my hands crossed *à la* Napoleon, I stood waiting. My temples were damp with sweat, and I could feel that I was turning pale all over. But at last, thank God, he had some compassion upon me. Relinquishing his thread, he slowly rose, pushed his chair back in the same manner, took off his spectacles with equal deliberation, counted his money at a similar pace, and, after asking me over his shoulder how much tea he was to purchase, departed as lethargically as he had executed his previous movements. On the way to rejoin Lisa I could not help debating whether my best plan were not to flee away, no matter whither, in my dressing-gown, just as I was.

In the end I reseated myself. As I did so she looked at me anxiously, and for a few moments silence reigned.

"I will *kill* him!" suddenly I exclaimed as I struck the table with my fist—struck it so violently that the ink fairly spurted out of the inkstand.

"What do you mean?" she asked, trembling all over.

"I will *kill* him, I will *kill* him!" I repeated, barking out the words like a dog and (keenly though I felt the absurdity of my behaviour) continuing to thump the table with my fist.

"Oh, Lisa, you cannot think what a torment the man is!" I went on. "You must know that he is my rascal of a servant. Just now he has gone out to get some tea and sugar. Oh, Lisa!"—and I burst into tears.

Here was a situation! How ashamed I felt of my weakness! Yet, do what I would, I could not master myself.

Lisa was terrified.

"What *is* the matter?" she exclaimed, as she came fluttering towards me.

"Some water! Give me some water!" I stuttered in a strangled voice (though, as a matter of fact, I knew that I had no real use for water, any more than there was any real reason for my stuttering). "The water is over there." *Per se* the situation was real enough, but at the same time it may be said that at that moment I was only playing a comedy, to keep up appearances.

In great agitation she fetched what I had asked for, and presently Apollon entered with the tea. It seemed to me that anything so *bizarre* and prosaic as tea was a terribly unsuitable commodity after all that had just happened. So I turned a little red in the face. Lisa looked at Apollon with a timid air, but he went out without giving us even a glance.

"How you must despise me, Lisa!" I said as I stared at her with an almost agonised anxiety to know what she was thinking. However, she was too confused to reply. Angry with myself though I was, I laid the bulk of the blame upon *her*. A horrible sort of resentment against her was rising in my heart, and I felt that I could even have killed her. To revenge myself I registered an inward vow that never again on this earth would I address to her a single word.

"*She* is the cause of everything," I reflected.

The silence continued for something like five minutes, while the tea remained untouched upon the table. Such was my perversity that I purposely refrained from drinking any, that I might make her feel the more uncomfortable (since it would not have been proper for her to take the initiative). But from time to time she kept throwing covert glances at me, with astonishment and distress in her looks. I remained obstinately silent. It was *I* now that was undergoing martyrdom, for, although I recognised the abominable baseness of my folly and rancour, I could not, for the world, help myself.

"I—I wish to leave that place for good," she began—probably her object having been, by some means, no matter what, to break the intolerable silence. Poor woman! She had begun, as I had, precisely as she ought *not* to have begun. To think of mentioning *that,* at such a moment, and to such a man! For a few seconds my heart contracted with pity for her clumsiness and futile frankness; but to this feeling there succeeded, almost instantly, a renewed access of spleen. Indeed, the slight instinct towards compassion which I had experienced only served to redouble my fury. "Let everything go to the devil!" I said to myself; and again there followed a five minutes of silence.

Presently she rose; saying in a tone which was scarcely articulate—

"Am I in any way inconveniencing you?"

In her tone there were both weariness and offended dignity; whereat my anger burst all bounds, and I too rose—trembling and well-nigh suffocated with rage.

"Why did you come here?" I shouted. "Tell me, if you please!"

The logical order of my words I did not heed, for I felt as though I must say *all* that I had to say at once, in a volley, and without caring in the least at what point I began.

"Why did you come here?" I repeated. "Tell me, tell me! Ah, *I* will tell you, my good woman—*I* will tell you why you came here. You came here because, the other night, I said to you a few words of compassion which touched your heart, and made you long for more. Let me inform you, then, that I was only making fun of you that night, and that I am making fun of you *now*. Yes, I have only been amusing myself a little. At dinner I had been insulted by some friends of mine, and had gone to your house to challenge one of them, an officer, whom I thought to find at your house before me. But I happened just to miss him, and felt that I must revenge myself upon some one, and get my own back. *You* chanced to be at hand, and so I vented all my rage and venom upon *you*. I had been humiliated, so I humiliated *you*. I had been rinsed out like a rag, so I exerted my strength upon *you*. There you have the whole truth of the matter. Yet you—you actually thought that I had gone there to save you! Is it not so? Is not that what you are thinking?"

I guessed that, though some of the details of my harangue might escape her, she would nevertheless catch the main gist of it. Nor was I wrong. She turned as white as a sheet, and tried to speak, as, with lips twisting painfully, she fell backwards across her chair like a woman who has been felled with a hatchet. All the while that I continued declaiming she listened to me with her mouth open, her eyes distended, and her whole form trembling with horror. The utter cynicism of my words seemed simply to stupefy her senses.

"To save you, indeed!" I went on as I leapt from my chair and began pacing the room. "*Why* should I save you, seeing that, for all I know, I am even worse than yourself? Why did you not give me a slap in the face while I was doing all that moralising, and say, 'Why have you come here, then? To read me a lesson?' . . . No, power, power over some one, is what I want. I wanted to play the game of forcing your tears, your humiliation, your hysterics. *That* was my object the other night. Yet I felt loathsome even to myself, for I knew that I was both a villain and a coward, and God knows why I gave *you*—yes, gave *you*, you wretched woman—my address. As soon as I reached home I fell to cursing you, for all I was worth, because I *had* given you the address. I hated you because I had lied to you; I hated you also because I had only juggled with words, and dreamed dreams, while all the while I wanted—well, what do you think?— to see you go hang! What I wish for is rest and quietness, and, to gain it, I would sell the whole world for a song. Indeed, if I were given the choice between the world coming to an end and my retaining my liberty to drink tea, I tell you that the universe might go to the devil so long only as I could go on drinking tea. Did you guess this the other night, or did you not? Of course I know that I am a brute, a villain, an egotist, a poltroon—so much so that for three whole days I have been trembling with fear lest you should come. And do you know what most disquieted me during those three days? It was the thought that I had seemed to you a hero, whereas at any moment you might come here and surprise me, looking dirty and out-at-elbows, in this old, torn dressing-gown! A little while ago I said that I am not ashamed of my poverty; yet I tell you that I *am* ashamed of it— more ashamed, more afraid, of it than of anything else in the world, even of being accounted a thief, since I am so full of vanity that every moment I feel as though my skin were being stripped from me, and I were being exposed to the outer air. Surely, too, you have divined that I shall never be able to pardon you for having surprised me in this dressing-gown at a moment when, like a savage dog, I was flinging myself upon Apollon? To think that the saviour, the former hero, should be brawling with his servant like a scabby vagabond, and so give you the laugh over him! Nor shall I ever be able to pardon you for the tears which, like an old woman who has been put out of countenance, I was shedding just now in your presence, despite my best efforts to restrain them. Nor shall I ever be able to pardon you the reason why I am confessing this to you. For it is you, and you alone, who must answer for it all, since it is you who have chanced to cross my path—the path of the foulest, the most blackguardly, the most ridiculous, the most trivial, the most obtuse, the most ill-grained worm upon earth. Other worms may be no better than I am, yet at least, for some

God-only-known reason, they seem never to look foolish as I do, who all my life shall have to be slapped on the cheek by lice, since that is my *métier*. But what does it matter to me whether you understand this or not? And what does it matter to me whether you meet your ruin in that house or not? And cannot you understand that, having told you all this, I shall for ever hate you for having heard it? Man but once in his life makes such confessions as mine, and then only when he is in a fit of hysteria. And, after it all, how is it that you are still here to flout and torture me, instead of taking your departure?"

At this point a strange thing happened.

I have such an inveterate habit of thinking and meditating in purely bookish fashion—of regarding persons as I may have previously pictured them in fancy, that at first I did not grasp the inwardness of this strange occurrence. Yet the poor outraged, insulted Lisa had gauged the position of affairs with far greater accuracy than I had done. In spite of all that had passed, she had divined what at once becomes clear to every woman who truly loves a man. She had divined that the wretch who had spoken to her in such terms was himself desperately unhappy.

Instantly the look of fear and resentment in her face gave place to a sort of mournful sympathy; and when I called myself a scoundrel and a blackguard, as also when my tears began to flow (for I wept a good deal during the course of my harangue), I saw her features contract as she rose and tried to interrupt me. Even when I had finished she did not seem frightened at my violence, nor appear to hear my reproaches to her for lingering; on the contrary her face expressed nothing but the fact that she was aware how greatly I must be suffering to make me speak thus. Besides, the poor woman was feeling so crushed and cowed, and thought herself so immeasurably inferior to me, that it never occurred to her to grow angry or to take offence. With a sort of impulse at once shy and irresistible she advanced towards me. Then, not daring to approach any nearer, she held out to me her arms. For a moment my heart contracted, and as she saw my face change she threw herself upon me, clasped me round the neck, and burst into tears. I too could no longer restrain myself, and fell to sobbing as never in my life had I sobbed before.

"I cannot be—I have not a chance to be—a good man," I murmured brokenly as, sinking upon the sofa, I sobbed for a quarter of an hour in a perfectly hysterical way. She clasped me to herself, and, folding me in her arms, seemed to forget the whole world as she did so.

But in time (and therein lay the mockery of it all) the fit passed (I wish but to reveal the sordid truth, and nothing else) as, with my form prone upon the sofa, and my face buried in its shabby leather cushions, I began, little by little, yet involuntarily and irresistibly, to feel that it would be an effort to raise my head and look Lisa in the eyes. Of what, then, was I ashamed? I do not know. I only know that I *was* ashamed. Also, my clouded brain had taken unto itself an idea that our respective rôles had now changed; that she was now the heroine, and I the wounded, humiliated creature whom, four nights ago, *she* had appeared to be. All this passed through my mind as I lay there on the sofa.

My God! Is it possible that I *really* hated Lisa? I do not know. Even to this day I have no clear idea of how things were. I only know that never at any time in my life have I found it possible to live without playing the tyrant over some one, and—— But reasoning is a useless pursuit; so why reason?

After a while I so far got the better of myself as to venture to raise my head. Yet I wonder whether it was precisely because I felt ashamed to look Lisa in the face that there suddenly revived in me a sense of domination, of possession. All unexpectedly my eyes began to blaze with passion as I clasped her hands in mine.

Yet how (so it seemed to me) I hated her! And how strangely that very hatred drew me to her arms! The one feeling spurred the other, until both of them came to resemble a desire for revenge. At first she appeared overcome with surprise—a surprise which amounted almost to terror; but that lasted only for a moment. Almost before I was aware of it she had strained me to herself in a passionate embrace.

X

A QUARTER of an hour later I was pacing the room with feverish strides. At intervals I would approach the screen, and, through a crack in it, take a peep at Lisa. Seated on the floor, with her head against the bed, she seemed to be weeping. Yet she had not gone away, and that irritated me. By this time she knew all. She knew that I had outraged her to the core, and that (how am I to express it?) my short-lived passion had sprung only from a desire for vengeance, from a yearning to subject her to a new indignity; that to my formless enmity there had succeeded a *personal* hatred which was founded upon jealousy. However, I do not say that all this was manifest to her. I only know that henceforth she was bound to look upon me as a man utterly vile and, above all things, incapable of loving her.

Yes, I am aware that I shall be told that to have acted with such blackguardism and cruelty was an impossibility. Perhaps you will even add that not to have loved such a woman as Lisa—at all events, not to have appreciated her love—was also an impossibility. But wherein does the impossibility lie? In the first place, I could not love her, for the reason that, to me, love always connotes tyrannisation and moral ascendancy. Any other love has never come within my purview, and I have even gone so far as to arrive at the firm conclusion that, properly speaking, love lies in the peculiar right of tyrannisation which the fact of being loved confers. Even in my most secret soul I have never been able to think of love as aught but a struggle which begins with hatred and ends with moral subjection. And, in the second place, I did not know what to do with the woman after I had subjected her. Again, therefore, I ask—wherein does the impossibility lie? Was I not depraved beyond belief? Had I not so fallen out of touch with everyday life as to think of taunting Lisa with having come to hear "further words of compassion" when all the time she had come to me for *love* (for it is in love alone that woman can find salvation and refuge from shipwreck; it is in love, and love alone, that she can attain regeneration)? So once again I ask—was it hatred, and *nothing but* hatred, that I felt for Lisa during the time that I was pacing the room, and stopping, at intervals, to peep at her through the screen? I do not think so. Rather it was that I could not bear to feel that she was there, for I wanted her to go, and was longing for peace and solitude. I had lost the sociable habit, and she disturbed me to such an extent that she hindered my very breathing.

A few moments passed, but still she did not stir from her profound stupor. At last I was callous enough to tap the screen, to recall her to herself; whereupon she gave a violent start, rose in haste, and resumed her hat, shawl and furs, as though her one desire were to get away from me, no matter whither. Two minutes later she issued slowly from behind the screen, and stood looking at me with sombre gaze. In return I smiled a smile which I forced for the occasion. Yet the moment that her eyes met mine I found myself forced to avert my gaze.

"Good-bye," she said as she moved towards the door.

I ran to her, took and opened her hand, put something into it, and closed the fingers again. Next, turning my back upon her, I retired precipitately into a corner, where at least I could not see her. . . .

I was going to have lied to you, my readers—to have pretended to you that it was without thinking, and purely through absence of mind and stupidity, that I put that something into her hand. Yet I will not lie. No; I will tell you frankly that it was out of sheer malice that I opened her hand and put the money into it. The idea had occurred to me while I was pacing up and down the room and Lisa was seated on the floor behind the screen. At the same time I can honestly say that the factor which caused me to perpetrate that gratuitous insult was malice of the brain rather than depravity of the heart. True, the act *was* an insult, but only a calculated, bookish, unreal one; and the moment that it had been perpetrated I retired, as I have said, into a corner—thence almost as instantly to dart back again in a storm of shame and despair. But Lisa had gone. I opened the door, and shouted down the staircase (nervously, and in an undertone): "Lisa, Lisa!"

No answer came, though I thought I could hear her footsteps on the bottom flight of stairs.

"Lisa!" I cried once more—this time a little louder.

Still no answer came, except that the glass entrance-door of the building opened with a creak, and then shut to with a bang. The sound reached me even where I stood at the head of the staircase.

She had gone!

I returned thoughtfully to my room. My heart was heavy within me, and for a moment or two I remained standing before the table at which Lisa, on her arrival, had seated herself. I gazed with unseeing eyes. But suddenly I started. Lying right

L

in front of me I had just discerned the crumpled bank-note for five roubles which I had a moment or two ago put into her hand! It was the same note, and no other, for it had been the only one that I had possessed. She had taken advantage of the moment when my back was turned to throw it upon the table!

Well, I might have foreseen that. Yet *could* I have foreseen it? No; I was too much of an egotist to have done that; I had too great a contempt for the world to have thought *her*, of all persons, capable of such an act.

The sight was unendurable to me. With all speed I dressed myself (taking for the purpose the first garments which came to hand) and darted off in pursuit. As yet she could not have covered more than two hundred paces.

The air was so still that snow was falling almost perpendicularly, and forming a thick coverlet upon the pavements of the deserted streets. Not a sound was there to be heard, nor a soul to be seen. The street lamps seemed to be burning with a curious sort of dimness. Running a couple of hundred paces to the nearest corner, I stopped.

Where could she have got to? And why was I running after her at all?

Ah, why indeed? To go upon my knees to her, to weep out tears of repentance, to kiss her feet, to ask of her pardon? Yes, all these things I, at that instant, longed to do. My breast seemed to be bursting with a longing to do them. Never to the end of my days shall I be able to remember that moment without a spasm of emotion.

"Yet what good would it do us?" I went on. "Should I not, to-morrow, be hating her for the very reason that to-night I had kissed her feet? And should I ever be able to make her happy? Have I not to-night proved to myself—for about the hundredth time—what I am worth? Should I not be a constant torture to her?"

For a long while I remained standing in the snow —standing in the dark, shadowy street—plunged in meditation.

"Surely things are best as they are?" I continued as I regained my room and set myself to drown with fancies the terrible aching of my heart. "Surely it is best that to the end she should carry the remembrance of her humbling? Of her humbling? May it not, rather, prove a cleansing—a painful, yet an intimate, reminder to her of her human dignity? To-morrow I should only have soiled her soul and wounded her heart; whereas the insult will *never* fade from her recollection. Yes, despite the filth and the horrors of the end which is awaiting her, the offence will never cease to raise and purify her —through hatred of the offender. Hm! And through pardon too? . . . *Will* she be happier so?"

In philosophic style I next proceeded to put to myself the following question—to be studied at leisure : Which of the two is better—moderate happiness or splendid suffering? . . . Which of them *is* the better?

To the solution of that problem I devoted the remainder of that agonising night. I felt half-dead for the pain in my heart. Never before nor since have I suffered, have I repented, as I did then.

Yet I still believe that, at the very moment when I left my rooms to go in pursuit of her, I was aware that I should return after going two hundred paces !

Never since that night have I seen her, nor have I heard of her.

To this I may add that, though for a time I derived considerable pleasure from my formula concerning the respective uses of insult and hatred, the agitation which I had suffered brought me near to being seriously ill.

Even now, after all these years, I find these bitter memories to recall; and though I can recollect many another bitter memory, had I not better, at this point, bring these "Letters" to an end? For it

seems to me that I have made a mistake in writing
them at all.   At all events I know that, from start
to finish, I have felt ashamed while writing the story
which I have just related.   Truly its inditing has
been, for me, not so much literature as a well-merited
punishment!   Nor can it interest any one that I
should spin long tales as to how I have wasted my
life in moral corruption—wasted it in solitude and
poverty and detachment from reality—wasted it in
vain-glorious searchings of heart in the underworld.
A romance requires a hero, and in me fate seems
to have combined only the materials for a *non*-hero.
Consequently the whole thing is bound to produce
an unpleasant impression, since all of us stand
divorced from reality—all of us halt in greater or
less degree.   So unfamiliar with life have we become
that at times we feel for reality a positive loathing,
and cannot bear to have it brought to our notice.
Indeed, so far have we advanced as to look upon
real life almost as a burden, a term of servitude,
and to agree that the better course is to live strictly
in the bookish manner.   But why do we also, at
times, grow restless, captious and querulous?   Even
you do not know the reason.   Yet if our querulous
petitions were to be granted we should find ourselves
in a far worse plight.   For suppose we were given
complete independence, and freedom to bestow our
love where we willed, and a wider sphere of activity,
and increased exemption from tutelage.   Why, I
assure you that we should very soon be asking to
be taken in hand again!   I know that you will be
angry with me for saying this, and raise an uproar,
and stamp your feet.   "Speak for yourself and your
own miseries in the underworld," you will cry; "but
do not dare to use the expression ' *all* of us.' "
Well, gentlemen, heaven forbid that I should justify
myself by seeking to include all my fellowmen with
myself; yet, so far as I am concerned, I have but
carried to a finish, in my life, what you have never
even dared to carry half-way, although you have

constantly mistaken your cowardice for prudence, you have constantly cheated yourself with comforting reflections. The truth is that I have been more *alive* than you. That is all. But look a little closer. We do not even know where present-day reality is to be found, nor what it is called. Whenever we are left to our own devices, and deprived of our bookish rules, we at once grow confused, and lose our way —we know not what to do, nor what to observe, nor what to love, nor what to hate, nor what to respect, nor what to despise. We grow weary of being human beings at all—of possessing real, individual flesh and blood. We are *ashamed* of being human —we account it beneath our dignity. Rather, we aim at becoming personalities of a general, a fictitious type. Yes, all of us are still-born creatures, not children sprung of living fathers; and that fact is coming more and more to please us. Soon we shall have invented a way of being born of nothing but ideas! But enough of this: I intend to bring these "Letters from the Underworld" to a close.

*   *   *   *   *

It may be added that the "Letters" of this dealer in paradoxes did *not* end here, since the writer could not forbear continuing them; but I who have been responsible for their transcription choose no longer to perform the task.

THE GENTLE MAIDEN

PREFACE BY THE AUTHOR

To begin with, let me beg pardon of my readers that this time it is not the usual "Diary" which I am giving them, but a story. Yet that story has taken me the greater portion of a month to write, and therefore I must once more ask my readers' indulgence.

Next, for the story itself. Although I have called it a "fantastic" story, I regard it as one in the highest degree realistic. True, its *form* is "fantastic," and of that I will furnish a preliminary explanation.

The story is not a story at all, nor yet a series of note-takings. Imagine a man by whose side, on a table, there lies the dead body of his wife. Though some hours have elapsed since she hurled herself from a window, the man is still so distracted with the shock that he cannot collect his thoughts. He passes from room to room of the house, and endeavours vainly to realise what has happened, and to rally his faculties. He is an inveterate hypochondriac—the kind of man who is for ever talking to himself; and this he is now doing, as he recounts the history of the affair, and tries to devise some explanation for it. As for consecutiveness of speech, he only contradicts himself, both in logic and sentiment. The one moment he is trying to justify himself, and to lay the blame on her, and the next moment he is launching out into a string of extraneous reasonings. Grief and profound agitation have possession of him. Yet by degrees he begins to understand better, and to focus his thoughts. The flood of recollections irresistibly aroused in him at last leads to the truth: and that truth ends by uplifting him in soul and in spirit. Indeed, towards the close of the story the whole tone of his soliloquy differs from its disorderly beginning, for there has dawned upon the unfortunate man the reality of things—or what he conceives to be such.

That is the theme of my tale. Of course, its action takes several hours to pass, while the tale itself is interrupted by many breaks and hiatuses, and is confused in form. Throughout, the man soliloquises to himself, with only occasional references to some unseen auditor—to some unseen judge, as it were. Always, in the realm of actuality, it is so. Had I been able to *stenograph* the words of the speaker, they might have issued even more rough and unwrought than I have conceived them : yet, for me, their psychological order would still have remained the same. In this sketch I have tried to imagine myself such a stenographer : and it is to that factor in the work that I have applied the term "fantastic." The same thing has been done before in Art. For example, Victor Hugo employs a similar method in his *chef d'œuvre,* "The Last Day of the Condemned Criminal." True, without producing an actual stenographic record, he has introduced into his masterpiece an element of unreality, through supposing that a condemned man could, or would have the time to, continue his jottings up to the very last day—up to the very last hour, the very last minute —of his life : yet, had not Victor Hugo permitted himself this licence, there would never have resulted what constitutes at once the most realistic and the most true of all his writings.

PART I

THE GENTLE MAIDEN

CHAPTER I

WHO WE WERE

So there she lies—beautiful, as always! From time to time I approach and gaze upon her face. To-morrow she will be taken away, and I shall be left alone. To-day she lies on two card-tables placed together in the *salon*, but to-morrow there await her the tomb and the white, white shroud. How it has happened I cannot tell. I try, again and again, to explain it to myself. Ever since six o'clock I have been trying to explain it, yet cannot bring my thoughts to a focus. Perhaps it is through trying so much that I fail. Perhaps it were better that I should once more recount these events in their proper order. Their proper order, indeed! O my God, I am no lettered man, as any one may see; yet, if I were to state these things as I understand them—— Yet *lest* I should understand them is what I fear.

However, if you would know (to begin from the beginning), she came to me that first day quite simply. She came to me to pledge some treasures of hers, to help her to pay for an advertisement in the *Golos* [1]—an advertisement to say that she was a governess who would give lessons at home or abroad. That was how it all started. Of course, at first I could see no difference between her and

---

[1] *The Voice of the People*—a Russian newspaper.

any one else—she came to me just as the rest
did; but in time I began to notice her. In those
days she was tall, flaxen-haired, and slender, and
always puckered her face at me as though shy
(though I believe she treated all strangers the same).
As for me, I treated her as I did every one else—not
as a pledger, but as a human being. As soon as
she had received her money, she always turned on
her heel, and took her departure. Never a word
did she utter. Others would begin disputing with
me, or beg and entreat me to give them more, but
she never found fault with what was given her.
Yet I always felt a little taken aback when she
called. To begin with, I was so astonished at the
things which she brought—things such as a pair of
silver-gilt earrings and a trashy medallion—the two
being worth, together, about twenty kopecks. She
herself, I believe, knew them to be worth but
ten kopecks apiece; but, for all that, I could see
from her face that they were very dear to her. Later
I learnt that they were sole treasures bequeathed
to her by her father and mother. Once, and once
only, did I permit myself to make fun of an article
of hers (you must remember that, as a rule, I never
forget myself—that my attitude towards the public
is always that of a gentleman. Few words, civility,
and strictness in business are my motto; above all,
strictness, strictness, and again strictness). However, it happened one day that she went so far as
to bring me the remnants—yes, literally the remnants—of an old hareskin rug. Well, I could not
contain myself, and made some sharp remark or
another. Heavens, but you should have seen how she
flared up! Her eyes were large, blue, thoughtful
ones: yet at that moment how they blazed! Never
a word did she speak, though—she just picked up
her fragments of hareskin, and departed. That was
when I first noticed her *specially*, or thought anything special about her—that is to say, anything out
of the common. Yes, still I remember that first

impression which she made upon me—the impression which struck me most. It was that she was very young—as young as, say, fourteen. As a matter of fact, she was three months short of sixteen. However, I said nothing, for I scarcely felt interested in her then. The next day she came to me again. Afterwards I learnt that she had taken her hareskin both to Dobronrov's and to Moser's, but that, as they are dealers only in silver and gold, they had had nothing to say to her. Well, once I myself took some pebbles of hers in pawn (such rubbish they were, too!). As I looked at them I was, as usual, astounded: yet, though *I* deal only in silver and gold, I accepted those pebbles of hers. That was the *second* time when I thought anything about her.

The third time she came to me (from Moser's) with an amber cigarette-holder—a pretty little thing enough, yet one of no use to those of us who deal only in gold. It was just after our encounter over the hareskin, so I received her coldly (though, with me, coldness always takes the form of civility). Yet, at the moment when I handed her a couple of roubles I could not refrain from saying with some irritation, "I am doing this *for you* only. Moser would never have accepted such a pledge from *any* one." I laid a peculiar emphasis upon the words "for you," and imparted to them a peculiar meaning, for I felt out of humour. On hearing these words she flared up as before. Yet she did not throw me my money back; she just took the coins and departed. So much for poverty! Yet what a passion she was in! I could see that I had wounded her. After she had gone I suddenly found myself asking myself, "Was the triumph worth two roubles? Ha, ha, ha!" Yes, I remember twice asking myself the question, "Was it worth it? Was it worth it?" and laughingly returning myself an answer in the affirmative, for I had now recovered my temper. There was no ill-feeling about me; I

had acted quite advisedly, and with fixed intention.
I had desired to prove her, for thoughts about her
would come straying through my brain. That
was the *third* time when I thought anything about
her.

So it all began. I tried to view the situation
from every aspect, and awaited her next visit with
impatience. Somehow I foresaw that it would not
be long before she came. When she did so I entered
into conversation with her with a feeling of intimacy
which surprised me. You see, I had not been badly
educated, and knew my manners. Hm!—Well,
already I had perceived that she was kind and good;
and kind, good people do not long remain at a
distance from one another. They may not express
their feelings openly, but they cannot help exchanging a word or two. They may answer briefly, but
they *do* answer, and the more so as time goes on.
One does not grow weary of talking if one feels
that one *must* talk. Of course, on that occasion she
told me nothing. It was only later that I learnt all
about the *Golos;* and so on. It seems that, as a
last resource, she had inserted into the paper an
advertisement which began grandly : "A young lady,
a governess, is willing to travel. Terms furnished on
application." Subsequently the advertisement came
to read : "A young lady will accept any situation,
whether as governess, companion, sick nurse, or
sempstress." To this further additions were made
until at length, despair coming upon her, the wording
concluded : "No salary required; only board and
lodging are expected." Yet she had not obtained
a situation. On the occasion of which I am speaking
I decided to try her for the last time. Accordingly,
taking up a copy of that day's *Golos*, I showed her
a notice in which it was said that "a young lady,
an orphan, seeks post as governess to young children,
preferably in a widower's household. Would assist
in housework."

"There, you see," I remarked. "This morning

a young lady is advertising, and by the evening she will probably have obtained a post. That is how *you* should go to work."

Again she fired up—again her eyes gleamed as she turned and walked straight out of the office. I was greatly pleased. I felt sure of everything now, and had no fear. No one else would take her cigarette-holders in pledge. Besides, she had no more cigarette-holders to pledge. Sure enough, she came back in three days—such a pale, agitated little damsel! I could see that something had happened at home, and happened in real earnest. What that something was I will state later, but at the moment I can only recall that suddenly I felt superior to and older than her. Also, I had suddenly conceived a plan. This time, you see, she had brought with her a little ikon—— Ah, but wait a minute, wait a minute. That was how it began, I know, yet I feel all confused. I try to remember everything—every little detail, every little feature, in her. · I try to bring my thoughts to a point. Yet I cannot, I cannot, and all those details and details have to be remembered——

What was it? Oh, an ikon of the Holy Mother. Now, an ikon of the Holy Mother and Child—an old family, domestic one like that one up there, with its silver-gilt vestment—is worth about six roubles. Yet I could see that the image was dear to her, and that she was pawning it *all*—that is to say, without first removing the vestment; so I said to her: "Would it not be better for me to take only the vestment, and to leave you the figure? Then you would still have your ikon."

"Then do you *mind* taking it all?"

"No; but perhaps *you* will mind?"

"No. Take the figure as well."

"I tell you what," said I reflectively. "Instead of taking the ikon in pledge, I will put it here in this case, with the other ikons, and place it under the lamp" (you must know that, on opening my shop,

I always first lighted the lamp [1]). "You can have ten roubles on it, if you wish."

"But I do not *want* ten roubles. Give me five, for I certainly mean to redeem it."

"What? You do not want ten roubles?—Why, the thing is fully worth it, I assure you," I added, noting that her eyes were flashing again. She made no reply, so I handed her five roubles.

"I do not despise any one for being hard up," I went on. "I have been like that myself, and even more than you. And though it is true that you see me engaged in this business—well, I have suffered——"

"Then you are revenging yourself on society, are you?" interrupted the girl with a smile which, though bitter, was quite innocent. That is to say, it was a general smile, for it was clear that she had paid me no special attention as yet, and did not care what she said to me.

"Aha!" I thought to myself. "So *that* is the kind of woman you are! Your character is developing in a new phase. Well," I added aloud, half-jestingly, but in some confusion, "I am one of those who wish to do evil only that good may come."

Instantly she fixed upon me a gaze which, though charged with curiosity, was also like that of a child.

"Stop!" she cried. "What do you mean by that? Where did you get those words from? I have heard them before somewhere."

"Do not trouble yourself. Mephistopheles used thus to commend himself to Faust. Have you read ' Faust'?"

"No—not very carefully."

"That is to say, you have not read it at all. Well, you ought to. I can see a scornful smile on your lips. You must not suppose that I am so lacking in taste as to be seeking to conceal my calling as a pawnbroker behind a recommendation of myself as

[1] The lamp which, in Russian dwellings, is always kept burning before the ikon or sacred image.

Mephistopheles. A pawnbroker will be a pawnbroker always. We all know that."

"What a strange man you are! I never supposed anything of the kind."

What she had meant to say was, of course, "I had never supposed you to be a man of education." Yes, I could read her thoughts. Clearly I had pleased her greatly.

"You see," I said, "one may do good in *any* field. Of course I am not speaking of myself; let us suppose that *I* never do aught but evil: yet——"

"Of a certainty one may do good *anywhere*," she said, with a swift and penetrating look. "Yes, *everywhere!*" she added abruptly. How well I remember each moment of that interview—how well *I* remember it all! How well, too, I remember that whenever this girl, this poor girl, tried to say something especially wise and discerning she always made it clear, by her unchangeably naïve and sincere face, that she was thinking to herself: "Is it not clever for a girl like myself to be saying such wise and wonderful things?"—and that, not out of boastfulness, like many people, but because clearly she put a great value upon her words, and believed in and respected them, and thought that every one else ought to do the same. O sincerity! To what can it not persuade one? And what an especially charming thing in her it seemed!

Ah yes, I remember everything; I have forgotten nothing. When that day she left me my mind was fully made up. That very day I made inquiries, until I had discovered every secret of her life. Certain details of the past I had already learnt from Lukeria, who acted as serving-woman at the house where she was living, and whom I had bribed some days ago. Those details were so dreadful that I cannot conceive how I could ever have remained as cheerful as this young girl was as she puzzled over those words of Mephistopheles—though herself in such a predicament. Well, she had youth on her side. In those

M

days I thought of her with joy and pride, since there was so much nobility in her. Even on the verge of the abyss Goethe's great words shed light around her. Youth is noble, no matter how small the measure, or how distorted the fashion. That was how I thought of her, and of her alone. Above all things, I regarded her as *mine*, and had no doubt now of my power. It is a most voluptuous feeling to have no further doubt of that!

Yet what am I saying? If I continue wandering on like this, how am I ever to steady my thoughts? I must hurry on and hurry on. I have nothing to do with that *now*, God knows!

CHAPTER II

THE MARRIAGE PROPOSAL

Such details as I learnt about her may be told in a few words. Her father and mother had been dead three years, leaving her to the care of two not over-respectable aunts. Perhaps it would be wrong to call them absolutely disreputable, since one of them was a widow with six children, and the other one was a nasty old maid. Both of them were dirty. Her father had been a civil service clerk—a gentleman merely by position. Everything, therefore, was in my favour. I came of a higher sphere than she did, for I was a retired staff-captain who had served in a good regiment, was a gentleman by birth, and was possessed of independent means. Hence, despite my loan office, the aunts could not well look upon me with anything but deference. Throughout those three years the girl had been the slave of her aunts, yet none the less had contrived to study for, and to pass, an examination, in spite of the pressure of unpaid daily labour. Clearly this showed a desire on her part to attain to higher and better things. Why, however, did I wish to marry her? I ought to have been spat upon for doing so. But that is to come later. At present she was forced to teach her aunt's children, to mend the clothes, and (to her very especial sorrow) to wash the floors. Also, to speak plainly, she was often beaten and corrected with the tongs. Finally the aunts decided to sell her. Phew! I will pass over the revolting details of it. Later on she told me them one by one. All this, for the space of a year, a fat shopman next door observed. Yet he was not a mere stallkeeper, for he possessed a couple of grocer's emporia. He had buried two wives, and was seeking a third, when his eye lit upon *her*. "This gentle girl has been brought up in poverty," he said to himself; "so I will marry her, as a mother for my orphaned children."

So he began to court her, and to bargain with the aunts—he, a man of fifty! She was horrified, and it was then that she first began to come to me for money, to pay for the advertisements in the *Golos*. Finally she had to beg of her aunts to allow her a moment in which to think the matter over. That moment they conceded her, but only one—not a second one; saying, in their abusive way, "We hardly know how to fill our own mouths, let alone a mouth too many." I had learnt of the affair, and that very morning, after breakfast, made up my mind. The same evening the shopkeeper paid her a visit; bringing with him a pound of bonbons (priced at half a rouble) from the shop. He was sitting beside her when I summoned Lukeria from the kitchen, and told her to go and tell the girl, in a whisper, that I was waiting outside with an urgent message I was feeling much pleased with myself. Indeed, I had been in a good humour all day.

At the gate, and in Lukeria's presence, I explained to the girl—agitated as she was at my having sent for her—that I had a care for her honour and her happiness, and that she must not be surprised at my manner, nor yet at the fact that I had stayed outside, seeing that I was "a straightforward man

who had studied all the circumstances of the affair."
Nor did I lie in calling myself a straightforward
man. Fool that I was, though, I ought not only
to have spoken *politely*—*i. e.* to have shown myself
to be a man of refinement—but also to have displayed some *originality*. Yet what harm is there in
that? I wish but to judge myself, and am so
judging. I am bound to state all the pros and
cons, and am stating them. Afterwards I remembered the occasion with complacency—though that
too was a foolish thing to do. I told her straight
out, and without any confusion, that I was not
especially clever, nor yet especially learned, nor yet
(perhaps) especially good; that I was but a cheap
sort of egoist (I remember the expression well, as
the idea of it had come to me *en passant*, and I was
much pleased with it); and that possibly I comprised
within myself a very, very great deal of what was
unpleasant in other respects. All this was said with
a peculiar sort of pride—every one knows how one
says such things. Of course I was artful enough
not to enlarge upon my good qualities after I had
set forth my bad. I was artful enough to refrain
from saying, "My dear young lady, on the other
hand I am so-and-so and so-and-so." I could see
that she was very nervous of me, but I put a gloss
upon nothing, and even increased my vehemence as
I perceived her trepidation. I said plainly that she
would find it dull living with me, and that for her
there would be no fine dresses, theatres or balls
until I had attained my ends. This stern way of
speaking had an attraction for me. I added (though
I touched lightly upon the point) that my reason for
adopting a calling like pawnbroking was that in
front of me I had one particular end, one particular
motive. Indeed, I had a right to say that, since
true enough, I had an end and a motive in view.
You see, I hated my loan office so much that at first
I used to comfort myself, half in jest and half in
earnest, with sundry phrases about "getting the

better of society," and so on. Consequently her sharp remark to me, the other morning, about "revenge" was not quite correct. That is to say, if I had said to her straight out, "I am revenging myself on society," she would just have laughed in girlish fashion, and the affair would have passed as a joke; whereas it seemed possible, if one let drop but a hint, a mere mysterious phrase, at once to excite the imagination. However, I had no fear now. I knew that the fat shopman was even more distasteful to her than I was myself, and that, as I stood there at the gate, I was figuring as her deliverer. Yes, I understood that well. Ah, how thoroughly a man understands baseness! But was it baseness? How is one to judge a man? Was I not, even in those days, in love with her?

Yet stay! Of course I said not a word to her about *benevolence*. On the contrary, it was all "It is *I* who am to benefit by this, not *you*." Yet, though I expressed this in words, I must have expressed it rather badly, for I noticed her features contract for a moment. However, I won in the end. As I am recalling the whole of this grossness, I may as well recall the ultimate grossness of all—the fact that, as I stood there, I kept whispering to myself: "You are tall and straight and well educated—you are, to speak plainly, far from bad-looking." That was what I kept playing with in my mind; until at length she said to me, as she stood at the gate, just "*Yes*"—though I ought to add, perhaps, that she stood for a long while thinking at that gate before she said just "*Yes*." Indeed, she remained so long plunged in reflection that at length I asked her, "Well, what?" and even said again, with a prolonged intonation, "Well, wha-a-at?"

"Wait a moment," she said. "I am thinking."

So serious was her little face—so serious, that I could not but respect it. Yet I also felt offended. "Is she choosing between me and that shopman?" I thought. Oh, how I misunderstood it all, how I misunderstood it all! Even to-day I do not understand it. I remember Lukeria running after me as I was departing, and stopping me on the road, and saying with enthusiasm, "God will repay you, sir, for preserving our young lady. Only, do not tell her so, for she is very proud."

Proud? Well, I love proud women. Proud women are splendid—except, perhaps, when one has reason to doubt one's power over them? Oh, villain, villain that I was! How complacent I felt! You know, I should have been astounded to know that, as she stood there at the gate, she had in her mind the thought, "Seeing that I shall be unhappy with either of them, would it not be better for me to choose the worst of the two—the fat shopman, so that the drunken brute may the sooner beat me to death?" Eh? How was I to conceive that she was capable of such a thought?

Yes, to this day, to this day, I do not understand it. I have just said that in her mind there may have been the thought: "Which of the two unhappinesses shall I choose? The shopman?" Yet *which* of us was the greater misfortune for her—the shopman or myself—the shopman or the pawnbroker who quoted Goethe? It still remains a question. Yet how so? Do you not understand that the answer to that question lies there on the table? Yet you say, "It is *still* a question!" But what is to become of me now? Does it concern me, or does it not? I cannot decide. Perhaps I ought to take some sleep, for my head is aching.

CHAPTER III

I, "THE MOST NOBLE OF MEN," HAVE NO BELIEF IN MYSELF

I HAVE not slept. Somewhere or other a pulse has been beating in my head as I tried and tried to remember this affair, with all its foulness. Aye, its foulness!—for from what foulness did I not then drag her? She might at least have understood that, and have appraised my conduct accordingly. In those days I used to hug myself with the thought that I was forty-one, and she but sixteen. The idea simply ravished me—this perception of our inequality of ages. I found it luscious, luscious, most luscious!

Also, I tried to have the marriage celebrated in the English style—that is to say, with none present but her and myself and two witnesses (Lukeria to be one of the latter); after which we would go straight away by train to, say, Moscow (it was there that my business lay), and spend a couple of weeks in an hotel. But she opposed this, and would not hear of it. No; when the ceremony was over I was to return in state to her aunts'—to the very kinsfolk from whom I was about to deliver her! In the end I had to give way; whereupon the aunts refused to do what was needful until I had presented the old harridans with a hundred roubles apiece, and promised them some more. After that they became complacent. Yet I said nothing to *her* about that transaction, for fear of distressing her with the meanness of it all. Next, a quarrel arose over the marriage gift. She possessed nothing—literally nothing, yet she would accept nothing. At last I succeeded in showing her that that could not be, and gave her a present because—well, because there was no one else to do it. Oh, fie upon me! Thereafter I lost no time in acquainting her with my views on matters, that she might at least know them. Possibly I was successful. At all events, from the first she did not fasten upon, but actually flung herself upon, me with affection. That is to say, she would run rapturously to meet me when I returned home in the evenings, and tell me, in her lisping way (oh, the charming lisp of innocence!), all about her childhood, and her youth, and the home where she was born, and her father and mother. Yet upon these raptures I would pour cold water. That was my idea of doing things. To her transports I would respond with silence—though with *benevolent* silence, of course; but she soon perceived that we were different, and that I was an enigma. Yet it was against an enigma that I myself was striving! It may have been the effort to unriddle it that made me perpetrate all this folly. Now, my first and principal rule was strictness—it was under that rule that I had taken her to my home. In short, my way of life and self-conceit led me to elaborate a whole system of rules. And how easily she wore herself out against them! Yet it was bound to be; I was forced by inevitable circumstances to create the system. Why should I do myself a wrong? The system was a good one. No, no! Listen to me. Judge a man only when you know the facts. Listen.

But how am I to begin?—for it is very difficult to do so. It is when one begins to *justify* oneself that one finds it so difficult. You see, things were like this. The young girl would say (for example) that she despised money; whereupon I would begin to insist upon money, to lay the greatest possible stress upon money. I would continue so to insist until she ceased speaking. Opening her great eyes, she would just gaze at me, and listen, and be silent. You see, she was a large-hearted girl—large-hearted and impulsive, but lacking in patience, and, in a way, contemptuous of me. I, on the other hand, was all for breadth of view, and desired to graft my breadth of view upon *her* mind, upon *her* mental outlook. Let us take a sordid example of this. How did I explain to such a character my loan office? Well, I never mentioned it directly, for then I might have had to apologise to her for it. Rather I adopted what I might call a *proud* tone, and spoke only through the method of holding my tongue. At that method, you must know, I am a master, and have practised it all my life, and have lived through many a difficult moment by its means. Ah, though none

have known of it, how unhappy I have always been
—cast out, cast out by every one—cast out and forgotten! Suddenly this sixteen-year-old girl found
out from some gossip or another some old details
about me, and at once thought that she knew everything, and that hidden in the breast of man there
lurked no more secrets for her. Yet still I kept
silence—always kept silence, and have kept it to
this day. But why so? What a proud creature a
man is! I wished her to learn the truth without
my help, but not from rascals. I wished her *of
herself* to guess the riddle of that man, and to
comprehend him. When I took her to my house I
hoped to win her full respect. I hoped that she
would stand always before me, to plead for my
sufferings—and I have paid the price for my hope!
Oh, but I was always proud, I always wished to
have everything or nothing. That is why I would
not go halves in happiness—why I wanted *all*—why
I was forced to act as I did. "Do *you*," I mutely
said to her, "unriddle and appraise me." Surely, if
I had begun to explain things and to suggest, to
wriggle about and to *ask* for her respect, it would
have been as though I had been beseeching her
pardon? Oh, to speak of it!——

Always I have been foolish, foolish, foolish! I
told her outright, and without any compunction (I
insist upon it, without any compunction), that the
nobility of youth is a beautiful thing, but—that it is
not worth a groat. Why, I said, is it not worth a
groat? Because it can be obtained cheaply, because
it is to be acquired without living, because those
so-called "first impressions of life" are to be
obtained merely by watching the labours of others.
Cheap nobility is always easy of attainment, as also
is surrender of one's existence, since at that age the
blood boils, and one desires but limitless strength
and beauty. Nay, give me an achievement of
nobility which is hidden, unheralded, and devoid of
glamour—which requires no calumniation of others

—which involves much sacrifice, but not a particle of glory. Give me a deed which holds you—you the man of virtue—up to the world as a villain, when all the while you are the most honourable man on earth. Come! Attempt the feat, or else retire from the struggle! I, I—well, all my life I have been engaged in such a struggle. At first she used to dispute things with me—ah, how hotly! Later on she began to hold her tongue better, and only opened her eyes very wide as she listened—yes, those great, great attentive eyes of hers. Then on her lips there would suddenly dawn a smile which was distrustful, furtive, and unpleasing to me. It was with such a smile on her face that I brought her to my home. In very truth she had nowhere else to go to.

CHAPTER IV

PLANS, AND YET PLANS

WHICH of us began it?

Neither of us. It began of itself. I have said that when I took her to my home I made a code of rules, and that only at times I relaxed them. I informed my bride that I was hiring her for myself in much the same way that money is hired or borrowed, and to this she made no reply—mark that. Indeed, she seemed to assent to the transaction with eagerness. My flat, my furniture, and so forth, are just as they were then. The flat contains two rooms, one of which is a large salon, with an office partitioned from it, and the other one our own room, which we use both for receiving company and for sleeping. The furniture is scanty; even her aunts had better. The ikon-case and lamp stand in the salon, where also the loan office is; while my own room contains a cupboard with some books, the pledges, and my keys. Yes, and there are in it a bed and a few tables and chairs. Also, I told my

bride that for the support of ourselves and Lukeria
(whom I had inveigled into becoming our servant)
I should advance her a dole of a rouble a day, and
no more. "I wish to make thirty thousand roubles
within the next three years," I said—"and, besides,
you earn no money." To that she raised no objection,
but, of my own accord, I afterwards increased her
daily allowance by thirty kopecks. The same with
the theatre. I told my bride from the first that she
must look for no playgoing at all, beyond that once
a month I should take her to a seat in the pit. We
went, I think, three times, and saw "The Pursuit
of Happiness" and "The Song Birds." We went
there in silence, and we returned in silence. Ah, why
did we begin doing things in silence (for there was
no quarrel at first—only that same silence)? I
remember how sometimes she would throw me a
stealthy glance, and how, on noting that glance, I
would redouble my silence. True, it was *I* who
insisted upon that silence, not *she*. On her side one
or two interruptions of it occurred at moments when
she was embracing me; but inasmuch as those interruptions were painful and hysterical, and I looked
only for assurances of happiness and respect from
her, I always received them coldly. And I was right,
too. Always on the morrow of those interruptions
there took place a quarrel.

Yet there was not so much a quarrel on those
occasions as once again a silence and—and then
more insolent glances from her. Insubordination
and independence—that is what it really was, though
she did not know it. Yes, I could see her gentle
face becoming more and more insolent every day.
Would you believe it, on my side I grew dirty in
my ways, and even taught her to be so too. There
could be no doubt that, however intermittent the
process, she was at last finding herself. Yet to
think that, after leaving all that grime and poverty,
all that washing of floors—to think that, after all
that, she should suddenly begin sniffing at *our*

poverty! You see, it was not really poverty, but *economy*—economy in what was necessary, in clothes and linen and cleanliness (for at that time I imagined cleanliness in a man to be offensive to a woman). Yet it was not economy that she objected to, but my *dirtiness* in economy. "Given an aim, the stronger character will point the way." She took to refusing to go to the theatre; her scornful demeanour became worse and worse, while I, for my part, grew more and more silent.

But had I no excuse? Our principal difference was over the loan office. Of course I know that a girl —especially one only of sixteen—cannot wholly give in to a man. Woman has no originality; it is an axiom, and for me it is an axiom still. That is why she is lying there now in the salon; for truth is truth, and even Mill himself could not alter that. But woman is also *loving*—she is *loving*. She will try to deify even the vices and the cruelties of her beloved. *He* could never find for his cruelties the excuses which *she* will find for them. Yet this is not originality; it is *nobility*. Lack of originality has been the undoing of women from the beginning. What that is original can you point out to me on that table? Is it original to be lying on a table? Ah!——

Listen. Of her *love* I felt assured. How she would rush upon me, and throw herself upon my neck! Of *course* she loved me—though, more truly speaking, she loved *to love*. Yes, that is it, rather —she loved to love, she had need of something which she could love. It is important to note that I never showed her any cruelty for which actual excuse needed to be sought. You may say, as every one else did, "He is only a pawnbroker": yet what is a pawnbroker? There must have been some reason for a man of refinement becoming a pawnbroker. You see, one may cherish an idea in such a way that, should one give vent to any other idea—put any other idea into words—it issues awkwardly, it

shames one. And why? For no reason that I know
of, unless it be that we are all of us worthless, and
unable to speak the truth. I do not know. Just
now I called myself "a man of refinement." That
is absurd—and, besides, it is not so. The real, the
indubitable, truth is that I *had the right*, if I so
wished it, to secure for myself a livelihood by opening a loan office. "You have dismissed me," I said
to myself (and by "you" I meant society)—"you
have driven me forth in contemptuous silence, and
have returned to my passionate protest an insult
which will abide with me for life. Thereby you
have given me the right to cut myself off from you,
to amass thirty thousand roubles, and to spend my
declining years in the Crimea—somewhere on its
southern shore, among the hills and vineyards. Yes,
you have given me the right to retire to a property
of my own there, bought with those thirty thousand
roubles, and far from you all. Yet I wish to live
without any enmity against you—only with an ideal,
and in the company of the woman who is beloved
of my soul, and of my family (if God should send
me one), and of the peasants who shall be my
protégés." All this is very well to say *to myself
now;* but what could have been more stupid of
me than to have said it *to her then?* Hence that
proud silence of mine—hence the fact that we used
to sit together without speaking. Besides, what
could she have made of it all? She was only in
her sixteenth year, in her first youth: what could
she have understood of all my excuses, of all my
sufferings? In her were the unbendingness, the
ignorance of life, the jejune, cheap convictions, the
gallinaceous blindness, of "the beautiful soul."
Again, there was the loan office. Well, was I at
all oppressive in my business? Could she not watch
me at it, and see that I never took more than
was my due? Oh, the injustice that there is in the
world! In her were charm, gentleness, even heaven
itself: yet at the same time she was the tyrant, the

pitiless tyrant and torturer, of my soul! I should be doing myself a wrong if I did not say so. Do you think that I did not love her? *Who* can say that I did not love her? Yet the irony, the cruel irony, of fate and nature stepped in there. We humans are accursed, and all our lives are accursed. Mine is so in particular. I can now see that somewhere I made a mistake—that something or other went wrong. Yet all seemed clear enough *then*. My plan was as clear as day. "I am a proud, stern man," I said to myself, "and have no need of moral diversion. I wish but to suffer in silence." And it befell so. I was not mistaken, I was not mistaken. "In time," I said, "she will see that this is nobility on my part, though she has not yet guessed it; and as soon as ever she reads the riddle of me she will value me tenfold, and fall upon her knees in prayer for me." That was my plan. Yet there must have been something which I forgot, or which I omitted, to do. Something or other there must have been which I failed to effect. But enough, enough! Whose pardon can I ask now? What is done is done. Be bold always, O mortal, and proud: it was not *your* fault.

Yes, I will speak out now; I will not fear to come face to face with the truth. It was *her* fault, and *her* fault alone.

CHAPTER V

THE GENTLE MAIDEN REBELS

OUR quarrels began with her taking it into her head to lend money on her own account, and to value pledges at more than their worth. Twice she presumed to enter into a dispute with me in this connection. Yes, that was how my dear lady began her interference.

One day an old woman brought me a medallion—

a sort of souvenir which her late husband had given her. I was for buying it outright for thirty roubles, but she only began to weep pitifully, and to beg of me to keep it for her in pawn. Accordingly I did so. Five days later she came to me again— this time with a request that I would exchange the medallion for a bracelet which was not worth even eight roubles. I refused to do so. She must have read something in my wife's eyes, for she returned to her, unknown to me, and induced *her* to effect the exchange.

I learnt of it the same day, and expressed myself on the subject with kindness, but also with firmness and good sense. She was sitting on the bed and looking at the floor as she tickled the right side of her nose with her forefinger (a favourite gesture of hers). Over her face there played an unpleasant smile. I explained to her quietly, and without raising my voice at all, that the money was *mine*, that I was entitled to view life through my own eyes, and that when I had married her I had concealed nothing from her.

Suddenly she jumped up, gave herself a shake, and—would you believe it?—fell to kicking me! She was like a wild beast—her fury was that of a wild beast gone mad. I stood quite petrified with astonishment, for I had never expected anything like this. None the less I soon recovered myself, and, without even moving, told her once more, and in the same quiet voice, that henceforth I forbade her to take part in my affairs. She laughed in my face, and left the flat.

As a matter of fact, she had no right to leave the flat. She could go nowhere without my leave—such was the marriage agreement. Towards evening she returned, but I said nothing more to her.

Next day also she went out in the morning, and again in the afternoon. I closed up the office, and set off to call upon the aunts. Ever since the wedding I had dropped their acquaintance—no visiting

had taken place on either side. However, she was
not there. The aunts listened to me with much
curiosity, and then laughed in my face. "It serves
you right," was all they said. This I had expected.
Nevertheless I bribed the younger of the two—the
spinster—with a hundred roubles, and paid her
twenty-five of them in advance. Two days later
she came to me, and said : "Colonel Efimovitch, a
former messmate of yours, is in this business." I
was furious, for not only had Efimovitch treated me
very badly when in the regiment, but on two occasions (a month ago) he had had the hardihood to
come to the office, under the pretence of raising a
loan, and (I now remembered) had laughed and
talked with my wife. I had approached him, and
told him, in view of our former relations, never to
dare to visit me again. Nevertheless I had had no
idea of *this* in connection with him—I had merely
thought of him as an impudent fellow. However,
the woman told me that a meeting had been arranged
at her house, and that the whole affair was under
the management of an old acquaintance of the aunts'
—one Julia Samsonovna, the widow of another
colonel. "Your wife," concluded my informant, "is
with her at this moment."

Let me cut the picture short. The affair cost me
altogether three hundred roubles, for it was decided
that I should take an adjoining room for a couple
of days, and, from behind closed doors, be a witness
to the first meeting between my wife and Efimovitch.
The previous evening there took place between us
a brief, but significant, scene.

She returned home before nightfall, and, seating
herself on the bed, fell to tapping the counterpane
with her fingers as she looked at me with a challenging smile. As I returned her look it occurred
to me that for the last month—or, rather, for the
last two weeks—she had not been herself. Indeed,
she had been the very *opposite* of herself, for she
had appeared a turbulent, aggressive person who,

if not absolutely shameless, was at all events unbalanced and desirous of quarrelling. She had
seemed actually to *invite* quarrels. When a woman
of her type takes to that sort of amusement she only
hurts and worries herself, since she cannot possibly
make her conduct harmonise with her natural reticence and modesty. Hence, on these occasions, such
a woman does not act according to rule, and one's
intellect cannot trust the evidence of one's senses.
The more she becomes inured to her mental *volte
face*, the more she tries to conceal it, and the worse
she grows—though always under the guise of an
instinct for order and decorum which is superior to
your own.

"Is it true that you were turned out of your
regiment for refusing to fight a duel?" suddenly she
asked me as she jumped up, her eyes flashing.

"Yes," I replied. "My brother officers requested
me to exchange into another corps, but I anticipated
them by resigning."

"Then you were expelled as a coward?"

"Yes—I was looked upon as a coward. All the
same, it was not through cowardice that I declined
the duel, but through the fact that I would not
submit to my comrades' tyrannical dictation, and
call out a man who was not at fault. Please
remember" (I could not help adding this) "that for
me to oppose such tyranny, and to take all the con-
sequences of my action, meant far more manliness
than the fighting of any duel would have required."

And I launched out—I could not help doing so—
into a full justification of myself. This new humility
of mine was precisely what she wanted, and she
looked at me with a malicious smile.

"And is it also true," she went on, "that for the
next three years you walked the streets of St. Petersburg, and begged for coppers, and slept under
billiard tables?"

"Yes, I used to sleep at Viazemski's, in the Hay
Market. It is true that for a long while after my

N

military service I experienced much hardship and degradation. Yet it was not *moral* degradation, since I detested all that I did. It was a mere lapse of will and intellect. It was due to the temptations of my position. But all that is over now."

"Yes; and *now* you are a financier!"

This was a hint at my loan office, but I kept myself in hand, since I saw that she was thirsting for explanations which would only have humiliated me—and I did not mean to give them. Just then a client called, and I went into the salon to meet him. An hour later she came to me, dressed for a walk, and said as she halted in front of me—

"But of all this you told me *not a word* before our marriage?" To that I made no reply, and she departed.

The next evening I was standing in the room of which I have spoken, and heard, through its closed doors, the decision of my fate. And in my pocket there was a loaded revolver. Dressed in her best, she sat at the table, and listened to Efimovitch as he poured out his soul before her. All this (and I say it to my credit) I had foreseen and presumed. Indeed, I had recognised that I had foreseen and presumed it. I do not know if I express myself clearly?

It happened as follows. For an hour I listened —for an hour I listened to this interview between my wife—the gentle and refined lady—and that gross, stupid, sensual rascal of grovelling soul.

"How," thought I as I listened, "does that meek, innocent, half-educated wife of mine come to know so much?" And, indeed, the most skilful writer of the most famous comedy could never have devised such a scene of sparkling repartee, imperturbable laughter, and serene contempt for vice. What sparkle there was in her speeches and interjections! —what wit in her swift replies!—what sincerity in her opinions! Yet also what girlish simplicity in her demeanour! She mocked at his protestations

of love, at his gestures, and at his proposals. At
length, and by a clumsy process, arrived at the point,
and meeting with no apparent opposition, he ventured to seat himself by her side.

"All this," thought I at the beginning, "is mere
coquetry on her part—the mere coquetry of a bad,
but clever, woman who is seeking to enhance her
own value."

But no; her sincerity was as clear as the day.
One could not doubt her. It was evident that her
detestation of me—a detestation both insistent and
impulsive—had enabled this inexperienced girl to plot
this meeting; but that, as soon as matters were
about to come to a head, her eyes were opened.
She had thought to wound me in some fashion, but,
after deciding upon this particular piece of mischief,
had found it intolerable to her modesty. How,
indeed, could Efimovitch, or any other rascal, have
pleased a pure and upright girl of ideals such as
hers? On the contrary, he excited her derision.
The truth had asserted itself again in her soul, and
made her vent her distaste in sarcasm. At length
this boor of a colonel took offence, and moved away
with such a frown upon his face that for a moment
I was afraid he would assault her out of base
revenge. Also (I repeat it to my own credit) I
witnessed the scene almost without surprise. I
had gone to the room to meet, as it were, an old
acquaintance. I had gone to it distrustful of everything, and of every accusation against her, although
I had a revolver in my pocket. How could I ever
have thought her to be other than what she was?
Why else should I have fallen in love with her, have
valued her, and have married her? Oh, I knew that
she hated me, but I also knew that she was no
wanton. I ended the scene by suddenly throwing
the doors open. Efimovitch leapt to his feet. Taking
her by the hand, I invited her to go with me. Upon
this he recovered himself sufficiently to exclaim in a
loud, rolling voice—

"Oh, I have nothing to say against the sacred rights of married people. Take her away, take her away. Yet," he went on, "though no decent man would care to meet you, for the sake of your good lady and of your previous service in the regiment I will—— Well, do you care to *risk* it?"

"You hear what he says?" I said to her as I stopped for a moment on the threshold.

Not another word passed between us as we walked home, but I took her hand, and she made no opposition—on the contrary she seemed struck by the act. Yet this lasted only until we had reached home. Entering the flat, she seated herself on a chair, and fixed me with a steady gaze. She was very pale, and, though her lips presently parted in a smile, she continued to gaze at me with a grim, triumphant, challenging sort of expression, as though she were sure I meant to shoot her. But all I did was to take the revolver out of my pocket quietly, and to lay it on the table. She gazed first at the weapon and then at myself (you must know that she knew the revolver well, since, whenever I opened my office for business, I always began by taking the weapon out and loading it. You see, when I first started in business I decided to keep neither a watchdog nor a giant commissionaire, as does Moser, but only to have the cook to open our door to visitors. Nevertheless persons in our profession cannot afford to dispense altogether with self-defence, so I kept a loaded revolver. For the first few days after our marriage she displayed much interest in the revolver, and made me answer many questions concerning its working and mechanism, and even persuaded me, on one occasion, to fire it at a mark. Please note all this). Well, paying no attention to her frightened face, I half-undressed myself, and lay down upon the bed. I was very tired, for it was now eleven o'clock. For another hour she continued to sit where she was; after which, putting out the light, she lay down, fully dressed, on the sofa by the wall.

This was the first time that she had gone to bed without me. Please also note *that*.

CHAPTER VI

A TERRIBLE REMINISCENCE

NEXT came a horrible incident. I awoke at (I think) eight o'clock, when the room was full of daylight. I awoke with all my senses about me, and opened my eyes quickly. She was standing near the table, with the revolver clutched in her hands. She had not perceived that I was awake and observing her. Suddenly I saw her move towards me, the revolver still in her grasp. Instantly I closed my eyes, and pretended to be asleep.

She advanced to the bedside, and stood over me. I could hear everything. A silence brooded, yet I could hear even that silence. Then came a grim movement—and in a flash, and despite my will, I opened my eyes. She was gazing into them, and the revolver was at my temple! Our eyes met. Yet only for a second did we gaze at one another. With a great effort I closed my eyes, and resolved at the same instant, and with all the strength of my soul, not to stir a limb, nor to open my eyes, whatsoever might await me.

Indeed, it is a common occurrence for a man who is sound asleep to open his eyes, and, raising his head for a second, to take a look round the room; after which, with the same suddenness and lack of volition as before, he will lay his head upon the pillow, and continue his slumbers without any recollection of what has happened. Consequently the fact that, after meeting her gaze and feeling the revolver at my temple, I closed my eyes and continued to lie still, as though sound asleep, may have led her to suppose that I was *really* asleep and had seen nothing : the more so since she would think it

improbable that, having seen what I had seen, I
should close my eyes again—and close them at such
a moment!

Yes, she would think it improbable. "All the
same, she may have guessed the truth," was the
thought which occurred to me just as instantly. Oh,
the hurricane of thoughts and sensations which
passed through my mind during that second of time!
How potent is the electric force of the human
consciousness!

"At all events," I reflected, "though she may
have guessed the truth, and be aware that I am not
asleep, I may have unnerved her with my indifference
to death, and her hand may tremble. Her former
decisiveness of purpose may fail before this new and
unaccustomed impression." They say that persons
standing on the verge of a precipice have a tendency
to throw themselves into the abyss. For my own
part, I believe that many a case of suicide and
murder has arisen from the mere fact of a revolver
having been taken into the hand. There lies the
abyss, there the slope which must not be impinged
upon if one is not to be impelled by some invincible
power to pull the trigger. Yet the conjecture that
I had seen all, that I knew all, that I could silently
await death at her hands, might check her on that
slope.

The silence continued—until suddenly I felt at my
temple, near my hair, the cold touch of steel! You
may ask me—Had I any certain hope of escaping?
To that I would answer as I would answer to God—
namely, that I had no hope at all, beyond a mere
chance in a hundred. And if you should further ask
me why I thus calmly awaited death, I would reply:
"Of what use was my life to me now that my own
adored wife had raised a revolver against me?"
Moreover, I knew with all the strength of my being
that between us, at that moment, there was in
progress a struggle, a dread duel of life and death,
in which one party was the man who, the evening

before, had been accused of expulsion from the service for cowardice. *I* knew this, and *she* knew it—if, indeed, she had guessed the truth, and was aware that I was not sleeping.

It *may* be that it was not so—it *may* be that I had no such thought in my mind : yet it can hardly have been otherwise, even unconsciously, since what I did then has remained with me every subsequent hour of my life.

Yet, again, you may ask me, Why did I do nothing to save myself from injury? That question I have asked myself a thousand times, and each time with a cold shiver down my back as I remember the occasion. But my spirit seemed to be in a trance; I had lost everything—I had lost everything through my own fault, and whom now should I save? Why should you think that I wished to save myself at that moment? How do you know that at that moment I could even feel?

Yet all the time consciousness was bubbling within me. The seconds passed, yet the silence remained as death. Still she was standing over me. Then suddenly I gave a shiver of hope. Quickly I raised my eyelids. She was no longer in the room ! I rose from the bed. *I* had won !—and *she*, she was conquered for ever !

I went into the other room to light the tea-urn, which was always kept in the salon, and which she usually superintended. I sat down at the table without a word, and took from her my glass of tea.[1] Five minutes later I looked at her. She was deadly pale—paler even than she had been the previous night—as she returned my glance. Then suddenly, on perceiving my intent look, she gave a wan smile with her white lips, and her eyes asked of me the timid question: "Is he thinking and puzzling over it? Does he, or does he not, know? Did he, or did he not, see?" I averted my gaze with an air of indifference. After luncheon I closed the

---

[1] Tea, in Russia, is usually served in tumblers, not in cups.

office, and went out to buy a screen and an iron bedstead.   On my return I had the bed set up in the
salon, and the screen disposed about it.   This was to
be *her* bed, though I did not tell her so.   Yet she
understood (without so much as a word spoken—
merely through the bed) that I had seen and knew
all, and that not a doubt remained.   That night,
too, I left the revolver on the table as usual.   She
lay down in silence upon her new bed.   The marriage
bond was broken.   She was conquered, but not pardoned.   As the night wore on she became light-
headed, and, when the morning had arrived, was in
a high fever.   In that state she lay for six weeks.

PART II

CHAPTER I

A DREAM OF PRIDE

Lukeria has just been in to tell me that she cannot remain with me any longer, but must leave as soon as my wife is buried. I have been down on my knees to her, and begged and prayed her to stay, but it is no good. I would have begged and prayed her thus for an hour. I keep thinking and thinking, and all my thoughts are painful. My head too is painful. Perhaps I did wrong in grovelling to that woman as I did. It is strange that I should have no desire to sleep. When a man is in great agony of mind, and the first dreadful throes are past, he usually feels a desire to sleep. They say that even men condemned to execution sleep soundly their last night. Well, I must do the same. It is only natural that I should do so, and my strength will not last if I do not. . . .

I have been lying on the sofa a little while, but I have not slept. . . .

All through the six weeks of her illness we looked after her night and day—I and Lukeria and a trained nurse whom I engaged from the hospital. I did not grudge the money, and even *wished* to spend it upon her. Also, I called in Doctor Schröeder, and paid him ten roubles a visit. When she returned to consciousness I began to be less expansive. How shall I describe it? The day she left her bed she went into my room, softly and without a word, and sat down at a table which I had specially bought for her. Neither of us spoke—it is a fact. True, later we began to talk to one another, but even then only on ordinary subjects. Of course, I was *purposely* reticent, while it was clear that she too was glad not to have to say a word too much. It seemed to me quite natural of her. "She is badly shaken and subdued," I thought, "and I must give her time to forget it all, and to recover her composure." So we still maintained our silence. Yet all the while I was preparing myself for the future. She seemed to me to be doing the same, and I found it interesting at times to wonder : "What is she thinking of now?"

No one can imagine what I suffered, or how I grieved, as I tended her during her illness. But I kept my grief to myself, and stifled my groans when in Lukeria's presence. I could not face, I could not even conceive, the idea of my wife dying without learning the truth. When she was out of danger, and recovering her health, I remember I suddenly became much calmer, and decided to "put off our future" indefinitely, and to leave things as they were for the present. Yes, some strange process then took place in me—I can call it nothing else. *I* had won, and the knowledge of the fact seemed to be all in all to me. Thus the winter passed. All that winter I was pleased with myself as I had never been before.

You see, there was in my life an external circumstance which hitherto (that is to say, up to the time of the catastrophe with my wife) weighed upon me daily and hourly. That circumstance was my loss of reputation and my expulsion from the regiment. In two words, it was the tyrannical injustice of which I had been the victim. My comrades had found me too serious-minded—perhaps too prone to sarcasm—for their taste, since frequently it happens that what a man likes and admires and respects his comrades only deride. I was never liked, not even in my schooldays. I have never been liked anywhere, nor at any time. Even Lukeria cannot abide me. My affair with the regiment was the outcome of that dislike. There is no misfortune more mortifying and unbearable than to be undone by an incident which might never have occurred but for a combination of conditions which themselves might have passed as a cloud. For a man of sensibility and feeling it is a most degrading thing. It all happened as follows.

One night at the theatre I went out, during an entr'acte, into the buffet. Presently A——ff, of the hussars, entered, and began telling two of his fellows, in a voice loud enough to be heard by all the other officers present, that a certain captain of ours, named Bezumtsev, had just caused a scandal in the corridor by "appearing to be drunk." As a matter of fact this was not so, since Captain Bezumtsev was *not* drunk that night, and the scandal was no scandal at all. After that the hussars went on to talk among themselves of other matters, and for the moment the affair ended. The next day, however, the report reached our regiment, and at once it was said that, though I had been the only man of our corps to be present in the buffet, I had neglected to approach A——ff, and to stop him with a word when he was speaking so insultingly of Captain Bezumtsev. Yet why should I have done so? If he and Bezumtsev had occasion for quarrel, it was personal to themselves alone, and need not have been fastened upon *me*. However, my comrades declared that the matter was *not* a personal one, but concerned the regiment as a whole, and that, since I alone of our officers had been present in the buffet, I had shown the bystanders and the public generally that our regiment contained officers who were not over-ticklish concerning the honour of themselves and their corps. With this opinion I could not agree. None the less I was given to understand that I could still set the matter right by having a formal meeting with A——ff; but this I did not choose to do, and, being much angered at the time, declined the suggestion with some brusqueness, and

sent in my papers. That is the whole story. I left
the regiment a proud, but a broken, man. I had
lost my power of will and my good sense; and when,
shortly afterwards, my brother-in-law in Moscow
squandered the last remnant of our family property,
including my own little portion, I found myself a
beggar in the street. I might have accepted private
employment, but I did not. After wearing a splendid
uniform I could not go and work on the railway!
Shame upon shame, therefore, ignominy upon
ignominy, lapse upon lapse, and the worse the better
—that is what I chose for my portion. Yes,
three years of murky recollections lie behind me,
including Viazemski's lodging-house. But about a
year and a half ago an old godmother of mine in
Moscow—a rich old woman—died unexpectedly, and
left me 3000 roubles. I considered the matter, and
finally resolved upon my course. I decided to open
a loan office, and to ask no one's leave to do so.
Money, and then a home, and then a new life far
from old memories—that was my plan. Nevertheless the murky past and the sense of my lost reputation for honour never ceased to weigh upon me.
As you know, I married—though whether by chance
I did so I know not. When I did so I thought
to introduce into my home a friend—for I stood
terribly in need of a friend; but this friend (I saw
clearly) would need to be put through a course of
preparation, to be made—even to be tamed. Would
it do to explain everything at once to a prejudiced
girl of sixteen? How, for instance, but for the
late terrible incident of the revolver, could I have
persuaded her that I was no coward, and that I
had been unjustly condemned by the regiment for
cowardice? Yes, the incident had happened oppor-
tunely. By successfully sustaining the ordeal of the
revolver I had avenged myself for all my sordid
past; and though no one else was aware of it, *she*
was so, and it helped me, since she herself helped
me by representing to me the one hope of my dreams.

She was the one human being whom I had marked out for myself, and I had no need of another. That too she knew. She knew also that she had made a false step in joining the number of my enemies. The thought simply ravished me. In her eyes it was now impossible for me to be a villain—impossible for me even to seem to be a strange personality. Yet this last idea was not so very pleasing to me, after all. Oddity is no vice, nor is it always unpleasing in a woman's sight. In short, I put the late catastrophe out of my mind. What had happened was overmuch for my faculties to envisage calmly—it included too many pictures, too great a store of material, for my intellect to grasp. Therein lay my folly as a dreamer : what had happened had *deprived* me of material, when all the time I thought that it still lay ready to my hand.

Thus the winter passed—in a sort of expectation of something. I loved to throw stealthy glances at her when she was sitting at her little table. She would be busy with her work (her sewing, that is to say), or, if it were evening, with books which she got from my cupboard. Even the selection of books in that cupboard was bound to tell in my favour. She almost never went out, except that, just at dusk, when dinner was over, I would take her for a walk, a constitutional. Yet we did not walk now in absolute silence, as formerly. On the contrary I always tried to make a show of keeping up an amicable conversation—though one that was not over-expansive on either side. This I did of set purpose—my idea being that she needed to be "given time." Yet it is a strange circumstance that never up to the very close of the winter did it once enter my head that, though I often threw stealthy glances at *her*, I never found her gaze resting upon *me*. I took this for diffidence on her part, since she had just the gentle, timid air which would come natural to one who had been through such an illness as she had. "No," I thought to myself, "it were

better to wait, and then of a sudden she will come
to you *of herself.*"

This notion had an inexpressible charm for me—
though I may add that, at times, I *purposely* egged
myself on until I had brought my spirit even to the
point of being stern with her. Thus, for a while,
things went on. Yet my resentment against her
never succeeded in ripening, or even in taking any
firm root in my soul. Somehow I always felt as
though I were playing a game. Although I had
violated the marriage tie by buying for her the new
bed and screen, I never found myself able to look
upon her as a sinner—not because I thought lightly
of her offence, but because from the very first day,
and even before I had bought her the bed, I had
made up my mind to forgive her. In a word, my
strange conduct arose only from my moral rigidity.
On the other hand, I looked upon her as so completely subjugated—as so completely crushed and
humiliated—that at times I was torn with pity for
her, notwithstanding that the idea of her subjugation
really pleased me. Yes, the idea of the inequality
between us really took my fancy.

Nevertheless I did a few good acts that winter.
For example, I remitted a couple of debts, and lent
a poor woman some money without security. I did
not tell my wife of these things, for I had not done
them for her approval; but it so happened that the
poor woman to whom I had lent the money came
back to thank me, and almost went upon her knees.
Thus the affair came out, and I think that my wife
was genuinely pleased when she learned of my
beneficence.

Then the spring came, and in the middle of April
we took out our double window-frames, and the sun
began to cheer our silent dwelling with its bright
spots of light. Yet before me there hung a curtain
which blinded my perception. A fateful, disastrous
curtain it was! At length my eyes were opened, and
I saw and knew all. Was it mere chance that that

happened? Was the fatal day bound to come? Did
the sun's rays fire my darkened soul to sense and
understanding? No; neither sense nor understanding were there. What happened was that a little
vein—a vein long dead—gave a little tremor, and
came to life, to illumine my murky conscience and
dispel my devilish pride. Yes, it all happened suddenly and unexpectedly. It happened one afternoon,
five hours after dinner. . . .

CHAPTER II

THE CURTAIN SUDDENLY FALLS FROM BEFORE MY
EYES

I CAN tell the story in two words. For a month
or so I had noticed in her a strange absent-mindedness—absent-mindedness, mark you, not silence.
My first intimation of it was sudden. One day she
was seated at her work—her head bowed over her
needle, and her mind oblivious of the fact that I was
looking at her. Then all at once it struck me that
she was looking thin and wasted, and that her face
and lips were pale. This, with her air of abstraction, gave me a sharp, momentary pang. Besides,
I had heard her coughing with a thin, dry cough,
especially at night. Instantly I rose, and went out
to send a message to Doctor Schröeder—though
without saying anything about it to my wife.

Next day the Doctor came. When he did so she
gazed from him to myself in astonishment.

"I am *quite* well," she said with an uncertain
laugh.

Schröeder hardly looked at her (only too frequently doctors are pompous and negligent), but in
the next room he told me that this was the after-
math of her illness, and that in the spring it would
not be a bad thing if I were to take her to the sea-
side—or, if that were impossible, simply into the

country. In short, he described the malady as mere
weakness. When he had gone my wife suddenly
said to me again, as she gazed at me with a serious
air—

"Really I am *quite* well."

Yet no sooner were the words out of her mouth
than she reddened—evidently from shame. Yes,
evidently from shame. How well I understand it
all now! She was ashamed of the fact that I was
still her husband—that I was taking so much thought
about her, like a *real* husband. At the time, though,
I did not understand this, but attributed her blush to
conciliatoriness (for the curtain was still before my
eyes).

A month later—at about five o'clock one sunny
day in April—I sat down to the desk in my loan
office, to cast up my accounts. Suddenly I heard
her begin singing to herself—heard her begin singing where she sat over her work at her table in
my room. Somehow the unusual incident produced
upon me a nerve-shattering impression which to
this day I cannot explain. Hitherto I had hardly
ever heard her sing, except during the first few days
after our marriage, when we could still sport
together, and fire at marks with my revolver. In
those days her voice had been a strong and full
(though not a true) one—an exceedingly pleasant
and healthy voice. Now, on the contrary, its song
sounded weak—not so much as though the voice
were depressed as though in the voice there were
something cracked and broken—as though the poor
little voice could not right itself and the song,
consequently, were ailing. She sang *mezza voce,*
until suddenly, when the pitch rose, the voice broke
—oh, that pitiful little voice, with the wistful break
in it! She stopped to cough, and then again—
softly, softly, and hardly so as to be heard—she
went on singing. . . .

You may smile at my agitation, but no one can
understand the reason of it. No, I was not sorry

for her—it was something quite different to that. During the first few moments, as I listened, there suddenly dawned in me a strange sort of doubt, a strange sort of surprise—doubt and surprise at once curious and terrible, at once painful and almost vindictive. "She is singing in my presence!" I thought to myself. "She has forgotten all about me!"

Shaking from head to foot, I remained rooted to the spot. Then I rose, took up my hat, and left the flat as though oblivious of everything. At all events I know not why or whither I went out. Lukeria helped me on with my coat.

"She is singing, then?" involuntarily I said to Lukeria. She did not understand, but continued gazing at me in a doubtful way. Indeed, I must have seemed quite unintelligible!

"Is this the first time that she has sung?" I went on.

"No; sometimes she has sung when you have been out," Lukeria answered.

How well I remember it all! I went on down the staircase into the street, and set forth at random. I halted at a street corner, and stood gazing before me. People jostled me as they passed, but I felt nothing. Suddenly I called a cab, and directed it to the Police Bridge—I do not know why. Next, I as suddenly leapt from the vehicle, and gave the driver twenty kopecks.

"This is for putting you about so much," I said with a meaningless smile. Yet in my heart I was beginning to feel a sort of elation.

I returned home hurriedly. The poor quavering, broken little note of the song was still in my soul, and catching at my breath. The curtain had fallen from my eyes. Since she could sing in my presence she had forgotten all about me—that was terribly clear to my mind. My heart was conscious of nothing else. Yet there was also rapture shining in my soul, and overcoming my doubts.

o

Oh, the irony of fate! Nothing else had my soul contained during the winter, or could it have contained, but rapture: yet where was *I myself*? Had *I* lived in that soul? I ran up the staircase and entered the flat—though whether with or without diffidence I do not know. I only remember that the floor seemed to be heaving in front of me, and that I swam in it as in a river. I entered the bedroom, to find her sewing where she had been before. Her head was still bent over her work, but she had ceased now to sing. She threw a cursory, incurious glance at me, of the ordinary, indifferent kind which one bestows upon a person entering a room.

I went up to her, and sat down by her side, like a man in a trance. She threw a swift glance at me—a sort of frightened look. I took her by the hand, and said something or another to her, but I know not what. That is to say, I *tried* to say something, for I could not speak connectedly—my voice kept breaking off and becoming inaudible, until I found myself at a loss for words and was reduced to sighs.

"Let us talk together. Say something," I murmured confusedly. Was I at that moment in my right mind? She shuddered a little, and drew back, with a pronounced alarm in her features as she regarded me. Then suddenly a look of stern surprise showed itself in her eyes—yes, of stern surprise as she gazed at me with those great eyes of hers. That look of astonishment, coupled with severity, completely unnerved me. "Have you any love for me still—any love?" was the question underlying that surprise, though she did not utter it. Yet *I* could read it, *I* could read it. My whole self seemed to tremble as I flung myself at her feet. Yes, I simply grovelled before her. She sprang up, but I caught her hands, and restrained her with extraordinary eagerness.

I quite understood this frenzy of mine. Yet—would you believe it?—rapture was so bubbling in my heart that I thought every moment would be my last. I kissed her feet in a transport of delight —yes, of delight, boundless and infinite, though coupled with an entire comprehension of my rapture. I wept, I tried to say something or other, but I could not utter the words. Then to fear and astonishment there suddenly succeeded, in her, a sort of anxious reflectiveness, a sort of questioning attitude, as she threw me a strange, and even a wild, look, as of one striving to comprehend something quickly. Then she smiled, as though she were filled with embarrassment at my kissing her feet, and drew them away from me. Nevertheless I even went on kissing the floor where they had rested. Presently, when she perceived this, she laughed with renewed embarrassment (you know how people laugh under such circumstances), until hysterics began to show themselves. I could see her hands trembling, but I paid no heed to that as I went on murmuring that I loved her, and that I would not get up from the floor.

"Only let me kiss your dress," I muttered, "and pray for you all my life."

I do not know—I do not remember clearly—but at all events she began to tremble all over, and then burst into sobbing. Finally the hysterical fit overcame her completely, for she was in a very nervous condition.

I picked her up, and carried her to bed. When the fit had passed she sat up, and, with a strangely moved countenance, seized my hands, and besought me to calm myself. "Quieter, then; do not worry," she said, and fell to weeping again. Never that evening did I leave her, but kept saying that I would take her to Boulogne for a course of the baths—now, at once, at most in a fortnight's time; that her voice was hoarse; that I had heard her cough; that I would shut up the loan office; that I would sell it to Dobronravov; that everything should begin anew; above all things, that we would go to

Boulogne, to Boulogne. She listened, yet seemed afraid. Indeed, she grew more and more so. But for me the important point was not that fact, but the fact that more and more the desire was growing upon me to prostrate myself at her feet, and to kiss and kiss the floor on which they rested, and to beseech her, and to——

"More than that, I ask nothing of you, nothing of you," I kept repeating. "Do not answer me, do not take any notice of me, but grant me only a corner whence I may look upon you, where I may be your property, where I may be your dog." But she only wept.

"I—I thought that you meant to leave me like this," came from her in a sudden, involuntary outburst—in an outburst so wholly involuntary that perhaps she did not know what she was saying. Yet, of all words that she had said that evening, these were, for me, the first and foremost, the most fateful, the most explanatory. They cut me to the heart as with a knife. They explained to me everything, everything. And, in view of the fact that she was here beside me—here, before my very eyes—they filled me with inextinguishable hope and marvellous happiness. I must have wearied her terribly that evening—indeed, I knew that I was doing so; yet I could not rid myself of the expectation that presently I was about to achieve *all*. At last, towards nightfall, her strength gave way. I persuaded her to go to sleep, and she did so, and slept soundly. Yet I expected fever, and, sure enough, it came—though only in a light form. Almost every minute throughout the night I arose, and went softly in my slippers to look at her. Yes, I wrung my hands as I stood gazing at the poor sick being who was lying prone upon the sorry little iron bedstead which I had bought for her for three roubles. Often I would go down upon my knees beside her, yet never dared to kiss the sleeper's feet without her permission. Next I began to say a prayer to God, but it was not long before I rose again. Lukeria kept an ever-watchful eye upon me, and was for ever coming out of her kitchen. At length I went to her, and told her to go to bed, since to-morrow we were going to "begin everything anew."

And, indeed, I so believed—believed it blindly, senselessly, and with absolute assurance. What rapture, what rapture possessed me! I waited only for to-morrow, for to-morrow. I foresaw no catastrophe, despite all the symptoms. Sense had not yet wholly returned to me, though the curtain had fallen; nor for a long while afterwards did it return. No, it was not until to-day, until to-day, that it returned. How, indeed, could it have returned to me *then*? *She* was still alive before my eyes, *she* was still present to my sight, as I to hers. "To-morrow," I said to myself, "she will ask of me pardon, and I shall tell her everything, and she will understand *all*." That was my expectation—clear and simple it was—for I was beside myself. Above all things I thought of the expedition to Boulogne. Somehow I expected Boulogne to mean everything —I expected Boulogne to be going to be the scene of the ultimate climax. "To Boulogne, to Boulogne!" I kept saying, and awaited the morrow with feverish impatience.

CHAPTER III

I UNDERSTAND BUT TOO WELL

ALL this took place a few days ago—but five, only five days ago. Yes, it all happened last Tuesday. It needed such a little while longer—such a mere atom of time—for the mist to be dissipated! Did she never become wholly reassured? Yet she listened to me next day with a smile, despite her confusion—and, mark you, during all the rest of the time (that is to say, during the last five days) I clearly perceived in her a sort of confusion, a sort of shamefacedness. She was afraid of me—yes, she was very much afraid of me. I will not dispute nor contradict that fact as a fool would do. Fear had full possession of her. Indeed, why should it not have had? We had been so long estranged from one another—had become so unfamiliar to one another—and then for *this* to happen! However, I paid no heed to her nervousness, for everything was bathed in new light for me. Without doubt I erred. Maybe I erred *frequently*. I erred the moment that we awoke next morning (it was Wednesday). I erred in making her my friend so soon. I was in too great a hurry over it. Further probation was needed, was absolutely indispensable. Yet what further probation was necessary? That morning I revealed to her that I had been living a secret life. I told her bluntly that, throughout the winter, my one aim had been to assure myself of her love. I explained to her that the loan office was a mere lapse of my will, of my better sense—that it was a mere personal notion of self-mortification and laudation. I made it clear to her that I had *really* been a coward that night in the theatre buffet, owing to the diffidence inseparable from my character. I was confused by my surroundings, by the buffet, by the doubt lest, if I intervened, I should intervene awkwardly. It was not the duel which I feared, but the risk of making a fool of myself. Yet I had never since tried to realise that fact, but had distressed myself on its account, and now had married her in order to distress her also. In fact, much of what I said to her that morning I spoke as in a delirium. She clasped me by the hand, and begged of me to cease. "You are exaggerating," she said. "You do but distress yourself," and again the tears flowed, and the fits of hysterics began, as she prayed me to say no more about it, to recall no more recollections.

But I paid no attention to her prayers—or only

very little. "Spring! Boulogne! *There* we shall
see the sun, our *new* sun!" was all that I could
say. I closed up the office, and handed over the
business to Dobronravov. Next I proposed to my
wife that we should give everything to the poor,
except the capital of 3000 roubles which I had
received from my godmother, and which I intended
to use for our trip to Boulogne; after which we
would return, and begin a life of purely manual toil.
That was what I proposed, but to it she said nothing
—she only smiled. I think it was out of politeness,
and to avoid offending me, that she smiled. I could
see that I wearied her—do not think me so stupid
and egotistical as not to have seen that. I saw
everything, down to the minutest detail—I saw and
was conscious of everything better than any one else
could be : but before my eyes there stood also the
vision of my happiness.

I talked of her, and of myself, and of Lukeria.
I said that I had wept—but no, I changed the
subject, and took care not to refer to that and certain
other matters. Once or twice she gathered a little
animation, I remember—yes, how well I remember
it ! (For could any one truly say that I saw and
understood nothing?). Indeed, had *this* not happened, all would have gone well. Only three days
ago the conversation turned upon reading, and upon
the fact that *she* had been reading during the winter,
and she actually laughed as she related to me the
scene between Gil Blas and the Archbishop of
Grenada ! Yes, she related it to me with the same
gentle, childlike smile as in the days when I was
courting her. How delighted I felt ! Yet I could
not help also feeling *this* about the story of the
Archbishop—that if she had only had sufficient
happiness and peace of mind to laugh at such
literary masterpieces during the winter it would have
been better ! Perhaps she had felt too resigned to the
belief that I meant to "leave" her "like this." "I
—I thought you meant to leave me like *this*," was

what she said to me last Tuesday. Oh, the mind of a girl in her teens! She really believed that I was going to "leave" her "like this"—with her sitting at her table, and myself at mine, until we were sixty! Yet here was I suddenly approaching her as a husband—as a husband who desired love! Oh, the blindness, the stupidity, of me!

Another error that I made was in looking upon her so unconstrainedly. I ought to have kept myself in hand, for transports only frightened her. Had I kept myself in hand I should never have done such things as, for instance, kiss her feet. I ought never to have displayed the least sign of being her *husband;* for, indeed, I was not so—I was only praying to be so. Yet I could not altogether keep silence; I could not omit to say a single word. For instance, all of a sudden I told her that her conversation enchanted me, and that she was incomparably cleverer and better-informed than I was. At this she reddened very much, and said, in a confused way, that I was exaggerating. Then, like a fool destitute of self-control, I told her how enraptured I had been when I was standing behind the closed doors of the room, and listening to her duel with Efimovitch—to the duel between her purity and that libertine—and how charmed I had been with her good sense and sparkling wit, coupled with childish simplicity. She gave a sort of shudder, and once more murmured that I was exaggerating. Then her face clouded, and, covering her face with her hands, she burst into tears. At this I could not contain myself—I went down upon my knees before her, and fell to kissing her feet again until the same kind of fit as had seized her on Tuesday put an end to the scene. This happened last night; and in the morning——

In the morning? Why, fool that I am, it was *this morning*—though a long while ago, such a long while ago!

Listen, and try to understand. When, that long,

long while ago (though it was only after her fit of yesterday), we met at supper I was struck by the calmness of her bearing, and all night through I lay throbbing with passionate expectation of the morrow. When the morrow arrived she came to me, and, clasping her hands together, told me she had done wrong; that she knew it but too well; that her wrong-doing had been torturing her all the winter, and was torturing her now; and that she valued my nobility of character beyond all words. "Henceforth I will be a faithful wife to you—I will always honour you," she said. And I—I leapt up, and embraced her like a madman. I kissed her—I kissed her face and lips—as her *husband*, and for the first time since our long estrangement had begun. Then I went out for a couple of hours, to arrange about our passports for abroad. My God, if only I had returned five minutes, just five minutes, sooner! Oh, the crowd at our door—oh, the looks thrown at me! My God!

Lukeria has told me (and I can never now let Lukeria go, since she knows all—she has been with me all the winter—she will be able to explain things to me), Lukeria has told me that, while I was out this morning, she went to my wife some twenty minutes before my return, to ask her some question or another (I do not remember what). She found that my wife had taken her little ikon (that little ikon there of the Holy Mother) out of its case, and placed it on the table before her, and that she seemed to be praying to it.

"What are you doing, *barina* [1]?" said Lukeria.

"Nothing, Lukeria; go away," replied my wife. "Stop a moment, though, Lukeria," she added, and then went up to her and kissed her.

"Are you happy?" asked Lukeria.

"Yes, Lukeria."

"Your husband ought to have come to you long ago to ask your pardon," Lukeria went on.

---

[1] Mistress or lady.

"God be thanked that at last you have become reconciled."

"Yes, it is a good thing," replied my wife. "Now go, Lukeria," and she smiled at her, though with a look so strange that, ten minutes later, Lukeria returned to watch her.

"She was standing against the wall, by the window," Lukeria has since told me, "with her arm resting against the wall, and her head bowed upon her arm. Yes, she was standing there and thinking. So deep in thought was she wrapped that she never heard me come and stand looking at her from the other room. I saw her give a kind of smile as she stood there—a kind of smile at her own thoughts. After watching her a little while I turned and went away. I too was thinking my own thoughts, when I heard the window open. At once I ran to tell her that the weather was cold, and that she must not catch a chill—when all at once I perceived that she had climbed upon the window-sill, and was standing, drawn to her full height, in the opening, with her back to me and her hands clasping her ikon. My heart seemed to stop, and I called out to her, "*Barina, barina!*" She heard me, and made a movement as though to turn round; but she did not actually turn—she just took a step forward, clasped her ikon to her breast, and threw herself from the window!"

I only remember that when I entered the yard gates she was still warm, and, above all things, that her eyes were turned towards me. At first there was a great outcry, but all at once a stillness supervened, the crowd parted before me, and—I saw *her* lying there, with her crucifix! I remember that I approached her as in a dream, and stood gazing upon her face. At intervals people approached me and said something, but I did not see even Lukeria—though she too was there. She tells me that she spoke to me, but I only recollect a gentleman who kept crying out, "It is the rush of blood from her

mouth that has choked her—the rush of blood from
her mouth," as he pointed to the blood on the stones.
I think he must have touched that blood with his
finger, and smeared himself a little, for I remember
seeing blood on his finger as he repeated the words
"that has choked her, that has choked her."

"What do you mean by ' choked her '? " I shouted
(so they tell me) as I rushed upon him with my fists
clenched.

Oh, it was terrible, terrible ! It was all such a
misunderstanding, it was all so unlikely, it was all
so impossible !

CHAPTER IV

HOW I WAS FIVE MINUTES TOO LATE

WAS it not, then? Was it likely? Can any one
say that it was possible? Why should this woman
have died?

Oh, believe me, I understand the matter as a
whole : yet it still remains a question why she killed
herself. It must have been because she was frightened by my amorousness—because she asked herself
seriously, "To consent or not to consent? " and,
unable to face the problem, preferred death. Yes,
I know it, I know it; there is no need to conjecture
further. By her promise to me she had under-
taken overmuch, and was frightened lest she should
not be able to perform it. All that is clear. It
explains at least *some* of these terrible circumstances.

Yet still it remains a question why she died. The
question keeps knocking and knocking at my brain.
I would have left her "like this " had she so wished
it. She did not trust me—that is it. Nay, but it is
not so. It was simply that, in my case, she would
have felt bound to be true, to love wholly, and not
as she would have loved that merchant; and inasmuch as she was too chaste, too pure, to agree to

such love as the merchant wanted she refused to
deceive me.   She would not cheat me with half-love
under the guise of love—still less with quarter-love.
She was too honourable—yes, that is it.   But, in
time, could I have instilled into her any greater
breadth of affection?   Nay, but that is an outrageous
thought !

Again, it interests me terribly to wonder, Did
she respect me?—for, indeed, I cannot rightly tell
whether she did so or not.   I never thought to
have been *despised* by her.   Yet why did it never
occur to me, the winter through, that she despised
me?   I was certain of the opposite only until the
occasion when she turned and looked at me with
that sternness and surprise in her face.   Yes, sternness especially.   *Then* I divined that she despised
me—I divined it irrefutably and for ever.   Ah, she
might have despised me, despised me all her life, if
only she would have gone on living !   Only a short
while ago she was walking and talking in this
room !   I cannot understand why she should have
thrown herself from the window.   How was I to
guess, even for a minute, that she was going to do
so?—I have just sent for Lukeria.   I could never
now let Lukeria go.

Oh, surely we might have come to some agreement?   We had been terribly estranged from one
another all the winter, yet could we not have become
intimates again?   Why could we not have come
together and begun a new life?   I was ready to
forgive, and so was she : *there* was our point of
union.   Only a few words, only a couple of days,
more—just that—and she would have understood
everything !

Above all things I am ashamed that this should
have happened so simply, so cruelly, so entirely
through my own tardiness.   In that lies the chief
shame of it—that I was too late by five minutes to
prevent her.   Had I returned five minutes earlier, the
crisis would have passed away like a cloud, and the

idea would never have occurred to her. It would all have ended in her understanding everything. But now there are only empty rooms here—now once more I am alone. The pendulum of the clock keeps beating, but it is not needed now, and no one heeds it. No one is here but sorrow.

I keep walking and walking about. Yes, I know, I know—you need not prompt me : I know that you think it ridiculous that I should be regretting the mischance of those five minutes. Yet at least I should have witnessed the affair. Just consider : she left nothing in writing behind her to say, "No one is to blame for my death," as people usually do. Did it never occur to her that it might be said to Lukeria, "You alone were with her at the time. *You* may have pushed her off the window-sill"? Yes, Lukeria might have been wrongfully accused had not no less than four persons seen (from the windows of the wing, and from the courtyard) my wife standing on the window-sill, with her ikon in her hands, and then throwing herself over. It was a mere chance that those four persons happened to be standing and looking at her. No, no; it must have come of an impulse on her part—of some irresponsible impulse. Oh, the fantastic unexpectedness of things ! What was she praying for when she was kneeling there by the table before the crucifix? It need not mean that she was then contemplating death. The impulse may have lasted ten minutes at the most—lasted only during the time when she was leaning against the wall, with her head on her arms, and smiling. Then the idea suddenly flashed into her brain—she turned giddy—and the idea was no longer to be withstood.

It was all a misunderstanding. She might have been alive with me now. What if it were mere giddiness, mere weakness of the vital force, that made her do it? The winter had enfeebled her. Yes, that must be it.

But I was too late ! ! !

How wasted she looks in her coffin—how sharp-
ened are her little features! Her eyelashes lie prone
upon her cheeks like arrows. It is as though she
had pined away. Her brains have not been
dashed out, nor has a bone been broken. There
was only that "rush of blood from the mouth"—
and only a dessert-spoonful at that! Internal
injuries, clearly. It is a curious thought, but what
if I should be able to prevent them from burying
her? If they should take her away—oh, but it is
almost impossible that they should take her away!
Yet I know that she must go. I am not mad, nor
yet in a fever. On the contrary, I have never in
my life been so sane. But to think that once more
there will be no one in the house, once more only
the two empty rooms, once more only I in my lonely
office! Oh, the fever, the fever of the thought that
I should have distressed her so!

What to me are your laws? What concern have
I with your customs, your morals, your life, your
State, your religion? Let your judges judge me;
hale me before your courts—before your egregious
justices. I will yet assert that I recognise *none* of
them. The judge may cry aloud to me, "Be silent,
officer!" but *I* will cry aloud to *him*, "Where is
your authority which can make me obey you? Why
has a halting mystery destroyed all that was dearest
in my eyes? What care I for your laws? Hereby
I cut myself off from them!" Oh, it will not matter
much to me.

You are blind, my wife—blind! You are dead,
and cannot hear me. You do not know with what
a paradise I would have surrounded you. Paradise
was in my heart, and around you too I would have
planted it. Perhaps you would not have loved me,
but what of that? It might have remained "like
this" had you wished it—it might *always* have
remained "like this." You might have spoken to
me only as a friend. We should still have been
joyous, and have laughed as we gazed into one

another's eyes. Thus we would have lived. And if you had loved another—well, it might have been so, it might have been so. You might have walked with him, and have laughed with him, and I would have looked at you from the other side of the street. Oh, it might all have been so if only you would open your eyes again!—for one moment—only for one moment! You might gaze on me as when, but a short while ago, you were standing here before me, and swearing to be my faithful wife! Oh, and in that one glance you would understand everything!

O void, O nature! Only men dwell upon the earth —and therein lies the calamity of it. "Is there in all the plain a man alive?" cries an old Russian hero. It is *I* who am crying that now—not a hero; yet there is no one to answer to my call. They say that the sun puts life into the universe. He rises, and one beholds him. Yet is not *he* dead also? Everything is dead, and dead men are everywhere. Only human beings are here, and over them there broods a silence. *That* is the world. "Men, love one another." Who said that? Whose command was it? The pendulum continues beating insensibly, malignantly. It is two o'clock in the morning. Her little boots stand there by the bed, as though awaiting her. Ah, but, in very truth, when they take her away to-morrow, what will become of me?

THE LANDLADY

PART I

I

At length Ordinov had to make up his mind to change his lodgings, since his landlady—the poor widow of a civil service official—unexpectedly found herself obliged to leave St. Petersburg, and to repair to her parents' house in the country without waiting for the first day of the month—the day when her tenancy was to expire. As the young man had hitherto had every expectation of completing his sub-tenancy with her, he was a good deal put out at this sudden eviction from his den. Besides, he was poor, and lodgings were dear. So, the day before his landlady left, he took his cap, and set forth into the back streets of the capital. As he went along he examined every bill of rooms to let which he saw affixed to a door; always choosing, for his purpose, the most dilapidated, the largest, and the most crowded of buildings, as places where he had the best chance of encountering not only such a room as he wanted, but also tenants who were as poor as himself.

Although for a time he held strictly to his quest, certain new and strange feelings gradually began to steal over him. At first in an absent-minded sort of way, then with some attention, and, lastly, with great curiosity he set himself to take note of his surroundings. The crowds, the din and life of the streets, the bustle and movement around him, the many unfamiliar sights which he beheld, his unfamiliar position—all this petty material of a daily existence which merely wearies the active, pre-occupied *habitué* of St. Petersburg in a strenuous and constant, but vain, struggle for rest and quiet

in the home which he has won by labour or otherwise—all this prosaic tedium and *banalité* evoked
in Ordinov's breast, rather, a sensation of calm,
bright cheerfulness. His pale cheeks took on a
faint tinge of colour, and his eyes shone with
new hope as he greedily inhaled deep draughts of
the chill, fresh air. Somehow he seemed to himself
extraordinarily light.

The life he had hitherto led had been a quiet,
absolutely solitary one. Three years ago, on taking
a university degree and becoming practically his own
master, he had been summoned to the house of an
old man whom hitherto he had known only by name.
There he had waited until at length the liveried
servant had condescended to announce his presence;
after which he had entered a lofty, dimly-lighted
drawing-room which was almost bare of furniture—
a room of the depressing type which is still to be
met with in old mansions which stand as survivals
from the epoch of great families and seigniorial
houses. In this room he had found himself confronted by a much-bemedalled, grey-haired dotard
—the friend and colleague of Ordinov's father, and
Ordinov's guardian—who had handed to his ward
what seemed to the latter a very small sum, as
representing a legacy derived from some property
which had just been sold under the hammer, to
liquidate a debt incident upon his grandfather's
estate. Ordinov had received the money with indifference, taken his first and last leave of his guardian, and departed. The evening had been a cold,
misty one in autumn, and Ordinov had felt in a
meditative mood, for a sort of unconscious depression had been chafing his heart. Also, his eyes had
been burning with fever, and every moment he could
feel hot and cold shivers running down his body.
He had calculated that, with the sum just received,
he could subsist for two, for three, or, if he stinted
himself carefully, even for four years. But darkness
was now coming on, and rain was falling, so he had

hired the first room which he had come across, and within an hour had moved his effects into it. There he had shut himself up as in a monastery where men renounced the world; and before two years were over he had become, to all intents and purposes, a savage.

Yes, he became a savage unawares. Of the fact that there might be *another* existence—an existence full of sound and fury, and constantly seething and changing—the existence which eternally appeals to a man and, sooner or later, absorbs him, since it will take no denial—he had not an inkling. True, it was not that he had never heard of it; it was, rather, that he had never himself known it, and had never sought such knowledge. From infancy upwards he had been sunk in a state of mental isolation which had gradually become confirmed through the fact of its being swallowed up by the deepest and most insatiable of all passions; by the passion which exhausts the vital forces without according such beings as Ordinov any foothold in the sphere of practical, everyday, strenuous activity. That passion was love of learning. Like a slow poison it was corroding his youth, destroying his capacity for sleep, and injuring his appetite both for healthy sustenance and for the fresh air which occasionally penetrated to his narrow retreat. Yet his state of morbid exaltation had never allowed of his noticing these things. He was young, and his wants were modest. Indeed, his passion for books had already rendered him an infant as regards any fitting of him for competition with his peers whenever it should become necessary for him to win a place in their ranks. In the hands of its more skilful devotees science is so much capital; whereas Ordinov's scientific devotion was a weapon which he was turning against himself.

Moreover, this devotion of his was an unconscious abstraction rather than a logically thought-out means for the acquisition of knowledge and culture; and

the same peculiarity had marked every other pursuit
—even the most petty—in which he had engaged.
From his earliest days he had had a reputation for
singularity, as being a boy between whom and his
comrades there was nothing in common. Parents he
had never known, and his strange, retiring nature
had earned for him, at school, much bad treatment
and brutality. Consequently, thrown back upon
himself, he had come to be shy, morose, and practically a world of his own. Yet in his solitary
pursuits there had not, at first, been any system or
ordered routine—everything had represented only
the first raptures, the first enthusiasms, the first
fever of an artist; but now he had created for himself a system which had grown with the years until
in his soul it had come to establish a vague, a dim,
yet a perfectly comfortable, form of ideas which were
gradually undergoing incarnation into such a new
and brilliant shape as his soul at once yearned for
and found a burden. Already he was faintly conscious of the originality of this form—of its truth
and of its power to stand alone. It was a creation
which corresponded to his strength; it was one which
was gradually materialising; it was one which was
ever gathering unto itself new vigour. But the term
of its incarnation and final fulfilment was yet a long
way off—perhaps a *very* long way off—perhaps
altogether beyond reach!

So this afternoon he walked the streets like a
stranger—like an ascetic who has left his dumb
solitude for the din and bustle of a town. Everything seemed to him novel and unfamiliar. Yet so
unused was he to this world which boiled and seethed
around him that he had no room even for astonishment at his own sensations. He had ceased now to
feel ill at ease, but, on the contrary, was filled with
a joy, an intoxication, which can be compared only
to that of a starving man who has just been given
meat and drink. Was it not curious that so trivial
a turn of fortune as a change of lodgings should be

able thus to agitate and bewilder an *habitué* of St.
Petersburg like Ordinov? The truth is that he had
hardly ever before been called upon to go out on a
business errand.

With increasing delight he pursued his way
through the streets; looking at everything in a
critical way, and, faithful to his mental habit, reading the pictures which unrolled themselves before
him in the same manner that a person reads between
the lines of a book. Everything made an impression
upon him, and not a single impression escaped him
as, with thoughtful gaze, he scanned the faces of the
passers-by, and also listened to any conversation
which was going on around him, as though he
wished to prove the conclusions at which, during
the quiet meditations of his lonely nights, he had
arrived. Frequently some new trifle would catch his
attention, and give rise to a new idea; whereupon
he would, for the first time in his life, feel vexed
that he should have buried himself alive in his
solitary cell. Everything here seemed to move
faster. Here his pulse beat more quickly and
vigorously; here his intellect, which solitude had
but cramped, seemed to be whetted and cheered
with its own intense, exultant activity, until it
worked with swift precision and assurance. He
would have liked to have plunged straight into all
this strange life which, as yet, had been wholly
unknown to him—or, rather, had been known to him
only through his artistic sense. His heart beat with
a gust of involuntary love and sympathy as eagerly
he set himself to consider the passers-by. Yet suddenly he perceived that some of them looked anxious
and absorbed! At this revelation his composure
vanished, and the reality of things began to impress
him with a sense of respect. He felt himself growing weary of the flood of new impressions which had
come upon him, in much the same manner that a
sick man, after walking a tentative step or two,
suddenly falls to the ground—blinded by the glitter

and sparkle and turmoil of life, stunned by the roar
of human activity, and confused by the sounds
emitted by the ever-changing, ever-seething crowd
around him.   By degrees Ordinov began to distrust
both the tendencies and activities of his present life
and his prospects for the future.   A thought which
particularly troubled him was the circumstance that
always he had been alone in the world, without love
or the prospect of love.   For example, some few
passers-by whom, early in his walk, he had tried
to engage in conversation had turned from him with
an air of *brusquerie* and estrangement (which,
indeed, they had some reason to do); and instantly
he had remembered that confidences of his had
always been repelled in this way, and that throughout his boyhood persons had invariably avoided him
as a youth of dogged, abstracted temperament.   In
short, he found himself struck with the fact that his
sympathy had never known any method of self-
disclosure than through ambiguous, painful efforts
which were devoid of moral balance.   Above all
things it had been the constant sorrow of his youth
to realise that he was unlike such other boys as were
his equals in age; and now that he remembered this
he made up his mind that always, and for ever, he
would find himself avoided—find himself left to his
own devices.

Insensibly he wandered into an outlying suburban
district; where, having dined at a shabby restaurant,
he resumed his perambulations.   Behind him
stretched long rows of grey and yellow walls, while,
in front, decrepit shanties were beginning to take
the place of the richer mansions, with, among them,
towering buildings cheek by jowl with factories—
buildings which were monstrous, blackened, reddish
in colour, and topped by tall chimneys.   Here the
prospect was empty and desolate; everything, to
Ordinov's eye, looked sullen and unfriendly under
the approach of night.   Traversing a long alley-way,
he issued into a square which encompassed a church.

Hardly knowing what he was doing, he entered the sacred edifice. A service had just come to an end, and the building was practically empty, save for two old women who were still kneeling near the entrance, and the verger (a little old man) who was engaged in extinguishing the candles. The slanting rays of the sun were throwing great waves of colour through the narrow windows of the dome, and flooding one of the transepts with a sea of light as they slowly ebbed; while the shadows, growing darker and darker as they massed themselves under the arches, were causing the gilt on the sacred images to glitter the more brightly in the intermittent, reddish gleam of lamps and candles. A prey to painful emotions and a sort of crushed feeling, Ordinov seated himself against the wall in one of the darkest corners of the church, and for a moment sank into oblivion. Presently he was recalled to himself by the sound of two persons entering the building with dull, measured footsteps. Looking up, he felt an indefinable curiosity possess him. The newcomers were an old man and a girl. The former —a man who, though tall, vigorous, and upright, was sadly wasted and unhealthily pale—might have been a merchant from some remote province. Clad in a long coat of black fur which, unfastened, showed a tunic neatly buttoned from chin to waist, he had his bare neck swathed in a scarlet muffler, and in his hand a fur cap. A long grey beard covered his breast, and from under menacing, bushy eyebrows his glance shone with a feverish light and a sort of slow, yet haughty and penetrating, air. As for the girl, she might have been about twenty. Marvellously beautiful, and dressed in a jacket of some rich, dark, glossy fur, with a white satin scarf tied over her head and knotted under her chin, she walked with her eyes cast down and a sort of meditative gravity on her face which imparted to the tender, gentle lines of her childlike countenance a sort of clear-cut, yet mournful, air. Somehow to

Ordinov there seemed something strange in the
aspect of this couple.

When half-way up the aisle, the old man halted,
and made the sign of the cross towards every side
of him, although the church was now empty. His
companion did the same. Then he took her by the
hand, and led her towards the statue of the Virgin,
the Lady Patroness of the church. The image stood
near the altar, and its ornaments of precious stones
and brilliant gold were glittering with a dazzling
sheen. The verger greeted the stranger with a
respectful bow, and was accorded, in return, a slight
acknowledgment of his salute; after which the young
girl fell upon her knees before the statue, and, the
old man having taken a church napkin and covered
her head with it, a sound of deep sobbing became
audible throughout the building.

So fascinated was Ordinov by the solemnity of the
scene that he awaited the end of it with impatience.
After a moment or two the girl raised her head, and
her beautiful face again shone clear under the light
of the lamps. Ordinov trembled, and advanced a
step or two, but she had now taken the old man's
arm, and was turning with him to leave the church.
Hot tears were still welling from her dark-blue eyes
(the long, pendant lashes of which stood out clearly
against the creamy whiteness of her complexion), and
running over her pale cheeks. True, there seemed
to be a smile on her lips, but her face bore traces of
a sort of childish, mysterious fear as, trembling with
emotion, she clung confidingly to the old man's arm.

Greatly agitated, and filled with a pleasurable
sensation which he could not repress, Ordinov
hastened after the couple, and overtook them on the
church *plaza*. The old man turned towards him with
a meaning scowl, and the girl too threw him a
glance, but only an incurious one which clearly
showed that her mind was occupied with something
else. For some reason which he could not account
for Ordinov still continued to follow the couple—

though at a distance, and under cover of the fast-gathering twilight. Turning into a long, dirty street near the fortifications, in the artisan quarter—a crowded street full of lodging-houses and corn-chandlers' establishments—they presently debouched into a narrow alley-way between two blank walls, and continued onwards until before them there rose the high, blackened walls of a four-storeyed building, the gates of which fronted upon a second long and populous street. As the three pedestrians approached this building the old man again turned round, and fixed Ordinov with an impatient stare. The young man halted, and stood rooted to the spot, for even to himself his impulse seemed a strange one. After giving him another look, as though to make sure that the silent menace had had its effect, the old man entered, with the young girl, the courtyard of the building, while Ordinov hastened to return homewards.

As he walked along he felt in a very bad humour, and severely reproached himself for having embarked upon a fatiguing expedition which had resulted only in the folly of painting an excessively trifling incident in all the colours of an adventure. Although, that morning, he had regretted having led such a secluded life, it was his instinct, rather, to avoid anything which could influence or distract or disturb his mind in its external and artificial world. Now, however, his mind turned gloomily, half-regretfully, to his solitary retreat, and he began to feel anxious and depressed about his indefinite position there, and all the worries which that involved. Also it irritated him to think that any such trifle could catch his attention. Indeed, it was only because he was so overcome with fatigue as to be incapable of properly connecting his ideas that at length he realised with a start that he had walked past the door of his abode. Irritably tossing his head at the thought that he had so far let his thoughts wander, and attributing his error to sheer weariness, he

climbed the staircase, and entered his garret. There
he lit a candle. Hardly, however, had he done so
when the image of the young girl came back to his
memory. So vivid, so strong was his impression
of her—so eagerly did he, in his mind's eye, set
himself to trace the gentle, tender lines of the face
which had been so agitated with fear, yet had had
such a mysterious affection shining through the tears
of its exaltation and childlike contrition—that his
eyes smarted, and fire rushed into his veins. But
presently the vision disappeared, and to his rapture
there succeeded first reflection, then vexation, then
a sort of impotent rage. Without removing his
clothes, he covered himself over with a blanket,
and lay down upon his rough pallet.

The morning was far advanced when, in a confused, dejected frame of mind, he awoke. Making
a hasty toilet, and almost forcing himself to think
of the minutiæ of the day, he went out, but took
the opposite direction to the one which he had taken
the previous afternoon. To make an end of things
he pitched upon some lodgings kept by a poor
German named Schpis, who had a daughter,
Tinchen; after which, the deposit paid, Schpis
removed the "To Let" notice which he had nailed
to the door of the room, and complimented Ordinov
upon his passion for learning, while also promising
to do his best to make him comfortable. Ordinov
replied that he would take possession of the room
that evening, and then set out again for his old
abode. On the way a sudden thought struck him,
and he turned in another direction. A spirit of
daring had come upon him, and he smiled to himself at the temerity of his impulse. His impatience
made the way seem long, but at length he reached
the church of the previous evening, and found a
service being held there. Choosing a seat whence
he could see all the worshippers present, he soon
perceived that the one in particular whom he was
seeking was absent; and, though he waited for a

considerable time, he was at length forced shamefacedly to leave. To divert the current of his
thoughts he set himself to think of indifferent
matters, and, considering the trifles of life, suddenly
remembered that the luncheon hour had arrived.
Sufficiently hungry, he entered the same restaurant
as he had dined at the previous evening; after which
he resumed his long, unconscious wanderings
through streets and alley-ways full of people, and
through empty squares, until he had reached a broad
space which was completely bare of houses, and
covered over with withered turf. The utter silence
of the place recalled him to himself, and aroused in
him feelings which were new or had long lain
dormant. The day was dry and frosty, as is often
the case in St. Petersburg during the month of
October, and at a little distance he perceived a hut,
with, beside it, some ricks of hay and a pony which,
with head down and muzzle pendent, was standing,
unharnessed, near a cart, and seemed to be deep in
meditation. Beside a broken wheel a watchdog was
growlingly gnawing a bone, and a three-year-old
child—clad only in a shirt, and scratching, at intervals, a flaxen, dishevelled head—had come out to
stare at the stranger who had wandered so far afield.
Behind the hut there stretched a number of meadows
and market-gardens, while, prominent against the
blue sky, dark lines of trees enclosed the horizon.
In the opposite direction a bank of snow clouds was
driving before the breeze, and the cloudbank, in its
turn, seemed to be driving before it a flock of
migratory birds which, in single file and with raucous
cries, were passing swiftly across the zenith. Everything was still, everything seemed charged with a
sort of solemn sadness, everything seemed to be
feeling dull and uneasy. Ordinov walked on a little
way, but soon began to find the solitude oppressive,
and turned backwards towards the city. There he
suddenly heard a bell beginning to summon worshippers to evening prayer; wherefore, redoubling his

pace, he had soon reached the church which, during the last twenty-four hours, had become so familiar to his thoughts.

The Unknown was there already. She was kneeling near the entrance, among a knot of other worshippers. Ordinov edged his way through the serried ranks of beggars, ragged old women, and sick and infirm persons who were waiting at the door for alms, and knelt down by the young girl's side. Their clothes were actually touching, and he could hear her fluttering breath as it came wafted from her half-opened lips with each burning prayer. As before, her features were eloquent of nothing but piety; as before, her hot cheeks kept blushing under the tears which spent and dried themselves there, as though to cleanse away some terrible sin. All around was in deep shadow, save that at intervals the flame of a lamp, shaken by the draught which entered through a small open window, shot intermittent gleams over the face of the Unknown—over the face every feature of which was graven upon Ordinov's memory, torturing his sight, and rending his heart with unspeakable pain. At length, unable any longer to bear the weight which oppressed his bosom, he burst into a storm of sobbing which brought with it relief as he bowed his aching head to the cold floor of the church. Nothing at that moment could he hear or feel save the beating of his heart and the sensation of sweet torment into which his pain had merged.

Was it solitude that had developed in him this excessive receptivity to impressions, that had left his senses so open to attack? Were the seeds of that restlessness sown during the long, long nights when he lay without sleeping, without light or air? Were all these disordered impulses and passionate emotions of the soul a necessary condition for the heart to expand and find an outlet? Or, rather, was it that the time had suddenly come for things to be as they were now, even as, on an oppressively hot

day, the sky suddenly darkens, and discharges upon
the thirsty land a warm rain which hangs in drops
from the boughs, and refreshes the grass in the
fields, and bends to earth the delicate crowns of
the flowers; until at last, at the first gleam of sunshine, everything rises again, everything springs to
meet the light, everything shoots heavenwards in its
desire to celebrate the rebirth of nature in a sweet,
abundant flood of joy and healthfulness? Ordinov
could not account for his condition. Indeed, he could
scarcely recognise himself. Though only dimly
aware that the service was coming to an end, he
rose when it did so, and followed the girl through
the crowd of worshippers who were making for the
entrance. More than once he encountered her quiet,
wondering glance; more than once, when stopped by
the surging of the crowd, he saw her turn in his
direction. Every moment her agitation kept increasing. Then her cheeks suddenly flamed like the dawn
as the old man appeared and took her by the hand;
and for the third time Ordinov found himself raked
by a disdainful, menacing glance. At it his heart
grew heavy with a sort of sullen resentment. But
soon the Unknown became lost to his sight in the
darkness; whereupon, recovering himself with almost
a superhuman effort, he rushed forward, and left the
church. Even the fresh air scarcely helped to revive
him. He drew his breath with difficulty, and felt
as though he would suffocate, so slowly, yet loudly
—loudly enough almost to break his chest—was his
heart now beating. In vain he tried to pick up the
trail of the mysterious couple, but no one resembling
them was to be seen in street or alley. Yet an idea
had sprung to birth in his mind; there had begun
to germinate in his brain one of those bold, fool-
hardy schemes which, however senseless they may
be, almost invariably succeed on such occasions.

Next morning, at eight o'clock, he repaired to the
building where he knew the old man and the girl to
reside, and entered a narrow, dirty court which more

resembled a house-sewer than anything else. In this court he found working a *dvornik* [1]—a little fellow of Tartar origin who, though not more than twenty-five years of age, had a prematurely wrinkled, senile face. On perceiving Ordinov the *dvornik* desisted from his labours, rested his chin upon his arms, surveyed the newcomer from head to foot, and asked him what he wanted.

"I want a lodging," replied Ordinov briefly.

"Which one?" inquired the *dvornik* with a grin, and a look as though he could read Ordinov's thoughts.

"A lodging to *rent*, of course," retorted the other.

"Well, there are none to be had in *that* house," said the *dvornik*, indicating the next-door tenement with a derisive glance.

"And what about this one?"

"There are none to be had here either," said the *dvornik*, resuming his work.

"Perhaps they *will* let me have one, after all?" went on Ordinov, as at the same moment he slipped a *grivennik* [2] into the man's hand.

The Tartar glanced at Ordinov, pocketed the coin, and once more resumed his work. After a moment's silence he said with an air of finality—

"No; there are no lodgings to be had here."

But the young man had ceased to take any notice of him. Stepping carefully across the yielding, half-mouldy planks which spanned the kennel, he made his way towards the only entrance which gave upon the foul, black, mud-encumbered yard of the wing of the building. He found the ground floor to be tenanted by a coffin-maker, so, passing by the workshop of this artisan, he ascended a winding, dilapidated, slippery staircase to the next floor, where, groping about in the dark, he soon happened upon a rough, stout wooden door which was screened by some curtains of ragged matting. Lastly, after

[1] A house-porter.
[2] A twenty-kopeck piece (= about 5d.).

further search, he found the latch, and lifted it.
He had not been mistaken. Before him stood the
old man, gazing at him with an air of extreme
surprise.

"What do you want?" he asked brusquely, and
almost in a whisper.

"Have you a room to let?" murmured the other,
hardly knowing what he said, for the reason that
behind the old man's shoulders he had just caught
sight of the Unknown.

The old man silently made a move as though to
shut his visitor outside; but at that moment Ordinov
heard the caressing voice of the young girl murmur—

"Yes, there *is* a room to let."

Upon this the old man released his hold of the
door.

"I only want quite a small one," said Ordinov,
hastening to enter, and addressing himself exclusively
to the girl. Then he stopped short in stupefaction as
his eyes, for the first time, got a good view of his
future hosts. Before him there was taking place a
dumb, unspoken drama. The old man had turned
as pale as death, and looked almost ready to faint
as he trained upon the girl a leaden-eyed, yet steady
and penetrating, glance. She too had turned pale;
but presently the blood remounted to her face, and
her eyes flashed with a strange light as she conducted
Ordinov into a neighbouring apartment.

The place consisted of a single large room,
divided into three compartments by a couple of par-
tition-walls. From the entrance a lobby led into a
diminutive chamber wherein a door in the further
wall evidently led into a bedroom. The former of
these rooms was so small, with two low windows
placed close together, that even the smallest
essential articles had the appearance of being cum-
bersome. Despite its niggardliness, however, the
furniture—which consisted only of a white wooden
table, two chairs, and a couple of benches placed
against the wall—was extremely clean. In one

Q

corner, also, there stood a large ikon, adorned with a golden crown, and supported on a ledge; while in front of it there was burning a lamp. This apartment and the bedroom shared a large, clumsy store between them, and in every way the tenement seemed to be ill-adapted for the accommodation of three persons.

Ordinov and the girl fell to discussing terms, but disconnectedly, and with little comprehension of one another. Standing but two paces from her, he could plainly hear the beating of her heart, and see that she was trembling with emotion and a kind of fear. At length an agreement was come to, and, stating that he would go and fetch his impedimenta immediately, Ordinov glanced at the old man, who all this while had remained standing near the entrance —looking as pale as before, but with a quiet, almost a meditative, smile playing on his lips. As soon, however, as he saw that Ordinov was looking at him he bent his brows again.

"Have you got a passport?" he asked in a loud, rude voice as he opened the front door.

"Yes," said Ordinov in an absent-minded way.

"Who are you, then?"

"Vassilii Ordinov—a gentleman—of no occupation—engaged on my own affairs." Ordinov spoke as brusquely as the old man had done.

"Well, I am Ilia Murin—burgher. Is that all you want? You may go."

An hour later Ordinov found himself installed. This surprised him more than it did Herr Schpis, who, with the gentle Tinchen, had already begun to suspect that his lodger was going to fail him. Ordinov himself hardly knew how things had come about, but he did not trouble his head much on the subject.

II

Soon his heart began to beat so forcibly that his eyes ached and his head swam. Mechanically he set to work to put his scanty effects in order—first of all unpacking his portmanteau of necessaries, and then his box of books, which he arranged in rows upon the table. After a little while the task grew wearisome to him, and, on his desisting from it, there recurred to his blurred vision the image of the girl whose aspect had so shaken his soul, and to whom his heart had turned with such a convulsive, such an irresistible, impulse. So great had been the plethora of happiness which had come into his dull existence that his thoughts were all in confusion, and his spirit was plunged in uneasiness and gloom.

Presently he bethought him of taking his passport to his landlord, in the hope that he would once again see his beloved; but Murin merely opened the door a chink, took the paper, and said—

"Very well. Do not trouble me any more."

Then the door closed again. For a moment Ordinov stood dumbfounded. Somehow the aspect of the old man, with its look of concentrated hatred and malice, hurt his feelings; but almost as instantly the disagreeable impression passed away, and for the next three days he lived in a whirlwind which contrasted curiously with his old inertia. He had neither the power nor the will to reflect. Everything was, as it were, in chaos. He only knew that his life had snapped in two, and that he had no more than a single desire—namely, to wait, to wait. No other thought occurred to his mind.

He re-entered his room, and found engaged in cooking at the stove a little old hunchbacked woman who was so dirty and ragged that he really felt sorry for her. Also, her temper seemed to be bad, for she was muttering to herself, and constantly making grimaces. This was the maid-of-all-work. Ordinov

tried to engage her in conversation, but she remained
obstinately silent—evidently out of spite. When the
dinner hour was arrived she drew from the stove
some cabbage soup, rolls, and a piece of meat, and
carried them to her master's room; after which she
allotted Ordinov a similar portion. Dinner over,
complete silence reigned in the flat.

Ordinov took a book, and slowly turned the leaves
of it. Yet, though for a long while he tried to force
himself to understand what he was reading, he never
wholly succeeded in doing so. Impatiently he threw
the book aside, and once more tried to produce order
among his effects. Finally he took down his hat and
coat, and went out. He walked at random as he
endeavoured to recover himself, to collect his scat-
tered thoughts, and to take stock of the situation;
but the effort only served to increase his sufferings.
Hot flushes and cold shivers kept seizing upon him
by turns, so that at times his heart beat with a
violence which forced him to lean against a wall.

"I would rather be dead," he thought to himself.
"Yes, I would rather be dead." Yet his inflamed,
quivering lips hardly knew what they were saying.

On, on he walked, until at length he realised that
he was wet through, and that rain was falling in
torrents; whereupon he turned homewards. As he
drew near his new abode he caught sight of his
acquaintance the *dvornik*. At once he became seized
with an idea that the Tartar had looked at him with
extreme curiosity, and then pretended to move away
when he found that Ordinov noticed his action.

"Good-evening," said Ordinov as he caught the
man up. "What is your name?"

"I am called the *dvornik*," the porter replied with
a grin.

"Have you been *dvornik* for long?"

"Yes; for a long, long time."

"And my landlord is a burgher, is he not?"

"Yes; certainly he is a burgher if he has told
you so."

"What does he do with himself?"

"He falls ill sometimes. He also lives, and prays to God."

"And is the lady his wife?"

"What lady?"

"The lady who lives with him."

"Yes; certainly she is his wife if he has told you so. Good-night, *barin*." And, with a touch of his cap, the *dvornik* retired to his lodge.

Ordinov went up to his room—the door being opened to him by the old woman, who, muttering and grumbling to herself, proceeded next to shoot the bolt, and then to withdraw to the garret where she spent most of her time. Night fell, and Ordinov had to go in search of a light; but since he found his landlord's door locked, he was forced again to summon the old woman, who, resting her arms akimbo, stared at him intently, and seemed uneasy at finding him near her master's door. At length she silently threw him a box of matches, and he re-entered his room. For about the hundredth time he made an attempt to put his books and belongings in order, but before long something compelled him to sink upon a bench, and to fall into a strange sort of torpor. At intervals he would come to himself, and know that his sleep was not really sleep, but a sick faint. Then he heard a door open, and guessed that his hosts were returning from evening prayer. Next, with an idea that he had a request to make of them, he rose, and believed himself to be walking, but in reality made a false step, and fell headlong over a bundle of wood which the old woman had just thrown into his room. There he lay unconscious, until, at length opening his eyes, he was surprised to find himself fully dressed on the bench, while over him, with tender solicitude, there was bending a woman's face—a beautiful face which was wet with compassionate, almost maternal, tears. Soon, too, he felt a pillow being thrust under his head, his body being covered with something warm,

and a fresh young hand touching his burning forehead. He would have liked to have said "Thank
you," and to have seized that hand, and to have
lifted it to his parched lips, and to have bathed it
with tears, and to have clasped it—yes, to have
clasped it for all eternity! He would have liked,
too, to have said many things, but could not think
how to do so. Above all he would have liked to have
died that very instant. His hands felt like lead, and
he could not move them at all as he lay there in his
helplessness. Nevertheless he could hear the blood
beating with such extraordinary violence in his
arteries as almost to lift him from the bed, as well
as feel that some one was bathing his temples. At
length he relapsed into unconsciousness.

When, towards eight o'clock, he awoke, the sun
was throwing broad shafts of light upon the tiles of
the floor. A delightful sensation of rest and quiet
and well-being was soothing all his limbs. Presently
he thought that some one seemed to move softly
away from his side, and he tried to rouse himself
and find out who that invisible some one had been,
since he would have liked to have embraced his
friend, and to have said to her, for the first time in
his life, "I greet you, my beloved!"

"What a long time you have been asleep!" came
in a gentle feminine voice.

Ordinov turned his head, and saw the face of his
beautiful landlady bending over him with a kindly
smile—a smile that was as clear as sunshine.

"And what a long time you have been ill, too!"
she went on. "But it is over now, and you must
get up. Why should you stay here in prison?
Liberty is better than bread, and more beautiful
even than the sun. Come, get up, my dear boy.
Try to get up."

Ordinov seized her hand, and pressed it. He
believed himself still to be dreaming.

"Wait a moment," she added, "and I will make
you some tea. Would you like some? You *must*

drink it, for it will do you good. Yes, I know it
will, for I have been ill myself."

"Yes, please get me something to drink," assented
Ordinov faintly as he raised himself up. He felt
perfectly strengthless. Shivers kept running down
his back, and his limbs were aching as though they
had been fractured. Yet his heart was light, for the
sun was shining warm upon him, and though his
head was swimming with weakness and vertigo, a
new and splendid, a new and unknown, life had
opened before him.

"Your name is Vassilii, is it not?" she asked.
"I only half heard what your landlord said to you
yesterday."

"Yes, it is Vassilii," said Ordinov. "And yours?"

He would have liked to have approached nearer to
her, but staggered as soon as he tried to stand.
Smiling, she steadied him with her arm.

"My name is Katherine," she replied, and looked
him straight in the face with her great clear blue
eyes. For a moment or two he and she stood
clasping one another's hands in silence.

"You have something to ask me?" she said at
length.

"Yes—I do not know," replied Ordinov with a
blush.

"Oh, but look at you! Nay, nay! Do not disturb yourself so. Sit down here by the table, where
the sunlight will catch you. Stop there, and do not
follow me" (this last she added on seeing him make
a movement to detain her). "I will come back
presently, and then you shall look at me as much
as you like."

Returning with the tea, she placed it upon the
table, and seated herself on the opposite side of the
latter to Ordinov.

"Drink some," she said. "Are you often ill like
this?"

"No. This is the first time that I have been
ill. . . . I do not know. *Have* I been ill? At all

events I am not going to be so any more. I have
had enough of illness. . . . Oh, I do not know
what is wrong with me!" he added in a choking
voice as he seized Katherine's hand. "Stay here
with me. Do not leave me alone. Give me your
hand, your hand! . . . You simply blind me! You
look to me like the sun himself!" He cried these
last words as though they were torn from his very
heart, while sobs choked his bosom.

"Poor boy! Probably you have always lived with
unkind people. Are you alone in the world—quite
alone? Have you no kinsfolk?"

"No, none at all. I am quite alone. . . . But
what does that matter? Everything will be better
now, for I am quite well again." He was speaking
almost deliriously. Indeed, the room seemed to be
turning round and round.

"I too have always been a lonely person," she
said after a pause. "But how you stare at me!
What is it? One would almost suppose my eyes
were scorching you! You know, when one is
in love—— But what am I saying? From the first
moment that I saw you I allotted you a warm corner
in my heart. If you are ill I will tend you as I
would myself. . . . But you must not be ill any
more. No. When you are quite well again we will
be as brother and sister to one another. Will we
not? Would you like it? A sister is such a difficult
person to find when God has not given one one."

"Who are you, and where do you come from?"
murmured Ordinov.

"From nowhere near here. . . . What do you
occupy your time with? . . . Do you know this
story? Once upon a time there were twelve brothers
who lived in a great forest; and one day, when they
were absent, a beautiful girl who had lost her way
in the forest entered their house, set it all to rights,
and left upon everything the imprint of her care.
On their return home the brothers guessed that a
woman had been to visit them, and sent for her,

and she appeared. Each of them called her his
' sister,' and permitted her to retain her cherished
liberty. So she remained at once their sister and
their equal. . . . Have you heard the story before?"

"Yes," said Ordinov.

"But life ought to be lived to the full. Do you
enjoy life?"

"Yes, yes!" cried Ordinov. "I should like to
live a long, long time—a whole century of existence!"

"I am not so sure about that," said Katherine
pensively. "I think that I would rather be dead.
However, it is right to love life and good people.
. . . But look at you! Why, you have turned as
white as a sheet!"

"Yes. My head seems to be swimming round
and round."

"Wait a moment, then, and I will get you a
mattress and another pillow. I will lay them here
for you, and you shall go to sleep on them, and
dream of me. The sickness will soon be gone. . . .
Our old servant is ill too."

As she spoke she was making up a bed—glancing
at Ordinov now and then, and smiling at him over
her shoulder.

"What a lot of books you have got!" she went
on as she lifted up the box in which they were
stored. Then she approached the young man, and,
taking him by the hand, led him to the spot where
she had made up the bed, and covered him with a
blanket.

"They say that books are not good for people,"
she added with a wise little toss of her head. "Do
you like books?"

"Yes," replied Ordinov, though only at a venture,
for he hardly knew whether he were really asleep
or awake. However, on pressing Katherine's hand,
he at once realised that he was at least not asleep.

"My protector also possesses a great many books.
Would you like to see them some time? He tells

me that they are devotional books, and is for ever reading to me out of them. Some day I will show them you, and then you shall explain to me what it is that he reads."

"Please go on talking to me," murmured Ordinov, his gaze bent intently upon her.

"Do you like saying your prayers?" she resumed after a pause. "You know, I am afraid—I am afraid that——"

Without finishing her sentence, she seemed to sink into a deep reverie. Ordinov lifted her hand to his lips.

"Why do you kiss my hand so?" she said with a blush. "Well, well! Take both of them, if you really must kiss them," and she gave him both her hands. Then, drawing one of them back, she laid it upon the young man's burning forehead, and set herself to stroke his hair, while blushing more and more every moment. At length she seated herself upon the floor near the bed, and, pressing her cheek against his, caressed his face with her warm, damp breath. Suddenly he became conscious that hot tears were falling upon his cheeks, like molten lead, while every moment he could feel himself growing weaker, and his hands becoming incapable of moving. All at once there came a knock at the front door, followed by the squeak of a bolt; and once more Ordinov felt sensible of the old man's presence behind the partition-wall. Also, he saw Katherine rise—though without either haste or embarrassment—and make the sign of the cross over his bed. Then he closed his eyes, and almost at the same moment there settled upon his lips a long, warm kiss. Instantly he felt as though a knife had been thrust through his heart as, heaving a deep sigh, he fainted away.

From that time onwards there began for him a new life. Sometimes, in a confused way, he would see himself condemned to live a sort of inevitable dream—a sort of extraordinary nightmare of bootless strugglings. In his horror he would strive to combat this fatality, but, at the very crisis of the contest, would find himself overthrown by some unknown power. Then he would lose consciousness again, and see gaping before him a fathomless abyss of infinite gloom—an abyss with nothing whatever beyond it—an abyss into which he would cast himself with a cry of anguish and despair. At other times he would experience moments of bliss which were almost too full, too transcendent, to be borne. At such times his body would take on a sort of convulsive suppleness, and the past would lighten behind him, and the future would have to offer him naught but joy and victory. From dreams of this kind he would awaken in unheard-of rapture. Indeed, who has not known such moments— moments when ineffable hope refreshes the soul with a shower of dew, and one could weep for very joy, and, what though the body be a prey to acute pangs, and one may feel that the woof of life is wearing thin, one still rejoices in this new birth, this new resurrection? Again, Ordinov would fall into a trance, and in that trance live over again the events of the last few days—though always with them appearing to him as so many strange, incomprehensible visions. Sometimes, too, the sick youth would lose his sense of memory, and wonder why he was no longer in his old den, under his old landlady. He would wonder why, at dusk, the old woman no longer came to see him—why the stove no longer threw fitful gleams into the dark corners of the room as she chafed her bony, trembling hands, or muttered to herself in a ceaseless monotone and threw glances of astonishment at the lodger whom she conceived to be a madman because of his passion for work. At other times he would recall that he really had changed his abode. Yet how had it come about? What had happened to him? Why had he moved into other lodgings? He did not know. His whole being was now divorced from his personality,

as well as held at a constant, an irresistible, tension.
Whither, too, was he being called, and who was it
that was calling him? Who had fired his blood with
the unbearable flame which was now consuming it?
He could not think, he had entirely forgotten.
Sometimes a shadow seemed to be hovering near
him, and he would try to seize it. Often, too, he
would think that he could hear the rustle of light
footsteps beside his bed, and the murmur of tender,
soothing words which seemed to him as sweet as
music. Fluttering, damp breath would come sweep-
ing across his face, until his whole being would
vibrate with tenderness. Then he would feel hot
tears falling upon his fevered cheeks, and a sudden,
long kiss would imprint its caressing sweetness upon
his lips. At such moments his very life seemed to
go out of him—the whole world around him seemed
to stop, and to have been dead for centuries and
centuries, and to be lying shrouded under a night
which had already lasted for a thousand years.

Other occasions there were when memories of his
childhood would return to him. Once more he
would relive those childish, untroubled years, with
their quiet pleasures and their endless happinesses.
Once more he would experience the first delightful
impressions of life which he had experienced when
swarms of good fairies had come flying out of every
flower which he picked, to talk to him in the luscious
meadow which lay in front of the little acacia-framed
villa. Other good fairies there were who smiled at
him from the end of the great clear lake on the
banks of which he had so often dozed the hours
away as he listened to the murmuring of the ripples.
Then there were fairies who were born of gorgeous,
smiling dreams; who lulled him to sleep with the
rustling of their wings at the hour when his mother
laid him in his little bed, and made the sign of the
cross over his forehead, and embraced him, and
soothed him to slumber with lullabies which should
prepare him for the long, quiet night. At this point

Ordinov's vision would also be confronted by a being
who, from the boy's childhood upwards, had caused
him terror, and had communicated to his life the
first baleful poison of melancholy. In a dim sort of
way Ordinov had felt that this being, this mysterious
old man, was destined to overshadow his future for
ever and ever; with the result that the child always
trembled when he beheld him, and could not take
his eyes off him, even for an instant. Besides, the
cursed old man constantly pursued him. In the
garden he would first come and spy him out, and
then throw him mocking salutes as he popped his
head, first over one bush, and then over another.
In the house, too, he would successively transform
himself into each doll that the boy possessed, and
laugh at and tease him, and make faces at him
through his hands, like some malicious gnome. And
at school, too, he would incite Ordinov's bullying
comrades to ill-treat their victim, or else take a seat
beside him on the bench, and mingle in a blurred
smudge with each letter in the grammar. Finally he
would settle himself at night beside Ordinov's pillow,
and chase away the bands of good fairies who had
been beating their gold and sapphire wings around
the cot, and put Ordinov's poor mother, too, to
flight, and banish her from her son, and then spend
the whole of the long, long night muttering some
fantastic legend which was quite incomprehensible
to poor little Ordinov, but which pained and agitated
him with its premature passions and terrors. Deaf
alike to prayers and sobs, the old man would continue his occupation until his victim had fallen into
a state of torpor which almost bordered upon a
fainting fit.

Suddenly Ordinov, the child, awoke to Ordinov,
the youth. The years had rolled away, and he found
himself rudely confronted with the actual position of
affairs, and forced to understand that he, a stranger,
was alone in the world—alone among mysterious,
dangerous people, among enemies who were gathered

together in a dark corner of the room, who were
whispering to one another, and exchanging signals
with the old hunchback as she crouched beside the
fire, while she pointed out the sick youth to them,
and chafed her wrinkled hands.   Extreme terror
would seize upon the dreamer, and he would begin
torturing himself with an agony of doubt as to
who those people were, and why he himself was
present with them.   As a matter of fact, he would
suspect that he had strayed into a nest of male-
factors, whither some unknown power had lured him
without first of all letting him see the aspect of its
inhabitants or its master.   At length his terror would
become absolutely unbearable as, in the darkness,
the old woman with the white, tremulous head would
begin to recite a long, long story in a low voice—
to recite it where she sat crouching by the dying
fire.   Then, to his still greater terror, the story
would begin to take actual shape before him, until
he could see actual gestures and faces, and could
witness a repetition of all the thoughts that ever had
passed through his mind—from the confused dreams
of childhood to his very latest thoughts and acts, as
well as all that he had ever read about, and all that
he had so long ago forgotten.   Then everything
would come to life again, and would take unto itself
forms which stretched to giddy heights, and whirled
themselves around him.   He would see stately, magic
gardens unrolling their vast spaces before him, and
great cities springing up and falling into decay, and
graveyards vomiting out their dead, and nations
rising and falling, and all his past thoughts materialising themselves around his sick pillow, and every
dream coming to birth again in corporeal shape;
until he would feel that no longer had he any spiritual
conceptions left, but only physical worlds and actual,
tangible edifices of ideas.   And he would see himself
lost, like a grain of sand, amid all this weird universe
of dreams which was at once so indestructible and
so infinite.   He would feel that life was pressing

with its whole weight upon his independence, and relentlessly pursuing him, like an eternal irony. And he would see himself dead, and crumbling to dust, without hope of either resurrection or eternity. And he would strive to flee, yet would find no corner wherein to hide himself from all this hateful world. At length, in a frenzy of horror, he summoned all his energies, and gave a loud cry, and——

He awoke to find himself bathed in sweat, with, around him, a silence as of death. Everywhere the darkness was profound. Yet still the old woman's story seemed to be going on somewhere; still there seemed to be in progress an interminable narrative, with the narrator's hoarse voice ringing familiarly to Ordinov's ear. The narrative was about a dark forest, and daring brigands, and a gallant leader of the type of Stenka Razin,[1] and that gallant leader's companions, and boatmen of the Volga, and a beautiful girl, and Mother Volga herself. Was it all an illusion? Did he hear aright? Fully an hour passed while he lay listening, with distended eyes, and held by a motionless, a painful, spell. At length he raised himself cautiously, and rejoiced to find himself strong with a strength which his grievous illness had failed to destroy. The delirium was gone, and reality had come in its place. He could see that he was still wearing the same clothes as he had been wearing when he last talked to Katherine; whence he arrived at the conclusion that no very great space of time could have elapsed since the morning when she left him. Also, a fever of longing was burning in his blood. Feeling his way cautiously along the wall, he soon came upon a large nail, fixed at a high point in the partition-wall against which his bed was placed. Clutching the nail with both hands, he then contrived to draw himself up until he had reached a crack through which there filtered

---

[1] Leader of a Cossack rebellion during the reign of Katherine the Great (1762–1796).

a feeble light into the room; after which, applying his eye to this crack, he held his breath, and proceeded guardedly to take observations.

In a corner of his landlord's room was a bed, with, in front of it, a table, covered over with a cloth on which there were heaped great books of antique shape, bound like missals. To the wall above the bed there was nailed an ikon which, in point of age, could almost vie with the one in Ordinov's room; while before the ikon there burnt a lamp. Upon the bed was stretched Murin. Looking ill and as white as a sheet, he had his limbs covered over with a fur coat, and his knees were supporting an open book. Besides him on a bench was stretched Katherine, with one of her arms around the old man's neck, and her head resting against his shoulder. From time to time she would look at him with eyes which shone with an almost childlike interest—so much so that the curiosity with which she was listening to his reading seemed to be absolutely boundless. Now and then the old man would raise his voice a little, and a trace of animation would show itself in his inert figure as, with a frown, and with his eyes shooting flashes, he would make Katherine begin to quiver with fear. Then something like a smile would dawn upon his features, and Katherine would smile sweetly in return; while at other times glittering tears would come welling to her eyes, and then the old man would caress her like a child, and she would press him closer to herself with her bare, white arm, and loll her head lovingly upon his bosom.

Ordinov found himself wondering whether all this were not a dream. Yet whenever he tried to think the matter out the blood came mounting to his head, and the veins in his temples would begin to swell. Presently he relaxed his hold of the nail, and, rising from the bed, and staggering, and hardly knowing what he did, walked like a somnambulist to the door of his landlord's room. There he fell headlong, and, the rusty lock yielding with a crash, Ordinov found himself actually in his landlord's chamber. He had just time to see Katherine give a shudder, and spring up with a start. He had just time to mark the fury which blazed in the old man's frowning, deepest eyes, as also the suddenness with which Murin's figure suddenly became a thing of menace. Yes, he had just time to see Murin seize a revolver from the wall, and the gleam of its barrel as, with an unsteady hand that was unnerved by rage, the old man trained the muzzle full upon him. A shot rang out, and then a wild, unnatural cry. When the smoke cleared away a terrible spectacle met Ordinov's gaze as, shaking with horror, he bent over the old man's form. Murin was lying prone upon the floor—twisted with convulsions, his face distorted, and his lips white with foam. In a flash the younger man divined that his unfortunate landlord had been seized with a severe epileptic fit; wherefore he at once proceeded to help Katherine to tend him.

III

IT was a terrible night for all concerned. Early next morning, despite his weakness and his still lingering fever, Ordinov went out for a walk. In the courtyard he encountered the *dvornik;* but this time the Tartar removed his cap as soon as ever he caught sight of the young man, and stood looking at him with a curiosity which he was at no pains to conceal. Next, as though regretting having done so, he resumed his broom, but still continued to throw covert glances at Ordinov as the latter slowly approached him.

"Did you hear anything last night?" the younger man began.

"Yes," replied the *dvornik.*

R

"What is the matter with that gentleman up there? What does he do?"

"You are his lodger, are you not? Well, then, you must find out these things for yourself. It is no business of mine."

"*Are* you going to answer my questions?" cried Ordinov, almost beside himself with nervous irritation.

"Why, what have I done? It was your own fault. Why did you go and disturb the gentleman? Let me tell you that the coffin-maker who lodges below him is deaf; yet *he* heard everything. And his wife too is deaf; yet *she* heard everything. And in the other court, too, they heard everything. I shall have to go and fetch a policeman."

"Well, I will go and fetch one too," said Ordinov as he turned away towards the door of the yard.

"Do as you like; you are his lodger. . . . But wait a moment, sir; wait a moment."

Ordinov returned, and the *dvornik* touched his cap politely.

"Well?" inquired the young man.

"If you go," said the *dvornik*, "then *I* must go to the proprietor."

"Well? And what then?"

"Only that you had better *not* go."

"Idiot!" cried Ordinov as for the second time he turned away.

"Sir, sir! Wait a moment!"

Again the *dvornik* touched his cap as he showed his teeth in a grin.

"Listen to me, sir. Do not be over-hasty. Why trouble the police, poor men? It would not be right to do so, God knows!"

"Well, listen to me. Take that, and tell me what is the matter with that gentleman."

"What is the matter with him?"

"Yes."

"I would have told you that without being paid for it."

The *dvornik* resumed his besom, swept a few strokes, and looked at Ordinov with a fixed and solemn air.

"You are a nice young gentleman," he went on, "but not the sort to have dealings with a fine gentleman like *him*. Mind your own business; that's my advice," and the Tartar communicated to his expression an earnest—almost an angry—look as he resumed his work. Finally, he approached Ordinov with a bearing full of mystery, and, accompanying his words with a very expressive gesture, said: "He's like *that*."

"Like what?"

"His head is all gone wrong."

"What do you mean?"

"That his head leaves him sometimes," repeated the *dvornik* with even greater *empressement* than before. "Yes, it leaves him, and he falls ill. You see, once upon a time he used to have a large ship —several ships, indeed—and to sail them on the Volga (I also am of the Volga country). And he used to run a factory besides, and it was burnt down, and—well, there you are! His head has turned with it all."

"You mean, he is mad?"

"No, no!" (here the *dvornik* struck an attitude). "He is *not* mad. On the contrary, he is very much himself. He knows everything, and has read everything—yes, everything in the world. He can foretell the future, and if any one comes to him, it costs the visitor two roubles, or three roubles, or four roubles, as the case may be, and *Hospodin* [1] Murin looks into a book, and turns its pages, and tells his customer the whole truth. But first of all there must be money on the table—yes, money on the table; nothing can be done without money." And the Tartar, who seemed to take a great interest in Murin's affairs, laughed in an appreciative manner.

"So he is a fortune-teller? He gives advice?"

[1] Mr.

"Yes," grunted the *dvornik*, with a quick nod of assent. "He foretells things just as they will be, and prays to God—yes, he prays a great deal; and then a fit comes upon him," the Tartar here repeated his expressive gesture, "and——"

At this point some one shouted to the *dvornik* from across the yard, and presently there came into view a little grey-headed hunchback who, clad in a peasant's smock, and with his eyes cast down, kept coughing, stumbling, and muttering prayers as he walked. He looked like a man who had been dropped in infancy.

"The master, the master!" murmured the *dvornik* in great excitement as he saluted Ordinov. Then, cap in hand, he ran to meet the little old man, whose face somehow seemed familiar to Ordinov. At all events he believed he had seen him before. Since, however, there seemed to him nothing remarkable in the circumstance, he departed—the *dvornik* escorting him to the gate as though he were a gentleman of the finest quality.

"The humbug was only playing with me," thought Ordinov. "God knows what sort of a mystery there may be hidden here."

However, he had not gone far when the current of his thoughts changed. The weather was dull and cold, and snow showers were falling. He felt quite frozen, and the ground seemed to be swaying beneath his feet. All at once a familiar voice—a voice at once genial and pleasant to the ear—wished him good-morning.

"Why, it is Yaroslav Ilyitch!" exclaimed Ordinov.

Before him there was standing a man of about thirty—a short, thick-set, red-faced individual who had small, dull-grey eyes, perpetually smiling lips, and raiment—well, such raiment as only a Yaroslav Ilyitch would wear. He offered Ordinov his hand respectfully, for the two had made each other's acquaintance only last year, and then by a mere accident in the street. To an easygoing nature

Yaroslav Ilyitch joined an extraordinary facility for scraping acquaintance with persons of good social standing—persons who at least had the manners of high society, and were well-informed, if not exactly clever. Also, though he had a pleasant tenor voice, certain intonations in his speech (even when he was conversing with intimate friends) assumed a note of overbearing self-assertion which swept aside contradiction, and may have been the outcome of habit.

"What a lucky chance!" cried Yaroslav, with an expression of the purest delight beaming on his countenance.

"You see, I live here now," explained Ordinov.

"But how long have you been doing so?" went on the other, already raising his voice a little. "I have known nothing of it, even though, as you surely remember, I am your 'cousin.' I too have been living in this quarter since I returned from Riazan a month ago. I look upon you, my good friend, as the oldest of my acquaintances," and he laughed in good-natured fashion. "Sergiev!" he then cried. "Wait for me at Tarassov's, and also tell Olsufiev's *dvornik* to come to my office immediately. I shall be there within an hour."

These brief orders given, the fine Yaroslav Ilyitch took Ordinov by the arm, and led him into a café.

"After such a long absence from one another," he said, "we must have a little talk. Well," he added in a tone of deference as he lowered his voice to the confidential note, "how are you getting on? Are you still working at science?"

"Yes—always," replied Ordinov in an absent-minded way.

"How splendid, Vassilii Michaelovitch — how splendid!"—and Yaroslav pressed Ordinov's hand with fervour. "Some day you will be an ornament to Russian society. May God speed you in the career which you have chosen! Heavens, how glad

I am to have met you! How often I have thought of you! How often I have said to myself, ' Where is our good, our generous, our talented Vassilii Michaelovitch? ' "

They engaged a private room, and after luncheon and vodka [1] had been ordered, Yaroslav Ilyitch seated himself, and gazed affectionately at his companion.

"I too have read much," he began in an insinuating voice. "I have read the whole of Pushkin [2]!"

Ordinov, still at sea, only looked at him.

"What an astonishing knowledge of love was Pushkin's!" Yaroslav went on. "But first of all let me thank you for all the good you have done me by so kindly suggesting to me noble thoughts."

"Oh, you exaggerate," murmured the other.

"No, I do *not*. I love truth, and am conscious of having ever consistently held fast to that principle."

"Oh, you are not fair to yourself; and as for me——"

"What I say is true," repeated Yaroslav warmly. "Who am *I* compared with you?"

"Oh, oh!"

"It *is* so, I tell you."

There ensued a pause.

"It was solely owing to your good advice that I left off frequenting bad company and amended my morals," continued Yaroslav impressively. "I now spend the greater part of my leisure at home, and in the evenings I read some improving book or other, and then—— In fact, I have but one desire now, Vassilii Michaelovitch; and that is, to serve my country."

"I always thought you a good fellow, Yaroslav Ilyitch."

"Ah, how you encourage me!" And Yaroslav pressed his friend's hand with even greater fervour than before.

[1] Corn brandy.
[2] The greatest of Russian poets (1799-1837).

"But why are you not drinking?" he said, when his emotion had somewhat subsided.

"I cannot do so; I am not very well."

"Not very well, eh? To think of that! Since when have you been ill? Would you like me to send for a really reliable physician? Would you? I will go at once and fetch him myself. He is a *very* clever man." Yaroslav Ilyitch was already reaching for his hat.

"Thank you, but I detest any kind of fuss, and have an innate distrust of doctors."

"Oh, how can you say so?" protested Yaroslav. "I repeat to you that this doctor is a *really* clever man. Not long ago (if you do not mind my telling you the story, my dear Vassilii?) there came to consult him a poor blacksmith. Said the blacksmith to the doctor, 'I have sent a tool right through my hand. Please cure me.' Upon this Simon Pafnutich —who at once perceived that the unfortunate man was standing in imminent danger of gangrene— decided to amputate the whole arm, and performed the operation in my presence. Yet so splendid, so truly wondrous, was the way in which he did it that I forgot my pity for the patient's suffering in my admiration of the simplicity, yet sheer impressiveness, of the feat performed. . . . When and where were you taken ill?"

"When I was changing my lodgings. I have only just come from a sick-bed."

"Then you are *still* unwell, and ought never to have come out! You are not in your old abode, are you? Why not?"

"Because my landlady had to leave St. Petersburg."

"Madame Savishna? Really? The good, the splendid old woman! Do you know, I had a respect for that lady that was almost filial. There was something about her decline that was so noble, so antique! In her one saw a sort of foretype of one's own declining days—that is to say, of one's own—

well, of—well, of something *poetical*." Yaroslav's voice ended almost in a shout, and he had grown confused and red in the face.

"Yes, she *was* a good woman."

"But where are you living now, might I ask?"

"Close by here—in Korschmarov's Buildings."

"*I* know them. Korschmarov is a very decent old man. I think I might even go so far as to say that I stand on a footing of intimacy with him. A health to the good old gentleman!" Yaroslav Ilyitch's lips fairly quivered with affection. Then he sent for a second bottle of vodka and a pipe.

"You are not actually in lodgings, I suppose?" he went on. "You have your own furnished rooms?"

"No, I am in lodgings."

"With whom, then? Perhaps I know him?"

"With Murin, a burgher—rather a fine old man."

"Murin, Murin? He lives in a back court, does he not—just over a coffin-maker's?"

"Yes, he does."

"Hm! So you are quite comfortable there?"

"As yet I could hardly say. I have only just moved in."

"Hm! Well, all I wished to say was—— Hm! You have observed nothing unusual about him?"

"Good heavens! What do you mean?"

"Only that you will be all right there, so long as your room pleases you. . . . To tell the truth, I was going to say something quite different—to give you a warning—but I know your character. . . . What do you think of the old burgher?"

"He seems to suffer from bad health."

"Yes, he *does* have rather bad health. But have you not noticed anything else? Have you had any talk with him?"

"Only a few words. His reserve and pride rather stand in the way."

"Hm!" Yaroslav Ilyitch seemed to become lost in thought.

"He is a very unfortunate man," he went on after a pause.

"Is he?"

"Yes; very unfortunate, as well as strange and interesting beyond measure. However, since he does not seem to trouble you, I must ask your pardon for having drawn your attention to the subject. Yet I wish I knew whether——"

"You have aroused my curiosity. Tell me all about him. Since I live with him, the subject very naturally interests me."

"Well, they say that he used to be very wealthy. He was (as you too may have heard) a merchant, and came to grief through several of his boats, with their cargoes, being sunk in a storm. Also, a factory of his which was managed by a relative was burnt to the ground, and the relative perished in the flames. What a category of misfortunes! Ever since then (so they say) Murin has been a prey to melancholy. At first there were fears for his reason; and, in truth, a quarrel with another merchant who owned boats on the Volga led to such an outburst that everything which he has done since that time has been set down to insanity. Personally I believe the story, for details of more than one extraordinary act on his part have since come to my ears. Finally he suffered yet another misfortune—a calamity which could only be ascribed to the malign influence of destiny."

"What was it?"

"It is said that, in a paroxysm of madness, he inflicted a grave injury upon a young merchant for whom, until then, he had cherished a great affection; as well as that, on recovering his senses, he was so shocked at what he had done that he came very near to committing suicide. At all events that is what I have been told—and I have had means of hearing of things which he has done. However, it is said that, during the last few years, he has been performing a sort of religious penance. . . . But what

is the matter with you, Vassilii Michaelovitch? Does
my story weary you?"

"No, no! Quite the contrary! Pray continue,
pray continue! You were saying that he performs
a sort of religious penance? Surely he was not the
only actor in the tragedy of which you speak, was
he?"

"I do not know. I only know that it is *said*
that he was—that no one else was implicated in
the affair. But now I have told you all that I know
of him, except that——"

"Except that what?"

"Well, I know—at least—— But no, I do not
know any more. I merely wished to warn you that,
if you should detect anything unusual in him, anything beyond the normal, you must set it down to
his numerous misfortunes."

"Then he is very religious—an actual fanatic?"

"Yes, I think so. But look at what he has
suffered! For myself, I believe him to be, at heart,
a good sort."

"He is not mad now, is he? He is quite sane?"

"Certainly. I can guarantee that. I would even
venture to assert that he has the full use of his
faculties. Only, as you have so truly remarked,
he is *exceedingly* strange and *exceedingly* religious.
Besides, he is a man of intellect, and can discourse
well and fluently and to the point. But it is strange
that he should be so well versed in book lore. His
chequered life has left its marks upon his face."

"He reads a great deal of devotional literature, I
understand?"

"Yes, he does. You see, he is a mystic."

"A what?"

"A mystic. I tell you this in confidence, and to
it I would add that for a long time he was regarded
with great suspicion, for the reason that he used to
exercise so strong an influence over persons who
came to consult him."

"What sort of an influence?"

"Well, you may, or you may not, believe it——
But I will give you an instance of what I mean.
Some years ago, before the old man came to live
in this quarter, there went to call upon him, one
day, a certain Alexander Ignatievitch (a gentleman
of honour and position who occupied a high post
and enjoyed universal esteem) and a lieutenant.
Their sole motive was curiosity. Well, Alexander
knocked at the door, which was opened to him by
Murin, who stood looking at his visitors in a strange,
fixed sort of a way. It was always his custom that,
if he had a mind to be civil, he looked his visitors
full in the face; but if he had no such mind, he just
sent them about their business. After a moment's
silence Murin said to them rudely, 'What do you
want of me, gentlemen?' to which Alexander
replied, 'Your art ought to have told you that we
have come to consult you.' 'Very well, then; come
with me into my study,' said Murin, addressing
himself unhesitatingly to the precise member of the
pair who had come to ask for his advice. Now,
although never, to this day, has Alexander told me
exactly what passed within, at all events he came
out with his face looking the colour of a sheet.
The same thing happened to a lady who stands high
in society. She too came out with a face the colour
of a sheet, as well as all dissolved in tears. She
came out looking both surprised at the eloquence of
the man and terrified at his predictions."

"How strange! Yet he does not go in for such
things *now*, does he?"

"No; he was warned not to do so. I might
quote other curious instances. For example, one
day a young sub-lieutenant, the only scion and hope
of a great family, was making fun of Murin. 'What
are you laughing at?' said the old man angrily.
'Do you not know what, in three days' time, you
will have become?' Crossing his hands on his
breast, he signified to the lieutenant that he would
have become a corpse."

"Indeed?"

"Yes. And though I hardly know whether to credit it or not, I have been told that the prediction was fulfilled. Yes, he *has* a gift of some sort, has that Murin. I can see you smiling. Well, of course you are much cleverer than I am, yet I *believe* in Murin, and am sure that he is no charlatan. Pushkin himself relates a similar occurrence."

"Hm! I do not wish to contradict you. . . . You say that he lives alone?"

"Oh, I do not actually *know*. In fact, I—er—believe that he has a daughter there."

"A *daughter?*"

"Yes; or, maybe, a wife. At all events there lives a woman of *some* sort in his tenement. I have spoken to her, but took little notice of her at the time."

"Hm! That is strange."

Ordinov fell into a reverie, and Yaroslav too became lost in thought. He felt pleased at having met his friend, as well as at having been able to tell him the interesting stories which he had related so well. So he sat contentedly smoking his pipe and contemplating his dear Vassilii Michaelovitch. But suddenly he rose, and assumed a businesslike air.

"What? A whole hour gone?" he cried. "Why, I am forgetting my appointment! My dear, good Vassilii Michaelovitch, though I bless fate once more for this happy meeting, really I must tear myself away. Allow me to come and visit you in your student's retreat."

"I beg of you to do so. I shall be most pleased. Also, I will return the compliment whenever I have the time."

"Then I shall count upon you; and you will be doing me a real service. You cannot think what pleasure you have given me to-day!"

Leaving the café, they encountered Sergiev, who was running to meet them with voluble explanations

to the effect that *Hospodin* Emelienovitch was prepared to wait upon Yaroslav Ilyitch immediately.
Presently there arrived also a buggy, drawn by two
smart trotters; whereafter, having shaken hands
with "one of his best friends" and touched his hat,
Yaroslav Ilyitch drove off to keep his appointment.
Yet, even while driving away, he twice turned round
to salute Ordinov, and to make significant signs to
him.

As for the latter, he felt so worn out (as also so
morally and physically relieved) that he could scarcely
drag himself along, and had much ado to regain his
lodgings. At the gate of the courtyard he once
more encountered the *dvornik*, who had been watching the leavetakings of Ordinov with Yaroslav
Ilyitch. The Tartar made a sign to the former
that he wished to speak to him, but Ordinov walked
on without paying him any attention.

On the staircase he came into violent collision
with a little man in grey who was leaving the
Murins' rooms with downcast eyes.

"Oh, I beg your pardon!" cried the little man,
rebounding against the wall with all the elasticity
of indiarubber.

"Have I hurt you?" asked Ordinov.

"Oh no!—though I humbly thank you for your
attention. . . . O my God, my God!" And the
little man went stumbling, gasping, and muttering
his prayers down the staircase. He was the proprietor of whom the *dvornik* had seemed to stand
so much in awe. Only when he was gone did
Ordinov recall that once before he had seen him
since his (Ordinov's) removal to Murin's. The
young man felt irritated and uneasy; but, knowing
that his imaginative and sensitive faculties had well-
nigh reached the breaking-point, he resolved to take
a little rest. Gradually he was falling into a sort
of torpor. He felt heavy, and as though his raw,
aching heart had been bathed in tears.

Throwing himself upon his bed (which he found

to have been made up during his absence), he set
himself to listen. The breathings of two persons
came to his ears—the one of them deep, laboured,
and convulsive, and the other one light, but
irregular, as though it were depressed in spirit,
as though it came from a heart which was beating
with the same force, the same passion, as possessed
the other one. Occasionally, also, the swish of a
dress and the gentle rustle of light footsteps could
be distinguished—sounds which awakened in Ordinov's heart a sweet, but mournful, echo. At length
he heard—or thought he heard—sobs, sighs, and
some muttered prayers. Instantly there occurred to
his vision a picture of *her*—of her kneeling there
before the ikon, with hands tightly clasped and her
arms raised. . . . Who was she? For whom was
she praying? To what invincible passion had she
surrendered her heart? Why was that heart such
an inexhaustible fountain of tears?

All that she had ever said to him now recurred to
his ears like the sound of music; and to each of her
words, as he eagerly recalled and repeated them, his
heart responded with a violent throb. . . . Yet,
stay! Was it not all a dream? . . . The late scene
between her and himself returned to his memory;
it passed again before his mind's eye. Once more
he beheld Katherine and her sad, sad face. Once
more he felt her warm breath upon his lips. And
at her kisses!——

Closing his eyes, he sank into a kind of doze. Far
away a clock struck the hour. It was getting late,
then, and night was falling. . . .

Suddenly, half-waking, he seemed to see her bending over him, and looking at him with those wonderful, those brilliant, eyes of hers—eyes which were
now sparkling with tears of joy—eyes which seemed
as clear and gentle as the azure vault of heaven on
a beautiful mid-summer's day. Her face looked so
bright, her smile was radiant with such profound
happiness, she leaned upon Ordinov's shoulder with

such a childlike, yet amorous, *abandon*, that he could bear his felicity no longer, and uttered a groan. She spoke to him, she murmured to him words of tenderness, until at length he recognised the music which had been fluttering in his heart. He drank in the warm air to which the young girl's ardent breath communicated such an electric fragrance; he stretched out his arms; he sighed; he opened his eyes. . . .

Yes, she *was* there! She *was* bending over him, all suffused with tears, shaking with emotion, pale with terror! She *was* speaking to him, she *was* imploring him to do something as she clasped her hands together and caressed him with her bare arms! He seized her, he drew her towards him, and she sank quivering upon his breast!

PART II

I

"What is the matter? What has frightened you so?" he said, now completely restored to consciousness, and clasping the girl eagerly to his breast. "What ails you, Katherine? What ails you, my dearest?"

She continued sobbing gently, with her eyes cast down and her face hidden in the young man's bosom. Indeed, it was long before she could speak, so racked was she with nervous tremors.

"I do not know," she said at length, half-choked with tears. "I do not know," she said again in a voice that was scarcely audible. "I cannot even think how I come to be here in your room."

As she spoke she clung to the young man, and, as though moved by some irresistible force, kissed his shoulders, hands, and breast. Finally, with the look of one who is overcome with despair, she sank to the floor before him, buried her face in her hands, and leaned her head against his knees.

He hastened to raise her, and to seat her by his side, but her face remained crimson with shame as with her eyes she mutely besought him not to look at her. Presently a painful smile showed itself on her lips—but a smile which presaged a new paroxysm of despair. All her terrors seemed to return, and she looked at Ordinov diffidently, appeared anxious to avoid his gaze, and answered his questions only in a whisper, and with downcast head.

"Perhaps you have had a nightmare?" said Ordinov. "You have been dreaming, have you not? Or perhaps *he* has frightened you again? Has he had another fit? Is he unconscious? Perhaps he has been telling you things which you ought not to have heard? Is it so?"

"No. I have not been dreaming," replied Katherine, with difficulty mastering her agitation. "Indeed, I have not even been to sleep. Nor has he said anything at all to me. He has long been gone to bed. True, once he called to me, and I ran to him, but he was still fast asleep. I spoke to him, but I received no answer. He did not even hear me. What a fit he had last night! May God help him! . . . Oh, the bitter anguish in this heart of mine! I have been praying—yes, praying a long, long time."

"Katherine, my darling! . . . But you are not as terrified as you were last night?"

"No, it is different this time."

"Then what has happened?"

"*It* has happened."

She shuddered, and clung to Ordinov as a child might do.

"Listen," she went on as suddenly she ceased to weep. "I had a good reason for not wishing to be alone there. . . . Do not grieve any more; do not weep for the misfortunes of others. Keep your tears for your own days of sorrow, when *you* will be lonely and unhappy, when *you* will have no one to comfort you. . . . Listen. Have you a sweetheart?"

"No. You are my first."

"*I*? Do you call *me* your sweetheart?"

Her face expressed the most profound surprise. She was just about to speak again when suddenly she checked herself, and lowered her eyes. Presently she blushed, and her eyes took on a brilliant glitter through the tears which were fringing her lashes. With a mien that was half-playful, half-diffident, she shot a single swift glance at Ordinov, and then looked down upon the floor again.

"No, *I* shall never be your first sweetheart," she said. "No, no!" she repeated thoughtfully, a smile just parting her lips. "No, no!" she said again—

s

this time breaking into frank laughter. "It is not *I*, my dear one, who will ever be your beloved."

But when she raised her eyes again it was clear that her brief access of gaiety had changed to a despair so profound—a despair that was so entirely a prey to agitation—that immense pity (the sort of unreasoning pity which is excited in the breast only by unknown misfortunes) seized upon Ordinov, and he looked at Katherine with inexpressible pain.

"Listen to me," she said as she took the young man's hands and forcibly checked her sobs. "Listen to me; listen carefully, my dear one. You must keep a watch over your heart. Love me if you will, but in another way than that, so that you may spare yourself many misfortunes, and escape making a terrible enemy, and have a sister in place of a sweetheart. But I will always come and see you if you wish, and caress you, and never regret that I have known you. Do you understand? Never during the whole two days of your illness have I left you. Take me, then, for your sister. It was not for nothing that I called you 'brother' just now; it was not for nothing that I have been tearfully interceding for you with the Virgin. Never will you find such a sister as I could be. Ah! A sweetheart? Is it a sweetheart that your soul craves for? I tell you that you might search the whole world over, yet never find a sweetheart like myself. I would love you to the end, even as I love you now, and I would love you because your soul is pure and transparent, and because from the first moment that I saw you I knew that you must one day come and lodge in this house, and be its welcome guest. So you see I *had* a reason for inviting you to enter when you first came. Yes, I should always be fond of you because, whenever your eyes look into mine, I can see that they are charged with love, and that they voice your heart. Yes, your eyes never speak but at once I know all that is passing in your breast. That is why, in return for your love, I would yield

you my life and my liberty; for it is sweet even to
be the *slave* of the man who has one's heart in his
keeping. Yet alas! my life is no longer my own,
and my cherished liberty is fled from me. Take me,
then, for your sister, and be to me as a brother.
Let me lie close to your heart when fresh troubles
and sicknesses shall come upon you; leave it in my
power to visit you without shame and without regret
—to pass a whole night with you even as I am
doing now. . . . Do you hear? Will you open your
heart to me as a sister? Do you understand all that
I have just said?"

She stopped, and looked at him in silence. Then
she sank exhausted upon his breast, and her voice
ended in a passionate sob, while her bosom heaved
convulsively. Yet her face bore the brightness of
the evening star.

"My darling!" whispered Ordinov, sight and
breath almost failing him. "My darling!" he
whispered again, scarcely knowing what to say, so
fearful was he lest his happiness should disappear
in smoke. He believed himself to be the sport of
an illusion. Everything was dancing before his eyes.

"My queen," he said at length, "I cannot understand you. I only know what you have just told me.
My ideas are all confused, and my heart is very
sore."

Again his voice failed him. Katherine pressed
the closer to his side, and as she did so he rose and
fell, in an abandonment of self-surrender, upon his
knees. His breast was swelling with sobs, and his
voice (which seemed to come straight from his heart)
was quivering like the string of a violin, in an
ecstasy of mysterious rapture and mysterious
happiness.

"Who *are* you, my beloved?" he cried, restrain-
ing his sobs only with a great effort of will. "Where
do you come from, my darling? From what heaven
have you flown into mine? Surely it must be from
some heaven of dreams, for I cannot believe that

you are a real being. Do not interrupt me; let me
speak, and tell you all—all—all. I have so long
wanted to do so ! . . . Who *are* you, my dearest—
who *are* you? How have you discovered the road
to my heart? How long have you been my ' sister '?
Tell me all your history, and what your life has
been, and the name of your native place, and who
was your first lover, and all your joys and sorrows.
Have you always lived in a warm country, under a
bright blue sky? Upon whom was your first affection spent? Who was your lover before I myself
became so? To whom did your soul first turn?
Have you a mother? Did she caress you when you
were a little girl, or did your eyes, like mine, open
upon a desolate hearth? Have you always lived as
you are doing now? What have your hopes for the
future been? Of what golden vistas have you
dreamed? How many of your hopes have come true,
and how many have been disappointed? Tell me all,
all, all. For whom did your youthful heart first ache?
Upon whom did you first bestow it? What must I
give you in order to win that heart for myself? What
must I give you in order to possess it completely?
Tell me all, my little sweetheart, the very light of
my eyes, my dearest sister ! Tell me how I may
reach you and touch your affections. . . ."

Again his voice broke, and he hung his head in
despair. When again he raised his eyes a sudden
terror froze his blood, and the hair stiffened on his
head.

For Katherine was lying there white and motionless, with lips as blue as those of a corpse, and her
eyes fixed and dim. Slowly she rose, took a step
or two forward, and fell with a piercing cry before
the ikon. A few incoherent words escaped her lips.
Then she fainted. Distractedly Ordinov raised her,
and carried her to his bed, where he seated himself,
in bewilderment, beside her. In a moment or two
she opened her eyes, raised herself a little, and
looked around her. Then, seizing Ordinov's hand,

she drew him towards her, and tried to speak; but
her voice only choked, and died away into sobbing,
while hot tears fell upon Ordinov's hand and
scorched it.

"Oh, how dreadful, how dreadful this is!" she
moaned in a voice of agony. "I think I must be
going to die."

Her parched tongue prevented her from saying
more; she could only gaze despairingly at Ordinov,
who was at a loss to understand her. As he bent
over her and listened, at length he heard her say in
a low, clear voice—

"Bewitched! . . . Yes, I have been bewitched!
. . . I am lost!"

Ordinov straightened himself as he looked with
stern astonishment at the young girl. A terrible
thought had crossed his mind, and manifested itself
in his face by a convulsive spasm.

"Yes—bewitched!" she continued. "That wicked
man has cast a spell over me. Yes, it is *he*, it is
he, who has ruined my life. I have sold him my
soul. . . . Why did you recall to me the memory
of my mother? Why did you come here to torment
me? May God judge and pardon you!" Again she
relapsed into tears.

"He keeps on saying," she continued in a low,
mysterious voice, "that when he is dead he will
return and claim my sinful soul. I am *his*—he has
taken my soul—he reads to me out of his books.
See, *there* is one of his books. He says that I have
committed a mortal sin. Look at the book for
yourself."

She tendered him a volume which he had not
before remarked. Taking it mechanically, he opened
its covers, and saw that it was a book which
resembled the devotional works affected by the
Raskolniki.[1] Yet he could not fix his attention

---

[1] The sect known as the Old Believers, who hold to the Scrip-
tures as they existed in the version before revival, in 1655, by the
Patriarch Nikon.

upon it; he only let it fall to the ground, and then, embracing Katherine, endeavoured to calm her.

"Come," he said, "you have been frightened, but *I* am near you now, so you may return to rest without fear, my sister, my love, the light of my eyes!"

"Ah, you do not understand, you do not understand," she replied as she twined her hands in Ordinov's. "I am *always* like this—I am *always* afraid. At such times I generally seek refuge with *him*, and sometimes, to comfort me, he recites an incantation, or at other times takes this book—the largest one that he possesses—and reads to me out of it. It is all about gloomy, terrible things. Sometimes I do not so much as know what he is reading about, and cannot understand it, and my terror redoubles. It seems to me as though not *he* were speaking, but some evil being whom it would be vain to entreat for mercy, who could never be propitiated. Then I feel such a weight, such a weight, pressing upon my breast! Then I suffer more than ever!"

"Then do not go to see him. Why should you?"

"Ah, I might reply, Why have I come to see *you?* All I know is that I *have* come. You see, he has only to say to me, 'Pray, pray,' and at once I find myself rising in the middle of the night, and going to pray for a long, long time—yes, for whole hours together. Often I feel half-dead for want of sleep, yet am kept awake by my terror. At such times storm-clouds seem to be gathering to destroy me, and an unknown calamity seems to be threatening my life. It is as though wicked people were conspiring to kill me, and all the saints and the angels were refusing to protect me. Then I return to my prayers, my prayers, my endless prayers, until at length a look of pity dawns on the face of the image of the Madonna, and I go back to my bed feeling almost like a dead woman. And sometimes I fall asleep on the floor where I am kneeling

before the ikon, and it is he himself who first
awakens me. He calls to me, caresses and reassures
me, and then I feel better. Yes, I feel strong again
in his presence, and fear evil things no longer. In
him there is power; in what he says there is virtue."

"But of what evil are you afraid? Of what kind
of evil?"

Katherine grew paler still, until to Ordinov she
looked like a woman who has been condemned to
death, and has no hope of reprieve.

"Of what evil am I afraid?" she re-echoed. "Do
you not know that I am a thing accursed—that I
have killed a soul—that my own mother has cursed
me—that I was the cause of my own mother's
death?"

Ordinov silently embraced her, and she pressed
herself to his side with a convulsive shudder.

"Yes, it was *I* who caused her death," she went
on with a shudder at her visions of the irremediable
past. "I have long wanted to tell that to some one,
but have always been forbidden to do so; he has
always bound me to silence on the subject, although
it is through *his* reproaches, through *his* fits of rage,
that I am constantly made to renew my sufferings.
He is my implacable foe, my murderer. In the night-
time all things come back to me, even as they are
doing now. Listen to me—listen! All that I am
telling you happened a long while ago—ever such a
long, long while ago. I do not so much as know
when it happened, although I am for ever seeing it
like a vision of yesterday, like a dream which has
been pressing upon one's heart since overnight.
Trouble, as you know, makes time as nothing.
. . . Press me closer to you, closer to you, and let
me tell you all my misfortunes; and if you can
free me from them—free *me* whom my own mother
has cursed!—I will give you my very life."

Ordinov tried to interrupt her, but, with hands
clasped, she besought him, by his love for her, not
to do so. Then, under the spell of an ever-growing

excitement, she began the following recital.   It was an inconsequential story, the devious wanderings of a storm-ridden soul; yet to Ordinov it seemed intelligible for the reason that her life and troubles were so closely intertwined with his.   In every word that she uttered he could detect and recognise *his own* old enemy—the old man who had figured in his childish dreams, but who was now hectoring it, rather, over the soul of this poor young unsophisticated girl, and profaning it with infinite wickedness.

"It was on such a night as this," she began. "Yet, if anything, it was even wilder, and the wind was howling through our forest as I had never heard it howl before.   (Or did it seem to me to do so only because that night was to prove the night of my undoing?)   Just under our windows it shattered a splendid oak-tree of which I had heard an old beggar say that, even in his boyhood, it had looked as tall and beautiful as it did then. . . . On the night in question (I can remember it as clearly as though it were yesterday) my father's boats were wrecked on the river; and ill though he was, the fishermen had no sooner come to tell him the news than he went out to the factory, to ascertain for himself the extent of the damage.   Thus we were left alone in the house, my mother and I.   I was asleep, and she was weeping bitterly.   Ah, I know now why she was weeping so bitterly! . . . She had been ill, and was as white as a sheet when she awoke me to tell me to prepare her shroud. . . . Suddenly we heard a rapping at the door.   I sprang up in bed, and my mother uttered a cry.   With a timid glance at her I took the lantern, and went out to open the door of the yard. . . . It was *he!* . . . As soon as ever I saw him my fears redoubled, for always—as long as I can remember—I had been afraid of him.   In those days his hair was not yet white, his beard was as black as coal, and his eyes were like two glowing cinders.   On more than one previous occasion they had looked at me with approval.

" ' Is your mother at home? ' he asked.

" ' My *father* is not at home,' I replied as I closed the wicket behind him.

" ' I know that.'

"Suddenly I saw him turn and look at me—look at me, oh, so strangely! It was the first time that he had so looked at me. I moved away towards the house, but he remained standing where he was.

" ' Why do you not come in? ' I said to him.

" ' Because a thought has just struck me.'

"Presently he changed his mind, and entered the house.

" ' Why did you tell me just now that your *father* was not at home when I asked whether your *mother* was? '

"I made no reply. My mother approached him nervously, but he scarcely noticed her. That I saw clearly, as well as that he was wet through and shivering, for the storm had followed him over twenty versts of road. Whence had he come, and where did he live? Neither I nor my mother knew. It was nine weeks since we had last seen him. Throwing down his cap, and pulling off his gloves, he offered no prayer before the ikon, nor yet saluted us as he took a seat before the fire."

At this point Katherine drew her hand across her eyes, as though to shut out some painful vision. Then she raised her head again, and resumed her story.

"He began to talk to my mother in the Tartar dialect—a dialect which I did not understand. As a rule I was sent out of the room whenever he came, but to-night my poor mother dared not utter a word, not even to her own child. And I—I whose soul was already in the toils of the unclean spirit—derived a kind of horrible pleasure from the spectacle of my mother's embarrassment. I could see that they were looking at me, and talking about me, and that she was weeping. Suddenly I saw him draw his knife (it was not the first time he had so threatened my mother). The moment he did so I rose, clung to his belt, and tried to seize the weapon. Indeed, though he ground his teeth, and struggled to repulse me and strike me on the breast, he could not rid himself of my weight. I thought that my last hour had come, for my eyes were closing, and I was gradually sinking to the floor; yet never once did I cry out. At last I saw him take off his belt and open his tunic. Then, tendering me the knife, and pointing to his bare breast, he said : ' Strike, for I have offended you. Take your revenge, my proud beauty. I will make no further resistance.' But I took the knife, and threw it away—doing so with my eyes lowered, yet also with a smile playing on my lips. Nay, on catching sight of my mother's sad face, I even looked at her with an insolent stare, and with the bold smile still curling my lips. She turned as pale as death."

To this rather incoherent narrative Ordinov listened absorbedly. Gradually the very vividness of her reminiscences was calming the poor girl. Like a wave of the sea, her present pain was disappearing before the troubles of the past.

"He replaced his cap, but did not offer to salute us. Once more I took the lantern, to prevent my mother from showing him out (she was too ill to do so, yet I knew that she would make the attempt), and, without a word spoken, we gained the door of the yard. I was just opening the wicket for him, and driving back the dogs, when suddenly he doffed his cap, and made me a low bow. Next, he drew from his pocket a little box of red leather, opened it, and showed it me full of gleaming diamonds. ' In the city,' he said, ' I have a sweetheart, and it was to her that I had meant to present these jewels; but now it shall be *you*, my fair one, that shall have them. Take them to adorn your beauty, or else trample them under your feet. Do with them just as you please.' I took them, but did not trample them under my feet, for I had no wish to pay him such honour. I took them out of sheer bravado, and at the same time with a certain fixed intention. Re-entering the sitting-room, I laid them on the table before my mother. For a moment or two she remained silent, as though in doubt what to say. Then she grew paler still, and said—

"' What are these, Katia?'

"' Some diamonds for you, mother. The merchant has brought them. That is all I know.'

"Tears were streaming from her eyes, and her breath was coming in short gasps.

"' They are *not* for me, Katia! They are *not* for me, you wicked girl! They are *not* for me——!'

"With what bitterness she uttered the words! Her very soul seemed to be weeping. As I looked at her I felt a momentary impulse to throw myself at her feet; but almost as instantly the evil spirit had me for its own again.

"' Very well,' I said. 'If they are not for you, they must be for my father. On his return I will hand him the box, and say to him, "Some merchants have been here, and have left their goods behind them." '

"My mother only wept the more—did my poor mother!

"' *I* will tell him who those merchants are,' she cried, ' as well as for what merchandise they came. *I* will let him know who is your rightful father, you heartless girl! You are no daughter of mine! You are a serpent! You are accursed!'

"I remained silent. No tears came to my eyes, for it was as though everything in me were dead. I returned to my room, and until morning listened to the storm. In *me* also there was a tempest raging.

"Five days passed, and towards evening on the fifth day my father returned, looking gloomy and out of temper. Although he told us that he had fallen ill on the journey, his bandaged hand told me that he had met with an enemy of former times.

Yes, I divined what his illness really meant, as also the precise identity of that enemy. Yes, I understood everything. Saying nothing to my mother—not even asking her where I myself was—my father called his workmen, and bid them cease work and put the house in a state of defence. These were ominous signs. Until nightfall we sat waiting and waiting. Again it turned out a night of tempest. For my part, I went to my window, opened it, and sat weeping there, for my heart was on fire. I felt as though I should have liked to escape from the room, and to flee to the farthest end of the world, where the daylight and the storms have their birth, for my virgin breast was beating tumultuously. Suddenly, at a late hour (in the meanwhile I must have been dozing, or my thoughts must have gone astray), I heard a knocking outside the window, and a voice calling, ' Open, open ! '

"Looking out, I saw a man climbing to the window by means of a rope. At once I recognised my unexpected guest. Opening the casement, I admitted him ; whereupon, without removing his cap, he collapsed upon a chair, and sat there panting and almost breathless, like a man who has been fleeing before tireless pursuers. I turned away, and for some reason grew pale.

"' Is your father at home ? '

"' Yes.'

"' And your mother ? '

"' Yes.'

"' Listen to me, then, and do not speak. Do you hear ? '

"' Yes, I hear.'

"' You hear what ? '

"' I hear a whistling outside the window.'

"' Good ! Now, fair lady, do you wish to bring about the downfall of your enemy ? If so, you have but to call your father, and, damn me, I will surrender. Take that rope and bind me, if you wish. Now is your chance for revenge.'

"I said nothing.

"'Speak!'

"'What do you want?'

"'I wish to rid myself of a woman for whom I no longer care—to say a last farewell to an old sweetheart of mine, and then to give my soul to a newer and younger love—to *you*, my beautiful damsel.'

"I burst out laughing. How was it that I so clearly understood his cynical language?

"'Very well,' he continued. 'But first of all let me into the house to greet my hosts.'

"I shuddered, and my teeth began to chatter, but I opened the door of the room, and admitted him to the other part of the house. Only when he was crossing the threshold did I sufficiently recover my faculties to say—

"'Take your diamonds with you, and bring me no more such presents;' and with that I threw him the little box."

At this point Katherine stopped to take breath. Though she was trembling like a leaf, the blood was once more mounting to her cheeks, her eyes were shining brightly through her tears, and the breath was coming from her lungs with a hissing sound. Presently she turned pale again, and went on in a tone that was at once low, tremulous, mournful, and agitated—

"My visitor gone, I found myself alone. The storm seemed to be hemming me in on every side. Then suddenly I heard a cry, and hasty footsteps in the courtyard below. Above all I could hear loud shouts of 'The factory is on fire!' I remained cowering in a corner of my room, though every one else went running out of doors, until only I and my mother were left in the house. I knew that she was dying, since it was three days since she had left the bed on which she was fated to breathe her last. Yes, I knew it, accursed woman that I was! . . . Then there came the sound of another cry—this time just below my room; a feeble cry like that of some dreaming child. Then again silence. . . . I put out my candle. My blood felt as though it were frozen, and I hid my face in my hands, for I had not the courage to look out of my eyes. Suddenly there arose a clamour close at hand. The workmen were returning from the factory. Leaning far out of the window, I could see the form of my father being borne along on a stretcher—*dead!* Also I could hear the workmen saying to one another, ' He tripped, and fell from a ladder into the white-hot cellar below. The Devil must have pushed him.' . . . Throwing myself upon my bed, I lay there shuddering—lay there hardly knowing whom or what I was expecting. How long I remained in that condition I do not remember. I only remember that my nerves were in an agony of suspense, that my head was aching, and that the smoke from the burning factory was making my eyes smart. Indeed, the thought that perhaps I was going to die seemed to me pleasant rather than otherwise. Suddenly I felt myself lifted up by the shoulders, and saw (so far as the smoke would permit me) *him, him,* with his clothes singed and full of cinders!

"'I have come to look for you, my fair one,' he said. ' Save me, for it is you who have wrought my ruin—it is you for whom I have lost my soul. How shall I ever atone for this accursed night? Suppose that we were to pray together?' He laughed, did that man of dread! 'Show me how I am to get out of the house and escape.'

"I took his arm, and led him along the passage (for I had the keys of all the doors) until we reached a dark cupboard, where I pointed out to him a window which gave upon the garden. Seizing me in his powerful arms, he leapt with me through the window, and for a long time we ran hand in hand, until we had reached a dense, dark forest. There he stopped a moment to listen.

"'We are being pursued, Katherine,' he said.

'We are being pursued. But the hour of my death is not yet come. Embrace me, fair one, in honour of our happiness and eternal love.'

"'But why are your hands all covered with blood?'

"'Because I was forced to cut the throats of your father's dogs, my dearest. They were baying God-speed to the lingering guest. Come!'

"Once more we ran, until, at a turn in the path, we suddenly came upon my father's horse. It had broken its halter, and fled from the stable, since it had no mind to perish in the flames.

"'Mount, Katia,' said my lover. 'God has sent us this means of escape. Will you not? Are you afraid of me? I am not a heretic or a libertine. I will make the sign of the cross if you wish.'

"He did so, and upon that I mounted: and as he clasped me to his breast I forgot everything, as though I were in a dream. On returning to my senses I found that we had arrived at the brink of a large river. Descending the bank, we plunged into a bed of bullrushes, where I soon caught sight of a small boat which my companion had previously concealed there.

"'Good-bye, brave horse,' he said. 'Good-bye. Seek now a new master, since your old one is gone.'

"I too ran to my father's horse, and embraced it. Then we took our seats in the boat, and, as soon as my companion had run out the sculls, we lost sight of the bank. Presently he ceased rowing, and looked all around him at the water.

"'Hail, Mother Volga!' he cried. 'Hail, my beautiful, my tempestuous river—the inexhaustible source at which all the children of God may drink! Foster-Mother, hast thou watched over my substance during my absence? Is my merchandise all in good order? Yet mayest thou take it all, thou stormy, thou insatiable one, if only thou wilt spare and be good to my pearl without price. . . . And, for thee,' he added to myself, 'do thou but speak to me a few words, my fair one—but a few words. Lighten my darkness, thou sun! Scatter my night, thou beacon!'

"He was laughing and talking in the same breath, in order to reassure me. Yet I could not meet his gaze, for I was burning with shame, and felt unable to utter a single word. The reason of this he understood.

"'Be it so!' he said, and his voice was full of tenderness now. 'There can be no striving against compulsion. May God pardon me, my darling—my proud, my beautiful darling! Do you still hate me? Am I still altogether repugnant to you?'

"As I listened there suddenly came upon me a storm of passion. But this time it was the passion of love.

"'Whether I hate you or not,' I replied, 'I would ask of you, Where else in the world would you have found a girl so bold, so insensate, as to admit you to her chamber in the dead of night? I have sold to you my soul for a mortal sin. My heart went suddenly mad, and I was powerless to restrain it. Of tears have I earned full measure. Yet it is not for *you* to gloat over the misfortunes of others; it is not for *you* to make sport of the heart of a young girl.'

"This I said despite myself. Then I relapsed into sobbing. He looked at me in silence for a while, and his eyes made me shiver.

"'Listen, fair one,' he replied—and his eyes were burning with more than human lustre. 'What I am about to say to you is no empty talk. So long as you shall give me happiness you shall be mine; but if ever the day shall come when you have ceased to love me, say nothing, waste not a single word, let there be no constraint between us. You will have but to bend your dark eyebrows, to avert your black eyes, to raise your little finger—and I will restore to you both your love and your liberty. *Only*, my tempestuous beauty, *that day will be the day of my death.*'

"At these words I felt my very flesh creep."

Profound emotion here interrupted Katherine's speech. Then a new flood of recollections caused her to recover her breath again, and to smile. Indeed, had not, at that moment, her eyes encountered Ordinov's fixed, ardent gaze, she would have continued her narrative. As it was, she shuddered and tried to speak, but the blood only mantled to her cheeks, and she was fain, as one demented, to bury her face in the pillow. Ordinov too felt profoundly moved. His very blood seemed to be turning to poison, and causing him an agony which was increasing with each successive word from Katherine. He felt filled at once with boundless resentment and with an invincible, yet bootless, passion. Indeed, there were moments when he could even have prayed Katherine to be silent, when he could have thrown himself at her feet and besought her to restore him the bliss of those early sufferings when, as yet, he had known nothing of her; to restore him his first passion, vague, yet pure; to restore him his first tears which, alas! had long since dried. Now that those tears could no longer flow he could feel the blood pouring into his heart at such a rate that he was ceasing to understand what Katherine was saying, and even growing afraid of her. How, in that hour, he cursed his love! He felt as though he were being suffocated—as though it were no longer blood, but a stream of lead, that was trickling through his veins.

"Yet that is not my greatest trouble," said Katherine as she raised her head again. "No, not that, not that!" she repeated in an altered voice as her face contracted and her eyes shone with a dry glitter. "Not that, not that, not that! One can have but one mother, and I have one no longer, but what does a mother matter, or the curse which she uttered when her last miserable hour had come, or

T

my former life, or my peace of heart, or my chastity, or my seduction, or my bartering away of my soul, or my commission of an eternal sin to gain a single moment's happiness? No. Though these things have been my ruin, they do not matter. My greatest trouble, and that which most embitters my heart, is to think that I am a *slave* to my own shame, that I love my infamy, that I hug the memory of my undoing as a blessed recollection. That is my greatest misery—the thought that my heart should be nerveless, that it should be incapable of feeling resentment at its own wickedness."

Again breath failed her, while an hysterical sob caught her by the throat. Her gasping lips looked parched, her breast kept convulsively rising and falling, and a curious anger was burning in her eyes. Yet her face was so replete with charm— each line of her features was vibrating with such beauty, was animated with such passion—that Ordinov's brooding thoughts once more took to flight, and he longed for one thing, and one thing only : to press his heart to that of the young girl, to let it forget everything as it beat to the same stormy rhythm as hers. Their eyes met, and she smiled. Instantly he felt as though he were caught between two rivers of fire.

"Mercy—have mercy !" he gasped. He was so close to her that their breaths were actually mingling. "It is *you* who have bewitched *me*. Wherein does your trouble lie? I do not know. I only know that my mind has for ever lost its peace. Forget those sorrows of yours, and tell me what you wish ; command me, and I will obey. Only come with me. Do not leave me here to die."

Katherine looked at him, but returned no answer. She had tried to interrupt him, and to take his hand, but the words had failed her. For the second time a curious smile dawned on her lips—there dawned something almost like laughter.

"Nay, but I have not told you all," she continued,

raising her voice a little. "I have yet many things to tell you. Do you wish to hear them? Do you, my poor, passionate lover? Listen, then, to your sister, for you do not yet understand the extent of her trouble. I could tell you how I spent a year with my protector, but I will not do so. At the end of that year he descended the river with some friends of his, and I was left at the house of a woman whom he called his mother—there to await his return. For a month, for two months, I waited. Then one day, when in the city, I met a young merchant. No sooner did I catch sight of him than the memory of my earlier and happier years came back to me.

"'Sweetheart,' he said, after he had exchanged a few words with me, 'I am Alesha,[1] your old betrothed. Do you remember how the old folk plighted us when we were children? Do you remember it? Or have you forgotten? Think a moment, for I am of your own country.'

"'And what say they of me in our own country?' I asked him.

"Alesha smiled.

"'They say that you are leading a bad life,' he replied, '—that you have lost your honour, and are living with a brigand, a robber of men.'

"'And what say you of me?'

"He shuddered.

"'I can say nothing good of you, nothing good. Yet never have I spoken ill of you since we last parted. . . . Ah, you have been my ruin! Pray buy my soul too, as you have bought his. Take my heart too, and make sport of my love. I am alone in the world—my own master now. My soul belongs to me alone. I have not acted as a certain girl acted—a girl who killed her own memory. I have not sold my soul. Why, then, do I say, "Buy it," seeing that it is not for sale? No, I will give

---

[1] A diminutive of Alexis.

it you for nothing. There is no reserve price upon it in the market.'

"I burst out laughing. This was not the first time, nor yet the second, that he spoke to me thus, since he remained in that spot a whole month, to the neglect alike of his business and of his friends. He lived there quite alone, until I began to feel sorry for his loneliness. At length, one morning, I said to him—

"'Alesha, meet me at dusk on the river bank, and we will go to your home together. I have had enough of my life of misery.'

"When night had fallen I made a bundle of my clothes. My heart was at once joyful and sad. Suddenly I saw my protector enter, though I had not been expecting him."

"'Good-evening,' he said. 'Come with me quickly, for a storm is brewing on the river, and we have little time to lose.'

"I rose and followed him, and we took the road to the river. What a long way it seemed! At length we sighted a small boat wherein there sat a rower whom I knew well. By his posture I could see that he was expecting some one.

"'Good-evening, Alesha,' said my protector. "God be with you! Perhaps something has delayed you, and you are waiting to return to your boats? Good fellow, pray ferry myself and my wife across the river to our friends. It is a long way thither, and I have allowed my own boat to depart, and it is over-far for us to swim.'

"'Come, then,' said Alesha; and my whole soul shivered at his voice.

"'Sit down,' he went on. 'The wind is blowing right for every one, so let every one take passage in my beautiful boat.'

"We stepped in. The night was dark, starless, and very stormy, and the waves were running high. No one spoke until we had left the bank a verst behind.

"'What a storm!' said my protector. 'Yes, it

is a heavy storm. Never within my memory have I seen its like on the river. Soon it will be a hurricane. The boat is top-heavy, and we can no longer ride three in it.'

"'No, we can no longer ride three in it. *One* of us is one too many.' As Alesha uttered these words his voice was quivering like the string of a violin.

"'Alesha, I have known you since you were a boy. I was your father's friend, and you and I have eaten bread and salt together. Tell me, therefore, Alesha, could you reach yonder bank without the boat, or would you prefer to lose your soul for nothing?'

"'*I* do not leave this boat,' replied Alesha. 'But what of yourself, good sir? If it should befall you to swallow a drop too much, it would mean no more than a somewhat comfortless moment.'

"'I too do not leave this boat. The water would never bear me up. Hold! Do you too listen, Katherine my treasure. I can recall just such a night as this, except that the waves were not so large, and the moon and the stars were shining. I would ask you, then—Have you forgotten that night?'

"'No—I have not forgotten it,' I replied.

"'Do you also remember a certain compact? Do you remember a man in love explaining to a fair maiden that, should the day ever come when he had ceased to find favour in her eyes, her liberty should be restored to her?'

"'Yes—that also I remember.' Yet at the moment I hardly knew whether I were alive or dead.

"'You remember that also? Good! Now, in this boat we are one too many. For one of us two men the hour must soon strike. Say, then, my dear one—decide now, my darling, which of us two—he or I—is to hear that hour sound? Speak but the word.'

"I could not answer."

Further than this Katherine did not get, for at

that moment a voice from behind them—a voice
hoarse and muffled—called her by name. Ordinov
started violently. In the doorway stood Murin—
clad in a fur coat, deadly pale, and glaring at the
couple with a semi-maniacal expression. Katherine
turned as pale as he, and sat returning his stare as
though fascinated.

"Return to my room, Katherine," said the sick
man, his voice scarcely intelligible. Then he left
them.

Katherine continued to gaze at the doorway as
intently as if the old man were still there. Then
the blood suddenly flamed into her white cheeks,
and with slow deliberation she rose. As she did so
the first meeting between her and himself recurred
to Ordinov's memory.

"Until to-morrow, then, my dear one," she said
with a strange smile. "Remember the point where
I left off—namely, at the point ' Choose between us
two, my beloved. Decide which of us you desire,
and which of us you do not.' You will remember
the place, will you not? You will wait until
to-morrow night? "

As she spoke she laid her hands upon the young
man's shoulders, and looked at him tenderly.

"Katherine, do not go away—do not go back to
him. He is mad."

"Katherine ! " called Murin again from behind the
partition-wall.

"What of that? " said Katherine with the same
strange smile as before. "What if he *does* kill me?
Good-night, my poor little brother—you whom I
ought never to have seen." Her head touched
Ordinov's breast for a moment, the tears bedewing
her face.

"They are my last tears," she murmured. . . .
"Now, dearest one, let all your troubles sleep
awhile. To-morrow you will awake the better for
them." With these words there went a passionate
embrace.

"Katherine, Katherine ! " cried Ordinov as he

fell upon his knees and sought to detain her.
"Katherine!"

She turned to him with a smiling nod as she left
the room. Then Ordinov heard her enter Murin's
apartment, and held his breath to listen. Not a
word came from the old man. Perhaps he had
once more sunk into oblivion? At all events no
sound reached Ordinov's ears. The young man
tried to rise and go himself to Murin's room, but
his legs failed him, and he sank back fainting upon
the bed.

II

For a long while after he had awakened Ordinov
could not imagine what the time was. Was it the
darkness of dawn or of twilight? How long had
he been asleep? In any case his sleep had been of
an unhealthy nature. He passed his hand over his
face, as though to drive away the phantoms of the
night, and tried to rise, but found his limbs refuse
their office. Not only was he shivering with cold,
but his head was aching badly. Yet with consciousness there was returning also memory, and he shuddered as a sudden flash of recollection recalled to
him the whole of the preceding night. So vivid
were his impressions of it that he could not believe
that several hours had passed between it and the
present moment. Surely it had all just happened?
Surely Katherine had but this moment left the room?
His eyes were wet with tears. Were those marks
of emotion the tears of the past terrible night, or
were they entirely new tears? Strangest fact of all,
his sufferings now seemed to him pleasant, even
though he was aware that his enfeebled frame could
not support another such ordeal. At one moment,
believing himself to be at the point of death (so
bewildered was he with his impressions), he felt
that death would come as a welcome guest; while,
the next moment, rapture filled his soul to such a

degree that his very vitality seemed to be bursting from him—his very soul seemed to be on fire, to be ready to break out into flame before expiring for ever !

Suddenly a voice began to sing such harmonies as occur to the soul only in hours of ineffable joy. Close at hand—almost (so it seemed to him) over his head—Katherine's clear, firm voice was singing a tender, recurrent melody. It rose, it fell, and died away in a plaintive cadence, as though it were consumed with a suppressed, yet insatiable, passion—a passion that was close-locked in the recesses of an amorous heart. Next it rose in trills like those of a nightingale (true symbol of inextinguishable affection), and diffused a sea of melody which had in it all the vitality of love's young dream. In the song Ordinov could distinguish certain simple, sentimental words which chimed wonderfully with the melody; yet it was not they which touched him, but the music itself. The simple, artless words which Katherine sang he found himself replacing with others which corresponded better to the hidden impulses of his passion—words which were full of *her*. First the song sounded like the last sob of hopeless passion. Anon it sounded like a cry of joy from a heart which has burst its chains, and is surrendering itself, in free and untrammelled serenity, to a noble devotion. Anon it spoke of the first accents of love, of modesty suffused with virgin blushes, of glittering tears, of timid, mysterious whisperings. Finally it seemed to voice the unsatisfied desire of a proud vestal who, rejoicing in her own strength, and standing unveiled to the light of day, opens to the full eyes which intoxicate the senses.

Ordinov could not await the end of the song. Yet he had hardly risen to his feet when the music ceased.

"It is neither ' good-morning ' nor ' good-afternoon ' that one must say to you, dearest one," continued the voice, "but ' good-evening.' Rise and come hither to our room. Come that I may have pleasure in your company. My protector and I are awaiting you, and are desirous of doing you a service. Pray, therefore, purge your love of all resentment (if still you feel any offence at the insult which has been done you), and come and talk to us."

Ordinov rose at Katherine's summons—though with no distinct idea in his mind beyond that, willy-nilly, he was going to his landlord's room. Presently a door opened before him, and, as clear as sunlight, there burst upon his vision the smile of his marvellous *inamorata*. Nothing could he see or hear but her, and his heart felt ready to burst with joy.

"Twice the sun has risen since we met," she said as she extended to him her hand. "Two dawns occur also in the heart of a young girl. The first dawn covers her face with the hue of virgin modesty, when her heart is beginning to awaken; the second dawn tinges it with the deeper hue of matured affection. Enter, then; enter, my dearest friend. Why should you halt upon the threshold? We tender you our love and honour. My protector also extends to you his greeting."

With a musical laugh she took Ordinov by the hand, and compelled him to enter. He did so with downcast eyes, for she seemed to him so marvellously beautiful that he could scarcely bear the sight of her. Never before had she appeared so entrancing, now that her features were wreathed in open, sparkling merriment. Yet her hand shook a little as it lay in his, and, had he raised his eyes to hers, he would have seen there a triumphant smile.

"Do you too rouse yourself, old man," she said, recovering herself with an effort. "Rise and greet our guest. A guest is a brother, and his host should rise to receive him. Salute our visitor, therefore, and tender him the right hand of good-fellowship."

For the first time the fact of Murin's presence

occurred to Ordinov's mind. In the old man's eyes
there was a dim look of pain, and he was staring
at his visitor with the same infuriated, insensate
expression which had struck Ordinov so forcibly
before. Though lying only in a half-dressed state
upon the bed, he had evidently been out during the
day, since around his neck there was wrapped a
scarlet comforter, and on his feet he was wearing a
pair of boots. Clearly, too, he was recovering from
his illness, though he still looked pale and wan.
Katherine approached him, and, with one hand resting upon the table, looked him fixedly in the face.
A smile which seemed to say that all that was being
done was being done at her good pleasure never
once left her lips.

"So it is *you?*" said Murin, rising from the bed,
and then reseating himself. "So it is *you*, my
lodger? I have done you a wrong, sir. I offended
you without knowing it, and then played the fool
with a revolver. Yet who the devil would have
supposed *you* to be an epileptic?" Then he
added with a frown, and hoarsely, as he involuntarily turned his eyes aside: "You see, when a
malady like mine comes upon one it does not first
give a warning knock at the door, but enters unawares, like a thief. Only the other day I nearly
put a bullet into Katherine's heart too. In short,
I am not very well, and have fits sometimes. Now
you know all. Pray sit down and be my guest."

Ordinov, in his turn, looked fixedly at his host.

"Sit down, sit down!" cried the old man impatiently. "Sit down, since *she* wishes it. You two
have become 'brother and sister' to one another,
I understand? You are as loving as a pair of
sweethearts, are you not?"

Ordinov seated himself.

"Look at your 'sister,' then," continued the old
man, with a laugh which revealed two rows of white
teeth whereof not a single one was missing. "Do
not be nervous about it. Do you *really* think your
'sister' very comely, my good sir? Tell me. Give

her a good look over, and pay homage to her beauty. Show us that your heart is bleeding for her."

Ordinov darted such a look of fury at the speaker that for the moment Murin quailed under it. The young man's breast was filled with rage that almost approached the boiling-point. Yet a sort of animal instinct warned him that, though he could not account for the interview (indeed, his mind seemed too paralysed for that), he was in the presence of a deadly enemy.

"Nay! Do *not* look at me!" said Katherine's voice from behind him.

He turned round.

"Nay, do *not* look at me, I beseech you, lest evil spirits should tempt your thoughts. Have some pity upon your beloved one."

Then, with a burst of laughter, she suddenly darted forward, and laid her hands over his eyes. Next, she as suddenly removed them, and buried her face in their palms. Yet she must have known that the rosiness of her face was still visible through her fingers; she must, therefore, have had no great objection to meeting the looks and smiles of the two men. Both Ordinov and Murin gazed at her in silence—Ordinov with a sort of loving astonishment, as though he were taking his first look at some famous beauty, and the old man with cold absorption. Nothing was to be read in Murin's impassive countenance; but his lips were turning blue, and beginning to tremble a little.

Katherine approached the table, cleared it of its books and papers, and placed it near the window. She was now breathing rapidly and in jerks, while at intervals she would inhale deeply, as though air were failing her, and her breast would rise and fall like the crest of a wave as it breaks upon the sea-shore. Beneath her downcast eyelids the lashes stood out like freshly-sharpened needles against the clarity of her cheeks.

"Daughter of the Tsar!" cried the old man.

"My queen!" murmured Ordinov. Yet almost

as he uttered the words he recovered his presence
of mind, for he realised that the old man's gaze
was bent upon him with a look of concentrated
malice and cold contempt.   He tried to rise, but
some invincible force nailed his feet to the floor,
and he was fain to reseat himself with fists
clenched.   He could not believe that the scene was
real; he believed himself to be the sport of some
nightmare, of some evil dream which was weighing
down his eyelids.   Strangest thing of all, he had no
desire from that dream to awaken.

Katherine removed the worn tablecloth, opened a
trunk, and took thence a more valuable cloth which
was embroidered in scarlet and gold silks.   With
this she recovered the table.   Next, from an antique
silver-mounted dressing-case she drew three silver
drinking-cups; one of which she presented, with a
solemn—almost a dreamy—air, to Ordinov and to
the old man respectively.

"Which of us," she said, "has not the good-will
of the other two?   In any case our guest has *mine*,
and he shall drink with me to-night.   Yes, both of
you are my ' brothers,' so let us drink to love and
to concord."

"Yes, yes!" cried the old man eagerly.   "Let us
drink together, and drown our cares in wine.   Pour
it out, Katherine."

"And *you*—do *you* also wish me to pour out the
wine?" Katherine asked of Ordinov.

For answer he held out his cup.

"One moment!" cried the old man with uplifted
hand.   "Let the one of us who cherishes an unsatisfied wish live some day to see it realised!"

They clinked their cups and drank.

"Next let us drink to you and to myself, old
man," said Katherine to her protector.   "If within
the recesses of your heart you still feel any tenderness for me, honour the toast.   Drink to our past
happiness; drink to the years which are gone.   If
you love me, bid me fill the cups again."

"Your wine is strong, my little one—so strong

that you do but wet your lips with it," retorted the
old man with a smile as again he tendered her his
goblet.

"At least I will *taste* of the wine, but *you*—you
shall drink your measure to the dregs. Why live
in company with sad thoughts, old man? Sad
thoughts only make the heart sick. To think is but
to grieve; therefore to live happily one should live
without thinking at all. Drink deep, old man, and
drown your care."

"Are you so well acquainted with care that you
know the best way to banish it? Come! I drink
to you, Katherine, my pure white dove! And you,
sir," he continued to Ordinov, "have you (if I might
make so bold) any acquaintance with care?"

"If I have I should prefer to keep it," murmured
Ordinov, who had never yet taken his eyes off
Katherine.

"Did you hear that?" she cried to Murin. "I
too have but a short acquaintance with introspection,
for time was when I gave no thought to the past;
but suddenly there came an hour when I could
remember all things : all that had ever happened to
me I lived over again in my insatiable soul."

"Ah, but it is ill work to congratulate oneself
only upon the past," remarked the old man despond-
ently. "The past is like wine which has been drunk.
What good does it contain? 'Tis like an old coat
—fit only to be thrown away."

"Yet it can *remake* itself," interrupted Katherine
with a forced smile, while two great tears which
had formed themselves on her eyelashes hung sus-
pended there, like diamonds. "No one can live their
whole life alone. The heart of a young girl is gay
—too gay even for yours to beat in full unison
with it. Do you understand what I say, old man?
. . . See, see! One of my tears has fallen into
your cup!"

"Have you received happiness—much happiness—
in return for your sorrow?" said Ordinov in a voice
which trembled with emotion.

"Perhaps, sir, you have 'much happiness' to sell?" interposed Murin. "Why do you interrupt when you have not been spoken to?" And he glared with a bitter, insolent smile.

"Yes, I *have* received a little happiness in return for my sorrow," said Katherine with a note of discontent in her tone. "What appears much to one person may appear very little to another. One person may wish always to be giving and never to receive, while another person may wish always to be receiving and never to be a giver. You at least" (this was said to Ordinov, accompanied with a look that was almost hard) "have no right to reproach me. One person may be of one kind, and another of another. Do you know *any one* to whom life has been wholly pleasant? . . . Old man, drink deep of your cup—drink deep! Drink to the happiness of your well-beloved—of her who has ever been your willing slave. Fill and drink."

"Be it so! But do you also drink," said the old man as he took the wine from her.

"As you will. But stay a moment. I would first say a word or two."

Katherine leaned her elbows upon the table, and sought to plumb the old man's eyes with her own. A curious air of resolve had settled upon her face. She seemed to be all on fire, and her movements were brusque and sudden. Undoubtedly a change had taken place in her mood. Her beauty, too, increased with her animation. Her lips, half-parted in a smile, revealed the whiteness of her teeth; her breath came in pants which made her nostrils dilate and contract; her temples were lightly spotted with sweat; and her hair—until now triply plaited upon the nape of her neck—had fallen, in disarray, over her left ear.

"Tell me the future, old man," she said. "Tell me my fate before your intellect has wholly immersed itself in wine. Here is my hand for you to look at. It is not for nothing that you are known as a mystic. Have you not studied books, and do you

not know the black art in its entirety? Look at my
hand, then, old man, and tell me what evils are
threatening my life. Yet do not lie; tell me only
what you *know*. Shall I ever be happy? Will you
ever pardon me, or do you propose always to strew
my path with misfortune? Shall I ever find a place
of refuge, or shall I, like a bird of passage, have to
spend lonely days among the righteous, seeking
always a place where I may lay my head? Who
loves me? Who hates me? Who would injure me?
Will my heart, now so young and ardent, always
be forced to pine in solitude? Will it fall to me
to spend my youth alone, and to go to the grave
before my time? On the other hand, will my heart
ever find a mate with whom it may beat in joyous
unison until a new sorrow arrive? Under what blue
skies, by what seas or forests, dwells now my true
lover? Will he love me well, or will he soon tire
of me? Will he always abide by his troth? . . .
Tell me also, old man, how long you and I will
abide together—here, in this murky den, among
your black books? Will the time ever come for me
to render you a last salute, to wish you health and
rest, and to bid you a final adieu? Will the time
ever come for me to thank you for your bread and
salt, for your meat and drink, and for all the pleasant
stories which you have so often related to me? . . .
Give me your best attention, and tell me the whole
truth. Do not lie to me, old man, but show me all
your skill."

Her animation had kept increasing until, at this
point, her voice broke. Though her eyes were
blazing, her upper lip was trembling; and though
in her words there was biting mockery, in her
accents there was also the note of tears. She
leaned across the table, and looked the old man full
in the face, while her heart beat loudly.

Ordinov uttered a painful cry, and tried to rise—
only to find himself once more nailed to his seat by
a swift, sidelong glance from the old man. In that
glance—a glance which made Ordinov tremble, and

cooled the utmost bitterness of his rage—were mingled irony, contempt, disquietude, and a sort of malicious curiosity.

When Katherine ceased to speak the old man smiled a dreamy, resigned smile. During her speech he had never once taken his eyes off her; but, now that his heart had received its death-blow, now that the fatal words had been spoken, he delivered his answer.

"It is a great deal that you wish to know at once, little bird who are trying your wings and burning to use them. Very well. Pour me out another cupful of wine, so that I may first drink to your liberation; otherwise I might be unable to avert the black eye from my will-power. For the devil, as you know, is strong, and evil is not very far from here."

With these words he raised his glass, and emptied it; but the more he drank, the paler he grew, and the more his eyes glowed like twin coals until, coupled with the fearful pallor of his countenance, they seemed almost to presage another fit. As for Ordinov, the wine was so strong that a single cupful of it had sufficed to obscure his vision, to inflame his blood, and to weaken his will-power. Consequently, in accepting a second cupful, he hardly knew the reason for his action—unless it was that he sought by its means to steady his nerves. Yet no sooner had he drunk it than the blood poured the faster through his veins, and he became a prey to such giddiness that, try as he might, he found it difficult to follow what was passing around him.

The old man dashed his cup upon the table.

"Fill it again, Katherine!" he cried. "Fill it again, O woman of misfortune! Fill it for me till death shall come—until the old man shall have sunk into his last long sleep, and you are rid of him at last! But for the present let us drink together. Why do you not drink? Do you suppose that I have not observed your failing to do so?"

Ordinov could not hear Katherine's answer—and, moreover, Murin did not let her finish, since, unable, apparently, to contain himself any longer, he seized her by the hand. His face was now deadly pale, and though his eyes kept glowing and growing dull by turns, his lips were trembling unsteadily as he began—

"Give me your hand, my little beauty. Give it to me. Yes, I will tell you your fortune, for in truth I am a mystic, as you have said. Your little heart of gold did not lead you astray when it told you that I am its soothsayer, and that I can foretell it the truth, whole and undefiled. But one thing have you forgotten. It is that, though one may tell a woman the truth, one can never impart to her intelligence and sagacity. No, intelligence is never a young girl's. She may hear the truth, but she cannot understand it. For, though in her head there may lurk a serpent of cunning, her heart is but a fountain of amorous tears. Yet always she will find her way unaided, and worm her way through any misfortune. Yes, a clever woman invariably succeeds—partly through her power of intuition, and partly through the power of her beauty (a single glance from which can intoxicate the soul). Yes, beauty will always overcome strength, and break in two even a heart of steel. . . . Will you know trouble, know adversity? No; for sorrow is not for the feeble heart. It is for the heart of strength —for the heart which can silently bathe itself in tears of blood. True sorrow will never be heard to complain; but *your* sorrow, maiden, is but a mark in the sand which the rain may wash out, and the sun efface, and the wind obliterate. . . . Will you ever be loved? At least you will never be the slave of the man who loves *you*. *You* will take from him his liberty—and you will never restore it. Yet when you, in your turn, shall seek a lover, you will never succeed in finding one. Always it will be as though you had sowed seed, and some one else had come and reaped the harvest of it. Just now, O tender child, O little creature of the sunshine, you let fall a tear into my cup—and with that tear you sowed a

U

thousand future tears, even before the words had
left your lips. Ah! *Some* day those tears will flow
in abundance! They will flow when, during long,
long nights of despair, sorrow shall come upon you,
and shall wrap you about with cankering memories.
Then will you remember the tear which you dropped
to-day! Yet will that tear never be to you aught
but an alien, a poisoned, tear—a little drop of water
which shall weigh heavier even than lead. It will
burn into the blood of your white bosom, and all
night, all night, until the weary dawn of a new day
of misery shall rise, you will toss upon your little
bed under the stress of a wound which will not heal
for many and many a day. . . . Come! Pour me
out another cupful of wine, Katherine, my dove.
Pour it out. Pour me out another cupful as a
reward for all my soothsaying, and let us have done
with idle talk."

His voice broke, and something like a sob escaped
his lips. Then he seized the wine, drank it down at
a draught, and dashed the cup upon the table. His
eyes were blazing.

"Let each man live the life he wills!" he cried.
"The past do you throw over your shoulder, and
then fill the cup again. Even though the soul perish,
a fig for wine's effects upon the unruly head, so
long only as the old man may sleep his last long
night away without dreams and without remembrance! Will he not have drunk all, have lived
all? And has not the merchandise already been
lying over-long in the merchant's store? Let him,
then, give it away for nothing. Yet a time there
was when he would not have yielded it for a single
groat under its value; when he would have shed in
its defence the blood both of friend and of foe;
when the purchaser would have had to give his very
soul to conclude the bargain. . . . Pour out the
wine again, Katherine!"

But even as he stretched out his hand it fell to his
side. He was now breathing with difficulty, and
his head was drooping. Again he shot a stern look

at Ordinov, but the fire of his gaze had grown much dimmer, and presently his eyelids closed, and a mortal pallor overspread his features. His lips moved as though he would have spoken again, while a tear which had sprung to his eyelashes started to roll slowly over his cheek.

Ordinov could bear the scene no longer. He rose, staggered forward, and took Katherine by the hand. Yet she never looked at him, but seemed to have forgotten his presence as completely as though she had never been acquainted with him. Moreover, she appeared to have lost all sense of reality, and to be a prey to some one fixed idea. Sinking upon her knees beside the unconscious Murin, she took him in her arms, and fixed her gaze upon him as though it were riveted to his form. For a time she seemed to be wholly unaware that Ordinov was still holding her hand; but at length she threw him a long and piercing look, while her lips curled with a bitter smile.

"Go! Away with you!" she said under her breath. "You are drunken! You are a villain! You are no longer our guest!"

Again she turned to the old man—listening to his breathing, and watching tensely over him as he slumbered.

Despair and rage crushed Ordinov's heart as in a vice.

"Katherine, Katherine!" he murmured as he pressed her hand. Her features contracted, and she raised her head; yet in her face there was such mockery, insolence, and contempt that Ordinov could scarcely bear the sight. Slowly she pointed to the old man, while in her eyes Ordinov could read all the disdainful hatred of his old enemy, all the wounding iciness of his glance.

"He will only kill you," he said, no longer able to contain his wrath.

At once there occurred to him an evil thought: and as instantly the devil seemed to whisper in his ear that the same thought was in Katherine's mind also.

"*I* will buy you of the merchant," was the thought which had occurred to him, "even though 'the purchaser must give his very soul to conclude the bargain.' Yet the blood which must be shed for you *shall not be shed by the vendor.*"

All this time a fixed smile—a smile which was striking death to Ordinov's heart—lingered upon Katherine's features. Beside himself, and almost insensible, he raised his hand, and unhooked from the wall an ancient dagger. As he did so astonishment and, for the first time, a sort of challenge showed themselves in Katherine's eyes. Then some one seemed to seize Ordinov's hand, and to impel him further towards the foolish deed. He drew the dagger from its sheath, while Katherine stared at him tensely, and almost without breathing.

Once more he glanced at the old man. He could have sworn that he saw one of the old man's eyes slowly open, and gaze into his (Ordinov's) face with a mocking smile! Yes, the eyes of the two men met and challenged one another! Ordinov stood petrified. Presently the smile seemed to overspread the whole face, and something like icy, death-like laughter rang through the room! Ordinov started so violently that the dagger slipped from his hand, and fell with a clatter to the floor. At the sound Katherine uttered a cry, as though she too were awaking from a nightmare, while Murin slowly rose, and with a movement of his foot pushed the weapon away into a corner of the room. For a while Katherine remained kneeling like a statue— bolt upright, her eyes closed and her features convulsed; but at length, sinking her head upon her hands, she fell forward, crying in heartrending accents—

"Alesha, Alesha!"

In a moment Murin had seized her in his powerful arms, and pressed her to his bosom with incredible violence. Yet when she sought to hide her face in his breast the old man's every feature grinned with such shameless, cynical laughter that Ordinov's

very being shuddered. The essence of fraud and
deceit, the essence of jealousy and calculated tyranny
—that is what spoke in the effrontery of that
laughter.

"The woman is mad—mad!" muttered Ordinov
as he turned and rushed from the house.

III

WHEN, at eight o'clock next morning, Ordinov—
his nerves still shaken with the events of the previous
night—opened Yaroslav Ilyitch's door (whither by
some unknown means he found himself wafted), he
started back, and stood petrified, on perceiving that
Murin was there before him. Yet, though the old
man looked scarcely able to hold himself upright,
he had refused Yaroslav's kindly offer of a chair.
As for Yaroslav, he uttered a cry of joy on perceiving
Ordinov; but his delight was short-lived, for the
next moment he was so seized with confusion that
he could only keep vacillating between his chair
and the table, without knowing exactly what next
to say or to do. Though conscious that it was in
the highest degree improper for him to be smoking
and neglecting his visitors at such a juncture, his
perturbation allowed him no choice but to continue
drawing at his pipe (and that with all his might) as
though there was some possible inspiration to be
derived therefrom.

Ordinov, on entering, threw a sidelong glance at
Murin, over whose face at that moment there
passed something like the malicious laugh which had
marked it the night before. Ordinov shuddered.
Almost instantly Murin's expression lost its appearance of enmity, and resumed its impenetrable air
as he saluted his lodger with a deferential bow.

This mute encounter gave Ordinov time to recover
himself. The better to take in the situation he
looked at Yaroslav Ilyitch, who, as yet, had by no
means regained his composure.

"Welcome!" cried Yaroslav. "Welcome, my dearest friend, Vassilii Michaelovitch! Enlighten us with your presence, and set your seal upon the common objects in this room." He pointed vaguely to a corner of the apartment, and then turned as red as a poppy—partly through confusion at his own awkwardness, and partly through displeasure at having murdered one of his choicest flowers of speech. With a sharp clatter he pushed forward another chair.

"I hope I am not putting you out at all?" said Ordinov. "I only wanted—er—to have two minutes' conversation with you."

"As long as you like!" cried Yaroslav. "*How* could you put me out, I should like to know? Have some tea, will you? Here, waiter!—You too will have another glassful,[1] I hope?" he added to Murin, who at once accepted the offer.

"Three more glasses!" was the stern order to the waiter when he entered; after which Yaroslav seated himself beside Ordinov, and spent several minutes in rolling his head from side to side (from Murin to Ordinov, and from Ordinov to Murin) like a china dog. Certainly he was in a very awkward position. Though he felt that he ought to go on talking, what he wished to say only came with difficulty, and suitable words failed him. For his part, Ordinov seemed once more to have sunk into a stupor. At length the pair of them began to speak at the same moment; whereupon the hitherto silent Murin, who had been observing them with some curiosity, exploded in a laugh which disclosed all his teeth.

"I came to tell you," said Ordinov to the old man, "that unfortunate circumstances compel me to give you notice."

"What a strange coincidence!" put in Yaroslav Ilyitch. "Why, I too was surprised, this morning, to hear this good gentleman acquaint me with your decision."

---

[1] In Russia tea is served in tumblers, not in cups.

"To hear *him* acquaint you?" re-echoed Ordinov, with a stare of astonishment at Murin. The latter only stroked his beard, the better to be able to laugh in his sleeve.

"Yes," continued Yaroslav. "For the rest, I may be wrong, but I ought to tell you frankly—indeed, I give you my word of honour on the point—that, so far as I know, this most estimable gentleman has said not a word to your discredit."

Again Yaroslav reddened as he mastered his confusion with an effort. Murin—who now, doubtless, had laughed his fill—saw good at this point to put in his oar.

"Yes, your nobility," he began, with a polite bow to Ordinov, "it is true that we have been talking of you. You yourself cannot fail to know that I and my ward would have been only too glad for things to continue as they have hitherto been, and that never a word would have occurred between you and ourselves. But you know my way of life, for you have seen something of it; and what all of us ask of heaven is, above all things, to be left to live in peace. Judge for yourself, sir. Am I to go down on my knees to you, and to beseech you with tears? What else could we do?"

Here Murin resumed the stroking of his beard. Ordinov felt anything but comfortable.

"Yes, yes," put in Yaroslav. " 'Tis as I told you. Monsieur Murin has bad health : *c'est le malheur*—— Excuse me, but sometimes I try to express myself in French, and am not over-good at it. That is to say——"

"Yes?"

"That is to say—er—well, *yes*."

Ordinov and Yaroslav Ilyitch bowed to one another without rising; after which they sought to cover their awkwardness with a burst of laughter. The naturally grave Yaroslav was the first to recover himself.

"On hearing of this I asked our good friend here for details," he went on. "He told me that his—er

—lady——" Yaroslav Ilyitch looked interrogatively at Murin (probably to conceal his embarrassment).

"Yes; my *ward*," assented Murin.

The delicate Yaroslav skated lightly over the point.

"Yes, your *ward*—that is to say, your *elderly* ward—has been ill. So," he turned to Ordinov, "Monsieur Murin informs me that this lady and himself disturb you in your work. . . . Vassilii Michaelovitch, you have concealed from me a very important circumstance."

"What is that?"

"The incident of the revolver."

Yaroslav Ilyitch spoke these last words softly, as though he would permit ever so small a shade of reproach to enter into the tone of his affectionate tenor voice.

"However," he went on with resumed vivacity, "I know the whole story, for Monsieur Murin has told it me from beginning to end. You have acted nobly, Vassilii Michaelovitch! What a fine thing is forgiveness! I tell you that this morning, when relating the story, Monsieur Murin had tears in his eyes!"

Yaroslav reddened anew, and his eyes shone as he fidgeted on his chair.

"Ah, sir! Ah, your Nobility!" put in Murin. "How I—how *we* (myself and my ward)—will ever pray to heaven for you both!"

Yaroslav Ilyitch could only struggle with unwonted emotion as he sat gazing fixedly at the speaker.

"You yourself know," Murin continued to Ordinov, "that my ward is but a sickly, as well as an untaught, maiden. And, for myself, I can scarcely hold myself upright."

"I quite agree," interrupted Ordinov with impatience. "Say no more on the point, I beg of you. Let us close the matter this very day—yes, this very moment, if you wish."

"No, no! That is to say, we are quite content

to keep you, sir." Here Murin bowed low again.
"It was not on *that* point that I wished to speak to
you, but on another one altogether. You must
know that she is a sort of a relation of mine—a fifth
cousin, or thereabouts, I am told. Do not misunder-
stand me, sir. We are plain people. From infancy
she has been as you have seen her—that is to say,
a little wrong in her head. She was born in the
wilds, and brought up with *burlaki*.[1] In fact, she
is only a peasant's daughter. One day her parents'
house was burnt to the ground, and her father and
mother perished in the flames. All this I tell you
for the reason that she herself may have told you a
different tale (though, as a rule, I let her say whatever she pleases). Well, a good while ago she
underwent examination by a medical board at
Moscow; and, to put things shortly, she was pronounced a little wanting. I give her house-room,
and we live, and pray to God, and repose all our
trust in the Supreme Goodness. Never in anything
do I seek to cross her."

All this while Ordinov's face had been undergoing
a gradual change, while Yaroslav Ilyitch, for his
part, kept looking anxiously from the one to the
other of the two men.

"Even that, sir," went on Murin, with a toss of
his head, "is not what I wanted to say to you. The
girl of whom I speak is a veritable whirlwind, a
perpetual tempest. What a loving, fiery young
creature she is, to be sure! Well, she cannot do
without some very particular friend—some (if I may
use the term) particular sweetheart. It is *that*
which has turned her brain. True, I can soothe her
a little by telling her stories—yes, I have done her
a great deal of good in that way; but I see clearly
(of course you must excuse my plain speaking, sir"
[here Murin bowed low again, and wiped his beard
on his sleeve)], "that she has a fancy for you; and
you, sir, I doubt not, were led by your passion for
her to come and lodge with us."

[1] Fishermen of the Volga.

Yaroslav Ilyitch threw a glance of disapproval at Murin—a glance which said plainly that he did not care for such disjointed utterances. Ordinov also could hardly contain himself.

"Yet," went on Murin, "even *that* is not what I meant to say, sir. I am only a simple peasant; we are but humble folk, she and I—but humble folk" (Murin again bowed), "but none the less we will always pray to God for you, my ward and I. . . . To continue—what do she and I need? Food and health. Yet, under the circumstances, what are we to do? Am I to go and hang myself? Judge for yourself, sir. It is a very simple matter. What is to become of us if she were to go and take a lover? Of course the term is rather a plain one (if you will excuse it, sir?), but you must not forget that I am a peasant speaking to a gentleman. You are yet young, your nobility, and lusty, and full of life. She too is young, sir—a mere inexperienced child. Would it, then, take much to send her astray? Remember that she is a *beautiful* child, and full-blooded and strong, and that I am only an old epileptic. Yet I shall know how to soothe her with tales when your nobility is gone; yes, yes, I shall know how to soothe her! And how she and I will ever pray to God for your nobility! I could not say *how* much we shall not pray! . . . Even if you were to fall in love with her, she could never be aught but a peasant-woman, a rough-and-ready stripling : and a peasant-woman, my good sir, ought to be no concern of yours. . . . Nevertheless, how we will pray for you, how we will pray for you!"

Once more Murin bowed to the ground, and in that posture continued stroking his beard. Yaroslav Ilyitch hardly knew what to do for the best.

"The splendid fellow!" he ventured at length (probably to conceal his embarrassment). "How could you go and have a misunderstanding with him, Vassilii Michaelovitch? . . . He tells me that you have been ill again?" he added, with tears in his eyes and unbounded embarrassment in his tone.

"Yes, I *have* been ill again," replied Ordinov. Then he added to Murin: "How much do I owe you?"

"Nay, nay, my good sir, my good sir! We are not the sort of people to sell Christ! Why should you be so ready to take offence? Are you not ashamed to do so? In what have we offended you, my ward and I? Come!"

"That is not the point," interrupted Yaroslav Ilyitch, who felt himself bound to point out to Murin the indelicacy of his procedure. "My friend here *hired* the room of you."

"Monsieur Ordinov," went on Murin, "I ask you once again—In what have we offended you? We took such trouble to make you comfortable! In fact, the doing of it simply wore us out. Of course, if you *must* go, you must, and may Christ go with you! But are we, for that reason, mere unbelievers and rascals? You might have continued to live with us, and to share our simple fare, and to shelter beneath our roof for ever, and we should never have had a single objection to make—never! No, we should never have had a single word to say! But the devil entered into you, and I fell ill, and my ward did so too. What, then, is to be done? There would be no one to look after you if you stayed— much as we should have liked things to have been otherwise. Yet we will pray for you, my ward and I," he added. "Yes, we will always pray for you." Again he bowed to his waist.

Tears of enthusiasm gushed from Yaroslav Ilyitch's eyes.

"What a noble disposition!" he cried. "O sacred hospitality of Russia!"

Ordinov looked at him severely, from head to foot.

"Yes, sir, by heavens!" cried Murin, catching at Yaroslav's last exclamation. "We Russians are nothing if not hospitable. Consequently we beg of you to stop with us a little longer" (here he buried his beard completely in his sleeve). "Yes, you *shall* stop!" he went on as he rose and approached

Ordinov. "You *shall* stop! Of that I intend to make a point. Stop at least one day, or two days, and we will ask of you no rent for doing so. But you must remember that my ward is ill. If only it had not been *she*! If only (for example) *I* had been living alone! What care I should have taken of you! That is to say, what care I should have taken of you as your landlord! Yes, I should simply have *heaped* favours upon your head—simply *heaped* them! However, I will manage so that you need never leave us. Yes, I swear that by God, much though it may sound. You know, you could stop with us permanently were it not for——"

"But, as a matter of fact, he *could* stop, could he not?" observed Yaroslav Ilyitch; then he became dumb again.

Ordinov had been wrong in casting such ferocious looks at Yaroslav, for, in reality, the latter was the most open and upright of men. But Ordinov was in a difficult position, while, for his part, Yaroslav was suffering from a mad desire to burst into laughter. Indeed, he would certainly have done so had he been closeted only with Ordinov, his bosom friend; after which he would have seized his friend's hand, and assured him, in all sincerity, that he felt for him a double measure of esteem—that he pardoned him, and that not for all the world would he blame his youthful indiscretions. However, under the circumstances, his extreme delicacy left him neither choice of attitude nor any means of withdrawing from the scene.

"You ask me if there is any way out of it?" resumed Murin, whose features had changed colour at Yaroslav's ill-timed question. "Well, sir, this is what I, in my uncouth peasant fashion, desire to say to Monsieur Ordinov. You have read too many books, sir—you have become too clever. We Russian peasants have a proverb that a man grows wise but to grow mad."

"Now, now!" put in Yaroslav Ilyitch, with a touch of severity in his tone.

"Thank you, but I *wish* to leave you," replied Ordinov. "Thank you too for all your trouble, Yaroslav. Some day I will come and pay you a visit" (this last was said in response to a polite, but unsuccessful, effort on the part of Yaroslav to detain him). "Good-bye, good-bye!"

"Good-bye, your nobility," said Murin. "Do not forget also to pay us peasants a visit."

But Ordinov departed without so much as noticing these adieus. He felt absolutely demented, he felt absolutely overcome, dumbfounded. Indeed, he felt as though he were suffocating—as though a severe internal chill were pressing upon his chest. He would gladly have died that very instant. Soon his legs began to tremble so violently that he was forced to rest against some railings, where he paid no heed to the looks and questionings of the throng which began to gather around him.

Suddenly, amid the babel, he heard Murin's voice, and, raising his head, saw the old man standing before him, his pale face so reflective and solemn that it no longer resembled the face of the man who, in Yaroslav Ilyitch's rooms, had been indulging in bitter mockery. Ordinov rose, and Murin, taking him by the arm, led him out of the throng.

"You have still to fetch your luggage from my tenement," he said with a covert glance at his companion. "Do not distress yourself, sir. You are still quite young. Why should you be distressed about *anything?*"

Ordinov said nothing.

"Perhaps you are offended, sir, and angry? Why so? Every one must look out for himself."

"I do not know you," retorted Ordinov, "nor have I any desire to pry into your secrets; but she— she——"

Suddenly a flood of tears gushed from his eyes, despite his attempting to stem it with the back of his hand. The gesture, as well as his expression and the convulsive quivering of his white lips, seemed to presage almost a fit of madness.

"I have already told you," said Murin, with a frown, "that she is practically insane. Why so, and how? That is no affair of yours. Whatever she may be, I love her—I love her more than my life, and will give her up to no one. *Now* do you understand?"

A flash of light sprang to Ordinov's eyes.

"What is it that makes me feel as though I were dead?" he cried. "What is it that makes my heart suffer so? Why was I ever fated to meet Katherine?"

"Ah, why?"

Murin smiled, but presently looked grave again.

"Why?" he went on. "How should I know? The heart of a woman is not exactly as deep as the sea. Some day you will learn that for yourself. It is true, sir, that at one time she had a mind to leave me for you. She misunderstood the old man, and thought that he had taken his fill of life. Possibly you pleased her at the outset, or possibly she wanted a change. However that may be, I cross her openly in nothing. Even if she were to cry for pigeon's milk I should give it her. Yet, though she is proud, and wanting her freedom, she would not know what to do with it when she had got it. Consequently things are best as they are. Eh, sir! You are young, and have an over-warm heart. At this moment you look like a forsaken maiden as you stand there wiping your eyes on your sleeve. You have had no experience. You do not know that a feeble soul like her is incapable of looking after itself. Even if it be given everything, it will still return, in the end, to its owner. Even if it be given a kingdom, it will still home to your call. Never can it really act for itself. In the same way, give it its liberty, and it will forge for itself new chains. No; liberty is not for feeble souls. I tell you this because you are so young. What are you to me? Come to-day and gone to-morrow, what are you, or any other man, to me? Yet from the first I knew that this must happen—though it was no duty of mine to warn you, seeing that if one is ever to live happily with a woman one must not cross her, even by a single word. However," went on Murin, with the air of a philosopher, "all that may be taken for granted. How, indeed, could things be otherwise? You yourself know that in a moment of rage a man may pick up a dagger. Again, a man may attack his enemy in his sleep, and bury his teeth in his throat. On the other hand, if some one *puts* a dagger into that man's hand, or if that man's enemy bares his throat *of himself*—well, then a man might recoil from such a deed."

Soon they entered the courtyard of Murin's abode. On perceiving them, the *dvornik* took off his cap, but threw a malicious glance at Ordinov.

"Is your mother in my tenement?" Murin asked of the Tartar.

"Yes."

"Then tell her to give this gentleman a hand in packing his luggage. And do you too make yourself generally useful."

Mounting the staircase, they induced the old serving-woman, who was also the *dvornik's* mother, to cease grumbling and roll Ordinov's effects into a bundle.

"Wait a moment," said Murin to Ordinov. "I have something else to bring you." With that he entered his room, and presently returned with a richly embroidered tablecloth—the one which Katherine had thrust under his (Ordinov's) head when he was first taken ill.

"*She* sends you this," said Murin. "Now, depart in peace, and may all good go with you. Yet take care. Do not again come prowling round here, or things may turn out badly for you."

This he said in a low—almost a paternal—voice, as though he feared to offend Ordinov. Yet his last glance at his departing lodger was full of nothing but infinite resentment, and he closed the door upon the young man with a look of unbounded disgust.

Two hours later Ordinov went to live with the German, Herr Schpis, whose daughter, Tinchen, exclaimed, "Ah! How delightful it is to see him again!" and demanded of him news. On hearing, however, that he was "not feeling very well," she promised to do her best for him; while Schpis, for his part, informed his lodger that he had not yet put up the "To Let" bill again, though in a day or two he would have done so, for the reason that the term covered by Ordinov's deposit money would then have expired. Finally the good Schpis took occasion to extol the honesty and correctitude of German folk in general.

That same day Ordinov again fell ill, and for three months never left his bed. Then, little by little, health returned to him, and he began to go out for walks. His life at Schpis's was an even, uneventful one, since the German was good-natured, and Tinchen too all that could be desired. Yet, for Ordinov, life had lost its charm. He became irritable, and subject to sickly impressions, until gradually he sank into a state of confirmed hypochondria. For weeks at a time he would never open a book, but, careless of the future, would let his money slip away without taking any thought for the needs of the morrow. Also, though there were times when his old feverish industry, his old ardour, his old visions, would return to his memory, those thoughts never became translated into action. He felt, as it were, sterilised—his dreams seemed to be sent to him for the express purpose of mocking his impotence (which, in his imagination, had come to assume gigantic proportions). In hours of depression he would even liken himself to the sorcerer's thoughtless apprentice who, after bidding water be turned on to his room, was drowned in the flood which it caused, through not knowing the magic word for "Cease!" Perhaps, had Ordinov ever conceived any original idea or cherished any hopes for the future, he would still have continued to believe in something—and a sincere faith is a safeguard against all the ills of life. Now, however, he only smiled at his own convictions, and ceased to take any interest in his erstwhile splendid schemes.

Six months ago he had simply lived in his ideas —sometimes working at them, sometimes, when temporarily weary, founding upon them (so young was he) airy hopes. The work upon which he had been engaged had been a History of the Church. With what burning fanaticism he had sketched its outline! But now he merely re-read his rough notes, corrected them, and then made a few researches. Finally he ended by abandoning his project altogether, without founding anything new upon its ruins. A sort of mysticism, of occult fatalism, had enveloped his soul. He could only suffer, and beseech God to end his sufferings. His landlord's servant—a devout old Russian dame—used to narrate with great gusto how her lodger would go to church and say his prayers, and then remain prone for hours, like a dead man, on the floor of the sacred building.

Ordinov never confided his trouble to any living soul; but often, at dusk, when the church bells were recalling to his memory that unforgettable moment when he had been kneeling near Katherine in God's house, and listening to the beating of the girl's heart, and baptising with tears of joy the hope which had newly sprung into his life—at such times there would arise in his murdered soul a veritable tempest, and his spirit would burst forth anew, and all the tortures of love would begin for him again. He suffered—oh, how he suffered! And he would feel that his love only increased with his suffering. Whole hours would pass while he sat motionless in his chair, forgetful of everything—forgetful of the world, of his grey existence, and of himself, now sad and lonely. Sometimes he would weep softly; at other times he would find himself whispering, "O Katherine, my only sister!"

To these tortures one terrible thought gave added poignancy. That thought clung to him, and grew from day to day, until it became an actual probability, an actual reality. It seemed to him (and he ended by believing it) that Katherine's mind had, throughout, been sane, but that Murin had had some secret purpose in dubbing her a "feeble soul." He believed that some undivulgeable mystery must have bound her to the old man, but that, inasmuch as it was not upon *her* conscience that the crime lay, she had innocently yielded to Murin's infamous domination. For what were they to one another? Ordinov's heart beat with impotent rage at the thought of the tyranny which was oppressing the poor young creature. His soul, thus enlightened, would follow with horrified eyes the gradual downfall which was being so cleverly, yet so traitorously, prepared for her. How that "feeble soul" was being tortured— how the girl was having Scripture quoted at her, how she was being blinded, how she was having her naturally ardent temperament exploited! Thus, little by little, the wings of that once free soul were being clipped until it should have become powerless to face the battle of life alone!

Yet, increasingly though Ordinov became a recluse (for it may be said that his German hosts did not interfere with him at all), there were times when he would take long, aimless walks through the streets, and always choose the most unfrequented hours and places for his purpose. One gloomy evening in spring he encountered, in one such deserted spot, Yaroslav Ilyitch. Certainly Yaroslav's health seemed visibly to have deteriorated, for his once kindly eyes had grown dull, and his general appearance looked dejected. Moreover, though in former days he had always appeared to be pressed for time and full of appointments, his clothes on the present occasion looked dirty and mud-stained, and the evening rain had turned his honest, though slightly empurpled, nose into a veritable water-spout. Even his side whiskers now hung neglected, and this fact, combined with a certain disposition to avoid an old friend, at once caught Ordinov's attention. Though himself only too anxious to escape condolences, he felt wounded and hurt at such behaviour. He preferred that Yaroslav should be as he had always been—namely, simple, outspoken, and a little uncouth, but never pretentious of being *blasé*, nor yet of being full of schemes for self-education. For is it not an annoying thing to find that a person whom hitherto we have loved precisely for his stupidity has suddenly become "clever"? However, Yaroslav's shyness did not last long. Out of love with life though he was, he could never wholly shed his true nature—the mantle which true *bons vivants* discard only in the grave. Delicately, as of old, he proceeded to probe the soul of his friend. After remarking that he (the speaker) was very busy, he went on to state that it was a long time "since you and I last met." Then the conversation took a strange turn—namely, that Yaroslav Ilyitch fell to discoursing on the hypocrisy of people in general, the vanity of looking for any happiness in this world, and the particular futility which is known as "life." *En passant*, of course, he dragged in the name of Pushkin, but this time with a marked air of indifference. Next he spoke of "good friends" in a cynical vein, and inveighed against the falseness and mendacity of persons who professed to be "friends," yet among whom sincere friendship did not exist, and never had existed. Yes, Yaroslav Ilyitch had indeed become "clever"! Ordinov said nothing to contradict him, but felt extremely depressed. In fact, he felt as though he were assisting at the interment of his best comrade.

"Just think, too!" said Yaroslav, as though suddenly recalling a very interesting item. "There is a piece of news which I had almost forgotten to tell you. I do so now in strict confidence. You remember the tenement where you used to lodge, do you not?"

Ordinov trembled and turned pale.

"Well, they have just unearthed a band of criminals there!—a regular association, a regular nest, of them!—smugglers, sharpers, and felons of all sorts! Some of them were arrested, and the others are still being looked for. The strictest instructions have been given for their capture. But the point which beats all others is this. You remember the *proprietor* of the buildings—a most pious, respectable, outwardly irreproachable old man? "

" Yes. Well? "

" Well, form your own opinion of humanity when I tell you that he was the *chief* of that band! Is it not incredible? "

Yaroslav Ilyitch was vastly excited over his story. Now he could form a true estimate of his fellow-men. Indeed, he had never failed to do so, for such was his way.

" And the rest of the band? And Murin? " asked Ordinov in a low voice.

" Ah! Murin, Murin! That noble, that venerable, old man! . . . But pardon me. You have suddenly inspired me with an idea. "

" An idea? Was *he too* one of the band? " Impatience was coming near to choking Ordinov's heart within his breast.

" Oh dear, no! What makes you ask *that?* " Yaroslav Ilyitch looked searchingly at his friend (a sure sign that he was reflecting). " Murin could not possibly have been one of them, since, quite three weeks ago, he left for the country, together with his wife. I had that straight from the *dvornik*, the little Tartar. Doubtless you remember him? "

Richard Clay & Sons, Limited, London and Bungay.

EVERYMAN,
I WILL GO WITH THEE,
& BE THY GVIDE
IN THY MOST NEED
TO GO BY THY SIDE